Larry Brown, born in 1951 in Oxford, Mississippi, is the author of six previous books, including *On Fire*, a non-fiction account of his seventeen years as an Oxford firefighter, and most recently the acclaimed novel *Father and Son*. He is the recipient of the Mississippi Institute of Arts and Letters Award for Literature, the Southern Critics Circle Award for Fiction in 1992 and 1997, and the Lila Wallace—*Reader's Digest* Award. A documentary, 'The Rough South of Larry Brown', premiered at the Center for Documentary Studies at Duke University in spring 2000.

Praise for *Fay*:

'American fiction at its best. Unlike most of his literary con-
temporaries, Brown is both unafraid and unashamed to tell
a whopping good story while dazzling us with the beauty of
his direct, finely detailed prose . . . his common, inarticulate
people act, and in the process enlighten us on the need for
love and family, and the struggle for survival in a violent
world. It's the honesty in the presentation of these characters, and the author's insistence on realistically depicting
the consequences of their very human choices, that lift this
novel above the pack. *Fay* is proof that important fiction can
be gritty, sexy and deeply moving . . . [Brown is] a writer
without gimmick who happens to possess a prodigious
natural talent. *Fay* illustrates, once again, that he's one of the
best we have' George P. Pelecanos, *Washington Post*

'With grim, stately beauty, Brown tracks Fay's wild and
bloody journey out of her troubled past, showing how – as
in Faulkner's universe – those who proceed from violence
will one day return to it . . . told in lapidary, perfect prose,
Fay limns the nervy psyche of a woman walking that line'
Time Out New York

'The accumulated everyday images and the metaphors of the
mundane fuse to create a work of grizzled beauty . . . through
it all, as always with Brown, his characters – particularly
Fay – retain an honesty and even a dignity that their actions
and surroundings would seem to render impossible. Brown
is a writer with the eye of a documentarian, his prose aim-
ing for nothing short of ruthlessly capturing the truth of the
world in which he has always lived. In *Fay*, he has created
an unforgettable heroine who seeks her place in a world she
hardly understands' *USA Today*

'The chapters flash by like fenceposts on the highway as the novel rushes towards its shattering conclusion. Mr Brown's Mississippi is hard to look at sometimes and his characters are not redeemed in traditional ways, but he tells their stories with a compelling, matter-of-fact compassion, and he never for a minute averts his eyes' *Wall Street Journal*

'For years Larry Brown has been known and respected as a writer's writer. But now, with *Fay*, this profoundly southern novelist may win the broad readership he so richly deserves . . . A marvellous creation, Fay has a catalytic, even explosive effect on the men and women who stop to pick her up. Brown, an ex-firefighter, does not write about genteel folk amid magnolia blossoms but about people often dismissed as white trash. His people live in trailers, work in strip joints and are given to sudden, irrevocable acts of violence, but he endows them with compelling moral lives. In *Fay*, Brown's magic is to make the reader wonder at his plucky heroine, then care about and finally root for her as she winds towards the novel's gripping conclusion'
People

'In this novel, his best work since *Dirty Work*, he evokes some of *All the Pretty Horses* author Cormac McCarthy's earthy, bloody, violence. That Brown reminds you of Faulkner and of McCarthy . . . is a compliment to each'
J. Ford Huffman, *USA Today*

FAY

Larry Brown

BLACK SWAN

FAY
A BLACK SWAN BOOK : 0 552 99917 2

First publication in Great Britain

PRINTING HISTORY
Black Swan edition published 2001

1 3 5 7 9 10 8 6 4 2

Copyright © Larry Brown 2000

The right of Larry Brown to be identified as the author
of this work has been asserted in accordance with sections
77 and 78 of the Copyright Designs and Patents Act 1988.

Set in 11/12pt Melior by
County Typesetters, Margate, Kent.

Black Swan Books are published by Transworld Publishers,
61–63 Uxbridge Road, London W5 5SA,
a division of The Random House Group Ltd,
in Australia by Random House Australia (Pty) Ltd,
20 Alfred Street, Milsons Point, Sydney, NSW 2061, Australia,
in New Zealand by Random House New Zealand Ltd,
18 Poland Road, Glenfield, Auckland 10, New Zealand
and in South Africa by Random House (Pty) Ltd,
Endulini, 5a Jubilee Road, Parktown 2193, South Africa.

Printed and bound in Great Britain by
Clays Ltd, St Ives plc.

For my uncle in all ways but blood: Harry Crews.

FAY

Book 1

She came down out of the hills that were growing black with night, and in the dusty road her feet found small broken stones that made her wince. Alone for the first time in the world and full dark coming quickly. House lights winked through the trees as she walked and swung her purse from her hand. She could hear cars passing down the asphalt but she was still a long way from that.

More than once she stopped and looked back up into the ridges that stood behind her, thinking things over, but each time she shook her head and went on.

South seemed best. She had vague ideas about a coast. She knew it would be warmer in the winter and that one thing drove her in that direction more than anything else. She imagined groves of citrus trees and sunny days picking the fruit and a tiny house where she would have her own groceries and watch television whenever she wanted to. She imagined one solid place where she could stay and maybe she could somehow send for the others then. Or ride a bicycle up and down the flat land with the water always shining out there beyond the shore and birds soaring like in the pictures she had seen of places like that. She kept her head down as she walked and she listened to the night things that called in the ditches and out past the stands of cane and in the clumps of trees that rose from the river bottom.

Once she stopped to rest on a narrow bridge and sat down on a timber studded with nailheads. A creek ran over snapped pilings and faintly gleaming rocks below her. She was thirsty but she feared picking her way down the muddy bank and the snakes she could not see. She sat hugging her knees and watching the specks of stars in the sky above her. All of it so still and unmoving, the stars so bright. She turned her head to the singing woods again. To go back would not take long. She got up and went on down the road.

Cows watched her progress from a quiet pasture like cows made of stone. She was afraid of them but she walked on by them. She didn't have a watch but she knew she'd been walking for about an hour.

When she rounded the last curve there was another bridge and she stopped again to rest before reaching a place where somebody might pick her up. She sat down and crossed her legs inside the skirt and opened the clasp of her purse. She rummaged through the few things that were in there and found the two dollar bills and pulled them out, smoothed the wrinkles, looked at them. She folded them and folded them again and undid the top button of her blouse and slid them into the left cup of the raveling bra, tucked them snugly in there and buttoned her blouse. Then she pushed herself up from the tarred wood with its hardened drippings of black goo and walked across it and out into the dusty gravel again. The moon was coming out.

She was afraid of the dogs that barked from the yards and sometimes came to the ends of the driveways and bared their teeth, but none came after her. She walked past a building set well back from the road and saw a dark cross set into the wood high up near the gable. She stopped. There was a light somewhere inside, a yellow beam that shone through stained glass windows. She wondered if there might be a water tap in the yard or on the side of the house. She turned down a neat drive covered with pea gravel, brushing the strands of her hair back from her face with her fingers. There was a light on a pole at the back and she could see a low wire fence and outcroppings of polished stones inside it. A whirling dance of insects hung around the pole. The light hummed with a low, steady drone and it cast a gauzy veil over everything. Crickets sounded from the dark woods back there.

She went cautiously even though there were no cars in the parking lot. Her steps were loud to her in the gravel. The west wall lay in shadow and there was a brick border for flowers near the entrance. She walked closer and saw a coil of garden hose in the damp grass and saw where it ended, a faucet protruding from a corner of the foundation. She went over to it and turned it on.

The water was cool and sweet. She was standing there drinking from the end of the hose when she heard it growling and turned her head to see a speckled knot of hair and bones with its head hung low between its shoulder blades standing thirty feet away. It moved closer and an odd clanking moved with it. She knew better than to run, so she let the hose drop from her hand and faced it. The dog seemed propped on its legs and a bit of drool swung from its jaw. The canines were bared in a bloody muzzle and its eyes were sick. Another ragged growl escaped it and it seemed hard-pressed to draw each breath. The foot that was caught in the rusty trap was nearly severed and the dog tried to hold it aloft as it came toward her, half whining, maybe for help. She backed toward the front porch and stepped onto it. There was a decorative iron column on each corner, leaves and vines hammered and painted, cool beneath her hands. The dog came closer. She turned to the double doors, the dark wood and the heavy brass knob. The door on the left opened when she twisted the knob and she stepped quickly inside, slammed it and stood with her back against it. The dog whined once and then there was nothing but the slight rattle of metal against gravel as the chain and trap were dragged away. She listened for a while but she couldn't hear anything else. She stepped away from the door and put the strap of her purse up over her shoulder. She

17

went forward reluctantly, uneasy in a stranger's home.

A room like none she'd ever been in. A carpeted hall-way that only whispered beneath her tennis shoes and long polished benches of wood shining faintly in the half gloom. She walked slowly, touching the dark brown pine. The ceiling pointed upward with long beams and chubby babies dressed in flowing swatches of cloth danced on air amid fields of flowers in a long painting across the back of the room or gathered at the feet of Jesus in a robe with a beard and long hair, seated on a stone. The tips of her fingers touched small brass plaques at the ends of the rows. The walls were lined with windows like the ones in front, beaded chips of glass in blue and red and gold, and at the front there sat a table holding bowls of polished metal. A white lace tablecloth. There were other paintings of Jesus and people, children, were always gathered about him. In all the paintings he wore a look of sorrow. There was no sound in that vast room at all. She wondered if the dog had gone away. She hoped it had. She thought it might be best to stay in here for a while, give it time to go somewhere else.

The long benches were covered with soft material that felt good under her hand. A small stage was beyond the table and on it stood a dark wooden plat-form. She opened a little side gate with a click and then went up the two steps to stand in front of the rows and rows of benches facing her. A Bible lay open before her, bound in leather, the pages so thin. She riffled through them, let them slide from her fingers. Somebody had to stand up here and talk to all these people.

'It's a church for rich folks,' she said. The sound of her voice reverberated in the room, echoed quietly off the walls. She stepped away from the book and went back down the steps, out through the gate, around the rail. There was a door set into the rear wall and she opened it and found herself in a kitchen. Only a dim light burned over a stove. Rows of long tables and metal folding chairs shoulder to shoulder.

There was a wall switch beside the door and she flipped it up. The lights in the ceiling flickered for a moment and then came on strong, a bright glare that showed dishes racked beside a sink and cans of coffee left on a counter and cabinets that lined the back side of the room. A white refrigerator.

She set her purse on the counter and opened the door to see milk in cartons, covered dishes with casseroles and fried chicken, sliced ham. The lights hummed in the ceiling.

She found a plate and a fork in one of the cabinets and a loaf of bread in a corner of the counter and heaped the plate with food and poured a glass of milk. She sat down at one of the long tables and began to eat. The chicken was dry but she didn't care. Crumbs fell to the table on each side of the plate. She wished she'd known of this place on those nights back in the woods when there was nothing to rock against her empty belly except for her knees, those times they'd waited for the old man to come in with something to eat and waited all night many nights and he never did.

After a while she got up and poured herself another glass of milk and rummaged through the cabinets again. There were some fresh doughnuts in a cardboard box. She got three of them and sat back down and ate them one by one and licked the icing from her fingers when she was done.

In her purse she found the mangled pack of cigarettes that her brother Gary had given her and she got one out, holding it between her fingers while she searched for the matches, that she found finally beneath tubes of cheap lipstick and plastic combs and hairbands, things she'd saved for years. She lit the cigarette and waved the match out and dropped it into her purse and then pulled out another chair to prop her feet on and stretched out, blowing smoke lazily at the ceiling, thumping the ashes into the chicken bones on her plate. There was only one more thing she could have asked for.

The instant coffee was in a drawer and she heated water in a pan, found sugar and stirred it into the swirling coffee and sat down again with the steaming cup in front of her. She had one more cigarette, but by then she felt she'd already been there too long. She put the dishes she'd taken food from back into the refrigerator and scraped the scraps into a trash can with a lid. She ran hot water into the sink and added detergent that was there and washed the plate and the glass and the cup and the spoon and the fork, put them back where they had been. Wiped the crumbs from the table with a paper towel. She put the chairs back in their places and put the pan away. When she was done, she got her purse and checked one last time to see that everything was as it had been. Then she turned the light off and went out.

In the middle of the big room she stopped again. Jesus seemed to gaze down upon her with his painted eyes. She looked at the table and the empty bowls. Even though she felt just from the expression on his face that he wouldn't mind her taking the food and eating it, she turned and went back up the quiet aisle to the table and reached inside her blouse for the folded money tucked into the bra. She unfolded the money, put one bill in a bowl, the other one back into the bra.

Nothing changed inside the room. It crossed her mind to find a corner to sleep in but she was still too close to the place she had left. When she cracked the heavy door open and peeked out, the dog had gone. She pulled the door shut behind her and went on up the drive toward the blacktop. And then she remembered that the water was still running at the side of the building and went back down there and turned it off.

The road climbed over hills where distant fields lay spread below her and the yard lights of houses were spots of blue shining and the red moving tails of cars crept along a far-off highway with only a hint of noise. The traffic was sparse and the two cars that passed her neither slowed nor stopped. An old country road where the pavement was lumpy with patches of hot mix and crumbled along the edges where tall grass grew. The dogs always barked when she walked past the houses. Through the big front window of one house she could see people moving, sitting down at a table, a man, a woman, a boy and a girl. She stopped for a minute and watched them. There were bicycles in the yard, a swing set. The man was laughing in his T-shirt and his glasses. The woman passed behind him carrying a bowl and she put one hand on his shoulder when she leaned over and set it on the table. The boy and the girl were helping their plates. It was like something she had seen once on a television in the window of a store somewhere in Florida and she remembered standing there looking at it until her father came back and jerked her by the arm and told her to come on. These people were almost like the people in that television show, a nice house, good clothes, plenty of food on the table. There were other things she wondered about, the father and his daughter. Did she lie awake, trying to keep the sleep away, and did she try to hide herself somewhere he could not find her before she closed her eyes? She turned away from the family and went on up the road.

The long muscles in her legs said they would be sore

in the morning from pulling the hills. But she seemed to be nearing the last one. Off to the north lay a low glow among the trees nestled at the top of the world and she knew it had to be a town. She thought it might be Oxford. She had heard her father mention that place. She thought that was where he went to get his whiskey, but she'd never been there. They had come in from the southeast, through Georgia and Alabama, the two-lane roads, the sleepy towns off the interstates where they spent the nights in the parks rolled in quilts or just stretched out on the grass. And back before he'd lost the truck, in the cab and the bed of it. But she was used to walking, a road in front of her. This one no different from any other in that they all led somewhere.

Biloxi. That was the name of the place. She was sure of it now. That was where she would tell people she was going. Biloxi.

She tried not to think about being alone as she walked. She hoped there wouldn't be any more dogs. But that dog had been hurting, wanting the trap taken off his foot. It had probably been half crazy with the pain. It might have been a good dog once, before it got into the trap. Maybe even somebody's pet. But she'd been bitten too many times to feel safe around any dog now. Maybe later when she got settled somewhere she could get a puppy, learn how to be friends with a dog.

She kept walking up the hill. She could see a lake off to the right in a deep clean hollow dotted with white forms that had to be sleeping cows. The moon was a hanging ball on the surface of the water and she knew the river was down there somewhere in that bottom. She couldn't think of the name of it. She'd cross it eventually, maybe even on the other side of this last hill. She was closer to the red lights of the cars now and she stopped suddenly to see if she could hear one. There was just the faintest sound coming to her as she watched another set of lights go through the trees. She wondered how far she'd come. Probably three or four miles and no way of knowing how much time had passed.

She started walking again, up toward the top of the hill where a new house was just being finished, the bricks still sitting stacked in the yard and lumber propped on sawhorses, a new concrete driveway that curved away from the old asphalt road. A low noise began to grow behind her and she looked over her shoulder to see light beginning to touch the roadside grasses and grow in intensity as the noise got louder and she could hear the motor straining. She stepped to the edge of the grass and kept walking. Whoever was driving let off the gas before it got to her and she turned her head when it went by, a Ford pickup with one tail-light, a boy's face in the window watching her. It kept slowing and went on up the road fifty feet more and then it stopped. She stopped too. The brake light was shining red and there was a boat in the back end, resting against the cab. A light flashed in the lens and the truck started backing toward her. She stood there and waited for it.

There were three boys in the truck. The one looking out the window had blond hair and a thin beard that she could see dimly. The other two were dark, indistinct. Some music was playing inside the cab but the driver reached over and turned it down.

'Hey,' the boy in the window said.

'Hey,' she answered.

The one in the middle and the driver were having a discussion. The blond boy looked her up and down and took a long drink of his beer, then stuck his head out and hung both arms down the side of the truck. She couldn't tell much about his face. He had a tattoo on his left forearm. The truck rattled as it idled.

She heard one of them tell the blond boy to ask her where she was going. And then she heard the other one tell him to ask her if she wanted to fuck.

'Where you headed?' the blond boy said.

She wished she could see his face better so that

23

maybe she could tell something about him. She never had talked to a whole lot of boys.

'Biloxi,' she said.

The one in the middle muttered something and leaned forward a little. The blond boy took another drink of his beer.

'Well you a long ways from there,' he said. 'What, your car tore up?'

'I ain't got no car,' she said.

The driver killed the motor. The headlights showed stubby pine trees and rotted fence and the front edge of the road going out into nothing before he pushed them off. The truck rolled back a few inches. But she wasn't afraid yet. She figured she could always run if something looked like it was about to happen.

'We been down on the river fishin,' the blond boy said. 'We got some lines out down there. You live around here?'

She pointed back down the dark road to the hills she'd left behind.

'I lived back over yonder. I want to go to Biloxi. Are y'all goin that way?'

The blond boy laughed softly and scratched at the side of his jaw. She liked him even when he shook his head.

'We ain't headed to Biloxi. You know how far that is?'

'No. Is it a long way?'

'I don't know how many miles it is. You got to go down through the whole state.'

She raised her eyes to the bottom of the sky where the wide soft light still glowed within the distant trees.

'Is that Oxford up there?' she said.

'Up where?'

She nodded toward the hills.

'Up there. Where you can see them lights.'

The boy glanced that way and she saw his head move quickly up and down.

'Aw. Yeah, that's Oxford.'

'Is that the way to go?'

He pulled back from the window and opened the door. When he got out and stood up, she took one step back. The middle boy slid over in the seat but he didn't get out. She could feel him watching her but she couldn't see his eyes. She thought he was the one who'd said what he said. The blond boy pointed with his beer toward the lights. He was tall and he had big muscles in his arms and she could smell the scent of fish on him.

'You can go through there,' he said. 'But you'd need to get on over to Batesville and then get on Fifty-five highway and go all the way down. It runs clean to Louisiana. You'd be pretty close to Biloxi if you got down there.'

He turned back to her and she noticed that he was barefoot.

'My name's Jerry,' he said. 'What's yours?'

'Fay,' she said. 'Fay Jones.'

'Well. You want a beer, Fay Jones?'

'I reckon so. If y'all got plenty.'

It was breezy in the back of the truck and the wind kept her hair in her face. He sat beside her with his shoulders against the rear glass of the cab and he had trouble getting his cigarettes lit. There were two coolers in the boat, and they perched on the stern seat and propped their feet on one.

He was recently out of the navy and he talked about all the places he had been, Singapore, Hong Kong, Manila. He told her he lived with the two other boys in a trailer near town and that they all worked the second shift at Georgia-Pacific, made plywood. They'd been on vacation three days, he said, and had four more to go, counting the weekend.

At first she wouldn't hold his hand and then after a while she did. She let him kiss her a few times, but when he tried to touch her titties she pushed his hand away. Sometimes she wished they were smaller. People were always looking at her, men, boys like this. He didn't protest. She held her knees together and tried to hold her hair.

She drank one beer quickly and he opened another one for her. She could see the muscles in his back through the threadbare shirt he wore. After he gave her the beer he leaned over and kissed her again. She let him.

The road reeled out behind them and the white center line dotted out beyond the tailgate, faded, fell into darkness. Houses they passed growing smaller and smaller in the night. His body was warm next to her and the wind had become chilly on her skin, little pimples of flesh standing erect like her puckered nipples she could feel inside the bra. She didn't know what they would do when they got to where they were going. She didn't want the other boys around and she told him she'd heard what one of them had said.

'He's just drunk,' he said.

They halted at a red light and she crossed her legs on the boat seat as cars pulled in behind them. The truck turned and went down a long hill past shopping centers and video stores and fast food joints. At another red light a cop in a cruiser never took his eyes off them, but the blond boy had already told her to hold her beer down while they were in town. The cop watched them until they pulled away and she was afraid he would pull in behind them, but he didn't.

They went up the next hill in light traffic, kids in Jeeps and Japanese pickups cruising up and down the street. She wondered how kids got money for new vehicles like that. They seemed to be everywhere, pulled up in parking lots talking to others like them, gathered in groups laughing and leaning out the windows.

'What are all these kids up to?' she said.

'Aw they just hangin out. They ain't got nothin better to do I don't reckon.'

He seemed quieter now that they were in town. The

26

pickup rumbled beneath them and turned and went up another street and then slowed to travel halfway around a massive white building lit by floodlights and surrounded by tall oaks. Going away from it and watching it she said, 'What's that?'

'Courthouse,' he said. 'Ain't you ever been to town?'

'Not this town.'

The truck gained speed and now the wind was colder. She leaned in closer to him for warmth, her hair fluttering on her cheek and her eyes closed sometimes. His hand rubbed her back and her ribs. She could feel his fingers pause to outline the shape of a bone and she was ashamed of how thin she was and didn't want anybody to see.

Then they were moving again, out of town, down a bumpy road with unlighted buildings and kudzu gullies where mangled cars were piled high behind chain link fences. A blue water tank stood high on blue legs, bathed in smoky light like the cars in the parking lot beneath it, steam rising from a flat factory roof. Walls of pine trees rushing past. They swayed on the boat seat in the curves, not talking much, just hiding from the slap of the wind and drinking their beer in small sips. The truck was going faster now and it went down into a hollow of black trees and wooden fences running out down the road behind them as far as she could see into the darkness chasing them. The brake light began to cast a dim red pall over the fence posts and patches of tar in the road. The truck slowed, screeched once, and turned into a dirt driveway. Tree limbs hung down and green leaves brushed the top of the cab and the truck lurched and swayed over holes and bumps in the drive. Beer sloshed from the can in her hand onto her skirt and one dark spot made a cold place on her leg.

'I need to go to the bathroom,' she said.

'Yeah. Just a minute.'

He took his arm from around her and sat straighter against the cab and turned up the last of the beer and

27

tossed the can into the bushes they were going past. They made a swift little circle and the truck stopped with a jerk. The blond boy got up and went over the side of the bed and said something to the middle boy as he was shutting his door. She looked at the place they had come to. It was a grove of young pines with a double-wide trailer sitting in the middle of it. Sawn stumps still showed beneath it. A droplight wired to one of the trees lit a half-finished wooden deck littered with sawdust and wood scraps, a sawhorse where planks leaned. She could hear a baby crying and music blaring inside the aluminum walls.

She stood up. The blond boy had his arms uplifted to help her down. She put her legs over the side of the bed and half jumped, half slid, his hard hands holding her by the ribs until he lowered her feet to the gravel. He stood watching her for a moment. Then he stepped away and leaned over the side of the bed and tugged on one of the big coolers. The driver climbed up in the boat and stepped down between the seats and got ahold of the other handle and together they lifted it up onto the side of the bed. The blond boy held it there until the middle boy came over and helped him set it on the ground.

'We got to dress all these fish,' the blond boy said.

'We got one in there weighs about ten pounds,' the middle boy said. 'You want to see him?'

'Yeah,' she said.

They moved it closer to the light and the middle boy raised the lid so that she could see down into the crushed ice where slick catfish lay black and shiny with their whiskered mouths and their dead eyes.

'Lord what a mess of fish,' she said. 'What y'all gonna do with that many?'

The driver had gotten down from the truck and walked up beside them. The middle boy was sorting through the slimed bodies, trying to find the big one to show her.

'We gonna have a fish fry one night,' he said, grinning

at her over his shoulder. 'Drink some beer. Have a party. You like to party?'

'I reckon so,' she said. She smiled at them and took another sip of her beer. Her purse was hanging on her arm and she really needed to get to the bathroom, but she didn't want to ask in front of everybody. From the depths of the cooler the middle boy pulled the curved and ice-cold corpse of a flathead nearly two feet long and held the dripping thing out to her like a present.

'He's a nice one, ain't he?'

'Sure is,' she said. She touched the slick flesh with her fingertip and then the boy dropped it back into the ice and wiped his hands on his pants.

'You can go on in if you want to,' the blond boy said.

She moved closer to him and stood there until the other two had picked up the cooler and started moving away with it.

'Where's the bathroom at?' she said.

He turned and pointed toward the south end of the trailer.

'It's down the hall. Linda's in there but just tell her you're with us. We'll be on in after we get through with these fish.'

He didn't wait for an answer but went to a toolbox on the deck and started looking through it. She saw him take out something and walk down toward the other two where they had gone around the end of the trailer. One of them had a flashlight and she could see glimpses of a rough table and the legs of their blue jeans.

She stood there alone and took another drink of her beer. Linda. And there was a baby but she didn't hear it now. The music was still going inside, some strange guitar like none she'd ever heard, but then she hadn't heard much, just what was on the radio when they had the truck or sometimes when the fruit pickers they used to work with brought a radio down to the groves. She'd always wanted one to carry around with her like she'd seen people do.

There was a path made from white stone chips leading up to the steps and somebody had spent some time laying a wooden border along both sides of it and there were posts stubbed up in front of the trailer where she guessed the rest of the deck would go. She stepped across the orange extension cords and around a broken Big Wheel and up to the steps. She didn't know whether to knock or not so she just opened the door and went up the steps, poking her head in, looking around. There was carpet in the living room and shiny paneling on the walls. A cluttered kitchen to the right and something in a pan steaming on the stove. She stepped inside and pulled the door shut behind her. The strange and uneasy wail of the baby started up again somewhere. Down the hall to her left. But he'd pointed to the right.

A big stereo system stood against the back wall of the living room beside a television and music was coming from the speakers, loud and strong, the bass booming. She looked at the new furniture and all the record albums they had and saw how thick the carpet was and how nice everything was and knew now that she had done the right thing by leaving except that already she missed her brother.

She set her beer on a counter and started down the hall. It was narrow, and as she turned to edge past a folding clothes rack she bumped directly into a chubby young woman who screamed in her face and fell back against the wall with scared eyes and an awful look.

'Who in the hell are you?' she said, and Fay backed up.

'I was huntin the bathroom. He said it was down the hall.'

'Who said? You like to scared the living shit out of me.'

Fay motioned toward the front.

'Jerry? That boy out there? They got a big mess of fish they caught.'

The baby wailed louder at the other end of the trailer,

a sound of anguish that trailed off under the thunder of the guitars screaming in the living room.

'I think that music woke him up,' Fay said.

The woman went past her and muttered, 'What do you know about it?'

Fay turned to watch her go. 'I don't know nothin about it,' she said to her back. 'I just wanted to go to the bathroom.'

She stood watching the woman go across the living room and down the hall to the other end of the trailer and then a door shut somewhere and there was nothing to hear but the music pounding in there. She didn't know what to do. She was used to going in the woods but those boys were back there and she was afraid they would see her. So she just waited. A minute passed and then the woman came out of a room down there carrying a baby dressed in a sleeper. When she came by the stereo she reached out and turned it down. She stopped at the edge of the hall and rubbed the child's back, jostled it up and down. The child was looking at Fay with its fingers in its mouth.

'It's down the hall there,' the woman said. 'Two doors down.'

Fay didn't say anything. She turned and went down there and saw the commode and stepped inside and shut the door, raised her skirt and lowered her panties to her knees and sat down. She closed her eyes and breathed a long sigh of relief and leaned forward until she was through. It smelled kind of funny in the bathroom and there were float toys for the child lined up on the floor in front of the tub, pajamas and socks folded neatly on a shelf. She dabbed at herself with some tissue she pulled off the roll and got up and fixed her clothes and flushed the commode. She never had turned loose of her purse.

When she stepped back out into the hall she didn't see anybody. The rest of her beer was still sitting on the counter and she picked it up and took another drink of it, but now it was warm and tasted flat. She didn't feel

31

like she ought to go and sit on the couch. What she wanted was to lie down somewhere for a while and find out what to do next.

She went into the living room and listened to the music for a few minutes. There were a few framed pictures of the woman on the walls, taken when she was younger, thinner, her hair a lighter color. A .22 rifle leaned in one corner, the stock painted red. Magazines were piled beside the couch, spilling onto the floor.

She sipped her beer again and saw a window in the back wall beside the stereo and walked over there. By cupping her hand over her eyes and pressing her face close to the glass she could see the boys out back, working their pliers at the fish hanging on the trees by their heads, stripping the skin away, the light dancing and moving on bloody hands, bloody meat. She pulled back lest they see her watching them and went across the room again.

She opened the door and went down the steps and closed the door behind her. The woman was sitting in a lawn chair beside the path, letting the child stand, or try to. It didn't appear to be old enough to walk yet.

'Hey,' Fay said. 'I'm sorry if I scared you.'

'I don't never know who's here and who ain't,' the woman said.

'I caught a ride with them.'

'Where'd they pick you up at, across the river?'

'Yeah.'

'I don't know what they want to bring all their whores over here for.'

'I ain't no whore.'

The woman turned her head to something out across the dark trees. The floodlight was shining on her face and her eyes were red. The child tried to take a step and she turned loose of it, but it almost fell and grabbed her by the knee.

'If you're gonna stay here you'll have to help with the bills,' the woman said. 'And I've done ate tonight. If you want anything you'll have to fix it yourself.'

32

'I've done eat.'

The woman nodded to herself as if this seemed to satisfy her.

'They drunk?'

'I don't believe they are. I couldn't tell it if they was.'

'How many fish did they ketch?'

'They got a whole mess of em. They got one weighs about ten pound.'

'You ain't got a cigarette on you, have you?'

Fay turned to the light and opened her purse and dug in there for the crumpled pack. She pulled it out. There were two or three left. She shook one loose and stepped closer to her, held it out. The woman took it and put it in her lips and stretched one leg out, feeling around in her pocket.

'Shit. Left it in the house.'

'I got some matches,' Fay said, and searched through her purse again until she found them. When she handed them over, the woman turned loose of the baby and the baby was startled and waved its arms for a second and then fell. Even though it was too late to jump for it Fay almost did. The baby was lying on the ground and the woman was trying to get her cigarette lit.

'Shit,' she said. She picked the baby up and held it standing between her knees and finally got her smoke going and passed the matches back to Fay.

'Is that your baby?'

'Yeah. Stays sick half the time. I just about had it asleep when you come in.'

Fay could see a few stars shining through the branches of the sheltering pines. She could hear traffic on the road out front. She looked around for a place to sit but there didn't seem to be any more chairs. The baby had put part of its hand in its mouth and was watching her shyly, almost smiling, and she couldn't tell if it was a boy or a girl. It had been a long time she'd been this close to a baby, and she smiled back at it.

'Well I don't know where we gonna put em,' the

woman said. 'I told Charles he needed to buy another deep freeze and he said we ain't got no place to put it and I said well build somethin cause the one we got's full of deer meat already and I've done eat that till it's running out my ears. They's a chair over yonder if you want to sit down.'

'Where bouts?'

'Right over there. That blue and white one. Which one you with?' the woman said.

'You mean . . . which one of them boys?'

The woman glared at her and pulled hard on her cigarette. Fay didn't like the look in her eyes.

'Well I know you ain't with Charles. You by God better not be. If that son of a bitch has picked up and brought you over here I'll snatch him baldheaded. I've done missed two ball games cause of this fishin trip.'

'I was kind of talkin to Jerry,' Fay said. 'He set with me on the way up here.'

'Huh,' she said. 'You better be glad Brenda ain't over here.'

'Who's Brenda?'

'His wife. She's on my ball team. She plays short-stop and I play second base. You ever go to the ball games?'

'I don't guess so,' Fay said. The woman had turned in her seat and she wasn't watching the baby. It was trying to take a step or two, coming out from between her legs.

'We play for Rent-All,' the woman said. 'We're the Rent-All Lady Rambos, me, Brenda, Jo Ann, Rachel, Heather Patterson, and Kuwanda Starr, she's a black girl but she's got a good arm on her but she can't run too good cause she got run over by a car when her boyfriend was trying to kill her. Now last Thursday we was in a game with Handy Andy and Rachel was on second and I was on third and Kuwanda popped one over center field that went almost all the way to the fence and I come home but Rachel didn't.'

The baby had lifted its arms, maybe for balance, and

was swaying on its feet as if it moved to some private melody, its feet turned in toward each other. It looked up at Fay and tried to move toward her.

'They asked me to coach next year,' the woman said. 'I told em I'd do it but they was gonna have to get us some better uniforms.' She took the last drag from her smoke and flung it across the yard. She gazed up at the sky for a moment and leaned back in the chair. The baby had gone past the safety of her knee.

'I used to play for Northeast,' she said. 'But I didn't like the league we was in cause we didn't play nothin but niggers and had to go play tournaments in Holly Springs and there was always trouble. I told Ken, I said Ken, I ain't got nothin against a nigger if he'll act right. I ain't prejudice and I've been to lots of company picnics and stuff with Kuwanda and I run into her all the time at Wal-Mart. But I told Ken, If you think I'm gonna get my throat cut in Holly Springs by a bunch of spearchuckers over a damn ball trophy fuck you and the horse you rode in on. Are they not through back there yet?'

She turned in the chair to look over her shoulder and when the baby fell Fay could hear the ugly sound its head made when it landed on the wooden border. She got up.

'Can I hold it?' she said.

The woman turned back around in the chair and looked at her. She seemed to be sizing her up. Then she leaned up and lifted the child and handed it over.

'I guess so,' she said. 'Just don't drop it.'

'I wouldn't drop your baby,' Fay said, and then the baby was on her leg and she had her hands around its stomach and she was looking down into its pale face. It was chewing something.

'I'm gonna go around here and see whatall they caught,' the woman said, and got out of the chair. She went up the path and beside the pickup and her wide ass faded into the darkness on the other side of the trailer.

Fay put her finger into the baby's mouth and ran it along the soft and wet lower lip and hooked the tiny rock, but it slid into the smooth crevice in front of the gum and she peered down in there, pushing the mouth open with her finger, pulled it out, dropped it on the ground.

'You better not be eatin rocks,' she told the baby. She had decided now that it was a girl. She jiggled it on her knee a little and the baby laughed in a happily surprised way and swayed. The small chubby hands with the dimples just back of the knuckles, she remembered that from a long time ago. How good their hair smelled after a bath. The hair on this baby was a light wispy brown and she kissed it on the side of its face.

'I wish you's mine,' she said. 'I wouldn't let you fall down.' She thought for a moment. 'Or trade you for a car neither.'

The woman stayed gone for a long time. She heard some arguing one time, voices raised in protest, and she could sometimes see the beam of a flashlight shining on the ground past the corner of the trailer where masonry blocks held the frame aloft. They never had taken the wheels off and she wondered at how they had gotten it down in here. The baby started to fuss but she hugged it tighter and then when it started to cry she held it up to her chest and patted it on the back until it settled down and after a long while she could tell that it was asleep. There was laughter coming from the darkness now and she wondered if this Brenda would come over and if she had anything to fear from her if she did. Tomorrow was still too far away to think about how it would be or what she would eat. And no money much. She looked down at the torn tennis shoes on her feet, the laces broken and reknotted.

She shifted the baby in her arms and without waking it lowered it gently onto her lap and turned it on its side, rested its head on her thigh. The fat hands in her fingers were cool and unwrinkled. She looked at the tiny nails and the eyelids closed now, a thin trail of

36

drool shining down its chin that she wiped away with the ball of her thumb.

'Wouldn't let nothin happen to you,' she said in a whisper. Out there beyond the pine trees there was nothing but the night.

There was a single lamp burning now in the living room and the music was a live thing that moved through the air and touched Fay's skin. She'd never before been able to hear the individual notes so clearly, the strings and the drums and the horns and the piano keys. She was sitting cross-legged beside the coffee table, laughing easily, the beer at her fingertips still holding bits of ice on the sides of the can. They kept passing the pipe to her and she knew now that she was right to leave what she'd left behind her. It seemed almost like nothing more than a bad dream now, another life, one she'd had for a time before she found this one, and she'd never known that it was possible for a person to feel this good, to feel this loved and protected and happy. Last night she'd been sitting in that rotting black cabin in the woods. Now she was here, with music, and friends, and she was safe.

There was plenty to eat on the table: chips and dip and pretzels, and the blond boy and the middle boy had fileted some of the catfish and were frying them on the stove. She could smell the fish cooking and she could hear the oil sizzling and whenever she looked over at the blond boy he winked at her. She watched the muscles in his arms and the shapes of his legs in the blue jeans as he moved at the stove. But she needed to ask him about this Brenda. There was plenty of time to get to that. He'd already said she could spend the night. There would be plenty of time to talk. Right now all she wanted to do was keep drinking cold beer and listening to the music and feeling it in the marrow of her bones, the way it floated over the room and spoke from the corners.

'You want another bowl?' the driver said. He was on

the floor sitting next to her with his back against the couch and Linda was in a chair by the door, singing along with the music, her eyes closed. At some point she'd taken the baby back to a bedroom and stayed with it for a while. And at some other point she had re-appeared in the living room and had been there ever since.

'Sure,' Fay said. He handed her the bag and the pipe and set them down in front of her and took another drink of the beer. There was a bottle of whiskey on the table, too.

'You want a shot?' The driver picked up the bottle and held it out to her.

'Might as well,' she said. She took it and turned it up to her mouth, took a big drink. It was hot and it burned her mouth and then her stomach as she swallowed and she made a face and handed it back. It seemed to jolt something inside her and she let out a big breath, fanned her hand in front of her mouth.

'Rough, huh?' he said. He laughed at her and set the bottle back on the table. There was something playing on the television but she couldn't keep up with it. She reached into the bag and pinched up some of the grass and put it into the bowl. The driver was watching her. Some of the stuff fell off the edge of the bowl and landed on her skirt. She looked down at it. She reached and brushed it off onto the carpet.

'God*damn*,' he said over the music. 'That shit's fifty dollars a lid. Don't throw it on the fuckin floor.'

She looked up at him and saw real anger on his face.

'Sorry,' she said. 'You got a light?'

He slapped a lighter down in front of her and glared at the television screen. Linda rocked on in her recliner.

She got the pipe up to her mouth just as the blond boy sat down beside her. She half turned to him and struck the lighter and held the flame to the bowl, sucked on the mouthpiece, felt the sharp smoke going into her lungs and held it like they'd told her to.

38

'Let me have a hit,' he said, and took the pipe and the lighter from her.

Fay made a small hole with her lips and blew the smoke out in a thin stream the way she'd seen them do. She turned to watch the blond boy and saw the red seed of fire growing in the bowl of the pipe. After he sucked it all in and it went out he laid it down. He went into a fit of coughing and ducked his head, leaning back against the couch. He put his arm around her, coughing still.

'Damn,' he said. 'That old skunkweed is rough. Did you catch a buzz?'

'I feel fine,' she said. 'I ain't never felt this good. It sure is nice of y'all to let me stay with you.'

He turned her face to him and when she leaned closer he put his hands on the sides of her face and she could smell the fish on him again. The music was still loud and the smoke had begun to get heavy in the room and her stomach was rolling just a bit, the bass in the speakers just beginning to make a small hurtful pounding inside her eardrums. His hand casually cupped her and he kissed her, his breath hot and kind of sour and then he pushed his tongue into her mouth. She drew back and pulled his hand down and held it in her own and he twined his fingers in hers. She could feel her face getting red. His hand came up again and again she pulled back from him. When she turned to look at the driver he was staring at them. The middle boy was still cooking and hadn't noticed. Linda was in her chair with her eyes closed. Maybe she was asleep.

'Let's don't in front of them,' Fay said.

'Come on, then,' he said, and stood up.

She turned her face up to him and suddenly she was dizzy. His face seemed to whirl against the ceiling, the strands of his hair sticking out from the sides of his head.

'I thought we was gonna eat,' she said, but she suddenly had no desire to eat at all, and it was only something to say, to put things off, to stay sitting where she was, and his hand came down and caught her wrist and began to pull her up.

'Eat later,' she heard him say over the music. And then he was leading her around the coffee table and across the living room and the middle boy raised his face to watch her as they went past. The smell of the splattering oil hit her full in the face, a waft of steam rising toward the vent hood. Her stomach rolled again. She looked into the pan and saw the slabs of dead fish dusted with scorched cornmeal and saw the thin cracks of blood rising up through the meat and cold sweat leaped out on her forehead.

'I don't feel so good,' she said, but the blond boy didn't seem to hear her. He still had her by the hand and they were going down through the hall where she had first run into Linda but now it was dark and she bumped the walls with her shoulder as he led her back. Clothes were on the floor. They passed the open door of the bathroom. She hadn't known the hall was that long. Her bladder was full again from all the beer she'd drunk and she pulled back and tried to tell him to let her stop, but he was strong and he just kept pulling her. He pushed open a door at the end of the hall and turned on a lamp and as he passed by the unmade bed he kind of flung her toward it and closed the door. She landed sitting on the edge of the bed with her skirt high up on her legs and her mind dazed. She could see fishing tackle on the dresser, lures and spools of line, a snarled reel and behind it color posters of naked women thumbtacked to the walls.

'Oh,' she said, and moved her hands to her stomach to quiet the rebellion growing there. She lurched up to try and make it to the door but toppled over onto one of the pillows and tried to push herself upright with one shaky arm and hand. He was pulling his T-shirt up over his head.

A knock came at the door and a voice said, 'Are y'all gonna eat or what?' She tried to rise again.

Things seemed to have shifted inside her somehow and her right side felt heavier than her left. She couldn't get one of her legs to work and she was afraid she was going to wet herself. And then he was on her, his hot hungry mouth pressing down on hers and her hair in her face as the knocking and the voice came to the door again: 'Hey. How many hushpuppies can y'all eat?'

His hand was up inside her skirt and she could feel his fingers pushing the elastic of her panties aside, probing, the nails scratching at her skin. She drew back and tried to form some words to tell him she didn't feel like this and it was hot in the tiny room and she could smell the sweat of his body on the sheets and the next thing she knew he had stood up and unbuckled his pants and had caught her by the ears and was guiding her toward him. She put her hands out to push herself back from this, could see it coming toward her face. But he had her head in a steel grip and she could feel his hard fingers pressing against the bone of her skull and she saw that he was trying to get it in her mouth so she puked on him.

That was enough to make him stop. He gave out a short cry and backed up and she tried to make it off the bed before the next spasm churned her guts, but it went down the front of her and landed in the floor between them. She was trying to tell him to help her, but he had already turned to the door and opened it and run down the hall to the bathroom and slammed that door before she could get off the bed. And it wasn't over yet. She looked for a quick place to put it and saw a small plastic garbage can half filled with fast food wrappers and newspapers, and she lurched out for it and went to her knees and then to her hands and knees and knelt next to it with salty tears running into her mouth. She heaved the contents of her stomach out until the bile came up and forced another fit of gagging on her. Her mouth was stretched wide open, trying to take in air, and she'd even gotten some of it in her hair.

Then he was standing over her, screaming at her, and the rest of them were coming down the hall, one carrying a spatula. She saw them briefly, but they didn't seem real, and then she felt herself rapidly sinking down into a place she had never been before, heard more than felt her head when it hit the floor.

Music was playing somewhere. Fay opened her eyes when she came awake but she did not move, just stayed where she was and tried to remember it and then did remember it, hands pulling at her, lifting, turning her, being dragged down the hall and then blackness again and then coming awake in the tub with the cold water spraying down on her from the showerhead and all of them next to the tub and her in her underwear, her hair hanging in wet strings from her head, slipping in the tub as she tried to get up and the woman Linda pushing her back into the water, saying, 'Goddamn, what a mess.' And sitting shivering on the commode lid wrapped in a rough towel and all her undergarments hung on a shower rod and water dripping from her panties and her cold naked feet on the linoleum.

Now she raised her head and bumped it against something, hard. She almost cried out but instead sent her hand searching to see what she'd hit, found a smooth cool rim of something and then leaned over the edge of the seat to see the gas and brake pedals, some cassette tapes on the floorboards. She moved her head out from under the steering wheel and pulled herself up in the seat. She looked around. The boat was still in the back of the truck. She could see it darkly through the rear window, and the shape of the trailer out there in the yard, the droplight on the tree cut off now. The window was down on the driver's side and there was a full pack of cigarettes on the dash, a lighter next to it. She opened the pack and lit one and sat there smoking. Her stomach felt better now but there was no way to tell

43

how much time had passed. She figured it was late. She was fully dressed except for her shoes, but her clothes were all damp. Somebody had evidently wrapped her in a musty quilt but she must have pushed it off in her sleep because it was piled up on her legs. She pulled it up around her shoulders and sat huddled, the tip of the cigarette glowing against the dash when she puffed on it. Where was her purse? She felt around on the seat and pulled the quilt off and hunted for it with her hands, but it was not there. And her shoes, she needed them. Would they have locked the door and would she have to wait for morning to retrieve her purse and her shoes and face at least some of them again?

She put a finger down between her legs to see if anything had happened to her while she was asleep. She couldn't tell. And could she have fought him off if it had come to that? The old man had crept up on her twice and twice she had fought him off, but she had been afraid that it would happen sometime while she was asleep. So she had left. She wished she'd told Gary to leave, too. He could have been with her now. But she knew he'd never leave them, that he'd always stay to try and take care of them. At least until their little sister could leave, too. Maybe she'd done the wrong thing by leaving. But staying was wrong too.

She thought about Biloxi again. A day's travel, he'd said.

The cigarette was almost gone and with it she lit another one from the pack. Putting off trying to get back in there. But she needed her purse, and she had to have her shoes for the walking she had to do. She felt inside her bra quickly. The dollar was gone.

She pushed the quilt down in the floor and opened the driver's door quietly. She pushed against it. It yawned open with a scream of metal on metal and she climbed down and left it open. Her feet were tender on the gravel. A few stars were still shining when she raised her face up to see past the tall pines. Across the whole state, he'd said. She wondered how big the whole state was. She hoped it wasn't as big as Texas.

She eased up on the wooden steps and touched the doorknob. It turned under her hand and the door swung open. On silent feet she walked into the living room and pulled the door almost closed behind her. A tiny red dot was lit on the face of the stereo and somebody was moaning the last lines of a song, and then a deejay chatting conversationally in the hushed room. The voice of somebody talking who was not mad at her and it comforted her. She didn't want to wake them up. She didn't want them to think she was trying to steal anything. She just wanted her shoes and her purse, and, if she could find it, the dollar.

Another song started up. The door tried to swing open in the wind, bumped back against the frame, and she caught it and pulled it shut. Nobody got out of bed and came screaming at her. She moved across the floor to the kitchen and past the stove. Grease had congealed on it, plates thick with sodden paper towels and half-eaten fries spattered with ketchup. Bent and empty beer cans sat on the counter. She was hungry again and she picked up a french fry and ate it.

There was a light in the hall, a miniature bulb inserted into a wall socket with a plastic shield covering the top half of it. At the door to the bathroom her hand found the light switch and flipped it up. The bathroom was lit by bright bulbs in a row above a mirror. There her shoes were beside the tub. She turned to see if anybody was coming. There was nothing to hear but the music. She couldn't remember where she'd put her purse, but on the lavatory top a wet dollar bill lay. She picked it up. She thought it looked like hers, so she folded it and put it back inside her bra.

She got her shoes back on sitting on the commode lid again, and her hair was a little drier now. She broke one of the laces again and had to rethread it down to the bottom eyelets, but she thought maybe it would stay on her foot.

When she eased out into the hall and turned the light switch off, she heard the baby make a faint cry and then nothing. Back at the stove she could see her purse sitting on the couch. She walked to it and picked it up. That was when she heard a dull groaning, half words, the soft sounds of bodies moving. All she had to do was walk out the door. But the sounds pulled at her, and she knew she'd never heard anything like that before. She wondered what it was that would bring such sounds to the mouths of people. It was near, just beyond the dark corner of the other hall. She moved one step at a time, and her feet made no noise on the floor. Just down past the corner a bit of yellow light spilled onto the linoleum in the hall and it came from the same place as the sounds. And she grew nearer and nearer and put her face just past the edge of the door and there were three of them, the blond boy on his back and the woman bent over him, her wet mouth stretched open and sliding up and down on him and the driver kneeling behind her, the skin of her big ass trembling and shaking as he slammed into her with his face turned toward the ceiling and his eyes pinched shut.

She drew back as quietly as she had come, one step at a time, back across the living room, easing the door open and shut softly, down the steps into the yard and past the lawn chairs and up the path toward the drive, walking faster once she was away from them, and then running almost blindly in the blackness, her purse swinging from her hand, down the rutted drive toward more night while the voices of the crickets and tree frogs told her to hurry, hurry, that it was late, that morning was near.

In pockets of their own shade the trees stood clumped along the pasture fence and a hot wind stirred the grass at her feet. The concrete was throwing the heat of the sun back into her face after only two hours. She could hear the trucks whining long before they got to her and she was keeping off the highway so as not to be hit from behind. There was a deep median of grass between the lanes and she had been watching the orange tractors for a good while now, the trucks with their flat beds parked and the groups of men in hard hats from a distance.

She had rested for a time just on the edge of the city limits at dawn after asking directions at a gas station just as a man was opening the door. He had pointed, told her to go west to Batesville, then south, and he had gone on in and started turning on the lights. She stood there for a minute, looking around for a hose or a water tap, but there was only the concrete island with the gas pumps and the cubicle of glass with racks of cigarettes and the man sitting there fiddling with the register. So she went on down the street and out to the intersection and started following the highway west, the way he had pointed.

She was very thirsty now and the grass was littered with Styrofoam cups, aluminum cans, shredded pieces of truck tires. She stepped around a crushed armadillo with its shattered shell and hairy legs, the toes splayed on the stones along the roadway. Off to the right she could see some white horses gathered at a trough and drinking from it. One raised its head and shook its mane, then lowered its head again. But she didn't guess she was ready to be drinking from a horse's trough just yet and she kept on walking.

She didn't know if she could walk all day in this heat or not. She had done it before, though never when she was feeling like this. The headache had been steadily climbing up the back of her skull and now it had settled into a place somewhere just behind her eyeballs and it caused her to grind her back teeth together in an effort to keep her jaws clamped tight so that maybe her footsteps wouldn't make her head fly apart.

She could feel the blood jolting in her legs and sometimes she weaved as she walked. What she had seen beyond the door the night before was still running like a fragment of a movie in her head and she could still hear the sounds they had been making. She hadn't known such things could be done, two men with a woman like that, and she wondered now which one was the father of the little child she had held.

The cars kept passing her and even if she'd had her thumb out there was no place for them to pull over except for the places where side roads entered the main highway. She could see houses set back from the blacktop but no people moved in the yards. She was closer to the orange trucks now and she could see the mowers canted up on the hillsides and a thin stream of shorn grass and weeds spraying out behind the tractor, a cascade of green bits and pieces.

She waited until the road was clear, then stepped out into the highway and walked across the center line and down into the grass of the median and went toward the orange tractors again. She could hear them now, the diesel chug and the steady swish of the Bush Hog and she could see the black smoke jetting from the pipe as the driver turned to make another pass. The trucks were parked in a flat turnaround between the two sections of road and a few men were loading portable signs printed with large block letters MOWERS AHEAD and the cars kept whizzing by on the road above her, her head about level with the pavement now, walking through the clipped grass and the torn bits of aluminum from the shredded cans and here and there jagged bits of glass she had to watch for, the soles of her tennis shoes so thin now and not able to turn away something as sharp as that.

The men climbed into the truck and it pulled away, one man riding on the side step, a red light flashing on a dome mounted in the roof. The tractor climbed out of the wide ditch and went along the shoulder against the traffic until it had gone past the turnaround and then it swerved down and once more the grass began to fly out behind it.

An air horn blared on the road above her and she looked up at the moving face of an older man watching her from his high cab. The truck changed gears without slowing and rolled on. A car passed it. There was not one bit of shade now and the sun beat down on her shoulders and the top of her head. She swung the strap of the purse up on her shoulder and kept walking. The orange truck had gone ahead and she couldn't see it any-more. There was just the man on the tractor still mowing. He went at a slow pace, back and forth in narrow sweeps, ever deeper into the grass valley until he too went from sight and there was just the exhaust pipe with the smoke drifting from it to show her his location. He crossed to the other side and she saw him start making his passes, climbing steadily toward the road.

She stopped and sat down on the side of the hill and hung her head between her arms and her knees. Her breath was coming hard and a tick was crawling on her ankle. She picked it off, tried to rub it off her finger, finally flicked it away with her nail. The thing about catching a ride was that you never could tell who was going to pick you up. If they stopped and you didn't like their looks, then you had to tell them to go on, that you didn't want to ride after all. She saw that she was going to have to be careful of boys now and that she'd been lucky the night before. And then sometimes they'd cuss you if you didn't get in with them after they'd stopped, call you a bitch or a whore or say *Fuck you, then*, or throw gravel on your legs when they spun off from the side of the road.

She didn't want to keep sitting there and she didn't want to go on. The tractor had climbed out of the ditch once more and it was going over the hill where the truck had gone and in another minute she couldn't see any of them. Fay knew they had water. Men who worked in the sun all day had to have water.

She wished she'd taken a few extra cigarettes from the pack on the dash of the truck last night. She didn't have any now. She'd already looked through her purse, hoping, but she'd known there weren't any more in there before she'd even looked. And they cost more than a dollar. She thought they cost about a dollar and a half.

Another horn blew at her up on the road, kept blowing, faded away down the highway and then it stopped blowing and she could hear the rush of its tires on the pavement. Far away down the country in front of her the road curved into the distance of a pale green mass that lay at the edge of the sky and that sky was the lightest blue she had ever seen, almost without color, and in that emptiness one small black form drifted with wide wings spread, turning in the currents, riding loops down and then lifting, stalling for a moment before it rushed downward again. She looked up at the buzzard and muttered, 'You gonna have to wait a while if you waitin on me.'

She almost didn't hear the car for the noise of the other vehicles on the road, but she turned her head from where she was sitting on the edge of the grass and saw a set of wheels slowing to a stop behind her, pebbles embedded in the treads, and then she looked up at the whole car and saw who was driving it and her heart sank fast. She stood up quickly, brushing at the back of her skirt.

The trooper stopped the car in the center of the turnaround and picked up the radio mike and said something into it and then he was getting out, reaching back in for his hat, and she saw the black tips of his boots coming out from behind the door. Then he was standing there with his neatly pressed gray trousers, a blue stripe down each leg, a gun on his hip and a crisp shirt, his nameplate and his shiny brass and all the authority she feared. He put the hat on and then his face was in shade. She could see the short dark hair just under the rim of the hat and his clean-shaven cheeks where tiny red vessels had come to the surface of his skin and her own distorted face twinned in the sunglasses with the cars on the other highway passing into and out the other side of the little gold rims. He touched the brim of his hat with his fingers, nodded.

'Can I help you, ma'am?' he said.

'I don't know,' she said. 'I was just out walkin. I ain't done nothin wrong have I?'

'I don't guess.' He glanced up at the sky for a moment. 'Mighty hot for a stroll. You headed somewhere in particular?'

She didn't know anything about cops except that they rousted you from the park benches and stared at you when they saw you walking down the road. And sometimes they pulled over and asked you where you were going, like this one. She didn't want to say the wrong thing. She knew he had all the power.

'I'm headed to Biloxi,' she said. 'I was just settin here. I got hot. I wanted to rest a little.'

The radio chattered loudly inside the cruiser but he didn't pay any attention to it. He was as good-looking a man as she'd ever seen and she wondered how old he was. She put a little tease in her voice, trying it out. She was loose now. She could talk to men now. She didn't think she wanted any boys.

'You ain't gonna arrest me, are you?'

'I don't reckon so,' he said. 'You feeling OK?'

She wasn't, but she didn't want to tell him that. He might take her somewhere, do something with her.

'It sure is hot,' she said. 'I wanted to catch up with them fellers to get some water if they had some but I can't catch up with em.'

'Who?'

She pointed. The road crew was nothing but a knot of men with a truck beside them, vague and hazy through the heat.

'They been cuttin the grass but I can't catch up with em. I thought I could but I've done about give out. That's why I was settin down.'

She looked up at him but could read nothing on his face. He seemed to be waiting for something else.

'I didn't know whether to try and catch a ride with somebody or not,' she said. 'I don't know who to trust and who not to.'

He watched her and didn't say anything. Then he turned and leaned into the car and picked up the radio mike again. He took off his hat and tossed it onto the front seat beside some papers and a clipboard. She could see a shotgun in a steel rack behind the seat, a steel mesh divider in back of the gun. He said something into the mike and waited for an answer, and somebody replied, a woman's voice, and he spoke into it again and then hung it back on the dash. There were handcuffs on his wide belt and she could see the imprint of his wallet in his back pocket. When he came out he was taking the cap off a plastic bottle of water, which he handed to her.

'Here,' he said. 'You'll get dehydrated out in this sun.'

She turned a drink down her throat and felt it come alive again, and swallowed and swallowed again, and took it down and gasped for air, and then turned it up again and then it was all gone. The bottle was light, almost weightless in her hand. She gave it back to him.

'Thank you,' she said, and wiped her mouth. 'That was mighty good.'

He tapped the bottle against his leg and looked down the road, just a glance, and then he turned back to her.

'My car's got an air conditioner in it. Why don't you get in and sit down for a while?'

She was almost afraid to get in, but she figured she'd better do what he said.

'OK. Yes sir.'

He walked around with her, opened the door on the opposite side, and she looked in and stopped. He leaned in and pushed it all over to his side and got back out of her way. She sat down and was enveloped in a waft of cold air. He shut the door on her and she sat with her purse in her lap. The glass was tinted and now the outside world was not bright and hot like it had been. He got in on the other side and buckled his seat belt and told her to put hers on and she looked down at meaningless straps until he saw that she didn't know how to do what he was talking about and bent toward her, his arm brushing against her, pulled the strap across her without touching her again and fastened it into the holder on the seat.

'There,' he said. He reached up for the shifter and then stopped. He slumped back against the seat, tapped his fingers on the steering wheel. He took a pack of cigarettes from his shirt pocket and when he saw her looking at them, shook one loose from the pack and offered it. She took it and said thank you again.

He pushed in on the lighter in the dash and looked across the road at the newly clipped grass.

'Are you in trouble with somebody?'

'I don't reckon so,' she said. 'I just didn't want to stay where I was at.'

The lighter popped out and he reached for it, held the burning red coil up to her and she bent her face holding the cigarette with her fingers until it was lit. He lit his own and rolled the window down six inches. The car looked and smelled brand new and except for

53

the papers on the dash it was very clean. She couldn't even hear it running.

'This sure is a nice car,' she said.

He turned his head a bit when she said that. He seemed amused for a moment.

'You ever rode in one of these before?'

She took that to mean had she ever been arrested. She cracked the window and tipped her ashes out, but they blew back into the car. She fanned at them.

'Don't worry about that,' he said.

'I don't want to mess up your car.'

'It's not mine. I just use it for a while and then they give me another one. You never have rode in one?'

'No sir. I never have been in no trouble.'

'Why are you out walking down the road?'

She looked down at her lap. The cars were going slower on the highway now. The only reason she was scared to tell him the truth was because she was afraid he might take her back and as close as she could figure she'd only made it about fifteen miles maybe. In twenty minutes she could be right back.

'I left because of my daddy,' she said.

He relaxed in the seat and she studied him. There was a wedding band on his left hand and there were some fresh scratches on his right forearm, tiny black lines scabbed in little arcs.

'And you're headed to Biloxi?'

'Yes sir. They said it was a long way. But I heard it was nice down there. They supposed to have a beach and all.'

'Who said?'

'Some boys that picked me up last night.'

'Some boys? Where'd they pick you up at?'

'It was on this road close to where I used to live.'

'Did you know these boys?'

'No sir. I didn't know em. They just stopped and picked me up.'

She could tell he was getting agitated but she didn't know why. Maybe he could tell that she'd been drinking the night before. Or maybe she was keeping him from doing his work.

'How many boys?'

'It was three of em. They had this boat in the back of their pickup and they had a big mess of fish they'd caught.'

'And you didn't know them.'

'I didn't know em from Adam.'

And that made him mad. He nodded and she saw a muscle flex in his jaw. He turned his face to the half open window.

'How'd you know they wouldn't kill you?'

'They didn't look like they would.'

He turned to look into her eyes.

'Have you got any idea how dangerous it is for a girl like you to be out on this road at night? Or any road. There's people that drive around just looking for somebody hitching a ride.'

She put her hands in her lap and looked out the windshield.

'I was tired of walkin,' she said. 'I didn't know where I was and I'd done almost got dogbit one time already. I didn't think they was gonna try to hurt me.'

She thought back to what she had seen them doing in that room. He kept looking out the window for a while. He took a few more drags off the cigarette and then flipped it out and rolled up the window.

'You're headed west, right?'

'I guess so,' she said. 'They said go west and then south. What's the name of that place where you turn off? Batesville?'

'Yeah,' he said. 'That's where my office is. I ain't supposed to be giving rides but I guess I can take you that far if you want to go.'

'Well,' she said. 'If you don't care.'

He picked up the radio mike and told them that he was 10-8 again and looked both ways before he turned the car around. She tossed her smoke out and rolled up the window.

'That air too cool on you?' he said.

'It's fine.'

He waited until the road was clear and then the power in the motor pressed her back in the seat and they were running down the hill in the cool air and the world was softened and diffused and she felt that they were floating on a cushion of air, rushing headlong toward those distant hills and the green line of trees slightly shimmering beneath that awful sun.

His name was Sam Harris and he told her he was forty-two years old. His home was at Cole's Point, he said, a lakeside house on the reservoir at Sardis, and he got to telling her about crappie fishing and running trotlines for White River cats and deer hunting in the deep hollows of hardwood timber on the forty acres he owned. There was just him and his wife now, he said, and she liked gardening, and had some clubs she belonged to, but he said he liked to fish a lot and she didn't.

At the Sonic in Batesville he pulled in and bought lunch for her, a thick hamburger with melted cheese and pickles, fries, and a Coke in a tall cup, her cheeks stuffed and chewing when he pulled back out into traffic and turned up Highway 51. Out past the high school and into the country land where the cotton was growing and the rusted irrigators crept on their wheels spraying water over the sunburned rows and past deserted silos with their conical roofs punched in, the rotten boards hanging and crumbling down the sides. Fields of tall corn with the tassled tops swaying in the wind and old barns where black cows lay chewing their cuds inside new pipe fences. Climbing back into the hills and turning northeast toward Highway 4 and the fronds of kudzu that had crawled unceasingly to the sides of the road and held out their trembling vines to the air. Back down again to 7 south of Holly Springs, his district, he said, pretty big district, wasn't it? and then again among the lumbering trucks so docile and slow now with him behind them, their broad polished backs shining until they passed them and left them behind, the car always kept at a swift and steady gait that seemed to sweep everything before them past, as if there were some purpose to their travel, a certain destination, but he said that he was just cruising.

Once in a while he would flash his lights at an oncoming car after reading numbers in red from a machine mounted on the dash but he didn't pull anybody over.

The sun went slowly across the sky until it hung straight overhead and invisible, glaring down on the roadway and always the cars and trucks climbing and passing, trailing one another in a line. He let Fay out to use the bathroom at a barbecue joint just north of Lafayette County and when she got back in the cruiser he handed her an ice-cold bottle of lemonade and a BC Powder and after another ten miles she felt lots better.

With her stomach full and the cool bottle sitting in her lap and the window cracked to let the smoke out, she started telling him about her life up till now.

The wind sucked the smoke from the car as farms and houses rolled by and treelines appeared and gradually grew closer and then passed as new ones appeared far down the road. He drove without speaking and she felt by then that he wasn't going to make her go back home. They were almost back to the place where he had picked her up when she started telling him about the two times her father had crept up on her in the dark, how he'd ripped her clothes and put his hand around her throat and tried to choke her down, and of how she'd fought and kicked and scratched at his eyes until she was able to get away from him almost naked and run into the woods to hide, alone with the night birds and the tree frogs calling and her heart hammering finally slower inside her chest.

She told him about her little sister, Dorothy, and how

she had just stopped talking a long time ago, and about Gary, her brother, who had worked all summer and kept them from starving, and how, yesterday evening, she had told her mother she was leaving and had walked out of the yard.

It was midafternoon by then. He slowed down and then turned off the highway onto an asphalt road where signs advertised boat rentals and lots for sale, a state park with symbols for camping and boating. He took his time on this road, following the curves and hills where the grass had been neatly mowed and young trees had been planted. He drove for a couple of miles and they came to the near end of the great levee where short treated posts held lengths of chain stretched down both sides. Out across the bright water she could see boats moving across the waves, specks of blue and white and red that were other boats far out on the lake. And there were sharp-winged birds soaring in the air, flocks of them that lifted and turned, and when she rolled her window down she could hear their voices on the wind.

Sam slowed the car and drove along the levee for a while. He smiled some, looking out at it.

'Pretty, ain't it?'

'It sure is,' she said. 'I ain't never seen that much water before.'

'It used to be the biggest earthen dam in the world. Then I think they built a bigger one over in Iran or Iraq. Most of this one was built with mule power. Back in the thirties. You want to get out and look at it?'

'I'd like to go swimmin in it,' she said. 'If I knew how to swim.'

He grinned and pulled the car over to an observation point and parked it close to the chains and left it running. They got out. He walked around to the front of the car and put his hands in his pockets and leaned against a lamppost that was there, watching her.

'There's a beach on the other side,' he said, turning his head toward the lower lake. She looked down there

58

at the groves of trees and the picnic tables, tents and campers under the trees.

'This is nice,' she said. She was smiling. She stepped over the chain and stood there looking out across the water. It was out there as far as she could see.

'And you say you live over here?'

He came over to where she was and stopped beside her, stretched his hand and arm out and pointed to the south side.

'You can't see it from here,' he said. 'I mean you can't see the house, hardly. I can see this levee from my back deck. I go out there in the morning to drink my coffee. It's over there behind that bluff you can see there, where that red dirt is.'

She nodded, looking, trying to see it. It was cool there with the wind coming off the water and the boats rocking up and down on the waves.

'What are you going to do?' he said. He sat down on the post next to her and folded his fingers together, watching the water move.

'I don't know.' She turned to look at him. 'I guess I'll just head south. I don't know what else to do. I don't want to go back.'

His voice was quiet and he kept his fingers locked together. He drew in a deep breath.

'How will you live, though? What will you do for money? For food? And a place to stay. You can't just sleep on the side of the road. Somebody'll do something to you. It happens to young girls all the time. I've seen it.' He turned to look at her. 'I've seen it myself, with my own eyes.'

Down below them there was a slanting wall of big white rocks that went all the way down to the water that lapped against them and receded, was unending in its movement.

'I guess I'll try to find a job,' she said.

'But you'd have to find a place to stay. You can't sleep in a park, the cops'll roust you in any town you go to. Or they'll take you to a shelter. They might even send you back to where you came from. There's no telling what might happen to you.'

She looked down at her dirty fingernails and the nails of both her big toes sticking through the ragged tennis shoes. She knew she looked bad and she wished there was something she could do about it.

'What you think I ought to do?'

Sam got up from the post and put his hands back in his pockets. The wind was whipping the legs of his trousers and the radio was chattering inside the cruiser.

'I think you ought to come home with me and let me and my wife fix you some supper. You like steak?'

She gave him a small smile.

'I'd like to try it.'

'Come on, then,' he said.

She gazed out over the water and saw that today was better than yesterday, and decided to go with it. She got up and they walked back to the car.

The drive that led to his house curved through a big stand of mature pines. You couldn't see the house from the main road, he told her. The cruiser nosed along the drive and the trees were close on each side.

'Amy's probably out on the deck with her nose stuck in a book. We can take you swimming after while if you want to go.'

She didn't know what to expect here. She'd never imagined that a cop would have a house in the woods or like to fish.

'I might get in if it ain't in the deep. I ain't never had a chance to learn how to swim.'

'Everybody needs to know how to swim,' he said. 'What if you were on a boat and it sank? You ever thought about that?'

'I ain't never been on a boat.'

He slowed down going around the last curve and she caught a glimpse of the house then, a flash of tall windows and cypress siding, a high peaked roof.

'You hang around me very long you'll be on one.'

The drive went over a low wooden bridge and when he pulled up and stopped in front of the house, she could do nothing but look at it for a minute. It seemed to have grown in one piece out from the side of the hill, the entire side wall made of glass so that she could see the furniture inside and fans turning in the ceiling and potted plants hanging from big wooden beams. The old pines that grew beside it covered it in a deep shade and littered its top with their needles. A wide deck ran all across the back of it and there were padded lounging chairs and tables and past the corner of the deck she could see the water of the lake rippling out there.

'This is your house?' she said.

'Home sweet home,' he said, opening the door. He had already checked out on the radio and he grabbed his notebook and got his keys. 'Come on in and we'll find Amy. I know she's probably got a swimming suit you can wear.'

Her fingers went to the door handle but they were slow in opening it. He was standing in front of the car, waving her in with his keys. She opened the door and got out, still looking up at the house. Now she was even more ashamed of her torn tennis shoes, the blouse and the skirt that were too small for her. She shut the door and walked up beside the fender and stopped. Sam had already gone ahead to the steps and now he turned to look back at her.

'Well? You coming in or what?'

'You sure it's all right?' she said. 'You don't think your wife will get mad or nothin?'

He walked back to her and gently took one of her hands.

'Come on, Fay,' he said. 'It's all right.'

She followed him then, the two of them hand in hand going up the steps to the door that was mostly glass too and inside to the clean pine floors and the big stone fireplace and the stuffed animal heads and fish hanging on the walls. The fans turned overhead and she could see a big kitchen and a butcher block table under a rack of copper pans and utensils.

'There she is,' he said, and he turned loose of her hand and set his things on a table in the corner. 'Let's go out on the deck.'

She didn't know what to do with her purse so she just held on to it. He didn't wait for her but went to the double glass door and pushed one side of it back and stepped out. A small woman in shorts and T-shirt who looked a lot like him sat in her chair with a drink in her hand. A book lay open and facedown on the table. He said something to her and pointed back inside and she got up a little unsteadily and then they both came back inside.

The woman smiled at Fay and sipped her drink. Her black hair was streaked with bits of gray and she had pretty white teeth, bright brown eyes that seemed shy and careful. She came forward with her hand out, and she seemed to Fay no more than a girl herself. Then when Fay looked closer at her eyes she saw the tight wrinkles of skin that makeup couldn't hide.

'Amy,' Sam said, 'this is Fay. I've asked her to eat supper with us tonight.'

Fay turned loose of her purse with one hand and took the hand that was offered.

'Hey Fay.' Her hand was limp and cool, fragile as a bird's wing. It felt like it had no strength at all.

'Hey,' she said. She could feel her face turning red. She shook the hand quickly and released it, and then looked at Sam for what to do next.

'I told her we might take her swimming. You got me some beer iced down?'

'It's out on the deck. Why don't you come on out and let's sit down, Fay.'

'I'm gonna go change clothes,' Sam said, and he went past them unbuttoning his shirt and vanished somewhere in the house. But this Amy was still smiling at her.

'There's a good breeze out here,' she said. 'It's been awful hot today, hasn't it?'

'Yes ma'am. It sure has.'

She followed Amy out the door and watched her slide it shut behind them and then followed her across the deck, watching her walk very carefully.

'Let's sit down over here in the shade, Fay. Would you like a cold Coke or something?'

Amy took a seat in a rocking chair and Fay sat down on the bench that ran along the railing of the deck.

'Yes ma'am. That'd be real nice.'

There was an ice chest between them and Amy opened the lid and reached into it and pulled out a can and handed it to her.

'Thank you.'

'You're welcome. Sam's working the day shift now and he always wants a cold beer when he gets home. So I always have some iced down for him. Are you hungry? Would you like something to eat?'

Fay shook her head and opened the can.

'No ma'am. I'm fine, thank you. He bought me a hamburger a while ago. Best one I ever had.'

She still had her purse in her lap but she picked it up now and set it beside her feet and held the can with both hands. She smiled, looked down, took a drink of the Coke. Something unexpected happened in her throat and two spurts of it shot out of her nose, fizzing spots that landed on her skirt. She jumped up and wiped at her skirt and then at her nose, sidestepping, her face blushing hotly.

'Goddamn,' she said. 'I didn't mean to do that.' She paused and looked up. 'I'm sorry. I didn't mean to say that, either. I'm just nervous.'

Amy had already stepped to a table and pulled a paper towel off a roll there. She was still smiling when she moved up close and dabbed at the wet spots.

'Nothing to worry about,' she said. 'I had a date with this boy one time and we'd been swimming, went in this beer joint to get some ribs and I sat down on this chair and farted in my wet swimming suit and you could hear it all over the room.'

She stepped back and winked. 'Shit happens. Don't worry about it. Would you rather have a beer?'

Fay looked at the Coke in her hand and already she knew that she liked what was in the brown bottles better.

'I guess so,' she said.

'Or I can mix you a drink. I like Ruby Red grapefruit juice and Stoly. You ever drink that?'

'Nome. A beer's fine,' she said.

Amy got one and opened it after a few tries and handed it to her. They sat back down and Amy picked up her glass. She looked into it for a second and took a sip, looked out across the lake, and then her eyes moved back to Fay.

'We don't get much company out here. We're a couple of regular hermits. I go to the beauty shop and the grocery store. That's it, beauty shop, grocery store, over and over.'

'It sure is nice out here,' Fay said. 'I ain't never seen such a pretty house.'

'It's too big,' Amy said. 'Too much to clean.'

Fay tucked her feet under the bench so that her tennis shoes were hidden. She wished she had some better ones. The beer was very cold when she sipped from it.

'All this water,' she said. 'I'd love to live out here.'

Amy nodded and leaned back, holding her drink with both hands. She crossed her ankles.

'I don't never go out on it. It's pretty to set and look at, though.' She took another drink and looked back up. 'He likes to fish. He goes out on it a lot.' She studied the lake for a while. 'Yeah. A lot,' she said, and then she lifted the glass as if that explained something. She gave Fay a weak smile. 'I like to relax when I get off from work.'

Fay just smiled and bobbed her head and tried to think of something to say to her. She wanted Sam to come on back out now. But looking at the water was nice. She could have sat there and looked at it for a long time. It made her feel good. The water made her feel like she belonged beside it in some old familiar way.

Now that she was so close, Amy looked older than him. By a good bit.

Fay peeled at the label on her beer and then made herself stop. Little fritters of paper to pick up.

'I was afraid of him when he first stopped,' she said. 'I was afraid he was gonna arrest me or somethin. I'd done walked a long ways and I was wore out. But he give me a ride and bought me a hamburger. He's a nice man.'

'Yes,' Amy said uncertainly. 'A very nice man.'

'How long y'all been married?'

Amy picked at something on her shirt and looked back up.

'This year makes twenty-one years,' she said. 'We got married right out of college and he went to work for the highway patrol. We've lived all over but we're from Verona, over close to Tupelo. He got transferred a couple of times and we lived in Natchez for a while, stayed in Lucedale for a couple of years, had a house in Grenada for a year or so. We had a house in Batesville for eight years and then we built this one. He loves it out here, fishes every day it's pretty. You want to see his boats?'

She got up and walked over to the rail and Fay followed her. Amy was pointing down into a cove where there was a wooden dock. Two boats drifted on their ropes. One was a big shiny thing with a big outboard motor and the other one was a scratched and dented old metal one.

'I gave him that old one on our first anniversary,' Amy said. 'He still uses it to crappie fish. You like fish?'

'I've eat it some,' Fay said. She leaned up against the rail and set her beer down carefully on top of it and unpinned her hair and shook it loose. Amy turned and looked at her.

'You've got pretty hair,' she said.

'It always looks awful. I can't do nothin with it.'

She felt Amy's hand come out and touch the ends of her hair, turned her face just a bit and nervously took another sip of the beer. She wished she had a cigarette.

'It just needs a trim is all,' Amy said. 'I could trim it if you want me to. That's what I do for a living.'

'You do?'

'I'm a beautician. I've got my own shop over at Batesville. Sam bought it for me a long time ago. But I've got all the stuff in the house to do this. I could do it before supper if you want me to.'

The hand lingered for a moment and then she pulled it back, reluctantly it seemed. And she moved closer and looked into her eyes.

'Tell me something, Fay.'

'What's that?'

The glass door slid open and Sam stepped out onto the deck in blue jeans and a black shirt.

'Y'all having a conference already?' he said. He was happy, though. He looked smaller somehow without his uniform on and Fay began to see now that he was different at home. He pulled out a beer and twisted the top off and put his cigarettes and lighter on the table and then came over to stand beside them against the rail.

'So what you think?' he said. 'Is this a little piece of heaven or what?'

'It's nice,' Fay said. 'It's the nicest place I've ever seen.'

'You want to go for a ride in my boat? It's fast, now.'

'I don't know.' She looked kind of worried. 'That water looks deep.'

'I've got some life jackets. I won't let you drown.'

He turned his beer up and took a big drink from it. Amy was leaning against the rail, looking toward the house.

'She just got here, Sam. Maybe she wants to rest.'

'Oh. Yeah.' He nodded and Fay saw something pass across his face, saw something too in the way Amy spoke to him that was just a bit too hard, a bit too weary. He nodded. 'Well. Maybe after a while.'

Amy walked around him and reached up to touch Fay's hair again with her fingers.

'I told her I'd be glad to trim her hair for her. And I thought she might like a nice hot bath.'

'I would like to go for a ride,' Fay said quickly. 'I sure would like to get this messy hair of mine fixed, too.' She took another drink of her beer. 'And a bath sounds good.'

It didn't seem to bother him a bit. He stepped over to the table and shook out a cigarette.

'OK, sure,' he said. 'I've got some things I can be doing. It's pretty hot to be out in the boat right now anyway. Maybe we can take a ride when it cools off some. Then we'll come back and fix those steaks. How does that sound?'

'That sounds real nice,' Fay said. 'Can I get a cigarette from you?'

'Help yourself. There's a carton in there on the kitchen table, too.'

She got one of the cigarettes and they stood around and talked some more. He was still standing there drinking his beer at the rail when they went into the house. Fay looked back at him and he turned, gave her a wave with the bottle, and then she saw him go back to watching the water move under the wind, and the limbs of the big old pines swaying in the breeze.

Amy brought her another beer after she was in the deep tub, stretched out with her toes spread beneath the faucet and her head resting on an inflatable pillow and a mass of fragrant bubbles almost spilling over the side of the tub. The warmth of the water had seemed to soak into her bones and now she was half asleep and wanted nothing more than to lie here forever.

She sat up when Amy came back in and set the beer on the edge of the tub.

'You want some more hot water?' she said.

'No ma'am.'

'Stop calling me ma'am. I'm not but forty-one. How old are you?'

Amy put the lid down on the commode and took a seat on it.

'Seventeen,' Fay said. 'I'll be eighteen in September.'

'So you're not out of school yet.'

Fay picked up the beer and looked at it for a second.

'I don't go to school. I ain't in a long time.'

'Why not? Did you not like school?'

'I liked it fine when I got to go. But we've moved around a lot. And we all had to work. The last school I had was in the fifth grade. My daddy wouldn't let me go no more after that. Said it was a waste of time and I needed to work and help the family. So that's what I did.'

She leaned back against the pillow and sipped on the beer. Amy had crossed her legs and she sat watching her with her hands in her lap.

'Do you still want to go to school?'

'It's too late now. I've done missed so much.'

'How's your reading?'

'Not too good. I needed glasses a long time ago but I never did get any. Daddy said they cost too much money. I can read somethin way off like a road sign but it's hard for me to read a piece of paper. I have to hold it way out. Like this beer bottle. I can read what kind it is but I can't read these little bitty words down here.'

She felt like she was talking too much so she slumped back down in the water and looked at the tile wall in front of her. She didn't even know these people and she was telling them all these things. But it was hard not to. Already she knew it was going to be hard to leave here, get back on the highway. Biloxi didn't sound like such a great idea now, now that she'd found this place. Amy was drunk but it was a kind and a soft drunk.

'I've got some clothes I want you to try on after while,' Amy said. She got her drink off the sink and turned it up. She lightly stroked her lip with two fingers. 'Some things that belonged to my daughter. I bet they'll fit you. I bet they will.'

'Thank you,' Fay said. 'I could sure use some more clothes. What, did she just outgrow em?'

'She doesn't need them anymore,' Amy said. She got up from where she was sitting. She had already hung some clean underwear and some jeans and a blouse on a rack on the wall. 'I'll lock this door on my way out so Sam won't accidentally walk in on you. You stay in here as long as you want. Then you can take that boat ride with him before we eat if you want to. OK?'

'OK. Thank you.'

Amy stepped out. Fay leaned back into the warm water and lifted the beer again and tilted a long cool drink down her throat. Oh yeah, it was going to be hard to leave this place.

The hull slapped at the water and bumped her in the seat. Then it lifted very high and she turned to wave at the figure of Amy growing smaller and smaller on the dock and then the hull came down and the boat leveled out and began to plane and the wind began to bring tears from her eyes. She huddled in her life jacket on the seat and crossed her arms over her stomach. Sam was smiling, guiding the boat toward the open water, and sheets of white spray plumed out and she looked back to see a wide trough of rolling waves left quickly behind them. In only a moment the boat was skimming at the very top of the water and she could hear the muted roar of the big outboard behind her and she could feel the vibration of the water on the hull in her bare feet.

They came out from behind the red dirt of the bluff and he turned the wheel to the left, and then growing out from the rough sand beach was the long looming shape of the distant levee and the spill of white rocks she had looked down on a few hours before. There were some stands of dead white trees off to the right where fishing boats were grouped and she could see people sitting in them. He eased off on the throttle just a bit and then he turned loose of it and steered the boat with one hand, casually, as if he were back on his highway again, and he watched everything around him just the way he did when he was driving the cruiser.

It was too loud for any talk, the rushing wind and the sound of the motor, and there was too much to see, the sun beginning to lower in the sky but still bright enough that she had to shade her eyes with one hand to study the levee and the distant shore where other landings jutted out into the lake. Everywhere boats pulling skiers towed white fans of water that crept across the surface of the reservoir.

It seemed to take a long time to get any closer to the levee, but whenever she looked back she could see how far they had come, and after five minutes the red dirt bluff was just a patch of color among the trees and the rocks and she couldn't see the dock that Sam had built with his own hands.

When the sun fell behind the levee he slowed the boat and made a gentle sweep to the right and raced along its length for a while. He took his sunglasses off and stowed them in a pocket beneath the console.

'What you think?' he yelled, and she nodded and smiled and pulled her hair out of her face again.

'We better get back,' she heard, and he turned the wheel away from the levee and pushed down on the throttle again. Most of the wind had died by now and the lake had started to slick over. The water seemed darker now and it was as if they were skidding across a plate of black glass, the boat driving like an arrowhead with hardly any spray coming out from the hull, just the clean smooth nose aimed at the red bluff and the trees flashing by on the right side, boys and girls in water up to their necks off the beaches and their dogs splashing in the shallows and the last rays of light in the tops of the woods and already the small coves back in the smooth fingers of water growing dark with night.

* * *

70

By lamplight he speared the marbled slabs of meat onto the grill and small yellow flames leapt up, the grease sizzling when it fell into the coals. She helped Amy bring out plates and napkins and a garden salad they had fixed in the kitchen together with the stereo playing. Fat potatoes wrapped in foil and piled on a dish in the center of the table, a loaf of brown bread slashed with cuts and butter dripping from the shining crust.

They sat and talked and she felt that she had never been as hungry as she was now, watching the steaks cook in their own juices and smelling them while the charcoal glowed red beneath them.

When the steaks were done, he brought them on an iron platter to the table and he turned on an overhead floodlight and they sat down. When she cut the first piece of meat and lifted it to her mouth she could feel them watching her, and she closed her eyes and chewed and let out a small moan and Sam laughed and then all of them were eating and talking.

'Oh hell, I almost forgot the wine,' he said, and he got up and went inside and brought it and stood it on the table, left again and returned with three crystal glasses and a corkscrew. He opened the wine and poured it and they held their glasses to hers, and they leaned forward and clinked them softly, and she could see the light from the lamp shining on their faces.

She ate slowly. She was enormously hungry and somehow she restrained herself from eating too quickly. She took her cues from Amy, kept her elbows off the table, her napkin in her lap, and after the first few times she didn't talk with her mouth full.

It was only nine o'clock by the time they finished. She helped Amy stack the plates and carry them in to the sink and then they sat out on the deck with the bugs and he lit a citronella candle and the mosquitoes left them alone. She could tell it when the wine and the beer began to get to her and she slowed down, took small sips, and sometime during all that conversation she woke in her chair alone. Amy was just stepping back onto the deck.

'I've got your bed ready,' she said. 'Come on.'

She didn't argue. She asked her where Sam was and she said he had already gone to bed, that he was going fishing early in the morning and that he'd wanted Fay to go with him, but that he'd wanted her to get some rest, too. Amy helped her undress in a room papered with roses, a bed with pillows trimmed in lace, a child's dolls sitting in a toddler's rocking chair and lined in rows against the walls staring with their dead dolls' eyes.

From somewhere Amy brought her a nightgown and Fay held her arms over her head and let her pull it down over her shoulders, her waist, and then the covers were pulled back and she crawled in beneath a comforter that smelled of flowers in the spring. She closed her eyes and felt one soft kiss on her cheek. And then the door was closing and the room was dark and out there past the window in the night somewhere she could hear an owl hooting, but it was old and familiar, a song from deep woods, something she had heard before.

Sam was going slowly across the glassy water in the old aluminum boat when the first pale light of dawn began to show beyond the ragged teeth of the dark trees that lined the lake, steering with one hand and trying not to spill the cup of coffee on his knees. The big dead trunks stood together a mile or a mile and a half out and the boat drew steadily nearer them, wakes of lapping water fanning out and growing ever gentler and wider, where they ran to the shore and floated sticks up and down, broke softly on the red sand and receded.

Looking back he could see the lights on his deck still burning, and far off to the west he could see the lights of vehicles inching across the levee, the glow of them swirled in the mist that stood on the water like smoke. There were running lights of red and green far off across the lake, but he couldn't hear the motors. The boats seemed to move very slowly and faint spumes of water ran along their sides. He wondered if she knew how to ski. But then of course she didn't if she didn't even know how to swim. Well. He could teach her to swim and ski both.

It was still almost too dark to see so he cut back on his speed even more and it wallowed back in the water and dragged sluggishly until he twisted the throttle just a bit more and pushed the speed back up and ran closer to the clump of trunks looming up out of the water. He saw an eagle rise up out of one of the nests and sail out into the darkness, just the bob of its snowy tail until it vanished into the gloom that still lay over the northern shore.

When he got closer he finished the coffee and set the cup in the bottom of the boat. He pulled the throttle back to an idle and when he was within fifty feet of his line he cut it off and let it drift closer, reached down for the long paddle and turned the motor to let the side of the boat slide gently against the tree, bumping, rising, and he pushed out with the paddle against the tree and came to a stop. Alesandra's thighs were like velvet.

He sat for a moment with his hand on the dead wood and then looked up into the naked branches outlined against the sky. They had been here for as long as he could remember and he could imagine them as they once were, standing in a forest with squirrels climbing through their heavy growths of leaves and lending shade down on a hot summer day. There would have been a carpet of dead leaves beneath them, dry and crackly underfoot. Now they had stood here in this water almost fifty years. He patted the trunk like the back of an old friend. Was she watching him even now?

Waiting for the sky to lighten a bit he poured more coffee from the Thermos. The boat moved in the water, shifting slowly among the trunks. He rested the cup on his knee and watched the morning come. He could hear trucks and cars pulling into loading ramps far up the lake. Faint sounds in the dawn, the creakings the boat made, a slap and swish of something turning up in the water, a groan the trunk made as it stood in its bed of mud. Finally he drained the cup and set it down for good to tend to his business.

But he hadn't baited his lines in two days and he doubted there were any fish still alive on them. There was a piece of pipe in the floor of the boat and he reached down for it and started unwrapping the cord he kept on it. Alesandra was asleep somewhere in a warm bed, probably. Some bent rods were welded to the side of the pipe and he got a good grip on the end of the cord and stood up carefully in the boat, it rocking some, and he swung the pipe back and forth a few times on the cord and then turned loose of it and let it fly out over the water. It made a deep *plunk* when it went in and the cord tightened quickly. He sat back down and started hauling the cord in hand over hand, letting it pile up between his feet until he felt the weight of his line. He hoped they were getting along OK. They seemed to like each other and maybe now Amy would feel better for a while, having another somebody to take care of. The only thing was how long. They couldn't just keep her like a stray dog and she had a family somewhere too but she'd left that on her own and how many kids had the guts to do something like that, just strike out on their own? He stopped for a moment to see if he could tell if there was anything on the trotline, but he couldn't tell. The line rose as he pulled, tight beads running down the slant of it back into the water or dripping to make tiny pools beneath it until he finally caught it with his hand and unhooked the pipe from it. He didn't even know how old she was but not old enough to be out walking around after dark on the roads, or even in daylight. Too many sickos running around out there. He held the line in one hand and dropped the pipe in the floor of the boat and then by pulling with both hands on the line he turned the boat sideways so that the line could pass over his knees. He leaned forward for the bucket and pulled it closer and began to draw himself and the boat under the line, hand over hand, looking for the first hook. Something was there in the water just under the line, something that did not move.

He cussed softly, his eyes intent upon the rising line. He hauled into the boat a dripping White River cat that weighed about six pounds, the eyes dead and pale in their sockets and the curved body stiff and hard.

'Damn it, Sam,' he said. He tore the hook from the fish's mouth and tossed it over the side. He pulled a half-thawed shrimp from the pile in the bucket and threaded it onto the hook, drew the line in, saw the next hook come up. Empty. And the one after that. And the one after that. He glanced up. Boats were beginning to move everywhere on the water now but he didn't pay any attention to them. He kept on baiting and pulling the line. This one had sixty-three hooks on it and he doubted he'd have enough bait for both lines. But he could check the other one and see if it had any fish on it.

He couldn't think of any reason she couldn't just stay with them for a while. She was undernourished, that was easy to see from looking at her, but her clothes were too small for her and that meant she must not have had any new ones for a long time. The fish kept coming up dead and he kept taking them off, working silently, the boat rocking slightly in the water and the line riding down the other side and back into the depths. She must not have had many chances at anything. And the thing of it was that she wasn't complaining about it. She'd just told him the way things were. He didn't blame her for being scared of him at first. She'd probably been told to stay away from cops, or had already seen the bad side of too many. Walking to Biloxi. Jesus. Somebody would find her dead somewhere in a field off an interstate and there would be a note in the local papers, nothing more. She probably didn't even have any identification on her. And nobody would ever know who she was, who she'd been, where she'd come from. It was just a lucky thing that he'd seen her. A lucky thing that he'd been on that particular road at that particular time, before she'd gotten in with somebody. Who would take her no telling where. And do to her no telling what.

By the time he got to the end of the line, the sun was rising up over the trees and the heat was already climbing. He had four live fish big enough to keep. He'd taken off fourteen dead ones and he was not happy with himself for wasting them. But he was eager to get back to the house and clean these and put them in the refrigerator, cook them for their supper tonight.

The long paddle was there beside his knee. He

picked it up and pushed off from the dead tree the line was tied to and then leaned it against the seat once again. The old outboard started on the second pull and he motored slowly out of the stand of dead trunks, a boiling trail of churned water following him, and then he opened it up and headed straight for his dock. It was a speck in the rising sun and the sun was on the windows of his house so tiny and far away across the moving water of the lake. But they were probably still asleep. He checked the time on his watch and it wasn't even seven o'clock yet. The catfish would live for a long time on their stringer and there wasn't any need to be in a hurry about dressing them. He twisted the throttle back a bit on the outboard, scanning the water around him. More boats were coming out from the levee and fisherfolk were finding their parking places among the stands of trees or up in mats of brush close to the shore. He could see the sun glinting on their cane poles when they swung out their jigs or minnows, but he didn't need any more crappie now. The deep freeze was already full of them.

He glanced at the dock and the house once again, then turned the motor to the left and goosed it up again until it was nearly planing and the hull was slapping the waves in a steady gait. He went past Pat's Bluff and the long line of pickups and boats already turned around and waiting to back down onto the ramp, people gathered in small groups, talking and waiting for the ones in front to unload and get going. He steered wide of them so as not to make a wake and moved back toward the center of the lake and pushed the throttle wide open. The old boat was dented and battered yet it moved across the water like a fleet and weightless thing now, skimming past the red sand banks and the anchored fishing boats nearly hidden in their copses of vegetation. The outboard roared in a low and throaty voice as it pushed him across the lake.

He went nearly a mile before he made a wide sweep to the right and throttled back just short of the landing at Coontown, then slowed it even more and edged into the shallower water and nearly to the shore. He cut the motor off and drifted closer, until the boat came to a halt in a group of young willows. There was a nylon rope coiled behind the seat and he picked it up and fastened it to the nearest tree with a brush hook. He picked up a chain stringer and snapped it into one of his belt loops and then went over the side carefully, rocking the boat until he felt his tennis shoes sink into the soft mud of the bottom. From the bow he retrieved his rod and reel, an old Johnson spinning rig. He stood there and cast his lure out into the open and let it settle, then wiped a bit of sweat from above his eyes and twitched the tip of the rod, turning the crank slowly, pulling the lure in. It darted and swam in the manner of a small baitfish. The water swirled behind it and he felt a fish grab it, but then it turned loose. The lure floated back up and he began to retrieve it again, more slowly now, making the lure dance and jerk as if it were an injured minnow. Nothing hit it. He pulled it on in without another strike, then walked some more.

The sun rose higher and it reflected back off the surface of the water into his eyes. He pitched the lure beside a half-submerged log and let it lie there for a moment, then twitched it gently, once, twice. He actually saw the fish come up in a green flash and suck the lure down, a tiny disturbance and then the rod was bowing in his hands and the fish was pulling off line and he was trying to keep the line free of stumps and bushes, holding it high in front of him, trying to horse the fish in before it could wrap the line around something and break it. It jumped once and he guessed its weight at three pounds, and then it was pulling again and he let the rod tip down a bit before he pulled on it again.

He smiled under the sun and towed it closer and closer until finally he leaned up and caught it by the jaw and lifted it out and held it for a moment, admiring it. It wasn't caught bad and he eased down on the thumb button on the reel and let a length of line slide out and held the rod between his knees while he worked the hook out and then it was free. He lowered the fish back into the water and it flashed away into the depths. He walked on in the water and cast his lure again. The morning grew warmer and the water lapped at the shore. Far up past the point where the water ended a red tractor turned in to the field and lowered its disk and began to break the land, the green earth turning under and coming up brown and the diesel engine chugging and jetting its black smoke from the high exhaust pipe and the big cleated tires turning. He fished on and let the rest of the world go on by.

It was nine o'clock when he nosed the boat into the dock and shut off the motor. He leaned down for the stringer of catfish and lifted them dripping from the water.

When he slid the patio door open he was careful to be quiet in case they were still asleep. Just as quietly he went back out and took off his wet tennis shoes and left them on the deck and then went back in. The house was silent except for the whisper of the fans slowly turning in the ceiling. His jeans were still wet but he took a minute to put on some fresh coffee before he went down the hall. He eased open the door to the dark bedroom and saw Amy huddled in sleep, just a bit of her hair sticking out from under the covers. She didn't move when he went to the closet and pulled a clean pair of jeans off a hanger and got some clean boxers from a drawer. She turned over and made a noise just as he was closing the door. He went to the hall bathroom and changed, knocking softly a few times at first to make sure Fay wasn't in there.

It was Wednesday morning, the first of his two days off, and he didn't have to go back on patrol until Friday at 10:00 a.m. He was thinking picnic, make some sandwiches and ice down some beer and take them over to the other side and let her play in the shallow water, maybe even get a life jacket and let Fay get used to being in the water, maybe even get out there with her and see if he could teach her to dog-paddle. Take his rod and reel, fish up in the willows while they worked on their tans. He could see the whole afternoon in his mind. He'd have the fish dressed before they left and he'd have them soaking in some salt water inside the refrigerator and late in the afternoon he could fire up his fish cooker and make some hush-puppies, slice up some potatoes, and then just when the sun was going down across the lake they could sit out on the deck and eat.

The phone rang inside and he went to catch it before it woke them up. Even going to it he was thinking about getting out the bacon and starting them some breakfast, get it almost ready and wake them up. It was almost nine-thirty. Time for them to get up anyway.

But it was the dispatcher on the phone from Batesville.

'Where?' he said.

He grabbed a pen and a pad from where they stayed beside the phone and jotted it down.

'OK,' he said. 'I'm on my way.'

He hung up the phone and tore the piece of paper off and wrote a quick note to Amy, then hurried down the hall to get his uniform on and put on his gun.

About seven minutes later he was screaming down the lake road with all his lights flashing and as he approached the intersection of Highway 6 he pumped the brakes hard several times and looked to the right. Two trucks way off, one passing, and to the left there was one car coming. He saw the smoke come squalling up from the front tires, some woman gripping the steering wheel with both hands.

'Thanks, lady,' he said, then pushed down hard on the accelerator and smoked his own rear tire coming out of the intersection. When he topped the first hill there was a car passing a truck and already heading back into the right lane. He turned the siren on and passed them at eighty, then turned it back off. Over the next hill there was traffic ahead and he slowed down and turned the siren on again. They all moved over and he flew by them, a rush of sound coming out against the doors each time he went by one, *shoom shoom shoom*. Trees and houses flashed by and he could hear the four-barrel carburetor suck in wind and gas each time he hit the pedal. He never liked going this fast because a dog could always trot out in the road in front of you, a deer could leap from the bushes.

He made it to the city limits of Oxford in about ten minutes and slowed for the caution light, swung wide around some cars that were waiting to turn, siren screaming, then floored it again and went on over the hill into heavy traffic. This was the worst part, cars all jammed together and passing or people cruising with their radios on and not hearing him until he was right behind them. Sometimes they did something stupid like slamming on the brakes or weaving into another lane without looking. He didn't want to cause anybody to have a wreck and he damn sure didn't want to have one himself before he got there.

He climbed the long hill on the east side of town and then he was back on a two-lane road and he had to be more careful. He passed when he could and when he couldn't he turned the siren on and got them to pull over and passed them then. When he glanced at his watch he realized that less than an hour ago he had been in the water with his rod and reel.

The traffic got lighter as he gained more distance from town. There were a few straight stretches where he hit a hundred. And then topping the last hill he saw before him the wreck at the bottom of it and he swerved over to the left lane to go past the line of stopped cars, that rushing sound coming against the doors again. He slowed down. An ambulance was already sitting there with its red light turning, and two county patrol cars were there as well.

He pulled in and parked on the shoulder of the road and picked up the mike and told the dispatcher that he was 10-6, put on his hat and got out. It was already very hot and he closed the door of his cruiser to keep the interior cool. The ambulance attendants were trying to free a woman pinned behind the steering wheel of a late model Grand Prix and he could hear her screaming. The other car was turned upside down in the ditch and he couldn't tell what it was, just a rusty undercarriage, some slick tires, shattered bits of metal and plastic lying around it. He walked over to one of the deputies who was trying to help the ambulance attendants. He could see the other one down on his knees in the ditch, looking into the overturned car.

Spectators had gotten out of their cars. The road was blocked both ways, the Grand Prix sitting dead on the center line. He could feel people looking at him but he ignored them and spoke to the deputy.

'What about it, Mike?'

'We're trying to get this lady out. I believe the man in the other car's dead.'

'You called the wreckers yet?'

'Yessir, they're on the way.'

He stepped around and looked into the car over an attendant's shoulder. They had bandaged a cut on the woman's head and put a neck brace on her.

'Can I help y'all in any way?' he said. One young man with red hair turned his face to him.

'Yessir. Can you hand us that backboard there? I think we're just about ready to try and bring her out. She's got a broke leg but there ain't enough room to splint it in here.'

Sam bent to the aluminum frame and spread it open and passed it into the car. The red-haired attendant climbed into the backseat and slid the frame behind the woman. She had stopped screaming now and was just gritting her teeth together. There was blood on her clothes.

'Y'all are killin me,' she said.

'Yes ma'am, we're just trying to help you,' the young man said. 'Now we're gonna slide this thing in behind you and I'm gonna hold your head real still. Now just take it easy and we'll have you out of there in a jiffy. Be on our way to the hospital in just a minute.'

Sam leaned in and spoke to the woman.

'Do you know what happened, ma'am?'

She didn't say anything for a moment and she closed her eyes. He could tell she was having a hard time breathing.

'He pulled right out in front of me,' she said. 'I tried to miss him. The son of a bitch. Where's he at?'

'The other car's over there in the ditch, ma'am. Were you headed west?'

'I was headed to Memphis,' she said in a breathless gasp.

'OK, let's get her on it,' the attendant in the backseat said. The other attendant in the front seat pulled forward on the woman's shoulder and Sam helped them slide the backboard behind her. He stepped out of the way and they quickly strapped her into it and started sliding her out. He caught the outside edge of it with his hands and they brought her out in a sitting position and then put her down in the road and she started screaming again. He figured they'd have her out of there in a couple of minutes and he looked up the hill to see if he could see the wreckers coming but there was still just that stopped line of traffic.

The deputy came around from the other side and they went down into the ditch together and squatted next to the driver's door and the other deputy, the really young one, who raised his face and shook his head. The top was crunched down on the car so that the headrest was pressing against it. Sam could smell booze when he poked his head in through the broken window. A man who looked to be in his late fifties was lying against the roof and he wasn't moving, his face coated in blood and already flies were on him. There was a piece of something shiny lying beside him and Sam reached out and picked it up. Ice. He dropped it on the grass and lay on his belly and crawled in far enough to find the man's wrist and pressed his thumb down hard on it just back from the heel of the hand. He watched the faces of the deputies watching him and he felt one drop of sweat fall from his nose and there was no beat of blood in that withered arm at all. He looked at his watch. It was twenty minutes after ten.

He crawled back out and stood up.

'Yeah,' he said. He looked up on the road and he could see the attendants putting an air splint on the woman's leg. He wanted to get this traffic moving again as soon as he could.

'Yonder comes the wrecker,' the young deputy said.

'And there's the Ford truck behind him,' the other one said. 'You want to move that Pontiac first, Sam?'

'That'd be real good, Jay. The sooner we can get this traffic moving the better I'd like it.'

When they stepped back up on the road the attendants had loaded the woman onto a wheeled stretcher and were lifting her up into the open back doors of the ambulance. One climbed in the back with her. The wreckers pulled in slowly and up the hill he saw another ambulance coming down for the body. He glanced at the overturned car in the ditch again. Somebody had some bad news coming.

It took another hour to get the Pontiac out of the road and to right the overturned car and retrieve the body, send it to the hospital. He got the traffic moving again, standing in the center of the highway and kicking bits of glass and metal onto the shoulder. He had sweated almost completely through his shirt by then and the only thing he was thinking about was getting back home and finding a cold beer. The deputies got called to a woods fire on Highway 7 and they went up the hill with their blue lights going. When a break in the traffic came he went back to his cruiser and sat down and started filling out the accident report and drew a sketch of what he believed had happened and signed everything. He put the car in gear and shut the door and turned around on the side of the road, then pulled out and turned his blue lights off and headed back toward town. There was sweat running down his face and his hair was wet with it. He called the dispatcher on the radio and told him that he was headed back home. The radio never ceased its chatter. There were wrecks on Highway 55. Troopers were pulling over people at Byhalia. Somebody was checking out for lunch at Pontotoc. He didn't know how they kept it straight who was doing what.

He was hoping he wouldn't get another call now and he turned down the volume some on the police radio and turned on the FM radio in the dash, punching buttons until he got a country station out of Tupelo. If they'd just let him get back home and get away from the house they wouldn't be able to call him back in. He figured Amy and Fay were up by now. He'd get a quick shower and clean those fish and pack a lunch and then they could take off.

He took the bypass around Oxford again and pulled over at a beer joint at the Panola County line and got a ham sandwich and a paper cup full of Coke and ice and ignored the young country boys with cutoff jeans eyeing him so uneasily with their arms full of cases of cold beer. He got back into his cruiser and unwrapped the sandwich and then pulled out. He cruised at fifty-five and nobody passed him. It never failed to amuse him how well they behaved whenever they could see his car. The Coke was nestled between his legs and he picked it up occasionally and sipped at it from a straw. He finished the sandwich and kicked his speed up a bit and soon he was turning onto the access road and taking the curves where the kudzu was deep and green, a lush landscape of vegetation that encroached on the edges of farmers' pastures and the yards of houses. He could see the shapes of old shacks set back from the road that the creeping vines had claimed totally, leaning forms sinking slowly back into the earth. Once in a while he met cars and trucks towing fishing boats or ski boats. Once in a while he waved to somebody.

He slowed and turned into his drive and stopped as he did many times to look again at the mailbox with its painted birds and flowers framing the name *Harris* and could remember the morning when Karen had been sitting on the deck with her brushes and tubes of paint creating it, smiling up at him for a moment before leaning forward to touch it with the tip of her brush. He sat there studying it with the window down and his hand resting on the side mirror. It was flaking some now, part of a bird's tail missing, a few petals from a daisy. He guessed the metal was galvanized and the paint wouldn't stick to it forever. He blew out a long sigh and went on down the drive.

When he came out of the pine forest and in view of his house, Amy's car was gone. He pulled the cruiser up beside his pickup and checked out on the radio, then got out and went up the steps. The radio was playing inside and there were breakfast dishes in the sink.

The note was lying beside the telephone, next to the one he'd left for her, but he didn't really want to go over there and read it. He opened a beer and took a long drink and looked out through the patio door. The lake was rough with wind and waves. He took another drink and walked over to the table and picked up the note:

Sam, I've taken Fay over to Tupelo to shop for some clothes. Be back later this evening.

A.

He balled up the note and threw it toward the trash can and stepped out on the deck. He leaned on the rail, a small muscle working in his jaw. The beer was cold in his hand and he turned it up again with the wind moving over his face. His boats were drifting and bumping against each other on their ropes below.

'Fuck it,' he said, and went over to the ice chest to take out the catfish he'd put in water there that morning. When he raised the lid they were all dead and stiff, their discolored backs hard and their pale eyes staring. He just shook his head and let the lid drop.

Light waves were breaking against the beach and he could see people lying on towels and children playing in knee-deep water. Ski boats were pulled up to the edge of the sand and young people in shorts and swimsuits were sitting on quilts or lying still in the sun. He cruised past them slowly and looked out over the lake. He had his black trunks on and he was just riding, letting the air wash over him, sipping a beer and watching everything as it went by. There was no telling when they might be back. Get over to Tupelo like that and get to talking and shopping and she wouldn't notice how late it was getting and it would be easy for them to just have supper over there. That was what she and Karen had done a lot of times. They'd see a movie together and go look at new cars or go visit Amy's parents. And thinking of that reminded him that he needed to get over there and see his own folks. But they'd always get to talking about Karen and that was always so hard. He didn't have any answers for them. He didn't even have any for himself.

The sun was straight overhead and the water had calmed. Some people were skiing up near the levee and he saw somebody fall and the splash of the water. The boat slowed and turned back to pick up the skier. It looked like Amy could have at least waited until he got back to ask him if he'd made any plans. But Fay would probably have a good time. She needed some new clothes and he didn't care anything about a shopping trip anyway.

He relaxed in the seat and just cruised with one foot stretched out on the nylon carpet and the wind whipping his hair. There was no need in sitting at the house by himself, watching television or something.

A boat came by him and ran alongside for just a minute, and the driver raised his hand and slowly waved and grinned. Sam waved back. It was Tony McCollum, the one who'd pulled Amy over that time and had been nice enough not to take her to jail for drunk driving. He probably had some lines out, too, or was going grabbling in some of the logs he had tied down all over the lake. Tony waved a final time and sped off, and Sam turned the boat east and away from the beach and pushed down on the throttle until the hull was skimming the water. He sipped his beer and watched the trees on the south side going by. He guessed he could always go back to the house and get in the pickup and drive up to the bait shop for some night crawlers and bait his lines. But it was still too hot to do that. And he knew if he kept on riding around in the boat drinking beer he'd still be doing that when it got dark. Unless he ran into her somewhere out here.

In three more years he could put in for retirement and what would he do then? A man could only fish so much. Or ride around in the boat and drink beer. It was about all he had to do when he was off. It might be best to not even think about retiring until they forced it on him. Go for thirty. He knew plenty of other troopers who were doing it. Maybe later they could travel, go to some places they'd never been. He could buy one of those big recreational vehicles and they could drive it out to Yellowstone and the Grand Canyon, or go up in New England in the fall and look at the leaves turning colors. He had to do something with her. She couldn't keep going the way she was. She was going to drive herself crazy, crying the way she did and asking him all those questions he could never answer.

Oh yeah he could see them, cruising up and down the highways of America, just another retired couple with nothing but time on their hands, no place to be at a certain time and nothing in particular to come home to.

The lake began to narrow down toward the mouth

of the Tallahatchie River and he slowed the boat some, started making a wide sweeping turn. The water was low and there were stumps in some places to be hit so he turned back toward the deeper water and headed toward the levee again. He looked at his watch and it wasn't even three o'clock. He didn't want to be drunk on his boat out on the lake. He thought he'd just cruise past the levee one more time. There wasn't anything else to do.

He pushed the throttle on down and went for a half mile and then he saw the boat coming out from the landing on the north shore. Instinctively he looked back toward his house but it was no more than a smudge of color over there. And he knew they weren't back yet anyway. He slowed and made a wide turn and the other boat turned with him without getting any closer than a hundred yards. The Chris Craft with its curved glass windshield and that big Mercury inboard was a high-dollar ride on this lake. She had her dark hair bound up in a red scarf. Bright spray kicked up from the mahogany hull and he could see her smiling at him. He didn't smile back. She turned the wheel to the right and swept over into his wake and trailed him, closing the gap slowly until she was running forty or fifty yards back of him, bouncing in the deep trough he was leaving. She probably tailgates cars, too, he thought. But then she pulled out and passed him just as they were getting closer to a stand of trees on the right. He slowed and she shot past, weaving back over in front of him. He saw the hull on her boat come up when she throttled back and he followed her into a cypress brake where the water was fairly still and they were sheltered from view. He slowed down almost to an idle, being careful, steering between the old trees into a cooler shade where floating logs lay under Spanish moss all hung down from the limbs. He had fished for crappie in here, early morning mist, the quiet splash of a jig, the birds crying, peace.

Up ahead there was a gap in the trees and in the

patch of sunlight slanting there in shafts between them she turned the boat around and headed back toward him. He pushed the throttle straight up and killed the engine. She stopped hers only when she was almost to him. He reached his hand out and let the boats come together with a soft bump.

'I've been expecting you,' she said.

He raised his face and looked again into her Lebanese eyes.

'I've been busy.'

It was what he always seemed to say. It was so hard to keep it quiet and he knew he'd been lucky. Just like with Tony a while ago. Seeing him then and not now. And anybody could pull up in here. But they had to talk somewhere.

'You're always busy,' she said, and he hoped she wouldn't cry again. Or threaten him with something. How much of it was an act and how much real? What if it was all real?

'What you want me to do, Alesandra? Quit my job?'

The water lapped at the trunks of the cypresses. A fish splashed near the base of one and formed a ripple there. The water settled very gradually and the boats squeaked when they rubbed together. He turned loose of hers and held on to her foot instead, couldn't help himself. The warm pad of her heel, wrinkled, tough. Her calves were velvet too. She took off her scarf and shook her hair loose, then reached for a plastic cup and drank from it. Probably gin. She smoked only five cigarettes a day and could squeeze him so tightly inside her it took his breath.

She let her hair fall across one eye. 'Where's the old bag?'

He turned loose of her foot but she didn't move it, just hooked the underside of her ankle to his boat and held it.

'Tupelo. Shopping.'

'Shops till she drops. A real eighties woman.'

'No need to get ugly. We already know you can.'

'You seeing somebody else?'

'No.'

'I catch you with somebody else I'll kill her.'

He thought she watched for him. Maybe with binoculars. She was always able to find him. He didn't know if what he felt was love. And wasn't it a little bit late to be still chasing after that? Everything was supposed to have been settled by now, with his life, with his family. He should have been expecting grandkids by now. But now here she was and there Karen was.

'I can't keep it up, Alesandra. I tell lies and forget what I told. I know she's caught me before. I think she probably knows I'm seeing somebody.'

'One time you said you didn't care if she did.'

The beer in his hand was almost empty. He drained it and tossed it over the side.

'All I know is we've had this conversation about twenty times. I can't leave her the way she is. I've been with her too long.'

'But you're not happy.'

'I'm like you see me.'

'You used to always be happy with me.'

'Maybe the fucking guilt has just weighed me down. Have you ever thought about that?'

'So now I make you feel guilty.'

He looked at her, the flat brown belly with its little slit of a navel, the full breasts with their line of cleavage in the flowered two-piece, and he thought of lying down with her soon, in ten or twenty minutes, maybe even now right here.

'Sometimes I feel guilty,' he said.

'But you're not blaming it on me.'

'No.'

'Good. Because it takes two people to fuck, Sam. I can't fuck you without your cooperation.'

Her temper was rising and she said crazy shit like that sometimes. She was just afraid he wasn't going to go with her, follow her to whatever place she had staked out this time. Sometimes it was a tent on the lower lake. There had been hotel rooms all up and down I-55 between Hernando and Grenada. He had even gone to one in Grenada in his uniform once, knowing how stupid it was when he did it, late at night, the parking lot jammed with cars.

'Where you staying?'

'Right across the lake. Holiday Lodge. I got cable TV. Twenty-two channels. Even the air conditioner works.'

'I probably better go home after while,' he said.

He heard a boat coming at a high rate of speed and he turned his head to see Tony McCollum race by, looking their way. It was too late to duck. She set her cup up on the wide railing and he knew what she was going to do even before she slipped her hands around behind her back. She pulled away the top half of the suit and then just dropped it in the floor of the boat.

'I know something more fun than that,' she said.

She picked up her drink and leaned back in the seat and let him have a good long look. Her lips on the rim of the cup and her eyes smiling to him and the rays of sun wavering over her. The thing of it was that she knew how weak he was and he hated himself for that. But he guessed it still wasn't enough to make him say no to her, was it? He wondered what Amy would do if she found out. If she'd even care.

'All right,' he said, finally. 'I can't stay all evening, though. We've got company. I need to get back before dark.'

'I'm sure that'll be plenty long enough, Sam,' she said, bending over for the top.

It was nearly seven when he got out of bed and walked to the window and pushed the curtains aside. Some boats were coming in to the marina and he could see that the sun would be going down before long.

She was lying on the bed having another drink, her head propped against a pillow and only one long brown leg under the covers. He let the curtain drop and went into the bathroom and got into the shower and turned it on and stood there while the hot water beat down on him. He was getting too old for this kind of stuff. After a while he turned the water off and reached for a blue towel on a rack there and dried himself off. He had to look at himself in the mirror then and he didn't much like what he saw. He turned away from it and went back into the bedroom and sat down beside her, then he stretched out again and put his hand on her belly. She set her drink down and rolled over to him. She kissed his knuckles and then his mouth. He put his hands around her and she was warm and good, her skin soft and tight under his fingers. Her hand moved down on him and he didn't think it would happen again but it did.

'You just took a shower for nothing,' she said.

'Yeah, I reckon so.'

It was almost dark before he could get away from her and even then she didn't want him to go. When he pulled away from the dock she was standing with her arms crossed in a short terry cloth robe and she didn't wave good-bye. He looked back once and waved. Far out across the lake he looked back and could see a white dot still standing there like something planted in concrete. After that darkness and the distance swallowed her up and he turned his face toward his home across the lake. He couldn't see any lights when he got a little closer.

The lake was smoothing over again and the water was turning blacker. He reached down to the switch for the running lights and turned them on. Other boats were going in to the landings and he could see their lights. He was ashamed of himself like always.

He saw their lights pull in from where he was sitting in the living room watching a Clint Eastwood movie on the television. They'd cut the cusswords from the movie and inserted other ones and commercials for dog food and paper towels. He looked at his watch and saw that it was nearly nine-thirty. He got up and went over and turned the volume down on the set and sat back down again to wait. But then he got up and turned on the porch light for them and he saw them coming up the steps, their arms full of packages and bags and he pushed open the door and held it for them. They were talking and laughing and Fay had on some new clothes.

'Hey Sam,' she said.

'Hey. Looks like y'all bought Tupelo out.'

'Just about,' Amy said. 'Would you go out there and get the rest of those bags for me? On the backseat.'

'Yeah. I been wondering where y'all were.'

'We just got to shopping,' she said. 'Go on in, Fay, let's set this stuff down.'

They went on in and he went down the steps and opened the door of her convertible and reached in for three big plastic bags. All full of clothes. When he shut the door he looked up at the house and could see them in there, moving around and putting their things down. He went up the steps and into the living room. He could hear them down the hall.

'Where you want this stuff?' he yelled.

She called for him to bring it back to Fay's room and it sounded strange hearing her say that, and to hear it coming from that room where he had gone and sat so many mornings before going in to work, sitting in the old rocking chair that Karen used to sit in when she was doing her homework or even before that when he would sit in it and read to her before bedtime even when she was too old for it. They were both sitting on the bed opening the bags and pulling out the clothes. He couldn't help but smile at them.

'My lord,' he said. 'What'd y'all do, buy a whole new wardrobe?' He set the bags on the bed and sat down in the rocking chair. Crossed his legs.

'We just got her a few things she needed,' Amy said.

'I got all kinds of shorts and blouses and stuff,' Fay said. 'I think we went to about ten different stores.'

She looked up at him and smiled, and he knew when he saw her face that Amy had told her about Karen. Had explained this room, maybe even the rocking chair he was sitting in.

He got up.

'Well, I'll let y'all get on with your stuff. Have you had anything to eat?'

Amy didn't even look up.

'We ate at the Red Lobster in Tupelo. Have you had anything?'

'I can make me a sandwich or something,' he said.

'I could fix you something,' Amy said, and then she did look up. 'We didn't mean to stay so long. We just got to talking and having such a good time. I figured you went fishing or something anyway.'

'Yeah, I did,' he said, and turned and went back up the hall. He stopped in front of the refrigerator and looked at the television. The movie was still on but he was hungry now and he wanted something to eat, so he opened the door on the refrigerator and started looking through there. He found some salami and bologna and cheese and built a huge sandwich with tomatoes and lettuce and lots of mayonnaise, sprinkled some salt and pepper on it and found some chips in the cabinet. He poured himself a glass of milk and took everything back over to his chair and turned the volume back up on the television and started watching the movie again. He knew they'd be tired now, would probably want to go to bed early. He guessed he could watch the movie until he got sleepy. But sleep came hard some nights. Amy always drank herself into a deep slumber, but many nights he lay awake beside her listening to her snore.

He had finished about half the sandwich when Amy came into the kitchen and fixed herself a drink. She moved in there with him and sat down on the couch.

'You tired?' he said, and picked up another potato chip.

'I am,' she said. 'But I feel pretty good. I bet she

95

thanked me twenty times for those clothes. What'd you do all day?'

'I had to go work a wreck,' he said. 'Then I just messed around on the lake. Rode around some. I started to bait up my lines again but I never did. What y'all got planned for tomorrow?'

'Nothing I don't guess. You didn't care for me taking her over to Tupelo and buying her some clothes, did you?'

'Why should I care?' he said, and took another bite of his sandwich.

'I just felt kind of bad about keeping her away from you all day.'

'You tell her about Karen?'

She got quiet and still. Took a sip from her drink and then looked at the television screen.

'Yes I did. We talked all day.'

'And?'

'She felt real bad about it. She feels bad now about staying in her room.'

'Ain't nobody using it. She might as well.'

'That's what I thought, too. We need to talk about her sometime.'

'About Fay?'

'Yes. About Fay and some other things, too.'

He picked up his milk and took a drink of it.

'Anytime you get ready,' he said. 'How about now?'

'Not now,' she said, and got up from the couch with her glass. 'I'm going to read.'

'What's Fay doing?'

'Taking a bath. Please lock the house before you go to bed.'

'I will,' he said. 'I might make me some coffee and go out on . . .' She was already going down the hall and he wondered how she could do him that way. Maybe she knew something after all. She was so cold. He wondered if Fay had noticed. Be hard for her not to probably. He looked down at his sandwich and suddenly didn't want any more of it. He got up and scraped his plate off into the trash and rinsed it off in the sink and left it there. He drank the last of his milk and fixed some coffee.

A good breeze was blowing out on the deck and now there was nothing to see out there but blackness, nothing to hear but a soft lap and swish of waves gently breaking on the shore down below. Distant white lights winked through the trees on the opposite side. He leaned against the rail and felt the wind on his face until enough time had passed for the coffee to be ready, then went back inside and fixed a cup. The movie was over now and the news was on. He didn't want to watch that or another movie either. He could hear a radio playing at a low volume in the bathroom down the hall. He was glad Amy had bought her the clothes. He figured she was probably trying them all on, so he went back out on the deck with his coffee and sat down to listen to the wind.

He pulled a chair back from the table and eased down in it and set his coffee down. He put his feet up on a low stool. Amy was probably under the covers already. And Alesandra lying in her bed across the water was probably still wide awake, her distant eyes staring up at the ceiling while the air conditioner hummed a low noise to help her sleep. He didn't know if she was dangerous or not. Sometimes he thought she was. Other times she seemed only glad to see him. Her eyes when he'd left tonight, he remembered them, vacant and filled with something like hate or maybe just disgust with herself for not rocking his boat a little. And they'd settled nothing. They never did. They just kept on like they'd been doing while her demands got more regular and she seemed to grow fingers that could reach out and get him. And something inside Amy had just up and died. That joy inside her, it didn't live there anymore. He'd seen a brief flash of it when they'd been bringing in Fay's new clothes, and when they'd been sitting on the bed opening the shopping bags, but by the time she had come up to the living room it was gone again. Maybe if Fay stayed with them for a while she could bring it back for good. And if that happened, he'd know what to tell Alesandra: Stay in Clarksdale.

He just had sat back down with his second cup when he heard the sliding door open. He looked over his shoulder to see Fay closing it. She had on some pajamas, a silky top and bottom with teddy bears sleeping on haystacks. She grinned, looked like she was embarrassed or blushing.

'Hey,' he said. 'I thought maybe you'd went to bed.'

'Not yet.' She walked over and leaned against the rail to look out over the water. 'Amy went to bed a while ago. Can I bum a cigarette? I know you get tired of me bummin.'

'I don't care.' He pushed the pack and the lighter across the table to her. 'You want some coffee? There's some fresh in there on the counter.'

'I believe I'll go get me some.'

She went in and then came back out and set her cup on the table.

'Pull you up a chair. I was just sitting out here looking at the stars. Saw a shooting star while ago.'

'It's a pretty night,' she said. She shook one of the cigarettes loose from the pack and lit it, then sat down and sipped at her coffee. 'I bet you come out here a good bit, don't you? I would if I lived here. I'd be out here all the time.'

'I sit out here a lot. It's pretty peaceful and all.' He stretched out in his chair and lifted his cup. 'It's really nice in the springtime. All the trees are budding out and you can smell it.'

'I always hated summertime,' she said. 'We was always in some hot place workin. That sun's so hot in the middle of the day. Just blisters you so bad and then it hurts at night. Just makes you wish you could sleep in a tub full of water all night or somethin.'

He nodded but didn't say anything.

'Was that a bad wreck you had to go to this mornin?'

'Pretty bad. Killed one man and hurt this lady. I reckon he was drunk. We had to get the cars out of the road and all.'

She nodded at this and pulled her feet up in the chair and wrapped her arms around her knees. Out of the corner of his eye he could see her rocking her body slightly in the seat. She kept looking out toward the water.

'How'd you learn all that stuff?'

Her question surprised him and he turned his head to her. She was still looking out past the rail.

'What stuff? You mean my job?'

She leaned over and flicked some ashes into the ashtray they were sharing and sipped at her coffee again.

'Well . . . yeah. Like how to get cars out of the road and stuff. And don't you have to learn all them laws?'

'Yeah. They send you to school for all that. You go and stay about two months with a bunch of other guys and then if you pass everything you graduate with your class and then you get assigned somewhere and then you might have to move for a while.'

'You ever had to shoot anybody?'

In a flash he remembered the shotgun in his face at the Greenville bridge and knowing he wasn't going to be able to get his revolver out in time and then how the man's face had disintegrated in a bloody mist from a deputy sheriff's rifle shot. How his hands had shaken that sunny afternoon leaning against the steel beams high over the Mississippi River and how the traffic had gone on by the body covered with the white sheet on the center line and the dark blood soaking into the white cloth.

'No,' he said. 'I never did. Came close to it a couple of times. I chased some folks who'd robbed a bank at Winona one time. But they wrecked.'

'Would you if you had to?'

'If I had to. If it was me or him or if somebody was fixing to hurt somebody . . . wouldn't you?'

'Yeah,' she said. 'I reckon I would.'

His coffee was growing cold in the cup but he didn't want to move. Didn't want to disrupt anything. She was talking to him again and he saw now that she was nothing like Karen, didn't sound or look like Karen.

'Amy told me about your daughter,' Fay said, quietly. 'I sure am sorry.'

He set the cup on the table and folded his hands in his lap. She had turned her face toward him and was watching him.

'It was a long time ago,' he said. 'Over five years now. Did she tell you what happened?'

'She just said it was a accident.'

He coughed in his throat to keep himself talking.

'Yeah. She'd slipped out of the house one night when I was on duty. Her mama had gone to bed and I was out on the road over close to Water Valley. There was this boy. I blame myself every day. She . . . Karen wanted to go out with him and I didn't much like his looks. He wouldn't look me in the eye. We'd had a lot of bad arguments about him. I guess I thought I was trying to protect her. Turned out there'd been a lot of times she'd already slipped out of the house to meet him. He'd park his car up here on an old road and walk through the woods over here. There was friends of his I went and talked to after Karen was dead.'

He picked up the coffee again and drank some more of it even though he knew it was cold. And then he just held the cup in his hands.

'But usually they wouldn't go anywhere. Karen knew when my shift ended and he'd always be gone by then. And her mama in there in the bed asleep, she didn't know nothing was going on. Neither one of us did. But I got a call that night about eleven o'clock while I had somebody pulled over writing em a ticket and the dispatcher said there was a wreck at the intersection of Three-fifteen and Six. Just right down the road here six or seven miles. And I was clean down in Yalobusha County. Took me a while to get over there but I was the closest one that wasn't tied up with something else. Big

100

crowd of people already there when I got there and an ambulance too so I knew it was bad. I got up and walked up the road there, I could see it turned over in the ditch. Old Plymouth Duster, I don't remember what year. He was outside and she was inside, both of em dead. I recognized her blouse.'

Fay turned her face away from him again and looked out over the black void beyond them and she was still rocking in her seat. He saw the tip of her cigarette glow when she pulled on it. She seemed so much older than Karen now, seemed not a child at all.

'Lord have mercy,' was all she said.

He studied his bare toes and set the cup back on the table. He could have stopped when he saw that she was crying but he had to get it out, tell it to somebody one more time. He knew he'd done it enough already, with troopers he knew in the passenger seat of his cruiser, prowling the midnight highways, the chattering of the radio an undercurrent to his story.

'I crawled in there with her. Somebody finally handed me a blanket in through the window and I wrapped her up in that. Wasn't a mark on her nowhere but her neck was broke. She just looked like she was asleep.'

He saw her wiping at her nose and he hushed. The wind had picked up again and it had turned cooler. He began to wish that he hadn't told her because he didn't want her to feel sorry for him. They sat there for a long time with neither of them saying anything. She leaned over and put the cigarette out, rattled the ashtray. When she got up he thought maybe she was going back into the house but instead she came over and leaned over him and put her arms around him. He wanted her to understand what he had been through and as she held him tightly he felt himself drawing strength from her.

'It's all right,' she kept saying. 'It's all right.'

Now bright days in the sun followed. On the lake she learned birds and trees from his pointing finger and began to study how he watched the weather and fished accordingly. Most times Amy wouldn't go, but she didn't seem to care that they spent so much time together, and they prowled the backwater. They would pull up into a shaded stand of cypresses and he would bait a cane pole for her, taking thrashing minnows from a foam bucket and threading them onto the hooks. She liked fishing and was good at it and he taught her how to dress them, how to cook them.

He would pull up close to a sandy bank and throw the anchor over the side and then help her out of the boat into water that was only shoulder deep. She was afraid of it but he was always right there beside her and he kept telling her that she needed to know how to swim. It was a long time before she could even dog-paddle around a bit but he was patient with her, and convinced her that he wouldn't let her drown. He would stand in the water and hold her in his arms, supporting her legs and her belly, and she would kick and splash while he guided her around. The water was warmer now from steady days of sun and she began to get browner and she was happy with the way she looked. Nobody said anything about her ever leaving.

They would stay out in the water for hours sometimes and if he ever got tired of it he never said anything. Then one day she suddenly started kicking with her feet and pulling with her hands and abruptly she was swimming. After that, he was firm in letting her know that she could not swim by herself. There were days when he had to work over, special details he sometimes got assigned to, always the wrecks on the highways, and on these afternoons Amy would come in from work and she and Fay would put on their suits and take a few blankets and towels and walk down the stairs behind the house with a small cooler and they would lie in the last weak rays of the sun while the water lapped at the red sand just below them, while the breeze blew over them. They talked about what they were going to have for supper that night or clothes and movies they liked, Amy almost always drunk. She only talked about Karen a few times, and Fay didn't tell her about being with Sam on the deck that night. She'd seen some of the pictures that stayed propped on a dresser in Amy and Sam's bedroom, a slightly smiling black-haired girl who looked like Amy. She never heard any sounds come from that bedroom at night. They seemed to get along. But what she had noticed was that they didn't touch. She never saw them kiss or hold hands. She was afraid to ask about these things.

Amy took her to an eye doctor in Oxford and she got a pair of glasses. At first she didn't try to read much of anything, but there were times when she was by herself in the middle of the day and she would pick up some of Amy's magazines and start going through them, reading the captions under the pictures, slowly and haltingly, touching the words with the tip of her finger, saying them out loud. She was rusty at reading and it was hard. But she kept at it and gradually she began to get better.

Some days she would fix a big glass of lemonade and retreat to the deck in her swimming suit and lie propped with her cigarettes and her drink and absorb the words, and work on the bigger ones she didn't know. Finally she began to read the articles themselves. How to Care for Your Baby. Ten Tips to Put the Romance Back into Your Marriage.

Amy would help her at night, the two of them on her

bed and the door closed while Sam piddled around outside or washed the supper dishes in the kitchen. Amy was a good teacher and she said once that when she was a girl she had wanted to be one.

But Fay's favorite times were with Sam out in the boat. There was nothing that could compare to that feeling of freedom when the blunt nose of the rig lifted and the spray started flying from the hull and the *slap slap slap* of the waves rolled under quicker and quicker until there was only the smooth cutting of the boat through the water, and the wind in her hair and the warm sun on her skin. Every day she thought of that other life that had been hers and she missed her mother and her brother and her sister. But she had no desire to go back to that life. She wondered how they were doing, but she figured they were probably doing about the same. One day when she was better and had plenty of money and a car she would go back. That's what she told herself: she would just go back and check on them. But it was easy to push that to the back of her mind when she was with Sam and Amy. There was always something to talk about, always something to do, another meal to fix, another trip to take, another afternoon of riding the water or swimming or fishing. The days grew in number and after a while it began to seem that she had never had any life but this one of friendship, good food, and a nice bed to sleep in at night.

One Saturday afternoon he took her to a beach that was screened from the lake by a stand of willows in a cove. She swam back and forth while he fished from a lawn chair on the sand and drank beer from a cooler beside the chair. She came wading out of the water and leaned into the boat where it sat drifting on a rope and reached in for a towel to dry her hair. He had already put down a quilt for her to sit on and she dropped down on it, rubbing the towel over her hair, drying her legs and arms. He pitched her a cigarette and a lighter without asking. There was a rod and reel stuck up in a holder nearby but he didn't seem to be paying much attention to it.

'Where's all the fish at today?' she said.

He pulled at his ear and crossed his leg. All he had on was a pair of blue jeans and they were wet to the knee, his feet covered with sand. Gray hairs on his chest that looked like wire.

'I don't know. They ain't here. You want some lemonade?'

'Did you bring me some?'

'I always do, don't I?'

She put the towel down and pulled her fingers through her hair.

'I wish I had a daddy good as you,' she said.

He muttered something in agreement and reached into the cooler beside him and retrieved a can and tossed it to her. She caught it and opened it and took a long drink from it, then leaned back on one elbow and lit the smoke and looked out over the water. She could hear a boat roaring by in the distance but she couldn't see it. And then she could, just a flash of something brown and shiny and the sound of it decreased.

The sun was very hot on her just then. There was no shade anywhere near and she rolled over onto her belly and lay there for a while.

'What you thinking about?' he said.

She pulled easily on the cigarette and let the smoke out slowly, and took another drink from her can.

'What the hell's Preparation H?'

'Ointment for hemorrhoids.'

'What's that?'

He laughed. 'Bumps on your butthole, girl. Truck drivers get em. So do highway cops. Where'd you see that?'

'TV. You wouldn't believe the stuff they sell on there.'

'Yeah I would.'

'You think Amy cares for us taking the boat out so much? Seems like we leave her at home all the time.'

He lifted his beer and sipped from it, then set it back on his belly.

'I reckon she can come with us if she wants to. I've asked her a million times but she'd rather set up there and read and have her a toddy. You worry about her too much.'

'Look what all she's done for me, though. She don't never seem to have any fun.'

'Long as she catches a buzz, she's fine.'

Far down the lake the sound of the boat had almost died away but now it sounded like it was getting closer and going faster. She saw it cruise past out there beyond the trees again. It kept going, the sound of it ebbing in the distance. She wrote her name in the sand with her finger, then scratched it out.

'Those glasses she got you OK?'

'They're fine. When you gonna teach me how to drive? You said we could start before long.'

'We'll get around to it.' He set his beer down beside his chair and bent over for the rod and started reeling it in.

'What you got on there for bait?'

'Chicken livers. I meant to pick up some shrimp but I forgot to. In a hurry to get home.'

He reeled it on in and she watched him. When he lifted the hook from the water the bait was still on it.

'Shit,' he said. He threw it back out and let it settle on the bottom, stuck the handle back in the holder. He leaned over and picked up the beer.

'I need to find someplace to take you where there ain't a bunch of traffic,' he said. 'Out in the country somewhere or something where you won't hit nothing.'

'Is it hard to learn how to drive?'

'Naw. There ain't nothing to it. But before you get your license you'll have to take the driver's test and pass the written exam. I'll go with you. Won't be nothing to it. You'll just have to study for the written. And practice on your driving a lot. Most kids your age already been driving for a couple of years.'

106

'We never did have nothin but a old piece of shit pickup. If we even had anything.'

He didn't comment. She'd noticed that many times when she brought up her family he didn't. She remembered how he'd gotten that first day when she'd told him all those things. She never had seen him mad since then. She watched his face and wondered what it would be like to kiss him.

She put her face down on the quilt and smoked the cigarette like that. Shit he was good-looking.

'Sam?'

'Yeah?'

'What's gonna happen to me?'

He waited so long before he answered that she thought maybe he wasn't going to, but then, quietly, he said: 'Nothing bad like what might have before.'

'I told you about my brother.'

'Yeah, you did.'

'And my little sister.'

'Yeah?'

'I don't know how I'll see em again.'

She knew he was thinking about his answer and she let him think.

'Well,' he said finally. 'I guess if you ever decide you want to go back and check on em you can.'

'Would you take me? I mean just to see?'

'You know I would.'

'What if they've moved by then?'

She heard him laugh softly and when she raised her face he was smiling down on her.

'You've got a lot of questions, girl.'

'I know it,' she said. Another one she had was why Amy drank so much but she didn't ask that because she thought she knew why. She didn't think Amy loved Sam. She never kissed him and she knew it wasn't right to think it but if he was hers she'd kiss him all the time. Do more than that with him too. She put her cigarette out in the sand and heard the boat out on the lake coming back. It was much closer now and going slower.

And when she pushed up with her arms to take a look it was gliding in toward them, a polished wooden hull pushing a gentle curve of wave, a beautiful woman steering it, her skin dark but not nearly black. Fay sat up.

'Who is that?'

He leaned over and set his beer in the sand.

'Trouble,' was all he said.

Something in his voice didn't sound quite right to her and he wasn't taking his eyes off the woman, who had cut the motor and was drifting closer.

'What you mean?'

'You're fixing to find out.'

Fay put one hand over her eyes to shade them from the sun, the water was so bright out there. The boat came closer to the bank and now the woman stood behind the wheel and steered it until it slid to a soft stop against the sand. Then she was climbing out and lowering herself into the water and Fay knew by the way she was looking at Sam that there was something between them. And in another heartbeat knew what that thing was. It was what those boys had been doing with that Linda in that bedroom in the trailer. What her daddy had tried to do to her and what boys had done to Barbara Lewis with her dress up over her chest. What she wanted to do with Sam if it wasn't for Amy. She wanted to see this. She looked at Sam and there was a pop and some sand exploded about six inches from her knee and she looked at it and saw Sam running and then another pop and the sand leaped four feet away from her and only then in that split second before she looked up did she know she was being shot at and Sam had reached the woman by then and they were fighting over the gun. Fay got up to see him pushing her back against the boat, but the weight of both of them was making it move. The gun popped again, such a small report, pointed up. It wasn't as loud as a gun in the movies, it was more like a toy gun or something, but Sam wouldn't have been gritting his teeth and straining so hard, even while she tried to claw at his face, if it wasn't real. She heard the woman scream out but she didn't stop struggling over the little shiny pistol Sam was trying to twist away from her until finally she dropped it with a shriek and maybe some broken fingers looking at the way one hand was feeling the other. She lay gasping in the water while he stepped back and looked around. He turned and started to give the gun a toss, stopped, checked something on it, then gave it a toss up on the beach, behind his chair. It didn't fire when it landed. He was trying to watch the woman while he got between her and Fay, and she didn't do anything for a while but just lie there in the water and watch him. Watch them. It was hard for Fay to keep from edging behind Sam once she'd taken a good look in those eyes and seen murder there without a doubt because she'd seen that before.

The woman raised a hand and wiped at her face, and then she squeezed her eyes shut for a moment and tried to move the hurt hand. Fay saw tears come from her eyes, saw her face reddening and puffing, heard her ragged breathing. She began to shake a little when she thought about the bullets, how fast and invisible they were, how silent but for the pop of the gun. In the movies some had silencers and only spat.

Sam moved closer to her, one hand out, searching for her. She grabbed it and held, and got up close behind him. She rested the other hand on his back and looked over his shoulder at the woman. She had cold eyes, Fay saw, eyes that had no light in them at all, something she must have been able to turn on and off when she wanted to and somehow Sam had not seen that. Even now she was looking for a new way to move, sizing things up. She wasn't whipped yet. Sam seemed afraid to take his eyes off her.

'You all right?'

'Yeah, yeah. She missed me. I didn't even know she was shootin at first.'

'I didn't either. Just stay where you are. Better still,

back up a little. Naw, just go over there where I threw that gun and stand next to it. She can't get to it now.'

She did like he said. She could hear him talking to the woman, didn't know what all he was saying, but the tone of his voice sounded like he was trying to get her to behave. The woman was saying things to him in a low voice. She looked down at the gun. It had sand on it. There was blood on Sam's face, a long scratch where she had gone at him with her nails. It was dripping down his cheek and she wondered if he knew it.

He knelt next to the woman, saying things to her, but she slapped at him and drew one of her legs back and kicked at him. Fay saw her pull loose when he tried to take her arm, heard her call him a son of a bitch and a lying bastard. Then she looked at Fay and said, 'Where in the hell did he find you?'

Fay took a few steps forward and the wind blew her hair. Her legs were long and brown and nicely sculpted, a skin of dark marble flowing. Little painted red toe-nails that splashed in the water.

'Walkin down the road if it's any of your business, bitch.'

'Why don't you come on down here?' Alesandra said.

Something old clicked in her. She could see the same hate she'd seen in Barbara Lewis. Way back in Florida when she would run out in the road for the food and the candy.

'Bring your ass on down here. I'll show you who you can fuck and who you can't. White trash piece of shit.'

'I'm fixin to whip your ass,' Fay said, wading out until Sam stopped her.

'Hold it. Right where you at, Fay. Come on, Alesandra. Get up and get in your boat.'

Fay had the whole picture now, and it explained everything, why Amy didn't kiss him. This was it right here. The bullets had come close and she started shaking more and she thought about Barbara Lewis showing her her food and telling her to come on over and get it if

110

she wanted it bad enough and she took more steps without knowing she was taking them and then Sam was pushing her back to tell her to quit, that this was enough, to stop it.

'Roll your blanket up, Fay. Roll it up and put it in the boat.'

She didn't want to keep looking into the woman's eyes so she moved back to the blanket and rolled it up and got her few things and carried everything down to Sam's boat. She looked at the rope and looked back. He had her up and she was saying something to him in a low voice, and Fay was watching when the woman pointed to her. She busied herself stashing the stuff behind the front seats and she was realizing that she was going to have to ride back across the lake with him. With one smooth-muscled move she hauled herself up the side of the boat with her hands and dropped into her seat with her feet hanging over, dripping. Sam was helping the woman into her boat, and she was crying. She tried not to listen. There was more crying and then begging because she kept hearing the word *please*. The engine fired and after a moment Fay looked up. The boat went slowly and blue exhaust churned up from the transom. Sam stood there watching after it. The woman sat sobbing over the steering wheel. It didn't move any faster. Sam turned his back on it and walked over.

'Well shit,' he said. He waited a moment. 'You all right?'

'I'm fine.'

'I didn't know she'd do something like that.'

'I guess you didn't know her too good. Your face is scratched,' she said, and touched the blood.

'How bad?'

'Not too bad.'

He leaned there and they watched the boat growing smaller, idling away. He went back for his cigarettes and lighter and his chair and everything, made a couple of trips while she sat there and watched the boat go away. She never had been called a white trash piece of shit before but she'd been called white trash.

He untied the boat from the willow it was moored to and coiled the rope and dropped it in the floor. He paddled out a ways before he started the outboard.

The sun had started to ease over in the sky and the air was cooler now. She reached back for her shirt and pulled it on. He put on his sunglasses and then she couldn't see his eyes. That woman thought she'd been in his bed.

They moved out from the red banks and the trees into open water and he turned the boat in the direction of his house but he didn't increase his speed. He seemed content to just motor along barely above an idle and she guessed he wasn't in any hurry to get home and see Amy. What else could he do but lie about the scratch? And what if Amy asked her about it? What would she say then? She'd have to lie too unless she wanted to get him in trouble. Maybe big trouble, maybe huge trouble.

Suddenly he killed the motor in the middle of the lake. It was very quiet then. The boat rocked in the waves and he took a look around and turned in his seat to face her. He took off the sunglasses and tossed them into the compartment on the dash.

The boat lay in the water. The lake looked empty.

'She thought you were with me,' Sam said. 'Seeing me.'

'I figured that part out.'

'Is this still bleeding?'

'Not bad now. It's scabbed over some.'

He rubbed at it, looked at his fingers. 'Well. I've either got to lay it off on something else or tell her the truth. I don't want to tell her the truth.' He paused. 'I don't know how much you've noticed about me and Amy.'

How close the bullets had come. How fast and unseen. How close she had come to winding up like Barbara Lewis.

'I mean you must have noticed that we're not real affectionate toward each other.'

She snapped herself back. 'Yeah. I've noticed. Why?'

He seemed to be struggling with something inside himself and he seemed embarrassed.

'Hell, you're grown, I'll just say it. I haven't been to bed with her in four years.'

She felt the blood going to her cheeks. He saw it too.

'I'm not trying to embarrass you. I'm just trying to explain this thing with Alesandra.'

'That woman.'

'Yeah. That woman.'

He seemed confused, a way she'd never seen him before, and he started out with some words and then stopped.

'Well here's what I can't do, Fay. I can't lay it off on my dead daughter. I can't say if she hadn't died this never would have happened. It mighta happened without it. I don't know.'

She chewed her bottom lip a little and felt some calmer. It looked like the boat with the woman in it was gone but she looked around just to make sure. He was waiting for her to say something.

'Can I ask some questions?'

'Yeah.'

'How old is she?'

'Thirty-one.'

'Where's she live?'

'Down at Clarksdale.'

'That's a nice big boat. She rich?'

'Oh yeah,' he said, and looked at a fingernail. He touched the scabbing scratch and looked at his finger. 'Too damn much money probably.'

'How long you . . . ?'

'Little over a year. I've met her in different places. Hotels mostly.' He looked around at the lake. 'But out here a good bit too.'

She felt her face burn as she said what she had to say. 'I don't know nothin personal about what men and

113

women do. But I've seen it,' she said, looking up then. 'I've seen it look awful and I've seen people enjoy it. You and her, do you . . . enjoy it?'

'Damn,' he said, and then he looked her in the eye and said, 'Yeah. We do.'

'More than with Amy?'

He looked down and thought about it and was slow to raise his eyes and say, 'Yeah, I think so. From what I remember.'

She thought about them doing it, them being on a bed with Sam on top of that woman and their mouths in different places and she started feeling warm inside and she thought about him naked and what he looked like and especially what he looked like down there and she wondered if that woman put her mouth on him the same way that Linda had done that boy Jerry. And what did it feel like when they put it in you? Did it hurt? She'd heard girls in camps say it hurt the first time. Her mother had tried to keep her close but she hadn't always been able to. They'd get on different rows of beans or tomatoes sometimes, different parts of the orange groves. Her mother never told her any of the things the girls told her. She looked at Sam's lips. What would it be like to touch his teeth with her tongue?

'You gonna see her anymore?'

'I can't. She tried to hurt you.'

'I'd say a limb scratched me, then.'

'Is that what you'd say?'

She nodded and pulled the shirt around her a little closer, giving him a satisfied smile. The motor came to life and he sent the boat toward the house. The world was becoming such a much more interesting place to live in. There would be a hot bath, clean clothes, good food for supper. It didn't hurt anything to think about him. Thinking about him didn't hurt anything. It was just thinking.

Amy closed her shop down early one day after Fay had been with them for a while. She did that sometimes, when the mood hit her. She had other appointments scheduled but she just couldn't stand there anymore. She told the girls to lock up when they finished and she walked out to the parking lot at Batesville under a hot sky at four o'clock.

The top was down on the Mustang and the seats were burning her legs. She had a little buzz starting. Traffic was bad. At the red light she had the radio going loud, tapping her fingers on the wheel to the beat of the tunes. She liked oldies stuff best, mostly hits from the sixties. Some boys in a pickup of mixed colors pulled up beside her and gave her a lookover, and she gave them back a blank face behind sunglasses.

She drove past used car lots with bright plastic pennants fluttering and snapping in the wind and by furniture stores and fast food joints sitting shoulder to shoulder, all of them so packed with cars it made you wonder how so many people could be off work at one time.

She went to the liquor store first, same one she always used. She only said what was necessary in there to get her little bottles, one from the cooler. She stashed the bottles in the car and walked over to the Winn-Dixie and was soon pushing a cart, getting things quickly, dropping them in, hurrying on down another aisle. Sam wasn't getting off until six and she and Fay would have plenty of time to lie out on the sand and talk. She got a cold six-pack of Bud tallboys and then backed up

115

and grabbed a four-pack of strawberry wine coolers and put them in the cart. Then she reached back and got another one.

At the seafood counter she looked down at pale gray shrimp clustered on their beds of chipped ice and rang the bell and got the young woman back there to weigh up two pounds of them. She waited and then saw the shrimp boil stacked in a display a few feet away and got a box of that, too. The girl handed over the white wrapped package and said Thank you ma'am and Amy went on down the floor, getting bacon, eggs and bread, lemons and cocktail sauce and mayonnaise and crackers. She got some pork chops and a bag of flour. She got a gallon of chocolate ice cream. The line wasn't long at the checkout counter and she had already begun writing her check when the cashier started ringing her things up. In just a few minutes she was out the door, walking fast, a tall boy behind her with a green apron carrying two bags. He leaned over into the backseat and set them down and she gave him a five-dollar bill just because she could.

'Thanks a lot, ma'am,' he said, and grinned.

She gave him a smile and got back into the car. There wasn't any reason she couldn't take off for an afternoon every once in a while. There was plenty of money in the bank and the house was almost paid for. And it didn't hurt to buy the things she'd been buying for Fay. The clothes were things she needed, the glasses, too.

She pulled back out into the street and turned east at an intersection beside monster trucks with loads of new lumber chained down tight or Low Boys with dozers sitting on their flat beds, mud crusted on them like mortar. The convertible wasn't good in town in the summer. But it was good out on the road. That was when she could turn the music way up and sing along with it, let the wind make a mess of her hair if it wanted to.

The traffic stopped and balked and went along and she went along with it, her arm hanging over the side of the door. She wished they'd all just get out of her way. But people kept turning off, and changing lanes, and she had to watch everything and be careful. In a little bit more she'd be out of it for good, could take a nip. Then she could open a beer and get on home. Ice down those wine coolers and walk down to the beach with Fay.

She got to the city limits and into a fifty miles per hour zone and reached down for one of the sacks. She held the wheel with her elbow long enough to push down the paper and twist off the top and get a sip. She reached into a grocery sack between the seats and got a beer, leaving town behind her, trucks and cars in the rearview, the cracked concrete road open and sunny and coming under her as she sped up.

She had a sudden craving for a cigarette and just pushed it to the back of her mind. She'd been quit four years now and it had been very hard for her. She always kept a pack in her purse, and a lighter, to remind herself that she could have one if she wanted it bad enough. But then she would think about how hard it had been to quit and what she would have to go through again if she started back, and that made it easier to try and push the craving away. But going down the road like this, the music playing, just having one between her fingers to trail smoke out . . . it would have been nice.

She went under the Highway 55 bridge and hit the sixty-five zone and pushed it up to seventy-five and held it there, passing what was coming off the ramp, swinging wide into the other lane. Trucks and more trucks, she didn't know how there could be so many. And all of them bound for different places, cities she'd never heard of up north and far south, too. Sam said he got sick of driving. She imagined truckers did too. But she didn't. She loved to drive and always had.

A tractor far up ahead was towing a hay baler, yellow lights flashing. She went around it and saw a man up on the seat in a felt hat, overalls, smoking the nub of a cigarette. What a hot job he had, turning and turning the wheel again in some dry green field, the chaff of the cut hay blowing over him, going down the neck of his shirt, getting into his eyes. That's what she thought as she passed him. An old man, had probably been at farming all his life.

The sky up above was clear and blue with scattered white clouds rolling high and far away. Such a good day to lay out on a blanket. She glanced at her watch. She'd be home soon.

The road was patched with black tar in wide melting ribbons and she went by some orange trucks with barricades set out for the guys. Somebody would come blasting along once in a while somewhere and run over somebody out working on the road. Sometimes they even ran over troopers who had somebody pulled over. Sam had seen it happen. She knew there was a lot of bad stuff he saw. She could tell it in the way he came in on some days that something bad had happened. He wouldn't have that happiness in his step like when he was going fishing. He'd just change clothes and get a beer and go sit out on the deck. She'd stand there at the door and look at him and wonder what smashed body he had seen or how many of them and if any of them had been children. That always tore him up worse than anything. Sometimes he would take the boat and go out and be gone for hours and wouldn't come in until dark or after. She tried to let herself think she didn't know what he could be doing out there on that water all by himself for so long at a time, but really, she knew he wasn't by himself, and what he was doing. It was OK. He evidently had to have somebody to do it to. Just as long as she didn't have to do it anymore. It wasn't fun anymore. So she didn't worry about it. And didn't think about him touching the bare skin of her breast inside her blouse in the backseat of his daddy's Impala. That was a long time ago. You couldn't bring that back.

Up ahead buzzards were sailing the sky in lowering circles, a big black whirling mass of them erupted from some dense cedar roost in a dim and hidden forest.

Nasty things and she hated to even look at them. Always eating something dead and so many of them they must have found a horse or a cow.

She kept her eyes on the road until she got to a place where she couldn't see them anymore. She passed the cemetery where Karen was buried, glancing out that way, knowing exactly where that little plot of ground lay behind a thin line of young trees. Sometimes she still wished that Karen was over at Verona, at her family's graveyard. But Sam had convinced her that it would be too far to go visit, and she guessed he'd been right. She was closer to them here and they could come more often to put down flowers and just sit. And weep. And weep and weep and weep. That had gotten old too. Now she didn't visit as much.

She wondered if Karen could see what was going on wherever she was, wondered if she knew about Fay taking her place kind of and if she would approve. She thought maybe she would. They'd just kept her in too tight, hadn't let her date, hadn't wanted anything to happen to her, and look where she wound up. Wasn't that the worst thing to fear, that your child would die? Wasn't it probably like that the world over? Now look where she was. Lying in a hole in the ground. She couldn't stop thinking about it. Awful things and awful thoughts like that all day long and even at night and sometimes especially at night. It was so much easier to go to sleep when you were drunk, and if you could function drunk and get yourself from place to place it was even better.

She really wanted a cigarette. They were right in there, too, a whole fresh pack of Salem 100s, and a lighter. He couldn't raise hell with her if she started back. He'd seemed glad she'd quit, had said he wished he could. And she said Well you can quit if you want to bad enough. She'd been proud of herself, and that pride would be seriously wounded if she finally broke down whizzing up the road like this and opened the pack and took one out and lit it.

119

She thought maybe it would pass if she just kept on driving, so that's what she did. For a while it worked. She looked at the houses set back from the road and admired the flowers the people had planted and listened to the music on the radio. She thought of what she needed to do in her own yard, trim the flower beds and prune some of the young trees she had planted, rake up some more of the pine needles. There wasn't much grass to cut and she was glad of that. Sam never had liked cutting grass. It was one of the few things he'd ever complained about. He always said it seemed like such a waste of time. But it wasn't, not if you wanted your place to look nice. Still she was glad their yard was mostly woods. It was one less thing for them to fuss about.

Once in a while she passed a solitary car. There wasn't much traffic on the road right now. She kept thinking about the cigarette and it wouldn't leave her alone. Just one or two puffs would do, then she could throw it over the top of the door.

She got her little bottle over in her lap again next to the beer and bobbled across the center line just a bit getting the top off. But there was nothing behind her and she took a good long drink, then capped it and put it in the other bucket seat within easy reach. She was about done with the first beer and she finished it just as a car topped the hill in her rearview mirror. She watched that mirror constantly when she was driving and drinking because she knew how easy they could slip up behind you if you weren't paying attention. She dropped the can into the floorboard behind her and wrenched another one loose from the sack.

And Fay smoked too. It wasn't easy being around them when they smoked all the time and all they wanted to. Fay would be smoking this afternoon while they were down on the beach and she'd have to lie there and smell it. And she could smell so good now. Before, when she'd smoked, she hadn't been able to smell hardly anything. That had come back, and her taste for food had come back. Sitting out on the deck now she could smell the trees and her flowers and sometimes even the fish that had washed up on the sand. Everything tasted so good.

She just didn't think she could wait any longer for one. She hated to go back to smoking. But she wanted one real bad. Worse than ever.

'Fuck it,' she said, and reached into her purse and found the slim package and pulled it out, her fingers almost shaking. She didn't let herself think about what she was doing. She pulled off the cellophane strip and tore the clear stuff off the top and flipped the box open. The car got closer behind her and started around to pass. She held the wheel steady with both hands on it and took out one cigarette. The car went around and pulled over in front of her and started drawing away. She took another sip of her beer and then put the pack down on the console and stuck the cigarette between her lips. She pushed in the lighter.

God it was good going down. She wasn't used to it and so she coughed a little at first, but oh it was good. Yeah, it was fine. How in the hell had she made it this long? And why in the hell would she have to hide it from him anyway? Didn't he do what he wanted to? Why couldn't she do the same?

Smoking again. Having one between her fingers. All the gum and the candy she'd put in her mouth and getting hypnotized in Tupelo and quitting over and over and for what? Just to wind up with one in her hand again anyway. If quitting made you unhappy then why in the hell quit? As far as it killing you, hell, she could get killed out on the road this afternoon but that didn't mean she was going to. You could get killed walking across the street in town. My God, a three hundred pound chunk of frozen shit could fall out of an airplane and come right down on you in your easy chair while you were reading the new Danielle Steel. Shit, you could get killed going to church. Heart attack. Bam. *Something* was going to get you.

She turned the radio up a bit more. Some more cars were coming around her now because she'd slowed down some. There wasn't any need in being in a hurry. That ice cream and stuff was back there, true, but it was wrapped up good and it probably wouldn't melt even if she did ride around a little before she went home. Get a buzz and then go home, that was the deal. And there wasn't any need in making a big deal out of her going back to smoking. Wasn't any need to try and hide it from him.

She thought about getting off Highway 6, maybe take a side road down through the country somewhere. There were roads she used just for that sometimes. Until Fay had come, there hadn't been any real reason to hurry home after work. Half the time or most of the time Sam wasn't there anyway, and even if he was, there wasn't much for them to talk about. She knew what being a state trooper was like by now and he knew what being a hairdresser was like by now. He stopped people and wrote tickets and she stood on her feet all day and fixed women's hair and in between customers went back to her office and took little drinks of this or that. The restaurant next door had a bar and it was always good for a couple at lunch. Nobody complained or stopped coming into her shop. She was careful. She never had messed up anybody's hair. But she remembered how nice and embarrassed that boy had been who'd pulled her over that time, that one who worked for the sheriff's department, what was his name? Tim? Tom? Tony. Tony McCollum. And he didn't do anything but make her sit there while he called Sam. She watched for cops behind her now. She wasn't going to get slipped up on again.

And it might be better to get off this road anyway. Everybody was going to get off work before long and they'd all be on this highway. You had to watch what you were doing. You just had to keep up with what was going on around you.

Up there she thought was the road she wanted. It

looked like the turnoff for that little crooked road that went up by that pretty church and that man's big silo and that garden he raised every year with those big watermelons. She put on her blinker a little too soon and started to turn it off and kept it on and noticed somebody pretty close behind her, not acting like they were going to pass. It wasn't a cop, it was just somebody. She hoped they weren't going up the same road she was going to turn onto. Because that would mess everything up. The whole idea was to get off on a pretty road where you could drive slow and look at everything while you drank and thought everything over and if somebody was right on your bumper then you couldn't even drink because then they'd be seeing what you were doing, riding around drinking.

The turnoff came up and she moved toward it and the other car behind her moved with her. Well shit. Goddamn it. Now everything was going to get messed up because of this person whoever it was following her. Not too close but close enough, too close for comfort because they could see her drinking from her can if she did and she didn't want anybody to see her drinking if she wasn't in a bar except Fay and Sam.

She got a drink anyway, shit, maybe the person couldn't tell what it was. Usually she had one of those foam deals, a coolie or whatever they called it, to put it in, and then nobody could tell what you were drinking, might be drinking a Coke for all they knew, and you could drink pretty openly like that. A cop would have to be driving right beside your window just as you took a drink to see that red-and-white Budweiser top, and that wasn't going to happen. But she'd lost her coolie somewhere.

She didn't take a drink when she was in a curve.

She didn't speed.

She kept her eye on the rearview mirror.

The person following her didn't follow too close but the person followed her all the way down to the stop sign. And here was a good place for the person to turn off and go to the right or the left and then not be behind her at all.

She came to a complete stop and looked both ways. The road was dead empty but she could hear the *chug chug chug* of a tractor and in looking up the other way to check for traffic she saw a boy working an old green John Deere slowly through a stand of young corn, the scratchers pulling at the dirt and dragging out the grass. She took off, glancing up at the driver behind her. The other car took off from the stop sign and didn't turn, just stayed right behind her. She took another drink of her beer and started to get a little pissed off. What were the chances of this shit happening? Of somebody just coming along, the exact same time she came along, maybe somebody who lived on this road and had been in Memphis shopping all day long or something, just coming in at the exact right time to get behind her and mess up her drinking and riding around?

And it wasn't like she did it all the time. But once in a while she liked to do it. It made her feel like back in the old days, when they rode around all the time in his daddy's car. And finally did it in there too. And pretty soon were doing it all the time in there. But Lord all that was a long time ago. She had been a girl then. It had been a long time since she'd been a girl. And once you lost that it was just lost forever. You didn't even know when it happened. One day it just was. You were a grown woman. And getting old was nothing but a drag. She wondered if Sam's woman was young, and if she was pretty. She bet she was. She wondered, idly, where they met when they did, how long they stayed together, what kind of things they might say to each other.

She didn't even need to be riding around, Fay was looking for her to be home. But Fay could always lie on the beach by herself. She wasn't ready to go home just yet. In a little while, sure, just not right now. There was too much to think about right now. Sometimes when you got out and rode around you could get in the right frame of mind to think about things and this felt like one of those times. You couldn't just call them up. They just arrived sometimes and you had to go with the flow of them.

The person behind her wasn't turning off and what if the person lived all the way at the end of the road? That was what, seven or eight miles. It looked like an old woman. Probably wouldn't make a shit if she drank in front of her. It would be better if they had a little distance between them, though. She sped up some, by about ten miles an hour, and thought maybe she could pull away from her, but the old woman sped up and stayed right with her. And then in the next straight-away, a clear half mile of road ahead and nothing coming, she wouldn't pass. Not even when Amy slowed down some more and kept looking through the rearview mirror at her. It was hard to see her plainly. Her hair was dark and seemed to shadow her face, but she could see an old woman's dress, fake pearls, medium big hair. A plastic bracelet on her wrist.

She got another drink of the vodka but the car behind her was taking all the fun out of it. And then like magic it slowed and turned into a driveway. Shit yeah. She turned up the beer and then set it back between her legs. Of course he was fucking somebody. She'd smelled it on him since she'd quit smoking, and now she was drinking worse.

Uh oh, now. She was weaving a little bit. Weaved over the center line right back there. And this road was narrow. She needed to watch it and be careful. Think about something good instead. Something like Fay. She'd head on home in just a few more minutes or just a few more miles. She wanted to look at the silo because it was a new one somebody had built a few months ago. She'd get right on home and go down to the beach with Fay and stretch out on those towels. What a wonderful girl to come into their lives. A way-faring stranger. Cooked and cleaned the house and was always cheerful. How could it be so? Had God said,

Well, sorry I had to mess over you like that, but now I'm giving you this? Not likely. God didn't do stuff like that. He didn't reach down and move people around. People did what they wanted to on their own.

The sky was bright overhead and the road was dotted with pretty houses, well-tended pastures. Here and there horses stood head to tail and snapped their tails at flies. Some man was baling his hay. She saw kids fishing on the bank of a pond. And there was the silo, dark blue with a silver top. She met a big truck and had to get over suddenly, her wheels almost at the ditch. It scared her for a second but she was OK. Her wheels threw up a little gravel from the side of the road but she jerked them back to the center of the road the moment the truck was past. Her heart was hammering just a bit. Might be best to get on up here somewhere and find a good place to turn around and head on back.

Lord God Fay could have him if she wanted him. If she wanted him. Limb scratched him? Bullshit. She hadn't made Fay back him up, because they both knew something she didn't, and she didn't really want to know what that something was. He could do whatever he wanted to just as long as she didn't have to hear about it. But how could they all live together like that? Could they live together like that? She knew it wouldn't bother her. She didn't even want to think about a dick.

She seemed to remember that there was a place up here somewhere to turn around. Seemed like it was on top of a hill where you could see off a long way in several different directions. And oh yeah, she could remember it now. She'd been through here in the winter before when the cows were wet and looked depressed huddled in their sodden pens. Skies gray and the crossroads lonely and windswept and the ragged sagegrass swaying at the edge of the road.

It was getting cooler. It was time to turn around. Fay'd be wondering where she was and she'd be ready and have her swimsuit on and hell she guessed she could just *tell* her Honey if you want to fuck my husband you just go right ahead cause I'm not gonna use him and I'd at least rather have him with some-body I like stead of somebody I don't even know. What was the need in getting divorced over it? Every-thing was pretty comfy, they had plenty of money, could do whatever they wanted to. She was pretty young was the only thing. She was pretty healthy too, though.

And his hands had just turned cold. It was that as much as anything. That's why she didn't want them on her now. Not on her legs, not on her titties, not on her face or her mouth.

She took another hit of the vodka and put it away and sped up a little. It was time to get on back. Hurrying now, she went weaving into the last curve before the intersection and barely squeezed by the first hurtling log truck and was trying to recover when the second one came barreling through so fast that she only had time for one last thought inside the screaming screech of air brakes: *Fay*.

Sam wasn't off duty yet so naturally they called him to it. It was a state road and he had to run it and he knew right where it was. He started shaking when he first saw it, the crumpled little Mustang with its bright red paint up under the log truck, and when he lost it another trooper who'd come in behind him led him away from it and made him stand there until he could get some more help. Sam headed over a couple of times and each time the other trooper convinced him to go back, that there wasn't going to be anything he could do.

Dark fell and lights were brought in, traffic stopped on the road and cops with flashlights keeping them still so that the emergency vehicles could get in and out. It went on and on and it took them a long time to get her out. He dropped his head and thought about Alesandra and the things he had done with her and wept openly, standing there on the side of the road in plain sight of anybody who cared to look, holding on to a whip antenna for strength, his hat off his head and lying in a ditch beside weeds and papers.

Two days later they buried her next to Karen. Sam was ill at ease in a new suit and Fay wore the first black stuff she'd ever owned. They'd made a quick trip to Batesville for clothes and she'd helped him pick out the casket.

The sun seared them until they were under the tent with the preacher saying his last words. Amy's parents were over from Verona and they were numb and they treated Fay with coldness and simple rudeness. Sam's daddy was sick and his mother had to stay with him. She'd kept calling him and crying, and he knew he'd have to talk to her some more when he got home.

It was over quickly, the people going back to their cars, all the cruisers waiting until the last as the men who drove them spoke quiet words to Sam and then turned away. Tony McCollum watched from a little hill, his hat in his hand.

His district chief was the last one, Grayton, a man nearly sixty with two silver stars on his uniform jacket. He limply shook Sam's hand and looked at Fay and then told him he wanted him to take a month off.

'Are you sure, sir?' he said. 'Who'll cover my district all that time?'

'I've already got somebody on it. I don't want to see you in that cruiser for thirty days, Harris.'

'Yes sir,' he said, and nodded. He didn't know Grayton too well. Most people said he was a prick. Thirty days to do what? Grieve? But he had to do what Grayton said.

In a few minutes most everybody was gone. He could

129

see a yellow backhoe parked up on the hill and he knew it was time for them to go. Fay had hung back by herself, watching him, and now he put his hand out for her and she came up to him and shook and shook when he put his arms around her. No sounds came out of her and then some did. He held her. Patted her back. A slow rocking waltz there without steps. He pulled back from her and raised her chin in his hand and looked at her eyes, at her shining cheek.

'You want to go on back home?'

'I'll fix you some supper,' she said. 'You need to eat. You ain't eat anything in two days.'

It was true. He was very hungry now.

'OK,' he said, and they turned together and walked across the grass as the people from the funeral home began packing up the chairs and pulling the velvet drapes from them, as another truck rolled slowly onto the green grass and stopped some distance back, waiting, letting them go on over to his pickup and get in and pull out. A black jet of smoke shot from the exhaust pipe on the backhoe and it rattled loudly in the silence and the cars passed as always on the highway.

It wasn't even close to dark when they got home. He said he was ready for a drink and went back to his room to change clothes. She went into hers and took off the black suit and hung it up carefully in the closet and then took it back down and wrapped it in the plastic bag it had come in and then hung it up again. Put the black flats neatly beneath it. What Sam had paid for with a piece of plastic. She listened to see if she could hear him, standing there in her slip and stockings, and he was on the phone. Probably his mother again. She found some shorts and a top and changed into them, brushed her hair in the mirror and put down the brush gently. Her mascara had smeared from her tears and she went into the bathroom and washed her face with cold water. She looked at her freckles. The only time she'd ever felt

130

worse than this was when her daddy traded her little
brother for that new car. It had taken her a long time
to get to where she could kind of live with that. And
she guessed this would take a long time, too, Amy.
Where did you go when you died? Did you go anywhere? Or did you just lie in a hole in the ground forever? She turned away from the mirror and switched
off the light and went up the hall. Sam's bedroom
door was open and she didn't see him. And she
needed a drink, too. She stopped by the icebox and
got a frigid beer out of it and opened it and took a sip
like ice. There was a rolled-up bag of potato chips on
top and she pulled it down and got her cigarettes and
lighter and stepped to the glass door where she could
see him leaning on the rail and looking out over the
water. She went out and pulled a chair up to the table
and sat down. He didn't turn around. A glass of
whiskey and ice sat at his elbow and she'd never seen
him drink that. She'd seen it in the cabinet, but she'd
never seen him take it down. He lifted the glass and
took a long drink from it and then set it back down.
She opened the potato chips and ate a few of them
but they were soft and almost tasteless. She pushed
them away. Who'd buy the groceries now?

'I've been thinking,' he said. 'The Mustang was paid
for and she had full coverage on it. They'll have to pay
whatever it was worth. Whenever we get that, we might
could take some of that money and buy you a used car
you could learn to drive on.'

He turned around and leaned back against the rail.

'I've got so much to do,' he said. 'I don't know where
to start. I've got to sell her shop. Start going through her
clothes. Maybe you could do some of that. Keep what
you want and throw the rest of it out.'

'Throw it out?'

'Why keep it?' He picked up the whiskey again and
drank from it. 'That closet was always too small for
both of us anyway. You might could wear some of her
clothes.'

131

She tipped the beer to her lips. She'd have to cook more now. Wash the clothes. But that would be OK. She'd have to stay by herself more. That might not be so OK. It was dark out here at night. And he worked so much at night. She'd have to find out about the doors, the locks.

'What you want for supper?' she said.

'Let's don't cook, let's go out and eat somewhere.'

'All right.'

'It might not look right to some folks, to go out and eat on the day you bury your wife. But we'd been meaning to take you to this good steak house up at Como. They got some about this thick.' He held his thumb two inches away from his finger to show her. 'We used to go there some. Long time ago. She'd still want you to go.'

There was not much of a breeze out there just then. Most days it was cool and steady, coming off the water with nothing to impede it. But the water was flat and calm, too, and nothing much seemed to be stirring out there. She didn't even know what day it was. She thought it was Thursday.

'We'll need to go over to the shop one day and get some of her stuff,' he said. 'I don't know what's in there much. A bunch of hair dryers and combs and stuff. I don't know what's hers and what's not. I guess I'll get one of those girls to help me. You met some of them, didn't you?'

'Yeah,' she said. 'I met Suzy and Amber. They're real nice. They were tore up about Amy.'

'Yeah. I don't know em that well. I think Amber's been working for her about five years and Suzy about two.'

'Maybe one of them would want to buy it,' she said.

He nodded and looked at the tabletop, thinking, thinking some more.

'May be,' he said. 'I need to get it appraised I guess.'

'What's that?'

'Find out what it's worth. I know it's worth a lot more than we paid for it. Real estate's high in Batesville.'

She didn't know what any of that meant so she just let it go. She wondered how he was fixed for money. He seemed to have plenty: the house, his boats, the new pickup.

'Feels funny, her not being here,' he said.

'Yeah,' Fay said. 'I may not lay out on the beach for a while.'

He picked up the drink and turned his head out toward the lake for a moment and took another sip from it and then came over to the table and sat down. She could see his fingers shaking where they held the glass, and how they trembled when he put his cigarette up to his mouth. A fine vibration going on there in his veins and small bones. She wanted to touch his hand, put her hand on his, but he was holding tight to the drink. He seemed afraid to look at her. Suddenly he did.

'You don't have to stay here with me. You know. All by yourself.'

That scared her. She'd been knowing this would have to be talked about, and she'd figured out all by herself what Amy's parents thought about her. They thought there was something between her and Sam. She could see it in their eyes. They thought she and Sam were fucking. And she guessed it could look like that.

'What you want me to do?' she said.

'Well.' He cleared his throat and kind of shook his shoulders. 'I just don't want you to think you have to stay here if you don't want to. I mean . . . I'm not even any kin to you. But if your own people can't take care of you . . .' He let the words trail off and said he was going back inside to mix another drink. He left the table and she heard the gentle thud of his feet on the boards and felt the slight trembling of the timbers beneath the deck and heard the door open and close. *If she didn't want to stay?* Did he think she wanted to get back out on that road and go to walking again? Go back to her daddy and the way he was? Not after all this. And maybe Gary had left by now, too. And what if he'd taken Dorothy with him? How would she ever know anything? Sam said he'd take her back someday. But they might all be gone by then. And he was trying to deal with all this, trying to decide what to do with her. She wanted to stay. It didn't matter that he wasn't any kin to her. He was a good man, a strong man, and that was what she needed. He could take care of her. And would he want her to take Amy's place like a wife? Would he? He'd said four years since he'd slept with Amy. But not that Alesandra. She was beautiful. He might go back to her now. No matter what he'd said. Things were different now.

The door opened again and it stayed open. He came back and sat down and the glass was full again with ice and whiskey, right up to the top. Somehow she was afraid to see him drinking it.

As if the conversation hadn't been interrupted he said, 'I mean it might look wrong to some people, but I'm not worried about what anybody thinks. I guess I'm just worried you might be scared of this.'

'Of what?'

'Just being out here at night with me. By yourself and Amy not here. Just me and you.'

She looked at his face until he turned it up to her and she saw the hurt and regret in his eyes. She put her hand on his wrist and said, 'That's all there is now, just me and you.'

He mixed another drink after they changed clothes and put it in a tall yellow cup and sipped on it while they were going down the road. He turned toward the dam and drove across the top of it just as the sun was going down so that below them the lower lake sat behind the clumps of oak trees deep and green with the orange ball on its surface slowly fading and dying. Campers and pickups and tents were clustered under the trees, the slight forms of people moving about, white gas lanterns already hanging and throwing their white light. People moving about, smoke rising from grills and hamburgers, night coming over the land.

He said that he used to like to camp and Fay said

she'd done it so much she didn't care anything about it.

'Camp out in a pickup for three months,' she told him. 'Try that for fun. It ain't none.'

They drove on into the gathering dusk and people had their headlights on. At Sardis he turned right and got up on the interstate and pushed the truck up to seventy and left it there.

By the time they got to Como it was full dark and cars were slanted at an angle in to a curb and they pulled in there beside the others and got out. They walked down a cracked sidewalk under a canopy of bent tin and past an antique shop and a dilapidated grocery store, down a concrete ramp to a glass-fronted place with hitching rails for horses still embedded in the concrete. Inside to a wide room filled with tables and people seated at them eating, a big grill at the back sending up smoke, a smiling waitress coming with plastic folders in her hands, noise and the smell of the sizzling meat, girls carrying drinks and silverware and coffee cups. Their girl led them to a table in an almost empty room with a dead fireplace and he ordered iced tea and helped her decide what she wanted. He told her the T-bone was good and she got that, Thousand Island for her salad, and the food when it came was the best she'd ever had. She could tell he was sobering up and he even laughed a few times and told her she looked nice in what she was wearing.

Going home down the black highway with the lights streaming toward them and glaring in her eyes she got sleepy and moved over in the seat closer to him and put her head up against his shoulder, told him she was tired. He said he knew she was and to go ahead and rest. For a long time she could feel the highway rolling by beneath the tires and she could hear the faint sound of a song on the radio and the wind whistling past the cab of the truck.

He woke her up when he shut it off and she opened her eyes and they were home. They climbed the stairs together and he locked all the doors but said he wasn't going to bed just yet. She saw him reaching for the whiskey bottle when she went down the hall to the bathroom. When she came out of there he had unlocked the glass door and was sitting there on the deck, looking out toward the water.

She didn't tell him good night because she didn't know what he was going to do. She went back to her room and undressed and put on a flowered silk camisole that Amy had bought for her and turned out the light and lay under the covers, trying to decide whether or not to stay awake.

Sometime just before sleep she heard him come back in and rattle around in the kitchen some, heard the dim clink of ice in a glass. She cried for a while about Amy, and thought about them burying her today.

Time passed and they fished and swam. Talked late on the deck at night. Several times he had to go see his folks and she cleaned the house or cooked. One day she started packing away the old clothes in the closet and trying on different things. She saved some shoes but only a few dresses since most of Amy's clothes were too small for her.

By the time she had spent all afternoon putting things in boxes and taping them shut, she was tired and she felt dirty from kneeling in the closet and hauling the boxes out to the front steps for loading. She wanted a long bath, a cold beer resting on the edge of the tub, her cigarette smoking in an ashtray on the toilet seat.

She drew the water and took her clothes off and dumped in some bath oil beads while the tub filled. She already had the beer and her smokes in there. She shut the door and turned on a plastic radio that always sat on a flowered rack with doodads and birds. Amy had collected pretty little things and they were all over the house.

She picked up one now and turned it this way and that, a crystal quail with faceted wings and a tiny beak and a frosted comb. She set it back among its minute brood, fledgling chicks of the same fine glass and no bigger than your thumbnail. She bent and got a magazine from a rack of them beside the tub and got her glasses and put them on and stepped into the tub and eased herself to rest against the rising bubbles and leaned back, and she read some in the magazine and sipped at her beer. When the tub filled halfway up she reached out one foot and with her toes turned off the water. When the temperature dropped some after five minutes she reached that foot out again and let some more hot water in. She stayed in it for thirty minutes, until all her toe pads had wrinkles all over them.

Not knowing he was home she came naked from the bathroom with the ends of her hair wet, rubbing at herself with a towel, and he was standing there at his bedroom door unbuttoning a striped shirt. Her heart leaped and she froze, and clutched the towel to her breasts for a moment, and then, slowly, her heart beating faster, pulled it down with her hands and went ahead and let him look, thinking: *I'm sorry, Amy, I am, but I need him and I'll take good care of him.*

He tried to avoid it. He turned his head and tried not to look at her. But she dropped the towel on the floor and moved toward him. He was a good man and she wouldn't find one better, so why not be like a wife to him?

'Don't, Fay,' he said, when she got up against him. 'It's wrong, and Amy,' he said but his words stalled as if they'd had no will behind them to start with and when she took his hand and placed it on her nipple she heard him moan. She kissed him and opened her mouth and reached down for him. When she felt it she turned him and pulled him into his bedroom and closed the door behind them.

Faint night sounds through the open window letting the breeze in, the creak and shift of the big boat at its mooring and the chill of the night air on their skins. He slept and thought he'd dreamed of fishing in a slow brown river and when he was a boy but came awake to find her again like a dream delivered with her mouth open and wet and her lower belly thinly pelted, her skin so smooth under his fingers and her hips arched up to meet him and her sweet lips pressing against his. Dawn found him cradling her next to him and her sleeping with her mouth open just the tiniest bit and the soft snoring that filled the room where light was just beginning to wash through the blinds.

She slept late and he stretched at the rail with his hands curled into fists and yawned scratching at his belly and looked down into the boat and could see the dew on the seats. Remembering the touch of her hands and the feel of her face. The hair that he'd twined between his fingers and how it felt inside her. He picked up his coffee and drained it and put on his tennis shoes and left her a note. He drove over to the bait shop at Pat's Bluff and got three boxes of redworms and then back at the house he cranked up the old outboard and motored out in the aluminum boat to bait his lines. He worked at that for a while so that he could do something with his hands and one line kept recurring in his head: *You sorry son of a bitch*. And no way to hide from that. But when he got back to the house she was fixing his breakfast and humming some happy little tune while she moved around the stove, winking at him.

He had her out around DeLay one day, trying to show her how to drive. She had the wheel in a death grip of both hands. An hour before this they'd been in the dark and cool bedroom, naked under the sheets. It surprised him that he was able to keep up with her.

'I guess it just takes some gettin used to,' she said, weaving a little over the road.

'You're doing fine,' he said, and patted her on the shoulder. When she got tired he started driving again and they rode down toward Calhoun County on the back roads, past the winched-up engines among rusting hulks and past row crops and pastures and old homes where homemade birdhouses swung gently in the breezes. They came back up 9 and turned and went toward Water Valley and rode down to Enid and had catfish just as the sun was going down at a roadside place where they could sit outside and watch it get dark as they ate, looked at each other, smiled.

She'd wake him in the middle of the night and he would open his eyes and she would be over him, strad-dling him, her hair hanging down over her heavy breasts and she would fling it back from her face and lower them to his lips and even though it was dark he could see her just fine.

Or she would lie on the deck and turn browner and browner. She cleaned the house and washed and ironed. The house was clean when he came in, the bed made, the dishes washed and put away.

They camped one night in an old tent of his on a spit of land out near Clear Creek. He set up a Coleman stove on a folding table and got out his black iron skillets and battered crappie filets and peanut oil and she watched the sputtering blue flames start up and even out, and she watched him carefully drop the pieces of fish into the skillet and saw how the edges curled up and how cautious he was with the size of the flame.

They made love in the tent almost all night instead of watching the rods and reels he'd propped on forked sticks beyond the campfire, where the water lapped softly.

She made him a cake one day by following the recipe on the side of the box. It was a rich chocolate cake with fudge frosting and he ate a quarter of it with milk in front of the television while they watched a show about the Civil War and she never said a word, just stared at what was being told on the screen. First she'd heard about it.

He took her grocery shopping in Batesville and she was careful with his money.

'Lord,' she said. 'I didn't know stuff was so high.'

'Just get what you want,' he said. 'I'll eat whatever you fix.'

On the third try she got up on his skis and shook the water from her face and soon was trying to do things with the rope, to weave and bob. She busted her ass a few times but she got back up and kept trying and pretty soon she could follow him wherever he wanted to tow her until her legs gave out, then she'd wave to him, drop the rope, and float in the water with her life jacket until he circled back around to pick her up.

Sometimes he rented movies, Westerns or films about cops in big cities. She learned how to use the VCR and

141

she still thought about Amy all the time and the guilt never did leave her. It was something she could feel on her as solid as her skin. But all she did was try to make him happy.

Sometimes in growing darkness they would cast their lines among the dead white trees for the big flatheads that came out of the depths at night to feed, old stubby things with wide heads and long whiskers. He would hold one up in the beam of the flashlight she held, and say, 'Now that's a nice one, baby, he'll eat good.'

And she would nod and smile in the rocking boat, unafraid of the dark or the water or any other thing simply because she was with him.

The phone rang one morning and he went to answer it and stayed out there for several minutes. He said *Yes sir* a lot. Fay listened to his end of the conversation from under her pile of covers in the bedroom where the blinds were pulled down against the light. They'd stayed up late the night before watching movies. She raised up for a moment and looked at the clock and it was 9:13. She closed her eyes and drifted for a while, and then he was in the room and on the bed with her, already dressed. She pulled at the sleep in her eyes with the tip of her finger, and rolled over in the bed toward him. She hadn't even heard him get up but sometimes she didn't. She seemed to need more sleep these days, was harder to rouse sometimes.

'Guess what?' he said. She could see the excitement on his face when she raised up and looked at him.

'What is it? They want you to go back to work?'

'Yeah. At four o'clock. Pete Turner had a wreck and Joe Price shot some woman in the eye over at Belzoni. They need me back today.'

She pulled her pillow up behind her head and slid backward a few inches, and reached her hand out to his. She'd been knowing it would have to end sometime but she just hadn't thought it would be this soon. But it wasn't like he was going away forever. He was just going back to work.

'Well,' she said, 'you think they're gonna put you back on the night shift?'

'I guess for now they are. But I'll get back on days

143

eventually, always do. You want to get up and eat some breakfast?'

She stretched her arms over her head and yawned. She didn't feel rested yet, and some more sleep, to slide back under the covers and drift away again, that sounded better than getting up to the bright sunshine she knew was outside.

'I don't know. I may sleep some more. What time you think you'll get in tonight?'

'I don't know. Maybe around one or two. Shouldn't be any later than that. You gonna be OK out here?'

'I want you to show me how to lock all the doors. I don't think I'll be afraid. I just want to make sure all the doors are locked. I'll sit up and watch TV until you get in. And I'll have you some supper fixed. What you want?'

He was already getting off the bed and going to the closet, pulling his shirt off, going for an old T-shirt in the closet.

'I don't care. Whatever you want to fix. I've got a lot to do before four. I'll have to leave about three-thirty. I need to wash my car and clean it out. Make sure it's running OK. I haven't had it out on the road in over three weeks. I'll have to gas it up, too.' He finished pulling the shirt over his head and turned back to her. 'You go ahead and sleep some more if you want to. I think I've got some pants ready but you may need to iron me a shirt when you get up. You mind?'

'I don't mind a bit.'

'What's wrong?'

'Nothin.'

She was looking toward the window and he came back around and sat down on the bed again.

'All right,' he said. 'What is it?'

'Nothin. I'm just gonna miss you.'

'I'll miss you too but that's not what's bothering you. What is it?'

She turned on her side so that she was almost speaking into his pillow.

'What you gonna tell your friends about me? A bunch of em saw me at Amy's funeral.'

'I'm not worried about that. What goes on between you and me is nobody's business but ours.'

'But don't you talk to your friends? I could tell you had a lot of em. How come they don't come over here any?'

He sat back and patted at his chest for his cigarettes but he'd left them somewhere else.

'They used to. Some of them. A long time ago, back before Karen died. But after she passed away I think they kind of got the picture that Amy didn't want people over. So they stopped coming.'

'Don't you miss em though?'

'I don't have to miss them anymore,' he said, and stood up. 'I'm going back to work today. We'll talk about all this whenever you want to, OK?'

'OK.'

'Go back to sleep.'

It was relatively cool under the shade of the big pines and he started spraying the car down with the water hose. He was sad to be leaving her by going back to work, but he'd missed being out on the road in the cruiser, waiting for something to happen, and she was right—he'd missed his friends. Going back to work would make coming back home even better, and he'd still have his regular two days off after five on. There were so many places he wanted to take her and so many things he wanted to show her.

Dried bugs were all over the windshield and he had to rub pretty hard on them to make them come loose. Damn things were everywhere at night and he drove so much at night. It took about ten minutes of rubbing to get the whole windshield clean but when he sprayed it off it looked pretty good. He moved to the back glass and did it. It wasn't nearly as bad. While he was back there he went ahead and did the trunk.

He'd already been thinking of a trip they could take

one weekend if she was up for it. The trailer the ski rig had come with was parked behind the house, the tongue propped up on a concrete block, but all he had to do was hook it up to the pickup, get her to drive it over to Pat's Bluff and wait for him. He could take the boat over there, back the trailer down to the water, and they could load the boat back on it and then they'd be free to haul it up to Arkabutla or down to Grenada or Enid. They could get a new tent or rent a cabin, fish all weekend.

He had to get down on his knees and scrub like hell on the headlights, one set at a time. The grille was the same way and he had to rub hard on the thin bars there and one of them broke under his hand.

'Why you plastic son of a bitch,' he said. He knelt and pulled the two broken ends back together so that you couldn't really tell that it was broken. He rubbed at it a little more.

'Shit,' he said softly.

He started moving around the cruiser, fender to door panel to door panel to fender with the sponge, dragging the hose by the nozzle behind him. He looked at his watch and it was almost fifteen after ten. He wondered if she was up yet and he looked toward the house but couldn't see her in the kitchen. She was like him, wanted a cup of coffee in the morning before anything else. But maybe she wouldn't get too lonely by herself. She could stay out on the beach and there was plenty of stuff to watch on the dish. He knew she liked those space movies, *Star Wars* and all that stuff. Hell, she probably never had gotten to see much of anything, growing up the way she had. He sure would like to run into her daddy sometime. Oh yeah. He'd like to have a little talk with that man. Maybe show him the error of his ways.

'Take you off in the middle of this lake and drown your ass,' he muttered under his breath.

But was he any better? He was forty-two years old. She was seventeen. He worried as he rubbed with the

146

sponge. But he wasn't any kin to her. It was a big age difference, sure, but it wasn't like other people hadn't done it before. Well it was twenty-five years. He was twenty-five when she was born. Hell, he'd been a state trooper for about five years when she was born. And had she ever said where she was born? He didn't much think she had. If she had he couldn't remember where she'd said. No telling, moving around like they had.

The car needed waxing but he wasn't going to wax it today. There wasn't enough time and he wanted to spend some time with her before he left. He wondered what Joe Price meant shooting some woman in the eye. No telling what the story was there. He guessed when he saw Price sometime he'd find out. And if Pete was in the hospital he needed to go see him. Maybe he needed to leave at three instead of three-thirty so he could go by the office for a while and sit around some and find out what all had been going on. Sit around and shoot the shit a little bit before he hit the road. Maybe Fay would fry him up some chicken if he asked her to. He could get one out of the deep freeze and thaw it out before he left. She was getting to be a pretty good cook. She was good on biscuits and mashed potatoes and gravy for damn sure.

He worked his way down the other side with the soap and the nozzle, rubbing and spraying. His feet were wet in his tennis shoes. The car sat dripping and clean and shiny. He poured the soap out of the bucket and rinsed it out good and turned off the water and coiled the hose beside the house. He walked around the car, looking for dirty spots, but he didn't see any. He looked up toward the house but he still couldn't see her. It was twenty till eleven and he'd thought she'd be up by now. But it didn't matter. Far as he was concerned she could do whatever she wanted to.

He checked the car again. Hell, he didn't need to rub it down with the chamois. He'd go in and make her some coffee, maybe have another cup himself. He needed to take her to the grocery store again sometime so she could get used to doing it whenever she got her driver's license. It would save him a lot of time and she'd probably be glad to do it. She was so good-natured. He hated to go off to work and leave her because he already knew she didn't like being by herself. She'd just have to get used to it. But it would be OK. Nothing was going to happen to her out here. All she had to do was keep the doors locked. He'd go on and get her up. She'd probably be ready to play.

But when he went in the door with that happy thought in his head and intending to make the coffee and then wander back to the bedroom and try to talk her into getting up, he heard a noise coming from the bathroom in there and his feet started moving faster and fear was rising in his throat and when he snatched open the door there she was, kneeling over the commode in nothing but her panties, holding her hair out of her face with both hands, her growing breasts full and swinging, retching the contents of her stomach, what was left of last night's meal, into the bowl of water that was already discolored with chunks of pink matter. She heard him and turned her face up to him with gobbets of half-digested things on her lips, her eyes full of tears, and then it hit him: *Oh, fuck, she's pregnant.*

He held her on the couch for a long time, rocking and calming her. She cried and cried. He had wrapped her in his arms and he kept patting her back and hugging her and talking to her in a low voice, trying to ease her. Thinking about that first night and no rubbers. Knowing better all the time and went ahead and did it anyway. Maybe she didn't know better but he did. Alesandra had always been on the pill and he'd never had to worry about it. But it was too fucking late to worry about it now.

He finally got her to put some clothes on and she went into the bathroom and stayed in there with the door closed while he made coffee and waited for her to come out. He drank a cup and waited some more and finally she did. She'd brushed her hair and had put on some white shorts and a dark blue T-shirt that had come from an oyster bar in Mobile, Alabama. And the weird thing was that she didn't look like anything was wrong. Totally normal happy Fay.

She fixed herself a cup of coffee and got her cigarettes and when she lit one he realized that he'd have to tell her that she needed to quit for the baby's sake. He'd have to get her to the doctor. She sat down at the kitchen table and he moved over there with her. She smiled at him and it struck him again how pretty she was. He could still remember what she'd looked like when he'd first seen her but that image bore only a vague resemblance to the woman who sat across from him now. What beauty in her nakedness, her hair down across her breasts, how white they were against the dark of her throat and face and arms. They had to marry. There was nothing else to do. No way they were going to get rid of it and no need even talking about it. He remembered her telling him about her little brother being traded for a car. This child had to have a home and this would be its home. He would take care of it, would raise it to wind and water, to trotlines and crappie poles and sun and rain and fishing. His child. His only child now. He put his head down on the table and rested it for a long time, feeling her slim cool fingers stroking easily across the back of his head. After a while he got up and even though he had only a few hours before he had to report for duty, he got a cold beer from the icebox and opened it and sat back down with it.

He almost opened his mouth and told her, but thought better of it and decided he would wait until tonight. He had to have time to think, and eight or nine hours of work would be good. They could eat a late supper and then they could talk about what they thought they needed to do, both of them, together.

She seemed to be waiting for him to speak. She wasn't that girl he'd picked up anymore. She didn't have dirt under her fingernails anymore and she'd gained weight that looked great on her. She was healthy and the baby would probably be healthy, too. And would it be a boy or a girl? It didn't matter. He'd take either one gladly. A girl could fish as well as a boy. Fay had proven that.

But there were other things nagging at him, too. Look how much difference there was in their ages. He was more than twice as old as her, and what if she didn't want to marry him? What if she thought he was too old to marry?

Finally she said, 'You want to talk?'

'Don't worry about anything,' he said. 'We'll talk tonight, when I get in.'

And they left it at that.

* * *

She fixed some ham and cheese sandwiches and he made her drink some milk. He thought he'd wait until later to bring it up about the smoking. Hell, he could quit, too, to support her, maybe switch to cigars or something.

She ironed his shirt and he shined his boots. He didn't drink another beer. He brushed his teeth a couple of times and used some mouthwash and found some Big Red in a kitchen drawer and chewed some of that while he was running the vacuum cleaner over the carpets in the cruiser. He got all his paperwork together, brushed his hat, took the car for a quick drive up the road in his civvies and gassed it up at the closest bait shop and talked fishing with the owner who came out and leaned against the pump while Sam held the nozzle in the fuel tank impatiently. He paid with a credit card and kicked the four-barrel in once on a straight stretch of road and it howled like a small jet engine. Satisfied, he turned back down the drive to his house and went back home.

His uniform was hanging neatly in the bedroom, the boots parked beneath the clothes, and she had pinned all his brass on the shirt exactly where it was all supposed to be. And Fay was lying under the covers with nothing but her head sticking up, her clothes and underwear in a pile beside the bed. She was smiling at him in a certain way he knew.

'Did I do good?' she said.

He sat down on the edge of the bed.

'You did real good. Amy never could get it straight which side my nameplate went on. So I always wound up putting the brass on myself.'

'She was good at a lot of other things,' Fay said.

He nodded.

'Yes she was.'

'What time is it?'

He held up his wrist and looked at his watch.

'It's almost two-thirty.'

'What time you need to leave?'

'I guess I need to leave about three.'

151

'Your car all ready?'

'Car's all ready.'

'Your pistol loaded?'

'Pistol's loaded.'

'Well then,' she said. 'I guess you're almost ready, ain't you?'

He grinned back at her.

'Almost.'

She stuck one finger out from under the covers and held it up in the air, the nail side toward him. She crooked it slowly, beckoning.

'C'mere,' she said softly.

After he left she cried for a little while and then she dried her tears and washed the lunch dishes and swept and mopped the kitchen floor. She didn't know anything about being pregnant or what you were supposed to do or if you were supposed to go to the doctor right away or stay in bed or what. She guessed she could read some of Amy's magazines about raising children or how to fix your hair or how to please your man. She thought she already knew how to please her man. Just keep him fucked down. Just keep it in his face all the time. He'd looked pretty happy when he left.

But she was all alone now, just like she had been when she'd first met him.

By four she had the house all cleaned up and she checked the chicken that he'd left in the sink. It still wasn't thawed out yet but it didn't matter, she wasn't going to try cooking it for a while yet. He said there wasn't anything to it, just mix up an egg in some milk and dip it in that, then roll it in flour, salt and pepper it, cook it on low heat with a lid over it and it would turn out all right. She hoped that was so. She didn't want to mess up his dinner after his first night of work.

Before Amy died she'd shown Fay where everything was in the kitchen, all the utensils and knives and pots and pans and graters and cutting boards, and where she kept all the food. She found the bag of red potatoes and pulled out four big ones and set them up on the counter to wash and peel and slice up later. She set out the flour and two bowls. Fried chicken and mashed potatoes and gravy. She thought she'd open a can of green beans from the cabinet and make some biscuits. That was one thing she had learned from her mother, how to make biscuits. She might not have been very good for anything else much, like protecting them from their father, but she knew how to make biscuits. She'd seen her make them out in the woods, out of canned milk and lard and flour, and bake them in an old dutch oven in the coals of a fire. Why hadn't she fought him harder? Why hadn't she run him off? Who knew? Who knew what the old man had put her through? Maybe she'd just gotten tired and had given up. A lot of times it had seemed that way. But there was no use wasting her time thinking about all that now. She was out of that shit now, for good. And she wanted this baby. She was plenty old enough to have one.

There wasn't really anything else she needed to take care of right now. She wasn't sleepy and didn't need a nap. She didn't really feel like reading right now and there was plenty of time for that later. The remote control was lying on the coffee table and she went over and picked it up and sat down on the couch and turned on the TV and started flipping through the channels. People in suits talking, somebody making a speech. Cartoons, some crazy rabbit hopping around with a black duck with a ring around his neck, and some fat little pink pig chasing them. Somebody was showing some jewelry on another channel and on another one some people in shorts and swimming suits were walking on some machine without getting anywhere. She was wanting to see a space movie but there didn't seem to be one on. Whoa. Wait a minute. Cowboys and Indians. She stopped right there and turned the volume up. Then she turned it up a little more. A bunch of people in some wooden wagons with round white tops on them had pulled their wagons in a circle and there was a shitload of Indians riding horses and wearing feathers all in their hair, circling them and shooting arrows at them.

'All *right*,' she said. She thought there was a bottle of wine in the icebox with the cork stuck back in. She got up and went to the cabinet and got down a wineglass and pulled the bottle out and poured the glass full. Then she stuck the wine back in the icebox and went back to the couch. She'd be horny again by the time he got back home. Some of the wagons were on fire now. People were hauling water in buckets and throwing it on the flames. This was how movies were supposed to be. She wondered if they ever made movies of people fucking.

Sam drove his cruiser in and parked it out near the edge of the grass where a man was mowing on a red Snapper and another man was trimming the grass along the curb behind him. They both wore prisoners' clothes and they didn't raise their heads when he parked the car and got out.

The lounge was near the back of the building and the door was open. Jimmy Joe Jacobs was pouring a cup of coffee when he walked in and he looked up and saw Sam and put the cup down quickly. Sam grinned at him.

'What's up, Jimmy Joe?'

'Hey boy,' he said. 'Bout time you got back to work.'

He gave Sam a hard handshake and patted him on the shoulder a couple of times. He had survived a terrible crash with a fire truck in a driving rainstorm near Sledge one night and it had left him with a permanent limp, all the bones of his right ankle having been fused together. Sam had known him for about twelve years and he was one of the ones who used to come to the house and fish with him.

'Take off your hat and set down a spell, Sam. You want me to pour you a cup of coffee?'

Sam took his hat off and put it on a table.

'I got time for a cup, I guess. I'm supposed to go on at four. I just thought I'd stop by here and see what's going on.'

Jimmy Joe poured him a cup and knew what to put in it, two spoons of sugar and a little Carnation that he pulled from a small refrigerator sitting next to the coffee machine. He dropped two quarters in a big coffee can and handed Sam the cup.

'Thanks, Jimmy.' They settled in some chairs near each other and Sam pulled the tall ash can closer to him and lit up.

'Aw, there ain't nothing going on,' Jimmy Joe said. 'I had to come by here and fill out some wreck sheets. The captain's on the phone for me, trying to find out when I've got to be in court next week. Same old shit. I heard you's coming back in today. It's good to see you, Sam.' He looked down into his coffee for a moment and then back up.

'I sure am sorry about Amy. She was about as good a woman as I ever met, I reckon. How you been doing?'

'Aw, I'm all right.'

'You been fishin any?'

'A little. I been going late in the evening and catching a few catfish.' He started to say 'You ought to come out sometime and go with me' but then thought of Fay and decided to wait. Instead he said, 'You been staying busy?'

'Aw yeah. Yeah, it's been pretty busy. We had a bad one down on Fifty-five the other day, tractor-trailer and a van full of retarded kids.'

'I saw it in the paper.'

Jimmy Joe took a sip of his coffee and crossed his ankles, wincing just the tiniest bit. Sam had seen that wince a hundred times.

'Yeah, it was awful. Poor little kids. Bad enough to be born like that and then have a damn truck run over you. Sometimes I don't know why I stay in this business.'

'Well, you ain't got long to go. What, two years?'

'Nineteen months. Nineteen months and then I'm

155

outta here. Ain't gonna do nothin but watch my cows eat grass. Fish and play with my grandkids.'

Another trooper stuck his head inside the door and Sam started to get up, but the trooper waved him back down.

'Don't get up, Sam,' he said. 'Sit there and rest. I heard you come in and just wanted to say hi. You doing all right?'

'Yes sir, I'm doing fine. Thanks for asking.'

'You welcome. You ready to roll at four?'

'Yes sir. I'm glad to be back.'

'Well we're glad to have you back. Sure am sorry about everything.'

'Well. I appreciate that.'

'All right. Good luck. Be careful.'

'I will.'

The trooper pulled back and went up the hall to an office and went in and closed the door.

'Boy he's had a cob up his ass today,' Jimmy Joe said in a low voice.

Sam sipped his coffee and tipped some ashes off his smoke. It felt good to be back in here, to have his uniform on again. He meant to call Fay after while.

'What over?'

Jimmy Joe kept talking in that same low voice and he leaned closer.

'Hell. You didn't hear what happened to Joe Price?'

'Well. I heard he shot some woman in the eye.'

'Yeah. He was pokin her in his patrol car.'

'What?'

'Oh it's going to be a hell of a stink,' Jimmy Joe said. He took another sip of his coffee and scratched at his knee. 'They trying to keep the governor from hearing about it but he's got spies all over the place. Somebody wantin a promotion, you know.'

Sam looked up the hall and saw a trooper cross from one office to another. He could hear the dispatcher talking dimly on the radio behind a closed door.

'He had some woman in his patrol car?'

156

'Aw you know how he is. He'll fuck anything. I believe he'd fuck a snake if somebody would hold its head. What I heard, now I ain't talked to Joe, what I heard was he pulled this woman over for weaving outside Belzoni and she was drunk and I reckon they worked it out to where he wouldn't get her for DUI if she'd give him a little.'

'Where the hell'd you get all this at, Jimmy Joe?'

Jimmy Joe sipped at his coffee again and then held the cup down on his good leg. The trooper up the hall crossed it again and shut his door.

'This is what he told Alvin on the phone the other night. Joe's scared to death his wife's gonna find out. Alvin told me, now don't tell nobody none of this, hear?'

'I won't.'

'Alvin told me he got the old girl to pull in down in this cotton patch on this dirt road and she got out of her car and got in his. Dumb son of a bitch. Looks like if he was gonna do something like that he'd of got out of his car and got in hers. But that ain't what he did. So he gets her back there on the backseat and strips her clothes off and takes his off and lays his pistol belt down in the floorboard. So they're back there fuckin like a couple of minks and they get done and gonna put their clothes back on and they set up and one of em somehow kicks the damn pistol and knocks the safety off and I think he told her to watch it, and then I reckon she bent over to pick up her britches or her blouse or somethin and either kicked it again or moved it or somethin and it went off and shot her right in the damn eye through the end of the holster.'

'Goddamn,' Sam said. He took the last drag off his cigarette and ground it out in the ashtray and leaned back in his chair. He looked at his watch and saw that it was getting close to three-thirty.

'What they gonna do to him, reckon?'

'Well, the woman's in the hospital over there. I think she's married, too.'

157

'Is she gonna live?'

'Aw yeah, she's gonna live but she ain't gonna have but one eye for the rest of her life. It turned and come out before it hit her brain. They put Joe on administrative leave but he's already been down to Jackson twice to talk to the big man. I expect they'll can his ass unless somebody can do some creative lying. And talk the woman into keeping her mouth shut.'

'What's her husband saying?'

'He ain't saying nothing. He's in Parchman doing twenty years for raising marijuana.'

They sat there for a bit, listening to the chatter of the radio in the room out there. And it was only a few more moments until a door opened and the dispatcher came walking down the hall toward where they sat. She was a woman about fifty years of age and her blond hair was puffed and swirled up on her head and she had an enormous set of titties that stretched out the front of her uniform almost beyond belief. She stuck her head in.

'Hey Sam.'

'Hey Gladys.'

'Are you on duty yet?'

He set his coffee down.

'I can be. What's up?'

'Oxford PD called and they've got some kind of disturbance over there on Jackson Avenue. Somebody's out in the street swinging a butcher knife at cars. They wanted to know if we could send somebody over but everybody's tied up right now with a roadblock down on Thirty-two. You want to go?'

'Yeah, I'll go. You want to go, Jimmy Joe?'

Sam got up and Jimmy Joe stayed in his seat.

'I got to stay here and see about that court date. I'm going off in thirty minutes anyway. If you need some help I can go, though.'

'Somebody's got to go,' Gladys said.

Sam got his hat off the table and left his coffee cup on it.

'I'm leaving right now,' he said.

158

'Take it easy, Sam,' Jimmy Joe called after him.

He went by Gladys and she moved back a little, but not enough to keep him from bumping up against one of her huge knockers. It was common knowledge around the station that Joe Price had been nailing her for years.

'You hear bout Joe?' he said.

'I hope his dick rots off,' said Gladys.

Just before he reached the city limits of Oxford he slowed just a bit and lit a cigarette, knowing it might be the last one he'd get for a while. He caught most of the lights on green and started slowing down when he saw the red trucks parked just past the overhead railroad trestle. One firefighter dressed in turnout pants and helmet stepped to the edge of the street and motioned him on, pointed up the street where about ten black-and-white police cars were parked with their lights going. He put his hat on and reached to the rack for the shotgun. He'd put some shells in his pocket before he'd left the station and now he slipped them into the magazine one at a time, chambering the first one with a quick shuck of the slide, then filled the magazine on up.

A police captain with a white shirt was standing next to a telephone pole when he walked up. The cop was giving him a subdued smile.

'You the one got the job, huh? I thought you's off.'

'Shit naw. Not no more.' He looked around at all the duffers assembled to watch a free show. 'You ought to be charging admission to all these folks.'

'Aw hell,' the cop said. 'I swear everbody from the post office and the paper and the welfare office, they all got to come out and see what's going on. We got it blocked on Jackson and down Ninth both ways. The goddamn radio station is right up yonder. Got that mobile son of a bitch they can use. Hell, I don't reckon we can shoot him now. Not in front of all these folks.'

'It's hard to get rid of this many,' Sam said.

159

'I reckon the whole town's heard about it. The chief don't want us to do nothing rash. There he is right there, up there on the corner. Three guesses who it is.'

Sam looked. A thin black youth with no shirt and a baggy pair of camouflage pants that were unbuttoned and sagging down below the waistband of his shorts was standing in the center of the street, brandishing a very big knife. He was encircled by a ring of police officers, none of them too close.

Sam shook his head.

'Why don't they put that crazy son of a bitch in the pen and just leave him in there?'

'I don't know,' the captain said. 'You want to go talk to him? We kinda hate to just shoot the poor bastard. Specially in front of all these people.'

'What'd he do this time?'

'He started out cuttin at cars comin down the street. He did that for a while till somebody called us. Hollerin a bunch of crazy old shit.'

'All right,' Sam said. 'Will you watch my shotgun?'

'Yeah, give it here. You better give me your hat, too.'

Sam handed them over and went on up the street. The boy's name was Mozell Washington and he had a long history of burning cars and Dumpsters, of insinuating himself, smelly and half-naked, at the tables of well-dressed dinner folk, and mooching quarters on the street. He was a semi-regular fixture around the city jail, and the grounds, and could be seen about half the time in coveralls picking up trash from the streets at dawn.

'How you doing today, Mozell?'

Tears were coming from the boy's eyes and he was rubbing snot from his nose with the back of his hand.

'Stay back, Mister Sam. Don't come no closer. They been messin over me again. Said I tried to cornhole James Louis.'

Sam glanced around at the faces behind Mozell watching them, still watching the knife, wondering where he'd gotten it. He brought food to the jail from

Smitty's sometimes. A farmer had caught him fucking one of his goats in the dark of his barn one day. He didn't figure he could reason with him but he thought he'd try anyway since he could always use the last resort.

'Folks need to get back to work, Mozell. You got the whole street stopped here. Why don't you put that knife down and we'll go over here in the shade and talk about it. You don't want Butch on you, do you?'

'I don't care if they bring him,' Mozell said. 'He'll be dead if they do.'

It was very hot there under the sun and on the black asphalt of the street and Sam could feel the sweat starting to bead on his face and growing under his arms already. All these people watching, that made him uneasy. It was relatively quiet now that all the traffic on the street was stopped. Other than the low hum of the police cars idling and the clicking of the control box for the traffic signal on the corner there wasn't much noise, and he knew the people could hear every word he said. So he was careful not to curse.

'Mozell, you listen to me. If Butch gets on you he ain't gonna turn you loose. So why don't you just put that butcher knife down and save everybody a lot of trouble? You don't want to get shot, do you?'

Something must have clicked in the young man's head at these words, for the expression on his face changed and he lowered his stance and spread his feet a little more. Sam could see how red his eyes were.

'Go on and shoot me, mister *po*lice officer. Mister big bad police *officer*. They ain't let me go to the sto in three days. Done took my cigarettes away from me.' His eyes narrowed and he gave Sam a mean grin. 'Come on, motherfucker, think you so bad with yo big pistol. Cut yo balls off for you.'

That was all he was willing to listen to and to have people hear. He backed up and then turned around and walked back down to the police captain.

'Well?' the cop said.

161

'Go ahead and turn the damn dog loose on him,' Sam said.

The captain had taken a megaphone out of a patrol car and he had waved up another cruiser that had been waiting down the street. The car pulled up beside Sam and he looked through the back window at the big black German shepherd standing on the backseat waving his tail slowly. The handler got out and opened the back door and fastened the dog to a chain lead and brought him out on the street. He told him to stay and the dog sat. Sam knew the dog but he didn't try to pet him now as he usually did whenever he went to the jail.

The cop pulled the trigger on the megaphone when he brought it up to his mouth and it made a few squawks at first. He told the people to move back and they did. All the cops stayed where they were. Mozell had seen the dog by now and the dog had seen him. Mozell was standing all alone, and he crouched a bit and held the knife out point first. Sam could hear him telling the dog to come on.

'If this ain't some small-time bullshit I don't know what is,' he said to nobody in particular.

'You ready, Captain Smith?' the handler said.

'Let him go,' the captain said, and the handler slipped the leash. A hush fell over everything as the dog started forward. He was running low and fast and it only took him a few moments to reach Mozell it seemed. He grabbed for that free hand and got it, and Mozell let him get a good grip before he swung the knife in a wide arc and sank it into the dog's ribs, just back of the shoulder. The dog whined sharply, once, like a puppy that had been accidentally stepped on, and then he fell to the pavement, snapping a few times at his side and then stretching out as if for sleep. Mozell pulled the knife free and looked back down the street at Sam.

'Come on, homeboy,' he said, and he motioned with the hand the dog had bitten and torn.

162

He had already put the shotgun down in the street and had taken off his hat again and was walking forward and pulling his slapstick out of his left hip pocket. He could see from the corner of his eye cops with their guns drawn at the edges of the sidewalks and he could see Mozell's lower lip hanging down slightly from his teeth and a thin strand of spittle dripping from his mouth and all the people watching from every side like fans at football. He could feel the sun on the top of his head and the dog was lying there bleeding, a dark stream that had begun to inch away from his body as the dog tried to pick up his head and see the thing that had been done to him.

He knew he'd have to let Mozell swing the knife at him one time anyway, and he just hoped he could be fast enough. If he wasn't, the ambulance was parked right there on the corner, and they could have him at the doors of the emergency room in four minutes, doctors and nurses waiting.

He didn't bother with saying anything else to him. He just walked straight up to him and when the knife came swinging to his belly he stepped back to let it pass, and in that fraction of a second when Mozell was trying to recover and bring it back, he swung the slapstick down like a carpenter with a framing hammer, right on his nose. He heard and felt the crunch of breaking cartilage under the lead shot that was sewn so snugly in its black leather pouch, and then Mozell was on his knees and cops were all over him, one kicking the knife away, others turning him facedown and putting the cuffs on him.

Out on the deck it was hot and Fay lay in the sun for a while after the Western was over. The chicken was in the refrigerator for safekeeping. It was still too early to start making supper so she was just killing time. She kept hoping Sam might call and she was listening for the phone inside.

The afternoon was almost windless and her skin had

beaded with sweat by five o'clock. She could raise her head just a bit and see out over the lake, but there didn't seem to be too much moving out there. Too hot. Occasionally she'd hear the roar of a ski boat coming by. Other than that it was fairly quiet.

She couldn't think of anything in the house she needed to be doing. The bed was made and the floors were clean and everything had been dusted. She thought she'd lay out for maybe another thirty minutes and then go inside and take a bath and relax in the water some before she started cooking. He wouldn't be in until late and there was plenty of time. She could nibble on some stuff and hold off on really eating until he came in, when she could meet him at the door with a cold beer and kiss him and ask him how it had gone. She wished he'd call. But he was probably busy. It was OK. She was patient. She could wait.

She went inside around five-thirty and started drawing the tub full of water, walking around inside the house with a towel wrapped around her, the stereo playing in the living room. She had her favorite tapes stacked beside the receiver, Merle and Willie and George Jones. He'd taught her music as well as fishing in these last weeks and months. The house was filled with the sweet notes of guitar and banjo and steel guitar, and she felt covered in the music. She thought about that night in the trailer with those boys and what Sam had said about that. And he was right. No telling what they might have done to her.

She put another tape on and went back to the bathroom and cut the water off. She'd already put some bubble bath in while it was filling up and now the tub was piled high with suds. She dropped the towel and got her glasses and a magazine and slipped in, propped up her feet, lit a cigarette and set the ashtray on the toilet lid.

By eight o'clock the potatoes were peeled and sliced and boiling in some water, and the chicken was frying at low heat on the stove beside them. She was sipping a small glass of wine and watching a show about elephants on the television. She was fascinated at how a herd of them could tear a forest apart eating the leaves and how long they stayed pregnant and about how well they all stuck together in general. She decided if there was any animal she could be, she'd want to be an elephant.

She missed him but she was OK by herself. It wouldn't be that much longer until he'd be in and then it would be like he never had been gone. And she'd get used to this. Other people had to do it, too. People had to work, and anyway, there was a lot to do. She guessed she'd have to go see a doctor about the baby and she was already getting nervous about that. She never had been to one but she'd heard people talk about that, how the doctor had to examine you, and she didn't want anybody examining her. There was so much she didn't know about the world and what was in it. If she'd stayed where she was, no telling what might have happened to her. No telling where she might have wound up. She wished she could see Gary. Maybe one day.

The sun was going down outside and she took her wine over to the sliding glass door and wandered out on the deck to watch the night come.

He still hadn't called. She guessed he was busy.

Out over the water the sky had paled up into hues of pink and there were scattered clouds of gray hanging there like smoke. There was an orange glow to the west that shot rays of light up through the sky and the drifting cirrus. She sipped her wine and watched the sun slowly sinking until the color of it ebbed and the darkness grew stronger, until the last bit of orange light was vanquished by the roll of the earth and she remembered the rest of the chicken still frying in the skillet and got up to go inside and see about it. One boat cruised on the water out there in the growing blackness that was coming but she could see nothing of it.

By ten she'd had two more glasses of wine and the food was sitting in the oven staying warm, the gravy made, the potatoes whipped with some sour cream and sprinkled with black pepper, the beans in a casserole dish. She was going to slice a fresh tomato and put the biscuits in to bake whenever he came in. The chicken had turned out fine. But now she was restless again and moved through the living room like a person who didn't stay there, picking up a magazine and looking at a few pages and then putting it down.

It was going to be a while longer before he came in. She located her sandals and slipped her feet into them and grabbed her smokes and lighter and pushed open the deck door and stood there looking out. The clouds were dark now and scuttling along the belly of the moon. A wind had come up, and she could smell the rain coming on the air.

For quite a while she leaned against the deck rail, looking at something that shone briefly or gave back a reflection when the clouds let the moon through. It was far up the beach at the back of the house, something there she thought was not usually there.

Flashes of light from far away came through the murky stuff in the sky. It was raining out there somewhere, but she couldn't tell which way it was headed.

She wasn't especially scared of the dark and she thought she'd take a walk down on the beach. It crossed her mind to get a flashlight but she went on without it. She told herself that it was just spending part of the night away from him that was making her feel so unsettled and uncertain. Once she got down on the sand there was a steady breeze and the lap of rising waves against the beach. She stopped and studied the sky for a while, thinking about what the baby might look like. She was never going to do anything mean to her baby. She was going to take care of it and give it everything it needed. She couldn't imagine what it was going to be like but there were images of infants in fluffy clothes sleeping in blankets going through her mind. You had to feed them at night if they woke up. Wash diapers. Heat bottles. Amy's magazines had lots of stuff like that in them. She knew about crib death and that they didn't know why babies died from it. She guessed she'd have to sit and watch it whenever it was asleep to make sure it was still breathing.

She hoped he'd ask her to marry him and she thought about herself dressed in white like she saw in movies. She'd have hers short. She'd let her legs show because she knew her legs were good. Sam had told her that and she'd seen men staring at her whenever they went to the grocery store in Batesville. More than once she'd stopped and looked up at the lettuce bin or the meat counter and seen some young man or boy or even older men looking at her. It pleased her now that they liked to look at her.

The beach felt good tonight. All the day's heat was gone and now there was just the breeze to lift her hair and cool it on her neck. She stood with her feet spread, and lifted her hair with her hands, and let the wind flow over her. The clouds parted and the moon looked through and she saw that shiny something up the beach there again. It was something curved, something a little way off either the sand or the water. She walked toward it and the clouds hid the moon again.

Now a feeling moved into the pit of her stomach that wasn't a good one, and it was stronger than what she'd felt before, and now she knew that something wasn't right. She looked back toward the house but there was nothing other than the lighted deck up there, deserted, silent. She walked a little more and now she was close enough to make out a boat pushed up against the shore, and she couldn't imagine why anybody would have left it there like that. But Sam had told her that he'd seen couples pull up and stop there and go off into the woods with blankets in their arms.

If that was the case she didn't want to bother anybody. She wouldn't want anybody bothering her while she was doing that. But it just seemed strange for it to be here so late. There were no lights around anywhere, no campfire light that she could see anywhere up or down the beach. It wasn't all Sam's land here anyway. He'd told her once that he had a hundred and forty feet of lakeside property behind the house and the rest belonged to the people on either side of them. Maybe it was some of them.

But the boat looked familiar, and as she got closer she recognized the shiny dark hull and the curved windshield. She could even see the silver letters on the side, near the back: Chris Craft. She turned. Alesandra came from the black trees and scattered grass and grew gradually into being in her dark clothes. The clouds parted and Fay saw the little gun in her hand again looking like the same one Sam had thrown up on the beach that day, and above it the eyes that were cold and staring under the moon. *That's what dead looks like*, she remembered.

It was behind the cook tent where the older boys took their turns with Barbara Lewis and where sometimes Fay watched from behind a tree. It was always hot and dusty there and the workers' backs were bent out across the fields. Once a day a bus rattled through and stopped and flapped open its door and waited for people to get on or off. Some left, others came in, and they didn't know anybody for very long.

She didn't know where they had been before this, only that it was a place with long fields of white where the workers carried sacks into the rows and dragged them along the ground after them, but then it had turned cold and they had come to this place down black and broken roads that went through low places of dark water for a long time, all of them piled in the cab that could get in there and her old daddy at the wheel with his whiskers and his stub of a cigar and his bottle nestled right next to his overalls. He'd smack them if they didn't be quiet.

She remembered walking around on a gravel lot near a stone barn and a fine farmhouse with roses in the yard as her daddy talked to a man, Gary and Dorothy and her mother sitting in the truck. Then a slow drive down a dirt road between fields, then the little camp of tents hidden near a river, out there where most of the fields lay, stretched out to the bordering timber that seemed miles away.

She was too small to work in some places and in some places they let her work. Her daddy told her that they'd eat better if she worked, so she did, but she never ate better. But working here was mixed in with watching the boys on top of Barbara Lewis. Her dress would be over her chest and her white legs would be spread and a boy with his pants slipped down over his ass going up and down on top of her, grunting and shaking, and then something would happen and he would scream out. And Barbara Lewis would turn her head while she was still on her back and see Fay watching her.

They worked the fields there for weeks and weeks, and she helped some, setting sweet potato slips, mounding up the good black dirt, the thin green plants so limp in rows behind them as they went along on their knees.

The workers struck the tents one day and the whole camp moved very slowly to new fields up near a black-top road, half the camp on one side and half on the other, and that was where Barbara Lewis began to tease her with her food. She would limp out on her crutch and her crooked legs and hold up her cans of Vienna sausage and her tins of sardines and she would show Fay candy bars.

'Come on over,' she'd say, from across the road, and another truck would roar by, shaking the ground almost as it came, an air horn blaring at the workers' children all scattered up and down the edge of the road. It was after her brother Tom was run over. The watermelon truck had gone over his head and they'd stood around him sprawled there dead in the dusty sunlight, and she'd looked at his eyes. For a long time after that they had money and good things to eat and lots of candy. But now they were here in this place called Florida and there was not enough food to go around in the pot her mother brought home from the cook tent each night. Her daddy ate most of it. Her mother would fight him over it but one time she spilled it and he beat her until blood came from her mouth. Gary fought him even then, what little good it did.

They stayed there and stayed there. She played with

some of the other kids and waded in a creek. In late evening she would wander back up to the cook tent where good smells floated out, not too close because they'd smack kids hanging around trying to get food, and she would see the older boys giving food and candy to Barbara Lewis and then helping her back behind the tent and she would watch them put her down in the trampled grass and give her a red box and then take her panties off and push her dress almost up over her head. And they would climb on while their friends waited and watched for their turns, while she lay on her back and scooped her hand into the box and stuffed the candy into her mouth and chewed it as they did what they did with her. She remembered wondering what was that they did and knowing that they were putting something of themselves inside of her. What her daddy peed with by the side of the road sometimes.

And every day Barbara Lewis propped herself on her crutch and chanted her little song:

Come on over and get it, Little Miss Chickenshit.

And she would set it down on the ground and let Fay look at it, bright peppermint candy still in its clear wrapping and the cans of meat, the fat round fingers of beef that were so good with crackers. Fay would watch her wait until a truck was in sight and make her way out to the road and set something down—a sucker, some pieces of gum, always a can of Vienna sausage. And Fay would turn her head as Barbara Lewis struggled back to her side, and try to judge how long it would take for the truck to get there, and she would go out tentatively, looking, afraid to jump, most times too hungry not to, and the horns on the truck would be blaring already, and sometimes she would go back. But sometimes she would not. Sometimes she would run out and grab whatever it was and snatch it almost from under the wheels of the truck, and it was a fine thing to open the sausages or unwrap the candy on her side of the road and look across at Barbara Lewis, leaning on

171

her crutch and yelling, already looking up the road for another truck.

But it became a harder trick to pull off. Barbara Lewis would wait longer, would let the truck get closer before she went and put something down.

Sometimes the fear was too great. Some days she was hungrier than others. Once she felt the side of her dress brushed by a towering truck that skidded and bucked and tried to stop and finally did, and then a man climbed down and screamed curses at them and sent them scattering back to their tents.

She wondered if Barbara Lewis hated her because she watched what the boys did to her. She wondered what it felt like when the older boys did that to her and if it hurt. It didn't seem to hurt her but it didn't seem like she got any fun out of it either.

One evening, late, Barbara Lewis's daddy came in early after a rainstorm and caught one of the boys on top of her. He slapped the boy and kept slapping him and then he pulled Barbara Lewis by her hair into their tent and the screaming started.

She didn't see Barbara Lewis for a while and then one day she was back, propped up across the road, her face swollen, both eyes still black, a tooth missing where one had not been missing before. They were standing on each edge of the road, looking at each other, and she could see that Barbara Lewis had nothing in her hands. She heard the truck grinding way off and she looked into Barbara Lewis's eyes and watched her wait until the truck was too close and then limp directly into the path of it. There was a noise and blood flew and the truck went past skidding. Then there was only Barbara Lewis broken and bleeding in the road and her eyes were not like they had been before. They were like Tom's eyes had been, only cold and staring. A voice inside her said: *That's what dead looks like.*

The flame blew by her cheek and she felt its hot kiss blossom against her skin and the bullet cut some of her hair. But she had her hands on the gun by then and she pointed it up as Sam had done and it didn't fire. She didn't say anything, and Alesandra didn't, only panted and struggled with her, and now that Fay had her hands on her she could feel the fear in the woman and could hear the breath coming in ragged gasps, and could hear her trying to suck it in like a fish in the bottom of the boat.

Then the gun did fire, once, and Fay didn't know how many it held, and she turned loose of it with one hand and doubled her fist and drove it hard into Alesandra's eye. It put her down and Fay had more leverage as she stood over her. She brought her knee up into Alesandra's nose and heard something give, and pulled the gun free. And she didn't even think about it, just pointed it down at her and squeezed the trigger and it bucked in her hand, those little barks you wouldn't think were loud enough, bright flashes of light like strobes that showed holes in Alesandra's falling face, and then the moon hid its face for good. A whippoor-will called from somewhere up the beach. Another one up in the woods somewhere answered him. She turned and threw the gun as far as she could into the lake. It went in without almost any noise at all and the black waves kept moving. Then she looked down at what she had done.

When the rain came she was far out in the lake and her fingers on the wheel of Alesandra's boat were slick with blood. She'd watched Sam operate his plenty of times. She had the running lights off and it was hard to see, but she was pretty sure the water was open, with no dead trees, for a long way out. She wasn't going to take her all the way to the levee or anything anyway. Just somewhere out here in this blackness she was going to stop.

The drops pelted her and she felt them matting her hair. The lake was getting rougher, and the boat rocked some in the chop. This was the only way to hide it. The rain would wash away the blood on the beach. If she was lucky she could make it back to the bank long before Sam got home. If she was unlucky or weak he might get there before her and ask her where she had been. And, soaking wet, what would she say?

It was probably best to go on out. She'd thought of trying to find the old trees, and of tying the boat to one of them and leaving her there. Some fisherman would find her in the morning. Somebody would take care of it. Of her. Somebody had to come to take care of Barbara Lewis. They had put her flattened head and her broken shins onto a stretcher and covered her up with a blanket, head to toe.

There was nothing but blackness around her and the rain stung her arms and legs. She didn't try to look at the body slumped next to her, its head almost down on the floor and still probably leaking blood. She was

174

too scared to do anything but just keep going. She could still see the light on Sam's deck and she knew that if she lost sight of that it was all over. She wouldn't be able to find her way out of this and she'd probably get caught. If she was still in this thing at daylight she knew she'd be caught. So she kept driving, trying to see what was in front of her, trying to remember what things looked like in daytime. There were stands of trees far out to the right, and some more groups of them way out in front. But she couldn't see anything of them now. It was all black, and moving, and the rain was bouncing on everything and getting in her eyes. Her hair was plastering to her neck.

She looked back at the light again. It was just about gone and she could not lose it. So she reached to the switch and killed the motor. The sudden silence of it barely registered in the noise of the wind and the rain.

She tried to see Alesandra in the seat next to her but she was just a wet thing. She had to get back to the house before he did and get cleaned up and maybe put her wet clothes away somewhere or maybe dry them. She would have to lie her way out of it when they found Alesandra. She was almost vomiting sick now with what she'd done, and shaking with the old knowledge of how it could happen so easily, so quickly. The cops in the movies always found out who killed somebody. They had fingerprints and bloodstains and they knew what kind of bullet came from what kind of gun and they'd keep messing around, smart son of a bitches asking you questions and waiting for you to slip up and then they'd catch you in a lie and it was all over. She'd say that of course she'd been home, that's what she'd tell them. She checked the straps on her life jacket to see that they were tight and then she slid over the side of the boat carefully, into the black water, and it was scary how fast the boat drifted away into the darkness and then disappeared. She kicked her feet in the water and swallowed a mouthful of it. The light at Sam's house was a tiny wavering dot that flickered and sometimes hid. It was bad to just leave her like that but there wasn't anything else she could do with her. Even now the rain was washing out the tracks from where she'd dragged her down the beach and loaded her into the boat. All she had to do was just keep kicking and she'd get there eventually. But the water kept pushing into her mouth and she let some get down in her lungs and had to stop and cough for a while before she could go on, the waves rising up over the back of her head. It pained her to have to crane her neck out of the water to keep it out of her mouth. Why would they even ask her any questions? The only person who might guess what happened would be Sam. She pulled hard against the waves and kicked her feet. The life jacket made it easier to stay up but it made it harder to move her arms.

But she could rest with the life jacket. That was the main thing. It might take a long time to get over there in these waves. But they might catch her. She might not be able to lie good enough whenever Sam asked her if she knew anything about it, which he would. He would for sure. And then, if she told the truth, what would happen to her? And how would he feel about it and about her now and what would happen to him since it happened at his house? His boss might drag him under. Somebody hateful and high up might see to it that he was ruined, and not let him be a cop anymore. They might send her to the pen.

The water was getting cold on her face and hands and legs and feet. The light seemed a little clearer, not quite so far away. The rain started moving across the tops of the waves in gusts, and she blinked her eyes and kept swimming, and even thinking that it might be best to just keep on going once she hit the bank. She could talk to him later maybe and try to explain it, try to tell him how it happened, and how scared she'd been. Damn crazy woman. Them having this baby and her trying to mess it up. She didn't have to come over like that, and sneak up to the house. Maybe she'd been watching through the windows. Maybe she'd been there before. Maybe she'd watched them make love on the couch at night. Why did people have to act the way they did? That one back there would still be alive if she'd left them alone. If she hadn't had that gun. Wasn't anything else she could have done, so the thing to do was just stick around and tell the truth about what happened. She stopped in the water and looked around. There was no telling where the boat was. This thing was done. There was no undoing it. She'd left a body in a boat and swum away from it. That was enough for cops. They'd find out she killed her, too. So she couldn't stick around here. She'd have to pack some clothes, get what little money she had, try to get out on the road and catch a ride quickly, just to get out of sight. She couldn't take a chance on hooking him up with this. She'd find some other place to stay for a while, and then later she'd come back. She didn't know how. She just knew she would.

She was weakening an hour later and the rain was still beating down on her, but the light was closer and the sky was as black as it had been before with the deepest part of night over her head. She sang songs to herself from the ones she'd heard on the radio or on the cassette player, tunes she could sway her hips to, and she didn't want to leave him. His hands were soft and warm and strong and they moved down between her legs and over her nipples and he put his face down there and kissed her until she'd scratch the side of his neck with her nails, didn't mean to, just got so excited. She kept spitting the water out but she had to swallow some of it and it was making her stomach feel bloated and she wanted to cry but she knew that wouldn't do any good because it never had before, not even when she couldn't pick up the watermelons and still he made her try, and she wondered where his sorry ass was tonight and hoped he was dead.

She kicked her feet and looked up at Sam's light shining out there, all alone by itself in the night.

Sam eased a cigarette out of his pocket and punched in the lighter on the dash and waited for it to pop out. His hat was on the seat beside him and he was off duty, had already checked out for home. He'd worked two wrecks, had run a roadblock for an hour and a half, and he had issued three tickets for speeding and pulled over one drunk that he took to jail in Coffeeville. He was done. Heading home. He'd eaten at the 444 truck stop on I-55 at Senatobia even though he wasn't supposed to be that far north.

He'd meant to call home, had intended several times to get to a phone, but they'd kept him running from place to place all night and he didn't even get to finish all his sandwich at the truck stop for the portable calling him away again.

But she was all right. She'd probably watched some television or read something. She'd get used to it.

He cracked the window to let the smoke out. He turned off Highway 6 and went up the access road toward the dam. There wasn't much traffic on the road now. Fay was young but he figured she'd be a good mother. He remembered the night Karen was born, how small she was, how red and wrinkled, how black her wet knot of hair. He wished things could have turned out differently for her. He wished he hadn't been so hard on her. And Amy now, done, finished, gone. And her stone not even up yet and he had to call them again about that. It was a big stone, a good stone. It had cost almost two thousand dollars. For that much money it looked like they could go ahead and get the damned thing up.

He turned off on his road and made the short drive down to his mailbox and went in past it, slowing down to a steady creep through these woods. The tires went quietly over the pine needles and bumped over the bridge and he pulled up in his yard and parked. He got his ticket book and his hat and locked the car after he got out. Looking up through the windows of the house he half expected to see her come to the door, but he thought maybe she was watching television and hadn't heard him pull up. It looked like it had rained hard here tonight.

But something seemed wrong when he went through the door. He called her name a couple of times and only the quiet house was there.

'Fay?' he said. The back door was standing open and the light was on over the deck. He set his stuff down. Maybe she'd gone for a walk on the beach. In the rain? Not likely. It was dark as shit out there away from the house. The oven light was on in the stove and he pulled the door down. Fried chicken and mashed potatoes and green beans. Everything looked a little dry. He closed the oven door and shut it off. It was one-thirty by the clock on the wall. He'd had to fill out some reports at the station.

If she was hiding it wasn't funny anymore.

'Hey Fay,' he said.

The television was playing, the volume low. Something on the Discovery Channel, looked like, animals living in the snow.

Nothing in the bathroom.

She wasn't in the bedroom but some drawers had been pulled out.

In the closet he couldn't tell if a suitcase was missing or not. He thought they'd had four. Now there were three.

Out on the deck he looked across the lake and couldn't see much of anything. He went down the steps calling for her. The only answer was the dying wind whistling past him. The moon was hung high and it showed a beach washed clean by rain.

He went back to the house and got a flashlight and put on some rubber boots and he walked and walked and called for her, even up on the road and as a solitary car came by. He looked until the batteries died in the flashlight and then he went back to the house and got some fresh ones and went out again, climbing up among the pine trees that covered his land and she was not there either.

Toward morning his legs had given out and he sat on the deck and watched dawn light the lake with pale streaks in the sky, and the birds began to fly from tree to tree. Boats moved across the water already, skimming over the surface, white shards of spray coming up from their sides.

Book 2

The truck rocked and the transmission made a grinding sound and then the air brakes went off with a loud hiss and the truck was moving away, rolling slowly at first, then picking up speed as it swung back into the road. She stood looking after it, and then she started walking out across the beach. The sun rose higher from the water, and the shrimp boats moved, towing their trawls, the birds lifting and circling over them, singing their rough cries to the morning.

The gulls were everywhere, moving in the air and walking along the white sand. Coke cans and used condoms and cigarette butts littered the beach. Early morning and only a few cars moving up and down the black highway and past the hotels and shell shops set back from the road and the fine old homes, the seafood restaurants, the strip clubs. The sea lapped slowly into the sand and a lone fisherman stood poised to fish on a rickety wooden walkway that ran a few hundred feet out into the water of Biloxi.

Just up the road a small brick building sat dilapidated and forlorn, lights still blazing around a sign where the dark silhouette of a naked woman reared rusting from the roof. An old man with a broom opened a side door and swept a few things out onto the sand and closed it again. Nothing much moved on the beach, just the birds and the light wash of the ocean.

She saw a police cruiser go by and she watched after it fearfully, but it went on down the road and out of sight.

Far out in the water slick black forms arced in and

out of the slight swells, wet and shiny, and she recognized them from television shows at Sam's house. Dolphins. She stood there for a little bit watching them, wondering if they had a certain place they called home.

The sky turned hazy and overcast with the threat of rain and it began to wear a gray overcoat across its expanse. There was a Denny's that was open about a mile past the gardened grounds of the Holiday Inn and Fay could see people sitting in there. The suitcase was fairly heavy and the purse was a newer one that Amy had given her months ago, and it held forty dollars, what Amy had said was kind of like an allowance for helping around the house. There was no sidewalk along this stretch of the road and it was hard to walk in the sand. She wasn't used to it and it was deep and loose. She could see a few dead fish floating in the surf and she wondered if that was where the smell came from. People had dropped trash in the sand and far away she could see the figure of a man spearing things and dropping them into a bag he wore at his side.

More traffic was coming down the highway now and a few cars began to pull into the public parking lots. People got out of them with their swimming suits on, pulling folding chairs and umbrellas and coolers from the trunks, toys for small children, bright plastic rings and beach balls. Fay was glad she had thought to bring a swimming suit, and there seemed to be some public restrooms where a person could change. She needed to eat.

She walked on and she could see people far down the beach going into the water. Some white buildings were clustered off in the distance and there were a great many boats harbored out beyond them. She could see others on the open water. And the water went out to what looked to her like the edge of the world. She stopped and studied it. It looked like it was going up-hill and that puzzled her.

The birds were wheeling in the sky and scurrying on their spindly legs along the sand. She almost sat down and rested, but more and more people were moving in around her and she was closer to the Denny's now so she kept walking across the sand until she stepped onto the asphalt of the parking lot. She was grateful to have some decent clothes, at least, and a little money, but she didn't know how long the money could last. She'd find a job. She'd get herself a place to stay. That was all she knew.

She walked past the few parked cars in the lot. Sand was everywhere and she could feel it gritting under her leather sandals. Somebody would have found Alesandra by now, lying in the open boat like that. It was too late to go back now.

She tried to make herself stop thinking about it. There was a glass door at the entrance and she opened it and stepped onto tan tiles and saw a few people sitting at a counter. She looked around for a second and then slid into a booth that was close to her. She set her suitcase and purse on the seat beside her and then saw a sign posted on the side of the table that requested customers to reserve the use of the booth for a minimum of two customers. But it wasn't crowded, what did it matter?

She didn't want to attract any attention to herself. She just wanted to get something to eat. She picked up her things and moved to a stool at the counter.

A couple of older men sitting together looked at her and she turned away. The menu was right in front of her in a steel stand. She picked it up and heard one of them mutter something and the other one laughed. She looked up and gave them the coldest glare she could manage and they both looked away and they shut up, too. She concentrated on the menu but didn't know what things ought to cost. The only times she'd been in a restaurant were when Sam and Amy had taken her. The glasses were in her purse and she took them out and slipped them on. She had some cigarettes too and she pulled them out and lit one up, slid a tin ashtray closer from a pile at the rear of the counter.

'Coffee, miss?'

She looked up to see a girl who looked only a bit older than her standing there with a glass pot of coffee.

She nodded.

'Yeah, please.'

The girl reached to a rack of cups and brought one down. She poured the cup full and Fay thanked her and found the sugar and milk and stirred them in.

'You know what you want?'

She glanced up again and the girl was standing there with her little pad, stifling a yawn. She cupped her hand at her mouth and said, 'Excuse me. Long night.'

'I know what you mean,' Fay said. Her eyes went back to the menu. All of it looked good. She didn't know what she wanted yet.

'You want a minute?'

She looked up again.

'What?'

'You want me to give you a minute to decide?'

'Naw, that's OK. How about givin me two of these eggs like this . . .' She pointed to the two perfect eggs with the yolks shining. 'And some sausage. And some toast. And . . . uh . . . some grape jelly.'

'You got it,' the girl said, and turned away, writing. She tore off the sheet and clipped it to a round metal thing stuck in a window at the back of the room and a man with a paper hat reached out and took it. He glanced out at Fay with a tired look on his face. She sipped her coffee and smoked her cigarette. Being inside now felt safer but she didn't know if she should use her real name. She'd caught three rides altogether and she'd made up names for all of them. One divorced woman with two kids sleeping in the backseat had given her a ride from Highway 6 all the way down to the Carrollton exit. Fay hadn't said much to her, only told her that her name was Betty and that she was going to see her uncle in Biloxi. She felt that the woman was afraid of her and that she'd regretted picking her up, and wasn't really going to Carrollton but had only said that to be rid of her. And, truly, once she was under the bridge by the edge of the interstate and resting some and smoking, she'd been pretty sure that she'd seen the woman's car come off the exit ramp up ahead and go on south down I-55. But that was OK. She was on down the road thirty or forty more miles from what she'd left behind.

The coffee was really good. She saw the door marked for the restrooms and got off the stool and went in there and sat on the commode. There was a machine for tampons. Wouldn't have to worry about that for a while.

When she went back out her coffee cup had been filled again and her food was there. The girl came over and asked her if she needed anything else but Fay had already started eating and she just shook her head and smiled. The waitress went away and started talking to the two older men down the counter. They didn't look her way anymore.

It was the best breakfast she'd ever had aside from the ones that Sam had made for her sometimes. He would whip up three eggs in a bowl and pour them into a greased skillet and dump in chopped ham and cheese and green peppers and make a thick omelette that would have her stuffed by the time she finished it. It was hard to think of him and not start crying but she kept sitting there and eating. Trying to calm down. She had to take care of herself now and find a job and she had to get to a doctor somewhere and she had to find a place to live. She ate her breakfast slowly and enjoyed it and even after she'd finished she kept sitting there and drinking coffee. Finally the waitress brought the bill and asked her if there was anything else she needed. She said no and looked at the bill and reached into her purse for the money. The bill was $4.37 and she put down a five-dollar bill and the waitress took it and rung it up and handed back the change. Fay dropped the coins into her purse and sat there finishing her coffee, looking through the windows at the beach. The waitress went down to the other end of the counter, lounging, smoking her own cigarette in a secretive manner, glancing around from time to time. It was still gray and cloudy outside, and she didn't want to go out there yet.

'Could I have some more coffee, please?'

The waitress looked at her and got up, a trace of annoyance on her face, but she lifted the coffeepot and brought it down.

'I thought you was through,' she said, but she went on and poured Fay another cup. 'No charge,' she said, and turned to go back.

'You know where there's a store around here any-where?' Fay said.

'There's a bunch of stores right on up the road here in that mini mall.'

'Which way?'

The girl pointed. 'Right up here. It's a couple of blocks.'

The place was deserted now. Fay could hear a radio playing somewhere in the back. She stirred sugar and milk into her coffee and lit another cigarette.

'You live here?' she said.

'Yeah. Why?'

'I just wondered. You like it down here?'

The girl looked down at her feet. She seemed bored and distracted. Fay thought she was pretty in a scary kind of way, like she wouldn't do to mess with.

'It's all right I guess. Sometimes I wish I was some-where else, but hell, it's probably that way anywhere you go. Don't you figure?'

'I hadn't never thought about it,' Fay said. She sat there for a bit.

'You just got into town, didn't you?' the girl said.

'How'd you know?'

The girl scratched at her chin.

'Suitcase. You look a little down on your luck. Where you headed?'

'I reckon I'm headed right here.'

'You got a place to stay?'

'Not yet. I thought maybe I'd go lay on the beach for a while.'

'It looks like it's going to rain,' the girl said.

'Yeah, it kinda does.'

'Depresses the shit out of me when it does.'

'How come?'

'You can't get out of the house to do anything. You can't go to the beach. You got a hell of an accent. Where you from, talking like that?'

'Up north.'

'Up north like where? You mean Minnesota or Michigan or somewhere like that?'

She grinned a little and suddenly Fay liked her.

'I mean north of here. Up around Oxford.'

By the time some more customers came in the girl had told her that her name was Reena and that she'd be getting off at eight and that maybe they could drive around and drink a beer or something. She said she could show her where she lived. And like the first day on the levee of Sardis dam with Sam it looked like a better thing and she decided to go with it.

Reena lived in a trailer thing at the end of a long street up from the beach. It was more like a large RV that you could drive to places and stay, hook up the electricity, the water. A rusting Japanese pickup was parked in the yard.

Inside was a man sleeping on a fold-out couch and two children were sleeping in the floor with pillows and sheets and quilts around them. A radio was playing, nobody awake to hear it. Reena snapped it off and reached into a small refrigerator and pulled out two beers. She motioned for them to go back outside but first she reached for Fay's suitcase and stuffed it into an overhead bed that was chained to the ceiling with hooks. She seemed not to want to wake anybody up.

There was a picnic table that looked homemade under a young catalpa tree and tiny black pellets were lying on top of the table. Reena swept her hand across them and raked them onto the ground and told Fay to have a seat.

'I don't want to wake em up before I have to,' she said. 'Chuck's good to watch em for me while I work, but I sure like to take a break when I get off.'

She opened her beer and took a drink from it. Fay opened hers and took a small sip. She wondered when the morning sickness would come again. She wondered what Sam could be thinking. The pellets kept dropping onto the table. Fay looked up and saw some strange green striped worms on the undersides of the leaves on the tree. They favored worms she'd seen on the plants in tomato fields.

'It's good fishbait,' Reena said.

'You don't know where I could get a job, do you?'

'Well. That depends on what kind of a job you want. You can work in the seafood plants. I did that for a while. You come home smelling like dead fish and shrimp every night. Or work in a restaurant like I do. Clean rooms in a hotel.'

Fay thought about it. She wouldn't be able to work all that long after she started showing probably.

'What are you on the run from?' Reena said.

'I ain't on the run from nothin.'

'That's bullshit. Something's after you. Somebody.'

'Ain't nobody after me,' Fay said. 'I just had to get away from where I was.'

Reena watched her. After a while she said, 'Well I could drive you around and show you what Biloxi looks like if you want to. You could ask around and see about a job somewhere. It ain't gonna be nothing but minimum wage around here. Unless you want to strip.'

'Strip?' Fay said. 'What's that?'

Reena rolled her eyes up and then closed them while she shook her head. She took another big drink of her beer.

'Damn, you are from back in the sticks, ain't you?'

'I know it.'

'Well. If you want to make some money that's where it's at. You can make three or four hundred a night if you're good. And you've got the body to be good.'

'What do you have to do?' Fay said.

'Nothing much. Just take off your clothes and dance in front of a bunch of perverts. They tip good, though. Unlike you.'

'What do you mean?'

'Girl, don't you even know what a tip is? Where did you grow up?'

'Just here and there.'

'I believe it,' Reena said. She got up. 'Come on and let's get in the car. We'll get us a six-pack and cruise the beach. You got a swimming suit?'

'It's in my suitcase.'

'I'll slip in here and get it and grab mine, too. They'll sleep another couple of hours probably. That'll be enough time for us to ride around some and talk. You got a lot to learn, honey.'

Thirty minutes later they were lying on the beach under a striped umbrella that Reena had stuck into the sand and there was a beer cooler between them big enough to hold a six-pack. They sipped from their cans and eyed the brown water out in front of them. It moved only a little.

'Is it always flat like that?'

Reena leaned back on her elbows on one of the towels she had brought from the thing she lived in.

'It is unless it comes up a storm.'

'I thought it was supposed to have waves.'

'I don't know what the reason is. You can go over to Gulf Shores and the waves come in all day. It's pretty over there but it's too expensive. It don't cost me nothing to come down here.'

The sky was still cloudy and far out in the Gulf it was overcast above the waterline.

'It's gonna rain,' Reena said. 'But at least we won't get blistered.'

'What time you need to get back?'

'I don't know. After while sometime. I got to get some sleep sometime today so I can work tonight. Tonight's my night at the club.'

Fay picked up her beer and took a drink.

'You mean to dance?'

'Yeah. I dance on Thursdays and Saturdays. I work my other job three nights a week. But I go over to the club sometimes even if I'm off.'

'Don't you ever get any time off?'

Reena gave a short bitter laugh.

'Time off? What's that?' She sat up and found her beer in the sand and poured a long drink down her throat. 'You start having babies like I did when you're sixteen and you're fucked. You don't get no time off. Less you're lucky enough to find you a rich husband. Or a good one. And you ain't gonna find no good one in a strip joint.'

Fay didn't say anything for a while. They sat side by side and watched the water and the people on the beach. Once in a while Reena would take a drink of her beer. There was some music playing somewhere near, and Fay turned her head and looked at some fortyish women lying back against webbed chairs. Their skins were dark and they rubbed themselves with oils that glistened. None of them had wedding rings on their fingers. Her mother had said that at one time she'd owned one. And Fay had asked where it had gone to but never had gotten an answer.

'What you going to do?' Reena said.

'About what?'

'Hell, a place to stay for one thing. You can't just sleep on the beach down here, the cops'll roust you. Or somebody'll cut your throat for you. You got any money?'

'I got a little. Not much.'

'You got enough to stay in a hotel room tonight?'

'I don't know. How much is that?'

'Shit. Probably about thirty dollars over here at the Holiday Inn. You might could find a cheaper place, though. There's a bunch of motels up and down the road here. They're probably cheaper than the Holiday Inn. As a matter of fact I know they are.'

'I don't think I've got enough for that,' Fay said. She was starting to get scared now, thinking about being out on this beach late at night where just anybody might come by. She was afraid the law might be looking for her.

'I'd offer to let you stay with me for a while but there ain't hardly enough room in there for us as it is,' Reena said. She rolled over onto her side and picked up a pair of sunglasses from the towel and put them on. 'You ever turned a trick?'

'You mean like trick or treat? Naw. They never did let us do that.'

Reena rolled over onto her belly and shook her head. She had a good tan and her dark hair was shiny and clean.

'I mean fucking a man for money. Sucking him off or something.'

Fay spoke quietly. 'I ain't never done nothin like that. I wouldn't, neither.'

Reena looked up.

'Don't say what you would or wouldn't do, honey. Cause one day you might have to. I turn a trick or two just about every night I work at the club. I have to. I ain't got no choice. My kids got to eat.'

'What about that guy at your place? Don't he work?'

'He did. He was a shrimper on one of these boats out here but business got bad when all these Vietnamese come in and they had to let him go. That was two months ago. He's been looking for a job but he ain't found one yet. So he watches the kids for me and cooks and cleans.'

'Does he know about this other?'

'You mean the tricks? He knows I dance. He don't know for sure about the other. It ain't none of his business and I'm about tired of his shit anyway. I'm just scared he might beat me up if I throw him out.'

'My lord,' Fay said.

Reena sat up and finished her beer and tossed her can onto the sand. She opened the lid on the cooler and got out a cold one. She sat with her knees up and grains of sand clinging to her feet.

'I hate to fuck somebody I don't even feel nothing for. But I'd feel a lot worse if my kids didn't have nothing to eat.'

She had turned her face away for a moment but now she turned back and rested her hand briefly on Fay's.

'I didn't have shit when I was growing up,' she said. 'And I ain't got nothing right now. I'm just trying to do better. I want my kids to have more than I did. It ain't their fault that I've done the way I've done. You want another beer?'

'Sure.'

Reena handed her one and Fay drank off the last of what was in the can and set it in the sand. She opened the fresh one and lay back on the towel.

'How hard is it to learn that dancin?' she said.

At Reena's Fay could see that the door was open on the RV and then she saw the man sitting on the front step wearing just a pair of jeans.

'I guess they're up,' Reena said, and pulled in and parked. 'Will you help me get my stuff out?'

'Yeah.'

She got out and opened the back door and reached in for the towels and the collapsed umbrella and her purse. Reena got the cooler and they went across the sandy yard in their swimming suits. Reena said something to him and he looked up at Fay. Not a happy look and she saw it.

'Chuck? This is Fay. We've been down to the beach for a while. The kids up?'

'Yeah,' he said. 'I fixed em some cereal and they're in there eating.'

He got up and stuck his hand out. Fay took it and shook and could see him looking at her titties, her legs. She didn't like him.

'Hi,' was all she said. She looked around. The black pellets covered the picnic table again. Chuck and Reena were talking. She went over to the table and put the towels and the umbrella on it and sat down. She was tired and wondered if maybe she couldn't just stretch the towels out under the tree and ball up one for a pillow and take a nap. The beer had made her sleepy on top of the big breakfast she'd eaten. She was used to taking a nap whenever she wanted to.

Reena set the cooler on the ground and Chuck bent over and took off the lid and got a beer from it. He sat back down on the steps and opened it, looking up at Reena. He had four or five tattoos on his arms and shoulders and he was burnt-looking from the sun, heavily muscled, dull reddened eyes behind sleepy lids. To Fay he looked lazy and maybe dangerous.

She tried not to listen but it was plain they were getting into an argument. She looked away, down to the end of the street where it stopped in a trash pile of split garbage bags and cardboard boxes, scattered beer cans and broken lawn chairs. Their voices were getting louder and it was something about money. She got off the picnic table and walked across the yard, away from them. It might be better to just go on, take her suitcase from inside the trailer and find someplace to change and go on down the road. Go somewhere, but where? She barely even knew where she was, only the coast. She almost wished she'd never left home. At least she hadn't killed anybody there. Why did Sam ever have to start

198

messing with her in the first place? But she knew all the answers to that. There wasn't any use in thinking about it. What happened had happened and it was too late to go back and change any of it. This was what her life was now. She'd just have to deal with it.

'Fay?' Reena called, and she turned. Chuck had put on a shirt and he was walking toward the little pickup, turning up the beer as he walked. Reena was standing at the door of the trailer and motioning for her to come on in.

'Come on and meet my kids,' Reena said. 'Then we'll lay down and take us a nap if you want to. Chuck's gone down to the dock for a while.'

She followed her up the steps and into the tiny living area where the two children sat with bowls of milk and cereal in their laps. They were watching a miniature television, a boy about three and a little girl who looked to be about five. They both wore shorts and T-shirts and both of them were very fair. Fay smiled at them.

'Hey,' she said.

'This is Jimmy, Fay,' Reena said. 'And this is Clara. Can y'all say hi to Fay?'

'Hey,' the little boy said. 'We got the cartoons on.'

The girl didn't say anything and barely looked up from the TV screen.

'They sure are cute,' Fay said.

'Yeah. Their daddy won't help me take care of em. Just set that stuff down anywhere, Fay.'

There didn't seem to be much room to put anything. Reena was going down a short hall and called back to her to follow.

There were two beds in the back room, short and compact, with thin mattresses. Reena reached over and turned on an air conditioner that had been fitted into the wall and then patched around messily with silver tape.

'Well this is it,' Reena said. 'You can sleep on that bed and we'll try to figure out something else when we get up. I got to get some sleep. Let me just go tell these kids something right quick.'

Fay sat down on the bed and it sagged. But she was so tired she could have slept on the ground. She pulled back the sheet and heard Reena telling the kids not to go across the road and not to wake them up. There was no door to the room. She could hear the TV playing, small explosions, laughter. Reena came back into the room and took off her swimming suit and looked at Fay. She looked like somebody who had lost weight.

Reena winked at her and slipped beneath the sheet on the bed, turned on her side and didn't move. There was just the mound of shiny hair, and the sheet stretched tight over the curve of her rump.

The TV played on in the front space. She heard the children talking. She didn't go to sleep for a long time. She didn't know if Reena was asleep or not.

'How bad does it hurt to have a baby, Reena?' she said, but Reena didn't answer, only shifted a little in the bed, and coughed lightly in maybe what was her sleep.

When she woke there was not any sound and the light had changed in the room. The air conditioner had been turned off and her thin pillow was damp with the sweat from her head and neck. The bed Reena had slept in was empty and she couldn't hear the children or the television.

She got up. There was still sand clinging to her feet and her legs. She rubbed at her arms going up the short hall and then she leaned forward and took a careful peek into the living area. It was empty of people and the screen door was closed. Her suitcase was still stuffed into the overhead bed and she pulled it down and went to see if there was a lock on the door. There was. She locked it and went back to the bedroom and pulled off the swimming suit and found a clean bra and panties, a blouse and some shorts. She put them on and put the swimming suit in her purse.

She went out the front door and stepped down into the yard, then looked up. The sun was over in the sky and she thought it looked like late afternoon. The car was gone and there wasn't any sign of the children. She went back inside to the living area where the sink was and the small refrigerator and looked around for a note, thinking maybe Reena had written her one, but there was nothing, just the two empty cereal bowls in the sink and two spoons. She opened the refrigerator and looked into it. Some bologna and some mustard and mayonnaise, a half-empty jar of pickles, some eggs and bacon and a few soft drinks. That was it. She closed it and got her purse and went back out into the yard. The little cooler was sitting there beside the step. She carried her purse and a beer over to a lawn chair. The beer was still cold when she opened it and took a sip.

She found her cigarettes. She only had about half a pack left. Maybe later if nobody showed up she could walk back down the beach road. There were some liquor stores and gas stations she'd seen earlier scattered up and down the road. But she didn't want to lug her suitcase and she didn't want to leave it here. She guessed she could hide it in some bushes along this street somewhere if she had to, come back and get it later.

Some of the children's toys were lying around in the yard: a bucket and a plastic shovel, a red-and-white tricycle, some tiny yellow trucks alongside balls and big plastic bats spattered with dirt that some former rain had kicked up on them. She drank the beer and eyed the clouds above. It looked like it was clearing off.

There was not much traffic on this street. Once in a while she would see a car or a truck turn into a driveway down the hill. She could hear a radio playing somewhere. An old woman across the road was down on her knees pulling at weeds in a flower garden. She looked up at Fay and waved one time and Fay waved back: Hey old lady.

She sat there and thought about Sam and the last time with him, that day before he had gone in to work, and all the times before with him and it got so bad she had to quit thinking about it. She never had been one to cry much but a few tears ran down her cheeks and dripped off her chin. She sniffed and rubbed slick mucus away from her nose with the back of her hand. Goddamn people. Always fucking something up. And wasn't this just a great place to be in? Nothing but a fucking dump. But it beat nothing, didn't it? She thought about Reena fucking people for money. She probably closed her eyes or something while it was going on. The dancing Reena had told her about sounded kind of good, the money part. But did you really have to take your clothes off? Couldn't you just dance in a swimming suit or something? She didn't want to get up in public and take her clothes off. And even if she did start doing it, how long could she keep on before her belly started swelling and everybody would be able to tell? Men who were paying to see a woman dance wouldn't want to see a pregnant one dance. And what exactly was a pervert? It sounded kind of nasty in some way. Maybe guys who jacked off or something. She'd asked Sam about that one time, about jacking off. He said every boy did it. Him too. She wished Reena would come on back. She just felt like she needed to know a little more before she jumped off into this thing. The money she had wasn't going to last long. It would buy cigarettes and a few sandwiches for a little while, and then that'd be all she wrote.

She got up and went back into the trailer and closed the suitcase. She came back out the door and walked around behind the trailer and looked off into the woods down there. There were dense pines, thick shade, snarled growths of honeysuckle and other plants whose names she didn't know.

Out of sight of the trailer she found an old mattress folded over against some boxes and jars and she raised it up, made sure no snakes were under it, and slid the suitcase down in there. Then she headed back up toward the yard and got her purse and put her smokes and lighter back in there and went down the road walking and looking around. The old lady had gone in or moved somewhere else in her yard.

There seemed to be a couple of daylight hours left before dark and she thought that would be enough time to walk down to the beach road, find a store, get another pack of cigarettes and walk back to Reena's trailer, be still sitting there in the yard when she came in. She had to find out about this dancing job and get Reena to show her how to do it.

She walked barefoot for a while and then had to get

out in the street where a portion of the sidewalk ran out. She dug the sandals from her purse and slipped her feet into them.

The neighborhood got better as she went along. The trailers started giving way to wooden houses with railed porches and barbecue grills sitting on them, neatly bricked homes with wire mesh fences and chickens in pens. There were some of the biggest roosters she'd ever seen in some of them, tall birds with black shiny feathers and blond tails. She saw groups of skinny children with black hair sitting in some of the yards and old men and women with the same features sitting on porches and reading newspapers or cooking on the grills.

She was trying to remember how Reena had gotten up to the trailer. There was a stop sign on down a ways and she seemed to remember her turning there. And when she got up to the corner and looked, she could see the water out in the bay. It didn't look that far.

Halfway down the hill, before she crossed the next street, she stopped beside an old house with gray and red paint, fancy woodwork on the edges of the roof and over the porch, all kinds of flowers planted and growing in the yard. There was a low stone wall that bordered the sidewalk and she sat down on it and rested for a while.

She hoped a store was close by. All she wanted to do now was find one, get what she needed, maybe a sandwich too if they sold them, and go back to her lawn chair to wait for Reena.

After a few minutes she picked up her purse and crossed the street at the stop sign. Cars and trucks were going down the road and people were still out on the beach. Some people were far out in the water but the water was only up to their waists. She couldn't get over it. Something about it just didn't look right. She hadn't thought it would be that shallow that far out.

When she got down to the beach road she didn't see anyplace to cross, so she stopped and watched the traffic for a while and waited until there was an opening and she darted halfway across. She had to wait in the middle of the road while some more cars and trucks came past and some blew their horns at her. When she saw another opening in the traffic she scooted across and stopped. The Denny's where she had eaten was way down the beach. She looked the other way and saw a gas station sign she recognized, but it was a long way off. Sometimes they sold beer. She'd seen her daddy buy beer in gas stations before. Sometimes they had sandwiches too. So she started walking that way, trudging through the sand again. People were lying everywhere on the beach now, children playing, music going, radios playing in cars where young people were grouped up near the road, talking and laughing. She heard a few whistles but she never looked to see who'd made them. She just kept walking. The gas station didn't seem to be getting any closer. And it wasn't as late as she'd thought it was. There must have been some clouds over the sun earlier because it was glaring down on her now and she could feel sweat beading across her brow. She wiped at it and kept walking.

Up ahead she could see a wooden walkway and after a while she reached it and got up on it. It was elevated above the beach and now she could see farther out into the water and along the beach where the people were packed in side by side, some drinking beer, some lying on their bellies under the sun, couples, older men and women, girls in groups of two and three wearing skimpy swimsuits and their legs and arms nearly black from the sun. The darkest white people she'd ever seen. She wondered how they could get enough time off from work to spend that much time lying in the sun. She guessed some of them were rich and didn't have to work. Maybe some of them were dancers like Reena and only worked at night.

The wooden walkway stretched for a long distance in front of her and there was a long white sign beside it that said WELCOME TO GULFPORT. When she got on the other side of it she looked back and it said WELCOME TO BILOXI. The gas station was closer now, but the walkway ran out, and she had to get back in the sand. She was really getting hungry now and she hoped they'd have some sandwiches.

The traffic passed beside her in a steady flow. On the high side of the road she saw old homes set back from another street that ran parallel to the one she was walking along.

She went on. The heat seemed to creep up on you here, to gather its forces slowly and then hit you all of a sudden. She could feel rings of sweat spreading under her arms, but there were no trees to rest under here on this side of the road. All the trees were up in the yards of the nice houses.

Past the houses there were some buildings she could see in the distance and they were narrow in front, all of them two stories, and cars were parked all around them. Red Carpet Inn, she read on one. Seaside Resorts, said another. She guessed they must be the motels Reena had been talking about. There were stripes across the road now and in the middle a concrete island where people stood. Fay saw some woman in a swimsuit with a group of children around her stop at a pole and push something on it with her hand and the light turned red and the traffic stopped and the woman came on across the road with her kids. The cars and trucks sat waiting and then the light turned green and they rushed on. And up there on the other side of the road there was a small store with beer signs in the windows.

There was a bench on up the sidewalk a short distance and she sat down once she got to it, leaning back against the painted boards and still watching the people across the road on their towels and under their umbrellas. There was a breeze blowing there and she wondered what her hair looked like. She ran her fingers through it a few times and then got her brush out of the purse and brushed it as well as she could and then tied it up in a ponytail and leaned back again. She sure wanted a shower. A motel would have one. But she was almost certain she didn't have enough money for a motel.

The traffic never seemed to lessen any. She was scared of hitchhiking after the things Sam had told her when he first met her, but there hadn't been any choice the other night. Leaving had been the only thing she could think of, and right now she couldn't think of anything else she could have done.

The store had a wide glass window and it advertised roast beef, tuna fish, hamburgers. Marlboro signs were on the window, Old Milwaukee, Schlitz, Budweiser. She went in and a little bell rang over her head. An old woman was watching television behind the counter. Fay nodded to her and went back to the coolers and looked in through the glass where the cold beer sat. She saw a six-pack of Bud in bottles and reached in and got it. There were chips on a rack nearby and she got a bag of them. Didn't want to spend too much money, not until she could make some more.

Up front in another glass case sat sandwiches already made and wrapped in clear plastic. She stood there trying to decide. Finally she took out a cold ham and cheese and reached for a couple of packs of mayonnaise there and carried her things over to the counter and set them down and opened her purse without looking at the woman too much.

'And I need a pack of Salem Lights, too,' she said.

The old woman didn't move, just kind of sat there and watched her.

'Young lady,' she said, 'are you eighteen?'

Fay looked up.

'Ma'am?'

'Are you eighteen?'

'No ma'am,' she said. 'I'm not but seventeen.'

She went back to digging for the money in her purse. It was buried somewhere down in there. She pushed aside lipstick and combs and packs of chewing gum and the swimsuit and finally found it, wadded in a loose roll. She pulled it out, dreading hearing how much it was going to cost. But she felt better now. She could have a few more cold beers now and have something to eat and something to smoke and maybe Reena might even be back by the time she walked up to the trailer park.

The woman wasn't ringing up her stuff, never even had moved off her stool. She turned back to her soap opera or whatever it was she was watching and said, 'You'll have to put that beer back, then.'

'Ma'am?' Fay said.

'I can sell you the sandwich and the chips,' she said. 'But I can't sell alcohol or tobacco to a minor.'

'Why?' Fay said.

'Because it's against the law!' the old woman said. 'Now go put my cold beer back in that cooler before it gets hot. Go on.'

Fay felt her cheeks flush hot.

'They's some up and down this beach don't care if you ain't but thirteen but I ain't one of em,' the woman said. 'You ain't old enough to be drinking anyway.'

It was the tone of the woman's voice that drove her out the door. Just before it shut behind her she heard the old woman call out for her to put the sandwich back where it had been but she didn't turn around. She just kept walking until she was back down by the bench. She looked back at the store and could see the woman watching her through the window. Nobody had ever told her you couldn't buy beer if you weren't eighteen. And what did that have to do with it anyway? Sam never had said anything about how old she was. Amy never had either. *It's the law*, she'd said. What law? The old woman had seemed to enjoy being mean to her and she didn't understand that. She didn't even know her and what could she have against her?

She didn't know what to do now. If she went to another store they might tell her the same thing. Or three stores might. She didn't think she had the energy to walk all up and down the beach trying to find a store that would sell her beer and cigarettes.

She counted the cigarettes she had left. Eight. They'd be gone by dark for sure. And she didn't know what she'd do then.

She lit another one of the cigarettes and sat there smoking it slowly, trying to make it last. Seven left. She'd need to stop again and rest if she headed back to Reena's right now, and she'd want one again then. Then there wouldn't be but six. If Reena had gone to work she probably wouldn't be in until late. Maybe real late.

She saw now that she never should have gotten off in Biloxi, never should have gone home with Sam. Out across the road the people were wading in the water and drinking their beer. She could see them lifting their cans and she could see the coolers next to them. They were rich people, rich enough to lie on the beach all day and not have to work. She decided to go back across the road and walk around some. She couldn't just sit here.

She could feel the men looking at her before she was a hundred feet away from the public bathrooms. She'd stuffed her clothes into the purse and she'd put on the sunglasses and she walked slowly, looking around. The swimsuit was nothing like the one Alesandra had worn that day but Fay knew she filled it out, felt now that maybe even it was a little bit too small for her, now that she'd gained some weight. She got over into the middle of the beach so that she could look everything over. She remembered what Sam had said one night when they were lying in bed, her head propped on his arm and her face resting against his chest, when she'd asked him why he was so crazy about her: *There's nothing like a pretty woman like you. The way you smell, the way your hair smells. Just touching you. Any man would give a lot for that.* She didn't know if that was true. Maybe it was only true for Sam.

'Hey honey, ain't you hot?'

She stopped to see who'd spoken so. A tall skinny

guy with legs white as the belly of a dead perch and wearing a dipshit hat was up under an umbrella with a can of beer on his stomach. His ribs stuck out. His chest was hairless, sunken, like maybe he'd been bad sick.

'Not too bad,' she said, and started walking again.

'Why hey, you can get up under here and cool off with me if you want to,' he said. 'I got a whole cooler full of beer right here. Nectar of the gods by God,' he said, and patted it like a good dog. She didn't look back.

'Well screw you, then,' she heard him mutter. She stopped. He was looking fearfully at her. She walked back to him.

'Screw me? Is that what you said? How about screw you, you skinny son of a bitch?' She started kicking sand at his face and he sputtered and spilled his beer. Asshole. He didn't look old enough to buy beer either. Probably lived here and knew where to go get it with no questions asked. She went on.

It wasn't nearly as hot now. The sun was still lowering in the sky and out across the water a pale blue had come up. All that water. How small Sardis seemed now. Sam in his boat would be a tiny dot out there. She wished she was still with him. She couldn't stop thinking about him and wondering what he was feeling. He never had come right out and said that he loved her, but she'd known it in the way he looked at her, the things he did for her, the way he'd kissed her, like each kiss was a great thrill for him. And then she told herself that she had to go on now, stop thinking about all that because it wasn't like that anymore and she wasn't there anymore. She was here now. And maybe would be for a long time.

She kept walking in between the rows of people, some on their stomachs with their eyes closed, past groups of girls who lay like they were dead, legs sprawled open in the sand. Little children on rubber rafts were splashing in the shallow water while mothers watched nearby. She'd be doing that one day if everything worked out.

The beach looked endless. As far as she could see there were people and umbrellas and running children, short chairs that sat directly in the sand, and up in the sky two kites floated and swayed. She stopped and stood looking up at them for a moment, trying to see the strings that held them or who on the ground was holding them.

'Wouldn't think there'd be enough wind, would you?' a voice said to her. She turned her head.

'What?' she said.

'I guess there's more wind up there than there is down here,' a smiling young guy said. She smiled back.

'I guess so,' she said. 'Sure ain't much down here, is it?'

'You hot?'

'A little.'

'Well,' he said, and shifted his chair to the left a bit. 'I got plenty of shade under here if you want to get out of that sun for a while. Got a towel right here you can sit on if you want to.'

She studied him. He had a good tan and he was heavyset, thick through the arms and legs and chest. His hair was coal black and she could see that his eyes were brown. Nothing bad was going to happen to her right here in daylight on a public beach. There were too many people around. And he looked OK anyway.

'Come on and sit down,' he said, so she did, not too close, right on the edge of the towel but up under the umbrella, in the shade. She put her purse down on the towel and almost reached for a cigarette, but then stopped. She had to make them last a while longer.

'I've got another chair in my van,' he said.

'Oh, no, this is fine. Thanks.'

'My name's Chris,' he said, and stuck out his hand. 'Chris Dodd.'

She took his hand and shook it. His fingers were warm and she could feel the strength in them. He squeezed her hand gently.

'My name's Fay Jones.'

'Pleased to meet you, Fay. You live around here?'

'No, I'm just . . . I'm kind of on vacation,' she said. 'I was just out for a walk.'

'Got a lot of stuff in that purse, looks like.'

She looked at it. Some of her clothes were bulging out of the top. She pushed down on them.

'Just some clothes. I just changed.' She felt her face getting red.

'That's what I figured,' he said. He turned the beer up and must have seen her watching him.

'You want a cold one?'

'A what?'

'You want a cold beer?'

She hesitated. She didn't want to seem too eager. But he was offering.

'I might drink one if you got plenty,' she said. 'I don't want to drink your last one or nothin.'

'Aw shit, I got a bunch. Reach over in there and get me one too while you're in there if you don't mind.'

She got up on her knees and turned around and opened the lid on his cooler. It looked like he had about a whole case in there. She reached in and it was so cold in there it hurt her fingers.

'Boy,' she said.

'Cold, ain't it?'

'It sure is.'

'I put some rock salt on top of it this morning. That'll make it almost freeze but not quite.'

She got two beers out and handed him one and closed the lid and turned back around. There was a small radio set on a towel beside the cooler and it was playing country songs at a low level. She opened the beer and took a sip and it was so cold it made her teeth ache for a moment.

'That's cold,' she said.

'Yep.'

On his left ankle there was a tattoo of leaves and tiny

flowers, red, blue, yellow, that encircled it. She pointed to it.

'Where'd you get that?' she said.

He looked where she was pointing.

'That? Oh I got that up in Philadelphia when I was in the marines. Me and a couple of my buddies got drunk one night in Chinatown and decided to go to the tattoo parlor. They both got devil dogs tattooed on their shoulders and I got this. They thought I was a wimp.'

'It's nice,' she said. 'I like it.'

'Thanks. I like it too. They say you get sick of a tattoo if you get it put on somewhere you have to look at it all the time, like your forearm. That's why I had it put there.'

She sipped at her beer and reached for her purse, pulled it closer. She pushed the clothes aside and dug down in there until she found her pack and the lighter.

'They put them on with a needle?'

'Yeah.'

'Don't it hurt?'

'It hurts like the devil. But you got to sit there and be still or he'll mess it up.'

She lit the cigarette and left the pack and the lighter on the towel. Then she picked them up and held them out to him.

'You want one?'

He waved his hand at her.

'I finally quit two years ago, but thanks anyway. I smoke a cigar once in a while. Don't figure that hurts me too bad. I sure get to wanting a cigarette when I'm drinking beer, though. How long you been smoking?'

She pulled her feet up and made a little circle with her legs and set the beer in between them.

'Aw, off and on, couple of years, I guess. I smoke more now than I used to.'

'That's what happens.'

It was always hard for her to talk to somebody she didn't know, somebody she didn't know anything about. He seemed friendly and nice enough, but she couldn't think of what to say to him. So for a while she just sat there and drank the beer and smoked her cigarette and looked at the people on the beach.

'Where you from?' he said.

'Up north of here. Up around Batesville and Oxford.'

'Say you on vacation?'

She looked away.

'Kind of. I'm just kind of visiting down here for a while. Trying to make up my mind if I want to stay.'

'Where else you thinking about going?'

She turned back to him.

'What's that?'

He was leaned back in his chair with his legs stretched out in front of him, holding the cold beer on his belly.

'I say where else you thinking about going if you don't stay here?'

'Well,' she said, 'I don't rightly know right now. I just thought I'd come down here and stay a while and see if I liked it. It ain't what I thought it would be.'

He sat up in the chair and tucked his feet back and held the beer with both hands between his knees.

'What do you mean?'

'I don't know,' she said. 'I just thought it would be different from this. I didn't think it'd be this many people down here. And all this traffic.'

He sipped at his beer and looked out over the crowd.

'Weekends are busy here,' he said with a nod. 'This place is geared for tourists. Did you see all the shell shops and stuff?'

'Naw,' she said.

'They got a little of everything down here. T-shirt shops, souvenir shops, tattoo parlors, strip clubs, restaurants. You name it.'

She sipped her beer and pulled on the cigarette.

'You reckon it's hard to find a job down here?' she said.

He reached for a pair of sunglasses and put them on

and leaned back in his chair again. She could feel him watching her.

'What kind of job you looking for?'

'I don't know. I ain't real choicey. I talked to this one girl but I don't know if I want to do what she does.'

'What's that?'

Fay looked up at him.

'She's a dancer.'

'What kind of a dancer? Not ballet down here I bet.'

'She's a stripper,' Fay said.

He looked down and seemed to turn that over in his mind for a few moments.

'Well,' he said finally, 'I guess there's a lot of girls who think they have to do that. I guess the money's easy to make.'

'She said it was.'

'Some of these clubs down here are rough, you know.'

'How rough?'

'Pretty damn rough. I doubt they treat the girls very well. I was in a few in the Philippines. And up in Washington, D.C. Years ago when I was in the service. I don't know you well enough to give you any advice but if I did I'd advise you to stay the hell out of those places.'

She didn't say anything for a while. And didn't really know why she'd told him all that.

'You like to swim?' he said.

'Some.'

'Hell,' he said, watching some children playing at the edge of the beach. 'You could clean rooms in a hotel before you'd have to go and do that.'

She just nodded. A little boy in front of her was slowly filling a pail with sand, then dumping it out, then filling it again.

'How old are you if you don't mind me asking?' Chris said.

She smiled at him and lifted her beer.

'How old do I look to you?'

He studied her critically, stroking at his chin with two fingers.

'Oh, I'd say about . . . nineteen or twenty.'

'I'm seventeen,' she said.

'You could have fooled me.'

'I'm big for my age,' she said.

'I guess you are. Are you out of high school yet?'

'I never did finish. I never did have a chance to finish.'

He fell silent again. She put her cigarette out in the sand and drank the rest of the beer, then eased the can down between her legs.

'I tried to buy some beer and some cigarettes and a sandwich a while ago but they wouldn't sell me the beer and the cigarettes. I didn't know you had to be eighteen. Nobody ever told me that.'

'You had anything to eat?' he said.

'I had breakfast.'

'Are you hungry?'

'I'm about to starve,' she said.

'You like oysters?'

It seemed like Amy had fried some one night, rolling them in yellow cornmeal like catfish and cooking them in a black iron skillet while the oil sizzled and spattered.

'I think I had some one time,' she said.

'Well, I tell you what.' He turned up his beer and finished it and put it in a plastic sack. 'Let me see your beer can there.' She handed it. 'I was going to go down to this bar down the road and have about a dozen on the half shell after while but since you just made me hungry talking about oysters I might as well go now. Why don't you go back and change into your clothes and I'll buy you something to eat?'

She hesitated. She felt like she had sand all over her. But she thought there was a faucet back there where you could wash your feet and legs off.

'You sure? I don't want to put you out none.' She

216

motioned toward all his stuff. 'You had a pretty good little nest built there.'

'I was about ready to go anyway. They got shrimp and steaks and stuff if you don't like oysters.'

'Well let me go change, then,' she said, and she got up. He was getting up, too.

'I'll be putting this stuff in the van,' he said. He pointed out toward the road. 'There's my van right over there. See that black one there?'

She looked.

'I see it.'

'Just come on over when you get through. I'll have it cranked up and the air going.'

'Don't you want me to help you with this stuff?'

'I can get it. Won't take me but two trips.'

'OK,' she said, and suddenly it seemed that everything in the world was right again, or at least better than it had been an hour ago. He probably wouldn't mind going in somewhere and getting her some cigarettes. She turned away and walked quickly through the sand. She looked back once to see him watching her. She waved.

The restaurant was cool and dark, the paneled walls hung with nets and mounted fish from the deep and shells and old anchors. The waiter led them to a table near the back where there was a glass window that let them look out over the harbor where all the boats were moored. When they were seated less than a minute the waiter reappeared and asked for their drink orders. She looked at Chris and he nodded almost imperceptibly and she ordered a beer. Chris asked for a frozen margarita and the waiter vanished. She looked around.

'Not crowded, is it?'

'We're early,' he said. 'About eight o'clock there'll be a line out to the parking lot.' He picked up his menu and looked at it. She reached for her glasses in the purse and slipped them on.

'They don't check to see how old you are in a restaurant?' she said. She picked up her menu and opened it.

'You're on the coast now,' was all he said.

The drinks came and the waiter poised with his pad and pen.

'How about giving us a few minutes?' Chris said. 'And may we have an ashtray, please?'

'Yes sir, certainly,' he said, and left to fetch it.

'Well, I know what I'm gonna eat,' Chris told her. 'I'm gonna have a dozen or two on the half shell and maybe a cup of the gumbo. They have good gumbo here.'

'What's that?'

He looked up from his menu to a spot somewhere just over her head.

'Well it's got rice, and shrimp, okra. It's kind of like a brown gravy with all this stuff in it.'

The waiter brought the ashtray and set it down.

'You think I'd like that?' she asked.

'It's real good. If you don't like it you can order something else.'

She was nervous about picking up the beer in front of the waiter, was afraid he might ask her how old she was.

'You want me to order for you?' Chris said.

'Yeah. Why don't you? I guess I'll try that gumbo.'

'I'll order you some oysters too.'

He ordered two dozen on the half shell and a cup and a bowl of the gumbo. He lifted his drink when she picked up hers, clinked his glass softly against her bottle.

'You like this place?' he said.

She nodded, smiling slightly. 'I like to look out at the water. Reckon who all them boats belong to?'

He sipped his drink and turned his head to them.

'Just different people. Some of them are working boats, shrimpers, oysterboats. Some of those tall ones with the platforms are sportfishermen. They take people out in the Gulf for a day of fishing or six hours or however long they want to go. It's a big business around here. And some people live on some of those sailboats and stuff.'

'What do you do?' she said.

He looked down at his drink and stirred it with his straw. He picked it up and sipped it again.

'I'm a pilot,' he said.

'Pilot?'

'Airplane pilot. I work for a company over in Gulf Shores, Alabama.'

She could only stare at him for a moment, then realized she was staring when the grin started to appear on his lips.

'What's the matter?' he said. 'You've not ever talked to a pilot before?'

'I've seen some of those crop dusters before. What kind of plane you fly?'

'Well I've done some crop dusting before. Right now I'm towing signs.'

'Signs?'

'Yeah. You know, those long ones that say Eat at Joe's or something. You've seen those, haven't you?'

'I don't think so.'

'Well, I make about two passes over the beach and then go back and unhook and put on another one. I do that all day long.'

He didn't sound happy about it and she wondered why. It sounded exciting to her.

'Don't you like it?' she said.

He took a big drink of his margarita and set it back down. He watched the table for a moment and then looked up.

'I can think of a hell of a lot of other things I'd rather be doing,' he said. 'But, it's flying.' He moved one of his shoulders as if that explained everything.

A few more people were coming in the front door now. Some of them settled at the bar up front and she watched them. Mostly they looked like older people and she had seen a lot of them down here already. She sipped at her beer.

'I've got some money,' she said. 'Would you get me some cigarettes somewhere later on?'

'What kind you smoke? Salem Lights? I'll go get you some.'

She reached for her purse. 'Wait a minute,' she said. 'Let me give you some money.'

'That's all right.'

He got up from the table and she watched him walk away and she noticed now that he walked with a slight limp. He disappeared around a corner and then the waiter came down the aisle of booths carrying a little table with their food.

'Here we are, ma'am,' he said. He set down the oysters and the gumbo and Fay looked at what was in front of her. Strange pale things on shells resting in beds of ice. A wedge of lemon speared with a narrow fork. A dish of red sauce and a paper container of something white and pasty beside it. She looked up at the waiter. He was laying out the silverware wrapped in napkins.

'All right, ma'am, two dozen on the half shell, cup of gumbo, bowl of gumbo, will there be anything else?'

'Ah . . . ,' she said.

'Would you like another beer?'

She looked at the half-empty one in front of her.

'I guess so.'

'And what about the gentleman? Will he be having another margarita do you think? That's OK, I'll come back in a few minutes.' And he folded up his table and was gone again.

She didn't know what to do with the things in front of her. There was a tray of crackers on the table that had appeared from somewhere. She decided she'd better wait for Chris and some instructions on how to eat these things. After a minute he came around the corner slapping a pack of cigarettes against his open palm.

'Salems were all they had in the machine,' he said. 'Hope that's all right. We can stop at a store later on if it's not.'

'Thanks,' she said, and put the smokes in her purse.

'Boy they look good don't they,' he said, and unrolled his napkin and put it in his lap. 'Yes sir, mighty good.' He took the lemon off the fork and squeezed some of the juice over them, then got some of the crackers. He took the paper cup of the white stuff and dipped some of it into the red sauce. She watched him. He looked up. 'Aren't you going to eat?'

'I never had this before,' she said.

He watched her for a moment.

'Oh, OK,' he said. 'Just do like me. Squeeze some of that juice on. Put a little of that horseradish in your cocktail sauce. Open you a pack of crackers.'

He dug right in. She did the things he'd told her to do. When she thought she had it ready she tried to spear one up with her fork but it kept sliding off.

'You've got to kind of scoop it out of the shell,' he said. 'Here. Watch me.' He slid one out, swirled it around in the sauce, popped it into his mouth and bit into a cracker. 'Man these things are good,' he said, chewing. He picked up his glass and waved it at the waiter across the room, and kept eating. She could tell he was really enjoying them but she didn't see how. To her they looked like some guts or something.

She finally got one out of the shell and dropped it into the sauce and then almost couldn't get it out. When she did it looked awful to her. She debated on putting something like that into her mouth. He was watching her. She was holding it in front of her mouth, just looking at it.

'You've got to get used to them,' he said.

She put it back into the shell.

'I don't think I can eat that,' she said. 'It looks like a worm or somethin.'

'A *worm*?'

'Or somethin. It don't look like nothin fit to eat.'

He bent to his plate again. 'Well if you don't eat them I will. Try the gumbo, why don't you?'

She slid the saucer and the white china bowl over in

221

front of her and smelled of it. Rich broth and rice and tiny shrimp that she could dip up with her spoon. She took a bite and it was delicious. It had some kind of leaves in it.

'That's not going to fill you up,' he said. 'You'd better order something else. How's that gumbo?'

'It's great,' she said, tearing open another pack of crackers. 'It's real good.'

'Why don't we order some shrimp to go along with this? I'm afraid you're not going to get enough with just that.'

'If you want to,' she said.

He signaled the waiter and handed him his empty tray and picked up hers and set it in front of him, then ordered a pound of boiled shrimp and kept eating. Once in a while he would smile up at her. She ate all the gumbo and the shrimp arrived just as she finished. Outside the window the light began to lessen and the boats in the harbor became less distinct, the masts starting to fade into the coming darkness. When she looked out again the people had started leaving from the beach. He didn't drink anything else but she had two more beers. At some point the waiter came and lit a candle and cleared the dishes away. He brought the bill and Chris handed him a credit card. The place was starting to fill up with people and it began to get noisier.

And then at some point he was leading her out and he was holding her hand and she felt like she had whenever Sam took her out and then drove her back home. Almost. The front seats of the van were high-backed and soft and deep and the stereo lulled her with clear string music and the sigh of brushes on cymbals. They drove up the highway and looked at the lights and the houses and Jefferson Davis's home with its long white fences and the big old trees standing in the yard. He reached back for another beer from the cooler. She had a cigarette going in her hand. The road led smoothly out of town somewhere, a soft sand road and houses set back from it with their mailboxes, horses standing in pastures and the smell of the ocean coming in through the windows. The van riding like a big boat itself and cushioning her from the bumps, him talking and her talking and the night stretching out before her and no worries now, just glad to be with somebody again once more taking care of her and letting her know that everything was going to be all right now, that she could ease up, that she was in good hands. In gratitude she leaned over and kissed him. His eyes glittered where they stared through the windshield at the trees passing by.

He was already inside her when she woke up. A dim bulb was burning in the ceiling over his head so that she saw first the top of his head thrusting against the backdrop of the light. At first she was scared and then she got mad. She tried to push him off but he threw a hard forearm like a steel bar against her throat and when she tried to push him again he rammed her head back against the armrest and told her to be still, but she could not. He started panting in her ear. And in just a moment it was over for him. He turned his face up and strained against her and she said, 'Why you chicken-shit.' He lay there for only a moment and then he was coming off her even as she was going for his eyes with her fingernails. He slapped her and knocked her back. He reached for his shorts and underwear. The jack handle was sticking out from under her front seat and she reached and got it and caught him half-turning, a look of surprise coming onto his face, and the lick she gave him slammed his head against the brown pile carpet that lined the walls. Blood came out of his mouth and he spit out a tooth and tried to say something but she hit him again and then he was still, lying there naked curled on his side with one foot almost into the leg hole of his underwear and his tiny dick shrinking as she watched it, glistening, leaking.

He had pulled only her panties and shorts off. One of her sandals was still on her foot. She found the other one in the floor and put it on and then took it back off and kicked the other one off and slipped on her panties and shorts and slid her feet back into the sandals. How to get out. She saw the handle for the door and pulled up on it but it wouldn't move. She tugged harder and the whole side of the van moved backward and she didn't know how he had gotten her back here in the first place. She had no idea where they were.

She stepped out onto the sand. A cool breeze was blowing and she could see mounds of sand with tall grass growing on them. It had to be open water out past that, it was so dark. The lights on the other side were far far away.

It took her a minute to find her purse. It was lying in the wheelwell by the front seat and she looked through it by the cab light to see that her money was still in there. He wasn't a thief evidently. She could feel what he had put into her oozing out. She stuffed everything back into her purse and then noticed that the keys were still in the ignition. She looked back at him. A small trickle of blood had come out over his lower lip and was seeping into the carpet. But he was breathing, little bubbles of blood frothing. Still she almost went ahead and hit him again.

She ended up dragging him by both feet out into the sand. She left his clothes in the back.

She slid the side door shut and closed the passenger door and went around and got behind the wheel. One more thing to thank Sam for.

It cranked at the first turn of the key. She groped for the lights and found the switch and pulled them on. She knew R was reverse and D was drive. Gas on the right, brake on the left. She slipped it into reverse and backed up until the lights were on both him and a clear trail that showed the tracks the tires had made on the way in. For a moment she considered running over him. Instead, she pulled it down into drive and pressed on the gas. She looked at the gauge. It was almost full.

She woke in the van beside the beach. It was not yet daylight but dawn was beginning to break out there at the rim of the water. She left the headlights on just to make sure that he'd have more trouble whenever he found it. And wishing more and more now as she started walking back up the street that she'd done something more to him. Thinking about him being up in there where her baby was where Sam had put it.

Only once in a while did a car or a truck come by. She crossed the road without any trouble and went up to the corner and turned up the hill.

It took her thirty minutes to get back up to the trailer park and when she stepped into the yard the car was there, parked beside a pretty new pickup, and she could see a light burning in the back room where she had slept. It was full light by now and she listened to hear what she could. A thin squeaking.

She moved around to the end of the trailer where a narrow screened window was cranked open near the roof. The trailer was shaking very gently, and she could hear some man saying, 'Oh God, baby, oh *fuck*, baby.'

She went back around to the front yard and walked over to the picnic table. It was wet with dew and she reached into her purse for the bottom half of her swimsuit and wiped a place dry to sit on. She sat. She unwrapped the pack of smokes Chris Dodd had bought her and tapped one out, found her lighter, lit it. The main thing she was wondering about was whether or not the children were in there, too.

After a while she got sick at her stomach and walked

out by the street and leaned against a tree and threw up a couple of times. She wiped her mouth and took another drag of the cigarette and headed back toward the picnic table. She didn't want to sit there and listen to it, but she was tired and she had to sit somewhere. She walked off to one corner of the yard but she could still hear it, the grunting and the panting. And she didn't want to sit on the ground. She went back to the table, and sat down to wait for the fucking to be over.

After a while the RV began to shake very gently again. She pulled her cigarettes out of her purse and laid them on the table beside her. The sun started coming up.

It was almost seven before a man emerged, an older guy in cowboy boots and jeans and a plaid shirt and a Western hat. He tipped this last to her, got into the truck, and spun out. The plates on the rear said Hinds County.

Fay started to get up. She wasn't feeling good. She was hoping that maybe Reena would let her lie down under the air conditioner again and rest. But another truck drove up the street and pulled in and parked beside the car. A man got out of it, glanced at her, then went over and knocked hard on the trailer door. She heard Reena say something and the man opened the door and went in. He pulled the door closed behind him. In less than a minute she heard yelling and things falling and then what sounded like the thud of a body hitting the floor. Then it was quiet. The man stepped out of the door holding some money in his hand. He gave Fay a long stare and she couldn't look away. He was short, with black hair slicked back, and he stood there at the trailer step and counted his money, then looked up.

'I got a job for a good-looking girl like you. Easy money. You could probably make about three hundred a night.'

She only dumbly shook her head. He crammed the

money deep into his pocket and winked at her and got into the truck and left.

She was scared now. She went over to the step and pushed open the door. Reena was on the floor in a red gown and she was pushing herself up on one hand, trying to get up.

When she saw Fay coming, she hung her head back down, and her dark locks shook. 'Aw shit,' she said.

Fay helped her get up to her knees, then up on one leg, and Reena's fingers dug into her arm for support. She led her over to one of the benches next to the table and helped her sit down. There was a splotch of color on Reena's cheek and a knot was growing under one of her eyes. She put her elbows up on the table and leaned over it with her head hanging down. She raised her face long enough to say, 'Get me that whiskey in the cabinet.'

She pointed and Fay went to it and opened it. There was tequila, bourbon, gin. She took down a pint of Jim Beam that was half full and looked in the cabinet next to it and found some glasses. She brought them over to the table and Reena leaned back and opened the bottle and picked up a glass and poured a drink. She held out the bottle.

'You want some?'

Fay shook her head and watched her drink a straight shot of the whiskey. Reena made a face and then poured another one. She turned sideways in the seat to sip at the next drink. She looked up at Fay.

'Be a sweetheart and get me my cigarettes and matches out of the bedroom. If you don't mind.'

Fay got up and went back there. The covers were mussed on both beds and there were glasses and beer bottles scattered around. The stubs of thinly rolled cigarettes lay in an ashtray.

'Bring me one of those roaches,' Reena called.

'What's that?'

'Those roaches in the ashtray. I know there's two or three in there. Bring me one.'

Fay picked up one that was about an inch long. She got the cigarettes and the matches and took them out to her.

'Thanks,' Reena said. She hung the roach in her mouth and slipped a match from the box and scratched it and held the wavering tip of fire to the joint and lit it. When she exhaled the first time Fay recognized the smell. What those boys had given her to smoke in the trailer. Only it was in a pipe then. She still remembered how bad she felt when she woke up that night.

Reena took three hits and offered it to Fay, but she shook her head. Reena ducked her face and finished it, sucked it down until it was only a tiny scrap of smoking paper that she had to hold tightly between the tips of two fingers. Then she dropped it into an ashtray and blew out a big cloud of smoke. She poured some more whiskey into the glass.

'Well. Do I look like hell?' she said.

'You gonna have a black eye,' Fay said. 'Who was that guy?'

Reena waved one hand to dismiss him.

'You don't want to know who that guy was.'

'What did he want?'

'He wanted some money and he got it, too. The son of a bitch. I wish Chuck had been here.'

'With that other man here?'

'What other man?'

'The one with the cowboy hat.'

'Where'd you see him at?'

'I saw him when he came outside. I was sittin on the picnic table.'

'Doing what?'

'Nothin. I was just kind of sittin there.'

'Shit,' Reena said. 'I was just about to go to sleep when that prick came in. Are you sure you don't want a drink?'

'I've had enough for one night I think. Why don't you let me help you to bed?'

Reena waved a shaky hand at her and took another drink.

'I can't go to bed now. I'm catching a buzz now. It'll be hours before I'll be able to get to sleep now. If that asshole had left me alone I'd be asleep. What happened to you? I come back right before dark and you were gone.'

'I took off down the street,' Fay said. 'I was almost out of cigarettes and I was hungry. Then I went down on the beach and I met this guy. He took me out to supper.'

'Yeah?' Reena was studying her and she seemed agitated. 'Yeah?' she said again.

'I drank a bunch of beer and I must've passed out. I woke up and he was on top of me. Had it in me.'

'God,' Reena whispered. 'Men are so mean.'

'I knocked some of his damn teeth out.'

'Good.'

'And left him naked in this place he took me to.'

Reena smiled. 'You did?'

'I drove his van back up here and left it.'

Reena looked at the glass and poured some more whiskey into it. She swirled it around in there and then just sat looking at it.

'I had it happen to me one time too,' she said. 'Coming home from work one night. I didn't even call the police.' She looked up. 'A person like me, some people can do like they want to with me.'

After a while Reena got up and made Fay some coffee, but kept drinking the whiskey until there was only a little left. When she finished that she got some gin and mixed something and sipped it. Fay got a cup of the coffee and Reena got down a pan and filled it with water and boiled a couple of eggs apiece for them. They peeled them and ate them with salt and pepper. Then they went back to the tiny bedroom, took off their clothes, and lay down and went to sleep.

Chuck woke them up at two o'clock calling Reena's name. Fay opened her eyes and saw her get up and pull on a robe and go out. She lay there with the sheet over her and heard the children's voices up front and out in the yard. The thought hit her that she needed to get out of this place and go somewhere else, but she could hardly think about moving right now. So she drifted back off to sleep with the sounds of arguing in her ears. Like so often before.

She woke finally and knew she had to go down in the bushes and get her suitcase. There were a few more changes of clothes in there and some clean underwear. She felt incredibly dirty and it seemed that already she had gone back to the way she had been living before she met Sam.

It was just as she'd thought it would be when she went out to the front room again: everybody gone. She went back for her sandals and picked her way down through the bushes behind the trailer and found again the mattress piled up against the boxes and retrieved her suitcase, carried it back to the trailer, opened it on Reena's bed and took out a few things, clean underwear, a ribbon for her hair. She closed the front door and found some soap and standing naked at the little sink washed herself as best she could and dressed in the clean clothes. Then at the same small sink she washed out the old underwear and the shorts and the blouse and the swimsuit and then looked through a window at the back of the trailer and saw a clothesline out there at the edge of the bushes. She carried the clothes out there and found some clothespins and hung her things up to dry. Eyeing the sky and the late hour and knowing they probably wouldn't be dry before dark. But where did she have to go anyway?

She ate a piece of bologna from the tiny icebox. It was curled and dry. She went out and sat on the picnic table again. The evening grew darker and she could hear the cars and the traffic down on the road that ran along the beach and she wondered if the van was still sitting there.

She was still sitting there when full dark came. Her supply of cigarettes was dwindling again, but there was nothing to do really but sit there and smoke and watch for the lights of cars coming up the street and try to tell if one of them was Reena coming in. There was some music playing up the street somewhere but she didn't think it came from a radio. It sounded more like a live band. She thought about walking down that way just to have something to do.

She decided to get up and get her purse and go down the sidewalk. She thought maybe she could find another store somewhere that had something to eat.

She went back inside and closed the suitcase and put it on the bed she'd been sleeping on. There wasn't much in it anyway, nothing worth stealing. She wasn't worried about Reena but she didn't like Chuck's looks. Her money was in her purse and she had that on her arm.

Going down the sidewalk the music got louder as she got closer. Before she got to the corner she could see cars and pickups parked all up and down the street and people moving around in a yard on the right. That was where the music was coming from. She saw people dancing and some of them looked to be about her age. Two boys with guitars were up on the porch with a couple of black boxes with red lights sitting between them. There was a drummer behind them and she stopped under a tree for a minute to see what was going on. It looked like everybody out there was drinking beer and smoking cigarettes. A pang of something went through her. She wondered what would happen if she went back to see Sam. Would he put her in jail if he found out what she'd done? There wouldn't be any way to find out unless she went back, and then if things were bad, it would be too late. She ached for him. And this baby she was carrying inside her, what was going to happen to it? She had to be in some place where she could raise it when it came and it had to be a safe place for both of them. She remembered her little sister being born in an old barn they had found and how her mother had lain in a pile of hay with only a few thin blankets for comfort for two days before she could get up and how scared she had been, thinking her mother was going to die. A long time ago, she guessed about twelve or thirteen years now. She wasn't really sure how old Dorothy was. And Gary. She thought about him less and less. Worrying about her own stuff. Living the good life with Sam those few short months. She could always hitchhike back home. But that would just put more of a burden on her mother than she already had now. She couldn't go back, not to Sam and not to her family. Maybe something would happen. Maybe tomorrow she could go out and try to find a job somewhere. She had to do something. She couldn't just keep staying in that trailer like that.

She moved out from under the tree and walked past the yard, watching the young people dancing and listening to the music. Several grills were going and she could smell food cooking and it made the spit start up in her mouth. She could see somebody turning hamburgers on one of the grills and dishing some of them out to other young people who stood with plates in their hands. She walked by, looking. A few people waved at her and she waved back and smiled. But they didn't invite her in to share their party and she went on down the street alone into the darkness that waited beyond the last street lamp she could see.

The sand below the crest of the beach was smooth and wet and there were lights moving far away out there in the distance. The beach was almost deserted except for an occasional solitary person still sitting on a beach towel in the darkness. She walked by two figures moaning and struggling against each other in the sand, the girl on her back with her legs locked around the boy's back and his white buttocks moving up and down on her. After a while she found a place where there was nobody close by and she sat down in the sand and studied the darkness. The cries of the birds were hushed now and there was only the sound of the traffic on the road, which had slowed down some. Sunday night and people going back home, back to jobs on Monday, children back to playing in their yards.

After she rested, she got up and brushed off the seat of her pants and headed toward the lights down the beach. Cafés and stores and gas stations. She walked slowly and ignored the occasional catcalls from boys in pickups and cars still cruising up and down the beach road. A long brown limo pulled up beside her at one point and kept pace with her for a while, but when she turned her head to look at it the black glass in the windows reflected only her own distorted face and the figure of her walking along beside it. She didn't know what to make of it but knew that somebody was inside watching her. Finally it sped on up the road and was gone.

She kept walking and looking out over the beach. It was almost completely empty now and once again she could see the trash that people had left, paper cups, beer cans, plastic bags. A small dog trotted along down there, stopped and watched her for a moment, then went on, disappearing into the blackness. She could see the harbor lights up ahead and knew she was close to the restaurant where they had eaten last night. She seemed to remember a gas station near there and a few stores. They had to have something to eat in some of those places.

By the time she got to the harbor the wind had begun to pick up and dark clouds scuttled along the belly of the sky. Thunder rumbled far off and in the distance through the clouds came flashes of light flickering. All she needed now was to be caught out in the rain. She started walking a little faster.

When she went by the restaurant it looked like a slow night. And she didn't want to go in there again. She kept walking.

A brightly lit service station was across the road. She could see people pumping gas and there were beer signs in the windows, a sign that said SANDWICHES. The traffic wasn't heavy right now so she went ahead and crossed both lanes, running just a bit on the other side when she saw cars coming. One car flashed its lights at her and as it zoomed by she saw that it was a police car. She watched for the brake lights to come on but they didn't. Maybe they had her description already. She'd get the sandwich and then she'd get off this main street. She didn't want to walk back up to Reena's trailer but she didn't know what else to do.

Another hundred feet and she was walking across the concrete in front of the station, angling past some trash barrels where two big cats were tearing into a bag of trash somebody had left on the ground there. Inside it was clean and bright and she went immediately to the big coolers in back and grabbed a cold drink from a rack of them and opened it and took a sip. She looked around. The other coolers were full of beer, juice, milk. She walked past them, looking into each. They had sandwich meat and cheese. There were racks of potato chips and shelves of candy bars. She picked up a Mounds bar and a bag of plain chips and went back down the coolers to another box sitting on a table. Inside it were all kinds of sandwiches. She leaned closer to look and saw ham and turkey, egg salad, pimiento, all kinds of things to eat. She opened the glass door and reached in for a thick ham and cheese, then carried her things up to the counter and waited. There was a short line and some kid was running the register. He looked like he was about fifteen or sixteen. Two men in front of her paid for gas and bought cigarettes and beer. She moved up after the last one had gone and set her things down, drew in a breath, said, 'Hey. How you doing tonight?'

The boy nodded and smiled shyly.

'Pretty good, I reckon. That all for you?'

'Let me have a pack of Salem Lights, please.'

234

She ducked her head and went for the money in her purse. When she raised her head he was searching in a rack over his head and he pulled down the cigarettes and tossed them onto the pile of stuff there and started ringing up her stuff. He looked up when he was done.

'That'll be five twenty-four, please.'

She pulled out a ten and handed it to him. He made change and gave it to her. She thanked him and went out the door sipping on the cold drink and wondering where she could go to eat.

Back on the sidewalk she looked both ways. Far up the street she could see a sign that said BUS STOP and she headed that way. Bugs were swarming around the street lamps set on top of the high poles and the traffic was sparse again and slow-moving. She knew there would be a bench at the bus stop where she could sit and eat. She didn't think she could wait until she got all the way back to Reena's trailer.

It took a minute or two to walk up there. She knew she had to get out tomorrow and look for a job. She figured she probably looked awful and she wished there was some way she could take a shower and wash her hair. But if there was a shower in Reena's trailer she hadn't seen it. She wondered how they stayed clean, and then remembered that for many years of her life she'd had not much of a way to stay clean, either.

It took her twenty minutes to eat and when she was done she stuck the candy bar in her purse and put the trash into the bag, took the last sip from the can and dropped it in there, too, got her purse up on her arm and stepped over to the trash can on the corner and threw the sack in there. There didn't seem to be anything else to do but walk back up to Reena's and wait for her to come in. But no telling what time that would be and she didn't look forward to sitting there waiting. She guessed she could go on in and get back on that bed and go to sleep.

But she didn't want to be alone in there if Chuck

came in by himself. She sat back down on the bench and looked across the road. Even the harbor lights were starting to dim now, and the restaurant where she had tried to eat the oysters had gone dead black. Suddenly she didn't want to be out on this street by herself, so she got up and started walking back the way she'd come, looking around as she went.

There was only one place down the beach that seemed to be still going. It was the little brick shack with the cutout of a woman in black silhouette rising from the roof. She had passed it on her way over here but she hadn't paid it much attention. It looked like a beer joint or something to her. When she got alongside it and looked at it from across the road, there under a pole that held a bright light was Reena's car, or at least it looked like her car. She stopped on the sidewalk to take a better look at it. It seemed to be the same shape, the same size, the same color, tan with a brown roof.

The wind blew at her hair and she held her purse in both hands. A light pierced the sky from somewhere far off the ground, a wide beam that traveled in an arc and then was gone.

The parking lot over there was full of cars. Maybe she was only in there drinking. But if she was, maybe she could sit down with her, talk to her, maybe try to figure out what she was going to do.

She was kind of scared to go over there. She remembered what Sam had said about beer joints and nightclubs and honky-tonks. But she was more scared to walk by herself all the way back up the hill to Reena's now that it had gotten so dark.

It wouldn't hurt anything to go over there for a few minutes. She could stick her head in the door and see if she could catch sight of Reena. If she did, she could stay. If she didn't, she could go. The traffic was light. And she didn't want to be by herself.

She stepped off the sidewalk and went down the slight slope of grass that bordered it, crossed both lanes of the road, and now she was in the parking lot and headed toward the door. There was music inside that she could hear.

Up near the door there was a big sign printed in chalk on a board:

SUNDAY NIGHT LADIES NIGHT
NO COVER
LADIES DRINK FREE

Shit, she thought, *is it Sunday*?

In the morning sun game wardens' boats were gathered in a group at the main landing, spectators between the trees around it, an ambulance with its red light whirling and the Panola County sheriff's cars, his uniformed deputies looking at Alesandra's boat where it was tethered to the bank. Even from that distance Sam could see Tony McCollum's flattopped head. The only question was whether or not his life was over. It was if Fay was in that boat.

He stood there beside his truck a little longer, looking down there, waiting, putting it off. A tarp was spread over the still thing on the front seats, the long form of a body. Going across the levee he'd seen the boat and all the varied uniforms, all the lawmen gathered around like they'd been invited to a party, with more arriving all the time, as if this were just happening. The dispatcher had probably called him at home just now.

Why was she gone and where was she? If she wasn't down there? And if she wasn't down there, who was? Somehow, someway, he should have called and checked on her. He should have made time to do it.

And there was Tony right in the middle of it. And he'd seen everybody, he'd seen a lot. He'd even seen Amy drunk behind the wheel of her car. And Fay at the funeral. Did he see them hug their little dance of grief when it was still just friends? All this trouble over a little blood rising up in an organ, and glances, and looks, and thoughts of the joining of flesh.

There was nothing to do but just go do it. He got back

238

into the truck and closed the door and headed down there before he could think beyond that.

Driving around the curve at the end of the levee it didn't seem real, the posts seemed to be moving by too slowly, and he thought about somebody putting each one of them in one at a time, years ago, some sweaty guy with a hard hat and a posthole digger and a truck with a water cooler strapped to the side. Something done a long time ago maybe under a bad sun.

Tony had turned to face him and he was looking up toward the road. He slowed and put on his blinker and waited for a car to come on past him, then turned down the hill and drove past maybe twenty scattered people watching, folks out for a little weekend fun.

He parked away from the crowd and got his keys. He knew some of these cops, had talked to a few of them at one roadblock or another, at a wreck, a fire. He pulled his own shades out of his pocket and slipped them on. He said a prayer that shamed him: *Lord God don't let it be Fay.*

He was aware of how bright the sun was and he was aware of all the little rocks in the road that he could kind of feel through the soles of his boots. It was going to be a real pretty day.

Tony met him, hand out: 'Hey Sam, we got something bad here.'

He squeezed Tony's hand for a moment, then let it go. He tried to look into his eyes.

'What's up?' he said. His heart was beating fast and to him his voice sounded shaky. Tony turned toward the boat and he turned with him, Tony keeping close to him, talking low.

'Feller out here fishin this mornin found it.' He looked up at Sam for a second. 'It's got a pretty dead lady in it.'

'A dead lady?'

'Oh God,' Tony said. 'She's beautiful. She's been shot.'

He saw woe and grief coming and knew for sure then

239

that he should have kept his dick in his pants.

'Have you . . . ?' he only managed to say. Tony ignored it. They were getting closer to the ambulance and the cluster of cruisers and the men who drove them. Another group of civilians stood under the trees at the edge of the asphalt beside some picnic tables, women with their arms folded and kids in shorts and swimsuits holding doughnuts and their quiet daddies with beer guts and tank tops or Grateful Dead T-shirts and trunks sipping cups of coffee with their elbows hoisted, trying not to miss a thing. You could see their ears cocked. Other people kept driving in and Sam saw a deputy sent by another to stop any more cars from coming down. He passed them and went up the hill, starting to jog, holding on to his gun, the sun shining on his back.

'She looks familiar,' Tony said. 'I don't believe I know her, though.' He sighed. 'How you been doing, Sam? I saw you out on the lake once or twice.'

'Yeah, I saw you,' he said, wondering at *What if it's Alesandra and I have to look at her dead and think about being in the bed with her? What you gonna do then, Sam?*

He nodded and spoke to a few of them, a deputy named Winfred, a game warden he'd eaten breakfast with once named Boo. They didn't have much to say. Nobody did. They were pretty quiet.

Tony stopped and said, kind of loud, 'We waiting on the coroner to move her of course. And David was in Memphis but he ought to be here in an hour or so. I don't reckon it matters to the lady none when she gets moved.' And then he stepped around the side of the boat, walking in water with his nice polished boots as he did so, and he grabbed a corner of the tarp and flipped it back and Sam leaned over and looked into the dead face of Alesandra. Now she wore two small dark holes, one in her cheek and one in her chin like pictures he'd seen of the Dalton gang laid out on boards and Clyde Barrow on his slab. Her face had been washed clean by the rain and even in death she twisted his heart.

And then Tony spoke up.

'You know her, Sam?'

It seemed later that it took him too long to answer, and he guessed that should have been answer enough to those watching him and probably had been. But he said, 'Yeah. I . . . it's her. I know her.'

Tony just nodded. 'I thought maybe you did, Sam.'

And he flipped the tarp back over and covered her face.

It took place at a picnic table up in the shade, the questions and answers, him smoking and trying to keep his head but unable to concentrate fully because of wondering how it had happened. Fay was gone because she had done it. It was not lost on him that he was the only other person who knew this. His hands were shaking from looking at Alesandra and he couldn't hide it.

Yeah, he knew her name, it was Alesandra Farris and she was from Jonestown outside Clarksdale and no he didn't know her daddy's name, never had met him. But he knew her?, Yeah, he knew her, How did he know her?, Well, he just knew her, he knew her, and then he just plain said it. Better now than on a witness stand when he'd have to take it back or lie: 'How do you think I know her, Tony? You saw me with her.'

And everything he'd been thinking about Tony and hoping wasn't true suddenly was. McCollum stepped back from the table, and he was pissed off, and the cuffs of his neat trousers had mud and grass on them, and he pointed down the hill where the coroner was snapping Polaroids and tossing the peel-off things into the water where they curled and floated like leaves.

'I've looked up to you for a long time, Sam,' he said. 'But that's a fuckin murder charge for somebody right there.' He dropped his finger. 'Cause that's a fuckin murder.'

'How you know it's murder?' he said, couldn't stop himself.

'She didn't shoot herself in the face twice.'

He had to look away. He could see McCollum studying him. He knew what would happen next. She'd be gone to Jackson now for an autopsy at the state crime lab. They would look inside her body at all of her parts, saw open her head, pull out some of her organs and cut little bits of them off for testing. He knew they would find alcohol, marijuana, cocaine too, he'd seen her use it. A man in a smock with a mask over his mouth would speak into a microphone mounted over a table while he cut with his scalpel and slowly learned all her secrets. And her family? What about them? What would they do and what would her daddy do if he had loved Alesandra as much as Sam had loved Karen?

He'll be like me, Sam thought, and he didn't believe there had been a time in his life when he'd been this scared. It was hard not to show it. Tony had always been polite and friendly before this, always waving, but now he'd changed. How much would he have to tell? And would it all get told? He thought he knew which question was coming next. He tried to be ready for it.

'Well,' Tony said. 'You don't know nothing about all this I assume.'

'I don't know anything about it,' he said. 'I ain't got a clue. But it's awful to see her like that.'

'When's the last time you did see her?'

He didn't even have to think. 'Weeks ago. I didn't even know she was up here,' he said, and was glad in one way that it was the truth. What the hell had she done to Fay to make her do that? And where in the hell did it happen? Down here? Not likely. Said a fisherman found her in a boat, where in a boat? Out by his place maybe? He was scared to ask anything and knew that would probably look wrong to Tony.

OK, then. Fay probably wasn't dead. Maybe. Fay might be on the bottom of the lake. Maybe. But there

242

wasn't any need in thinking that until there was a reason to.

Somebody came up and said something to Tony and he nodded and whoever it was went away. Tony put his hands in his pockets and Sam noticed he had a nice watch.

'I guess I need to talk to you some more later, Sam,' he said. 'I know you ain't mixed up in this no way. Just a personal question? If it ain't too personal?'

'OK,' Sam said. 'If it's not too personal.'

'How long you known this woman?' he said, which was just another way of asking him if this had been going on while Amy was still alive.

He thought about it. No answer seemed the wrong one now.

'I've known her for a while,' he said, and he thought that was all of it, and he got up from the bench and started to go.

'What about that girl who was with you at your wife's funeral? Who was she?'

'A friend of my wife's,' he said, and it was not a lie, and then he did turn away, and go on back to the truck.

At 9:14 and with full dark he was getting out of his cruiser just past the Prophet Bridge at the Yocona River where hundreds of swifts live and flare out over the water in waves of wings in the daytime. The broad current is slow and muddy and power boats glide up and down between the banks of the willow trees. But the birds were asleep now and the Ford Pinto stopped in front of him had been weaving in front of him for the last two miles. He had already radioed in for the tag and had gotten a name and a residence at Union West. The beer joint on 315 was back behind him and lots of drunks ran this road.

He could see two heads in the front seat. One of the heads bent over and did something in the floorboard and came back up. With a hard flip of his thumb he unsnapped the strap from around the hammer and put his hand around the cool checkered grip, the S and the W intertwined in a gunsmith's art. The flashlight's beam was strong and he stopped at the left quarter panel and told the driver to get out of the car slowly. The door opened, a leg came out, a foot rested on the gravel beside the road. Alesandra's face and the bullet holes.

'Get out and put your hands on the front fender.'

The driver tried to get out, leaned back, and Sam saw his hands come out and grip the door and the side of the car and pull himself erect. He tried to watch them both at the same time. Probably nothing worse than a couple of drunks but that might have been what Charlie Banks thought last year when he stopped somebody outside Clarksdale and got drilled four times with a .380, two of them just beside his nose.

He stood where he was. The driver had cut the motor off but had left the headlights on. They lit up the freshly mown grass and the Coke cans strewn out there in front of the car.

'Come on out and stand up,' he said. He kept waiting, not relaxing, ready to draw the gun if he had to. He wasn't worried about the driver. He was worried about that other head up front and what it had been doing in the floorboard. Maybe only hiding a bag of marijuana or a few cans of beer. Maybe reaching for a pistol.

'You better move it, man,' Sam said.

'I'm tryin,' the guy said, and finally came on out of the car, stood erect, shuffled past the door and around it and put his hands on the hood. He was an old man, with gray hair and saggy pants. His upper torso wore only a stained undershirt, and he had on some of those rubber sandals like people wear to the beach.

Sam eased up to the open door, slowly, the warm weight of the pistol grip in his hand. He shined the light in on the passenger and stopped. A young woman sat holding a baby in her arms. It was crying and she was rocking it, hushing it, trying to get it to stop crying. The woman looked up at him. She wasn't any older than Fay and her long black hair was snarled and tangled. The old man was still leaning against the hood. Sam put the flashlight on him. He looked away.

'You better cut those headlights off,' Sam said. 'You'll run your battery down.'

The old man started to move but Sam saw the girl lean over and reach forward and the lights went off. His own cruiser hummed steadily behind him and lit up the car he stood beside and he put the gun back in the holster and snapped the strap down. He checked the tag again. It was in date. He moved the flashlight around. The tires were slick and he could see a long broken place across the windshield. He knew it probably didn't have a current inspection sticker on it. It looked like folks down on their luck who'd just found some more. He stepped closer to the old man.

'Where you been tonight, sir? You can take your hands off the hood and turn around.' He glanced in at the girl. She was still rocking and trying to shush the baby. It looked to be only a few months old by the dim interior light.

The old man wobbled and faced him. He wiped at his stubbled chin with the back of one hand.

'I took my granddaughter and her baby to the hospital,' he said. 'I know I was weavin some. I don't see too good at night no more.'

'You been drinking anything?'

'No sir,' he said, and stood a little straighter. 'I quit that seven years ago.'

'Well.' Sam searched for some words. 'That's the reason I stopped you. Weaving. I thought you might be drinking.'

He could see now that the old man wasn't drunk. Hated like hell he'd even pulled him over.

He heard the girl say in a low voice close to the baby's head, 'It's OK now we'll be home in a little bit don't cry Mama's here,' and the baby start up again in a thin wail, shaky and tremulous and weak. And standing there somehow he knew for sure that it was going to die. And if he knew that, why couldn't he know where Fay was?

'You want to see my license?' the old man said.

'No,' Sam said, and he took a breath in and a step back. 'That's OK. Y'all headed home?'

The old man nodded eagerly.

'Yes sir, sure am. We got to git Rebecca back home. She's sick but they don't know whatall's wrong with her. We got to take her to Memphis tomorrow.'

He didn't want to look in at the girl and the baby again, but he did. The girl caught him with her eyes and her fear. She had one breast out now, and it was flat and white, and the baby had fastened to it, cheeks hollowing. The girl rocked it and stared at Sam as if he could lift her burden from her. But there was nothing he could do for her and he just told them to go on and be careful, to drive safely, thinking of how a road at night was dark and full of curves, and saying that he was sorry if he had scared them, that he sure hadn't meant to.

The sign outside said LOVE CAGE. Fay stepped closer and heard again the music, could see through the barred windows the play of blinking lights inside. Out front was a poster of a naked blonde. She opened the door and smoke rolled out as if the place were on fire. The first thing she saw was the stage. Her eyes were drawn to it because of the way it was lit up and there on a hardwood floor in front of a purple sequined curtain a young woman with white hair and wide hips shook her titties at the men gathered around her and cupped them in her hands as if she were offering them out to be taken. The music was thunderous and distorted, and the smoke hung heavy in all places in the room. A bar off to the right, shadowy figures drinking and talking.

She stayed by the door for a minute, looking around, trying to see Reena. The girl on the stage pranced in her high heels and she was naked except for a gold swatch of cloth between her legs where the corners of dollar bills poked out in little clusters that hid her navel from sight. The men in chairs at the edge of the stage were packed in two deep and they kept yelling to the girl and she kept leaning over as one or another half stood to put another bill in her little pants. She'd wink at them and smile, turn her backside to them, shake it, the flesh on it loose and wobbling, and the more she shook it the louder they yelled.

Fay wasn't sure what to do. There didn't seem to be any tables. Out of the gloom at the back of the room a man came forward with a cigar stuck in the side of his mouth and a stack of bills in his hand. He made his way

forward among the tables and the outstretched legs of
the patrons without looking at any of them and without
stumbling in the darkness or making a misstep. He was
tall, heavy, wearing a black shirt and black pants, white
cowboy boots, his red hair combed back straight and
shiny with something. His nose looked broken more
than once. He stopped beside her, ran his thumb across
the bills like a man riffling a deck of cards. He said,
'You want to sit down?'

She nodded. His eyes were squinched against the
smoke coming from the cigar and he turned and
pointed to the opposite corner: 'Over there's one.' And
he turned on his heel and left her, went back into the
shadows from which he had come. She looked where
he had pointed at one empty table sitting back against
the wall. Men were starting to turn and look at her
now. Other girls were moving among the tables carrying drinks and beer on round trays and they chewed
their gum and appraised her critically as she moved
among the tables and headed for the one chair she
could see. Men were talking to her and she couldn't
understand what they were saying. On the stage the
girl bent over with her backside to the audience and a
lean man stood up and shoved a five dollar bill in the
crack of her ass. She turned and blew him a kiss and
walked across the stage with the bill waving from her
behind until finally it fluttered to the floor. Two men
were on Fay before she ever got to her table. One
touched her elbow, the other her waist, and she pulled
their hands away from her. They moved closer to her
and she turned and backed to the wall and sat down
with both of them leaning into her.

'You want a drink?' one said.

'What you want?' the other one said. 'You want a
beer?'

She looked from one face to the other and saw a waitress watching her and the two men as she headed over
to where they were. Fay just wanted them to get away,
didn't want either one of them to buy her a drink

because she knew then he'd want to sit down with her.

'I saw her first, you son of a bitch,' one of them said to the other.

'Tough fuckin shit, buddy,' the other one said, and then they were pushing at each other. She drew back as they tumbled over a table and upset it, drinks falling to wet the floor. People jumped up from around them and the girl on the stage hesitated in her moves. The waitress with her tray stepped around the two rolling and cursing bodies and stood next to Fay.

'Didn't take you long to get something started,' she said. 'You want something to drink?' She scratched behind her ear with a pencil and studied the two fighting men without interest. 'One goddamn time in my life I'd like to work in a place that had a little class.'

'Why don't somebody stop em?' Fay said.

'Somebody will. In just a second. Now you want something to drink?'

'Can I get a beer?'

The waitress suddenly took three steps back and got up against the wall as the big man in the black clothes bent over her panting admirers. Their shirttails had come out of their pants and Fay saw one's hairy crack. The big guy hauled them to their feet by their collars and tugged them apart. They swung at the air half-heartedly, already winding down, but he held them for just a moment anyway and studied them, and then with one swift movement he slammed their heads together. It sounded like somebody dropping something wet that burst on the floor. He let them fall. They made not a sound and the music stopped. He turned his head to the stage.

'Turn that *fucking* music back on,' he said, and bent down and grabbed them up again by their collars and dragged them through cigarette butts and puddles on the floor toward the front door. Another tune started up, faster and louder than the last.

The waitress smiled a strange smile at Fay and rolled her eyes toward the bouncer as if to say *He don't play.*

She walked away. Fay watched him let go his hold on one of his customers long enough to open the door and hold it with his knee. He pulled the first one half erect and then booted him out the door, kicking him hard in the ass, then reached for the other one. That one left the same way and the door slammed shut. Once again the bouncer went back to his lair in the smoky gloom.

The white-headed woman had left the stage and a short girl took her place. She was very pretty with good legs and long brown hair and her beautiful breasts. She must have been a favorite because a great cheer went up when she came across the stage. She finished dancing to the number that was playing and then a slow song came on and she began to dance, waving her arms slowly, moving her hips gently side to side. They screamed and tossed dollars onto the stage. She turned and the lights on the stage dimmed, the voices hushed while she writhed upright. Colored round balls of light, yellow and orange and red, began to slide over her. She closed her eyes while they threw more money, balled it up and sent it toward her, the green wads sometimes bouncing off her back or legs to land and briefly on the stage roll and then come to a halt. Fay thought it was sad and beautiful. Wished she could move her body in that way. For Sam.

The number finished and the stage lights went off. It was totally black inside the joint for less than a minute and when the lights came on the stage was empty. The waitress walked over and set Fay's beer on the table. The beer was about four inches high.

'What I owe you?' Fay said, opening her purse.

The waitress wasn't looking at her when she spoke.

'Drinks are free for ladies tonight. You can tip me if you want to.'

'How much?' Fay said.

'That's up to you.'

'Is a dollar OK?'

The waitress wore her disgust plainly on her face.

'I reckon so if that's all you got.'

Fay dug a dollar out of her purse and put it on the tray. The waitress started to turn away but Fay put her hand out and touched her on the arm. She stopped and looked down at her arm as if she'd been burned.

'Yeah?'

'Is Reena here tonight? You know if she's here?'

The waitress cocked one hip and rested the tray on it.

'Who wants to know?'

'I do,' Fay said.

'Yeah? Who're you?'

'My name's Fay. I been kinda stayin with her some.'

The waitress chewed her gum lazily, pushed it out between her teeth and popped a small bubble with it.

'Oh yeah? She ain't said nothing to me about having company.'

'Is she here?'

'She might be. If she is she's busy right now.'

The waitress seemed to be waiting for her to say something else.

'I thought I saw her car out front,' Fay said. 'She never did come home and I just wondered if she was in here.'

'I'll go look,' the waitress said. 'Fay, right?'

'Yeah. Fay. Thanks.'

'I'll come back by after while,' the waitress said, and then she moved away through the smoke and the tables. The beer hadn't been opened but she popped the top and took a sip from it. It was barely cool. But she was inside. She could drink it slowly and wait to see if Reena was here.

Nobody else tried to come over and talk to her, but more than a few of them kept looking her way. She ignored them. She wondered if Chris Dodd had ever been in here. He probably had. A son of a bitch like him would probably just love a place like this where he could look at naked women and think about raping them.

She got to wondering about where the bathroom might be. Once in a while she saw a man get up and go toward the back, stay gone a few minutes, then come back. She put her cigarettes on the table to show that somebody was sitting there and with her purse in her hand went toward the back. Several men called out to her but she didn't look at them. At the corner she turned to the left and went down a dark hall to the end where two doors stood. The music was still throbbing behind her. She pushed open the door marked WOMEN and turned to see if there was a lock on it. There wasn't. She looked at it for a second. Surely nobody would come in on her. But she hadn't thought she'd ever wake up with somebody fucking her, either. There was a stall and a concrete floor that was wet and an empty paper towel dispenser and a tall gray machine on the wall with a scratched plastic label that said 25¢. She tried to read the tiny words at the top. There was a picture of a beach and an ocean and some palm trees and a woman and a man reclining on a towel in their swimming suits. There were three knobs on the machine. She read slowly, out loud in a low voice: 'Ribbed sen . . . shoo? Delight.'

Then she nodded. Oh. Fucking rubbers. Too bad Sam didn't have one on the first time they did it. He'd always used them later, after that first night. But it didn't make any difference now, did it?

She opened the stall door and looked to see if it had a latch on it. It had one but it was busted.

'Shit,' she said. She could hear the music blaring out there. The men started yelling again so she guessed another girl had come on the stage. It didn't look that hard, really. You probably wouldn't even have to dance that good if you had a good body. Just get up there and twist around some while they threw money at you. She thought she could do that. She might even be good at it if she tried it out.

She didn't want to stay much longer, but she didn't want to walk back up that black street by herself now. If she got another beer she was going to have to tip that girl again. And she was kind of a smartass anyway. Was kind of looking down her nose to her, seemed like. She wondered if she turned tricks too. If all of them did. Sam had been right. It was best to stay out of places like this.

A big woman was on the stage when she came out the door and went back up the hall. A very strange-looking big woman. Fay had picked up more than a few watermelons in Georgia that were not as big as the titties the woman had. It was amazing. She didn't know they could get that big. And how the hell did she carry them around? They were so big that she just had to stand there and look at her for a minute. The men were going crazy, leaping up and yelling and some of them howling like dogs. It was a long black walk back, all right, but this damn place, shit. And what if somebody followed her out? What would she do then? She suddenly wished she had a knife, a Coke bottle, something. The only thing she had was a fingernail file and she could jab that in somebody's eye if worse came to worst.

She made her way through the tables back to her own and felt some of them watching her again. The beer was gone when she sat down but her cigarettes were still there. She wondered why the waitress had taken it when it was plain to anybody who'd picked it up that it wasn't empty, that she wasn't done with it. And then she saw Reena coming by the bouncer back there who reached out an arm and stopped her. Reena had two Budweiser tallboys in her hands. She had on a short red bathrobe. The bouncer said something and she saw Reena shake her head. Then she leaned over and kissed him on the cheek and he patted her on the shoulder and she came out from behind the bar with the two beers. She was smiling at Fay. She tilted her head toward the big woman on the stage who was flopping her chest up and down, the customers still cheering her on. Reena made a crazy face and came on over and set the beers down, leaned over and gave Fay a hug.

'Hey, sweetie,' she said.

'Hey.'

'Let me get me a chair.' She went over to a table and got another chair and slid it over the floor and set it close to Fay. She sat down and reached for the beers, opened them and pushed one across the table. 'Cheers,' she said, and knocked her can against Fay's. She was either drunk or high, maybe both, some new combination Fay hadn't seen before. 'How long you been here?' she said.

Fay picked up the beer and took a sip of it. It was ice cold. Reena had on enough makeup that she couldn't see the black eye very much, but the swelling was still there.

'Not long,' she said. 'How's your eye?'

Reena turned her beer up and drank a long swallow of it, took a breath, then turned it up again. Finally she set it back down.

'Damn I needed that,' she said. 'Wanda come back and said somebody named Fay was out here to see me and I knew I didn't know but one. How you been?'

'I been OK,' Fay said. 'I thought today was one of your days to work at Denny's.'

Reena reached for one of Fay's cigarettes and stuck it in her mouth. Fay found her lighter in her purse and lit it for her. Reena inhaled deeply and blew out the smoke, tilted her head and blew it toward the ceiling. Behind her the big woman had gone into a hard bump and grind. To Fay her ass looked wide as a washtub.

'Aw shit. They fired me,' Reena said.

'Fired you? What for?'

'Little something on my breath. Who gives a fuck? Waiting tables for minimum wage?' She looked around. 'I was the star of this place.' She sipped at her beer again.

'I walked down and got me a sandwich,' Fay said. 'I saw your car so I came on in. I thought you might be in here.'

Reena swung her head slowly and Fay watched her. She didn't seem happy like before as she eyed the

254

people around her. Looking along with her Fay locked eyes with the bouncer. Those eyes seemed to pierce the gloom. Then he looked away. She felt something hard start in her chest, like almost falling asleep and thinking about falling from a high place.

'So what you gonna do?' Reena said. 'You gonna strip or what?'

She made Fay nervous and she sipped at her beer and thought about it.

'I hadn't really decided what to do,' she said. 'I wanted to talk to you some more.'

'And I ain't been around, have I?'

'Well.'

'You seen Chuck.'

'No. Not since the other day.'

'What day?'

'Yesterday, I guess it was.'

Reena lowered her head and Fay could see now that she was pretty drunk. She could see the bouncer watching her, too, but he was watching everything, his eyes moving around the room, constantly scanning. But she liked the way he looked.

'Who's the big guy?' she said, leaning closer.

Reena raised up some, as if she'd been about to go to sleep sitting there.

'Who?'

'Don't look at him,' Fay said. 'The one over there in the corner. The one you were talkin to fore you come over here.'

'Oh.' Reena moved her head. 'You mean Aaron?'

'He busted two guys' heads a while ago. Throwed em out. I thought he'd done killed em.'

'Oh yeah,' Reena said. 'Oh yeah. He's capable of that, too.'

Fay shrank from hearing this. She didn't dare raise her eyes to him now because she knew that if she did those eyes would be looking at her again.

So she faced Reena.

'You think he knows we're talking about him?'

Reena puffed on her cigarette without inhaling, like she didn't know how to smoke.

'That's Aaron,' she said in a low voice that seemed to hold some sort of pride. 'His brother owns this place. And he don't. 'Low. No trouble. See the sign?'

Reena turned and pointed and Fay saw it hanging up there near the ceiling, wreathed in smoke, words she could barely make out:

BE NICE OR LEAVE

Reena grinned.

'By God he means it too.'

She bent over the table and picked up her beer again, and shifted her legs so that the flap of her robe fell open for a moment and Fay could see, couldn't help but see, that she was naked below the waist beneath the robe. She saw Fay's glance and covered herself and giggled.

'Guess I need to get dressed, huh?'

Fay didn't know what to say but she knew now what Reena had been doing. She settled back in the chair and looked toward the stage again. The big woman had finished her act and was picking up the money from the floor and the men around her were clapping and yelling. With two fistfuls of money she walked off the stage and stopped and blew them a kiss as another girl was coming on. This one wasn't even a woman. She was a young girl, probably no more than fifteen or sixteen. The music started up and the girl began to dance and Fay turned back to Reena. She was nodding, almost nodding out. Fay thought her face was going to fall on the table and she pushed her by the shoulder, pushed her upright. Reena gave her a dreamy smile.

'Time to go my darling?' she said.

'I think it is. Let me help you up.'

In a weak and faint voice Reena said, 'That might be a good idea right about now.'

Fay took the cigarette from her fingers and stubbed it

256

out. She put her own cigarettes in her purse and tried to take the beer away from Reena but she wouldn't let her have it. Instead she pulled it to her chest almost like a pouting child and held it with both hands.

'All right,' Fay said, and she stood up. 'Let's go get your clothes.'

Reena motioned vaguely toward the bar.

'Back there,' she said, and she wobbled to her feet.

Fay got her purse and took Reena by the arm and then started trying to get her through the tables. It was tough going. Everybody in there seemed to be drunk by then and the little girl up on the stage had gotten down on her back and was pushing her middle up and down. Reena stumbled once and almost fell but she held on to her beer and Fay guided her by the arm and finally they were beside the bar and headed around the end when Fay saw that they were going to have to walk by the bouncer. He was there on his stool, watching everything, drinking a cup of what she guessed was coffee, but not paying any attention to them in particular.

'Back here,' Reena said, and Fay saw a door back there, and then they were going by him and he even moved his legs aside on the stool to let them pass. The bartender was mixing drinks back there and he barely gave them a glance as they went past. Fay looked at what was back there: a rubber mat on the floor, the butt of what looked like a gun sticking out from a waist-high shelf, tubs of ice and rows of glasses and a big cooler that was open and filled with rows of beer. A row of liquor. Reena pushed open the door and they went into a dim hall with scuffed black-and-white tiles on the floor. There were some doors on either side of the hall and Reena opened the first one on the right and pushed it open long enough for Fay to see the girl with the good legs down on her knees sucking a man with his pants and shorts down around his ankles and his shirttail over his butt.

She stopped what she was doing for a moment and looked up and said, 'Just come right on in.' Then she went back to what she'd been doing. The man was gibbering some stuff and his legs were shaking. Reena shut the door.

'Sorry about that,' she said. There was a door at the end of the hall and she weaved toward it. 'Let's go out here. Give her a few minutes. Get done with her hum job there.'

Fay followed, not too fast. Reena opened the door and stepped out.

'Hand me that brick right there,' she said, and took a sip from a flask that must have been in her pocket.

Fay looked around.

'Where?'

'Right there against the wall.'

Fay looked where she was pointing and stopped to pick up the brick.

'Put it right there, block that door so it won't lock. This door always stays locked. Keeps anybody from coming in the back side while everybody's up front.'

Fay knelt and put the brick down and Reena let the door close against it. There were some lawn chairs leaning against the back wall of the building and she unfolded two of them and set them down.

'Just sit down,' she said. 'She'll be done in a little bit and I can get my clothes. She stays so damn busy. You ain't got another cigarette I can bum, have you?'

Fay opened her purse and dug them out, handed one over, lit it for her. They sat down and looked out toward the water. Out across the black expanse of night and sea and distance came a low sad horn, a long note that hung in the air and gradually faded to nothing. Fay could see dim lights, specks in the night that was the world out there for somebody.

'What's those lights out there?' she said.

'Oil rigs. They're all over the Gulf out there.'

Fay was silent and they sat in silence. It was a few minutes before she noticed that Reena had dropped her head down on her chest and that she was crying. She sat watching her but made no move to comfort her.

After a while Reena raised her face and wiped at her eyes with the hand that held the cigarette and then a door slammed inside. Reena sat there. Another door slammed and then she stood up.

'OK,' she said. 'We can go back in now.'

Fay got up and stood there while Reena refolded the lawn chairs and put them back where they had been. She opened the door and kicked the brick out of the way and they went back in. The dressing room was empty now. Reena shut the door behind them and locked it. She came to Fay and tried to kiss her but Fay turned her face away and took it on her cheek and then Reena stepped back, tears leaking from her eyes and her eyes swimming in those tears, and then it was over. Fay's knees shivered and she shook inside.

A dressing table was there with three chairs and three mirrors with small bright bulbs up and down their sides. Makeup kits and hairbrushes and tubes of lipstick were scattered across the surface of the table.

'Go ahead and sit down while I get dressed,' Reena said. She slipped loose the belt around her waist and threw her shoulders back and she stood naked there in front of her. Fay tried not to look, but it was too easy to see that there was a bruise on her thigh like an egg and on her left arm, high up, near the shoulder, an even bigger one than that. Reena reached for some clothes hanging on a rack nearby. Back in a corner was a bed, the covers rumpled. Off past that was a tiny bathroom, the door open so that Fay could see part of the commode. She kept her hands in her lap and tried not to watch Reena get dressed. Through the thin wall she could hear the beat of the music out front and the dim shouts of the men surrounding the stage.

'How late's this place stay open?' she said.

Reena was trying to balance on one foot long enough to get the other foot through the waistband and into the leg hole of her red panties. She had to lean over and get a hold on the table for a moment.

'Sometimes it stays open all night,' she said. She got

259

that first foot in and turned and rested her butt on the lip of the table and poked the other foot through and pulled them up high on her waist. She reached for the red brassiere.

'Long as those suckers are paying money they ain't gonna shut the door. Help me fasten this,' she said, and she moved backward toward Fay, holding the cups onto her breasts, the straps over her shoulders and the back of it hanging down. Fay reached up and found the catches and pulled them together and fastened them. The bra was too small for Reena and the fabric cut into the flesh of her back.

'Thanks,' she said, and she wobbled over and picked up her blouse and put it on and started buttoning it. 'Is there anything to eat at home?' she said.

'There's some bologna and eggs and stuff.'

'How about milk? Those kids'll need some milk in the morning.'

'I don't think there's much,' Fay said.

'We'll stop by the store. Get a few things.'

'OK.'

Reena pulled on a skirt and with her toe fished a pair of brown flats from under the edge of the bed. She sat down in a chair beside Fay and looked into the mirror.

'Damn,' she said. 'I look like I been rode hard and put up wet.' She looked a little longer and said, 'Shit. Like the hind wheels of hell run over me.'

Fay didn't say anything. She watched her pick up a brush and run it through her hair a few times. Last of all she picked up the tallboy and drained the last few drinks from it. She tossed the can and got up.

'Let's go. I got to get my purse back from Aaron.'

Fay didn't much want to hear that, but she figured she could go on out to the parking lot and wait. She got up and followed Reena out the door and back up the hall. It looked like a few people had left when she went back by the bartender, who was sitting on a stool by then and reading a magazine. He didn't look up.

The music was still playing but the volume had

lowered some and there wasn't anybody on the stage now. She could see some of the girls who had been dancing earlier at tables near the front and talking to some of the men and drinking.

Aaron was sitting on his stool and Reena went to him and put her hand on his knee and said something to him. He looked at Fay and then leaned over sideways and reached his hand out and got a purse and gave it to Reena.

Fay could feel the big man's eyes on her but she didn't want to look at him. For something to do she got a cigarette out of her purse and lit it. She glanced toward Reena and saw that she was still talking to him and that he was shaking his head, not like he was mad, just disagreeing with her over something. She wished Reena'd come on. She was ready to get out of here and get some sleep. And already she was hungry again.

The door opened. Two men came in and looked around and headed toward the bar where she was standing. By now Reena was between the big man's opened legs and he was slowly rubbing one hand up and down her back, his head turned and his ear in close to her mouth to catch what she was saying to him. He must have liked what he was hearing because he smiled and nodded. Fay found an ashtray sitting on the bar and pulled it closer to her. The bartender closed his magazine and left it on his stool when the new customers leaned on the bar. They both looked at Fay and then one of them bent toward the bartender and she heard him order a bourbon and Coke and a beer. She turned away and hoped they'd leave her alone. But that wasn't to be. The one closest to her stepped over and put his hand up on the bar close to where hers rested, holding the cigarette.

'You work here?' he said.

She shook her head and looked away. 'No,' she said.

'Why don't you let me buy you a drink.'

She turned her face to him.

'No thank you,' she said. 'I'm ready to go.'

He picked up his wrist and held it close to his eyes, mock surprise showing on his face.

'Go?' he said. 'Why fuck baby, it ain't but eleven-thirty, what's your big hurry?'

'I ain't in no hurry. I'm just ready to get out of here.'

The bartender put the drink in front of him and he reached for it and took a sip. The other guy was paying, counting bills out and putting them on the bar.

'Say you don't work here?' the guy said again.

'No.'

'I be damn. I could have swore I'd seen you up on that stage before. Shaking your titties and all.'

She flung her hair off her face and whirled to face him.

'I don't know you, mister. And you ain't never seen me up on that stage.'

He took another sip of his drink and said, 'Well hell, all you whores are all alike. Long as a man's spending money on you you'll talk to him.'

'Why don't you just leave me alone,' she said.

'Why don't you suck my dick? I'll give you fifty bucks but you got to swallow.'

She couldn't say anything for a few seconds.

'I got fifty dollars right here,' he said. He was digging into the front pocket of his pants and he pulled out a roll of money. 'We'll just go out to my car and you can do it in the parking lot.'

He put the money on the bar while she stared at him.

'You better quit,' she said. 'You better stop talking to me that way.'

He put his hand on her shoulder and moved closer. She could see that he was drunk, could smell the whiskey on his breath now, could see his eyes tinged with red and the stubble of beard that had darkened his chin. She tried to pull back from him but he was strong. He was smiling at her.

'What you gonna do about it?' he said. His fingers had started moving toward her breast when another hand slid over from behind her and locked onto the one that was touching her. It was instantaneous. The man squeezed his eyes shut and showed his teeth and dropped his drink on the bar. The glass turned over and spilled, ice and Coke and whiskey all running back across the dented wood and dripping off the other side. She moved out from under it as the hand lifted from her shoulder and she turned to see the man in black standing there. She could see now that he was crushing the other man's hand in his, that the man's knees were going out from under him, that he was shaking his head and gritting his teeth and trying to form some words. But Aaron just kept leaning in and squeezing the hand and the man who was on his knees by now couldn't say anything at all. His friend was standing behind him with his face white and getting whiter. She heard what Aaron said when he leaned in even closer. It was almost a whisper, but the music had stopped now and so she heard what he said: 'Why didn't you leave her alone when she told you to?'

The man on his knees couldn't or wouldn't say. He just kept shaking his head and now Fay could see the tears pouched that had started to squeeze out between his pinched eyelids. And worse, she could hear the bones breaking in the man's hand. Tiny crackings, the ends of his fingers turning purple. She saw the dark stain spread on the front of his tan slacks when he wetted himself. And still Aaron squeezed him, bending lower and lower, not smiling, just looking into the face going lower and lower until the man was stretched out on the floor with only his hand extended as if Aaron was in the act of helping him up.

'Motherfucker must not a seen the sign!' Reena squealed behind her, and laughed wildly. She was leaning against the wall. She'd gotten another beer from somewhere and was drinking it.

Fay touched Aaron on the shoulder. She didn't think about what she was doing. She just touched him. His face jerked sideways and she saw the anger flash in his eyes but in a second or two it died away.

'Please,' she said.

'What?' Aaron said.

'Please let him go. I think he's learned his lesson.'

Aaron straightened a little but he didn't release his hold. He was looking at nobody but Fay. And then he turned his face back and stared down at the man and seemed surprised to find him holding on to his hand, sobbing quietly on the floor.

'Yeah,' he said, and started to come back from wherever he had been. 'I guess he has.'

He turned him loose then. He straightened fully and swept back a lock of his red hair that had fallen across one eye and put his back to the bar and crossed his arms over his chest.

'Be nice or leave, motherfucker,' Reena said, and took another drink of her beer. 'Let me have a cigarette, Fay.'

People were going out the door in twos and threes, the door shutting behind them. Some of the lights started to come on in the room.

Aaron nudged the man with his foot, prodded his shoulder with the toe of his white cowboy boot. But it was the man's friend he spoke to.

'Get him out of here,' he said. 'Don't bring him back.'

The other man turned up his beer and let it stand upside down against his mouth until he had drained it. He set the empty on the bar and said, 'What about me?'

Aaron didn't take his eyes off the man in the floor.

'You didn't do nothing. I reckon you can come back.'

And then he turned his back on them and went along the bar and over to where Fay was standing. He touched her on the shoulder, just the lightest pressure on that little bone just under the skin.

'You all right?'

She looked up at him. His hand was still very light on her shoulder and she liked it. A man like this could take pretty good care of you, she figured.

'Yeah,' she said.

'Nothing hurt but your feelings?'

'That's all.'

264

'Well,' he said, and took away his hand. 'Some people ain't got any manners. Some of em don't understand but one thing.'

'Thanks for taking up for me.'

'Anytime.'

He turned then and put one hand on the bar and scooted a stool up beneath himself and watched the man's friend trying to get him up out of the floor. Fay watched too. It took a while. The man was still crying and he was holding the broken hand with the unbroken one. He got up on his knees with his friend helping him and wiping at his face sometimes with the unbroken hand and then he was on his feet and his friend was helping him toward the door. But he looked back suddenly and it seemed he suddenly had murder on his mind.

'Don't say nothing,' Aaron said. 'Arthur,' he said. The bartender must have been waiting for him because the shotgun came sliding across the bar, through the puddle of Coke and ice and whiskey butt first and it slid into Aaron's hand and Fay looked at it as he swung it over the bar and into his lap and held the stock against his belly with his hands holding it by the pistol grip and the shortened barrels. It was a nasty-looking little thing, the side-by-side barrels only a foot long.

'Just in case you want to talk about it some more,' he said to the man with the broken hand.

The man just shook his head and he and his friend went on out the door.

'Sometimes they want to talk about it some more,' Aaron said. He sat there for a while, just watching the door. Some more people went out and more lights came on. It was if somebody unseen was switching them on by remote control. The shotgun never moved, never wavered. Then they heard a vehicle start up outside, saw the sweep of headlights past a window, heard the sound of it diminish out toward the road. When he got up from the stool and handed the shotgun back to the

265

bartender who turned and stuck it under the counter again, Fay saw at the small of his back the ivory grips of a pistol tucked tight against his black leather belt.

'Shut it down, Arthur,' he said. 'We're gone.'

It took Fay a minute to realize that she and Reena were leaving with him.

A Shoney's was up the beach three or four miles and now they sat at a booth with plates of eggs and sausage and biscuits and cups of coffee. He was on one side of the booth and she and Reena were on the other.

'You feeling better, Reena?' he said.

She was sipping coffee and orange juice and he'd made her eat a few pieces of bacon and some fruit. Fay was working on her eggs and she'd found some blackberry jelly on the buffet bar and she had a tall glass of cold milk and she was smearing the jelly on her biscuits.

'Not really,' Reena said. 'I was just about drunk.'

Fay hadn't said much, had mostly listened to them talk about the bar and then somebody named Gigi but it looked like Aaron got mad because his face turned red and Reena shut up about whoever she was. She thought it best to just be quiet and listen. But he kept looking at her, little glances she couldn't miss. He'd helped her fix her plate and said things that made her laugh and she'd watched him slip the pistol from his waistband and hide it under the seat of the El Camino he drove. She could see it through the window where she sat, a dark dark red, some kind of fancy shiny wheels, two chromed pipes out the back that had rumbled whenever he'd stepped on the gas.

'I need some more,' he said, and got up. 'How y'all?'

'I'm fine,' Reena said.

'I'm about full,' Fay said.

'You better eat some more.'

'I might get me some fruit in a minute.'

He walked away with his plate and Reena leaned into her, holding her cup at her mouth.

'What you think about him?' she said.

Fay picked up some more eggs and some sausage with her fork. She thought about the way he had slammed those two guys' heads together and what he had done to the man who'd been bothering her.

'Well,' she said. 'I'd say he don't take no shit off nobody.' She bit into the biscuit and scooped some more jelly from her plate. She turned her head a little and could see part of him on the other side of the steam table, his black pants and the bottom of his black shirt moving along slowly, his hands reaching out for more eggs, the spoon he held in his thick fingers.

'He takes care of us,' Reena said. 'He don't let nobody mess with us.'

'What do you mean?' Fay said. She didn't understand about the girl she'd seen on her knees with that man in her mouth. 'What about that girl we saw?'

'You mean the one who was giving that guy the blowjob? Cheryl? I mean you do know what a blowjob is, don't you?'

'I know what a blowjob is,' Fay said.

Reena was looking at her with some interest now, the beginnings of a small grin playing about her mouth.

'Oh yeah?'

'Yeah.' Fay picked up some eggs with her fork and ate them. She cut a link sausage in two and ate half of it.

'You ever give anybody one?' Reena said.

'What you want to know that for?'

'I just want to know. I bet you ain't never give anybody one, have you?'

'Yeah,' Fay said. 'I have.'

Reena sipped at her coffee and reached for the brown pitcher the waitress had left on the table and poured some more into her cup.

'Who?'

'I ain't gonna tell you that,' Fay said.

'That guy the other night?'

'No. I told you I woke up and he was on me.'

'You didn't do nothing with him beforehand.'

Fay sipped at her milk.

'I kissed him a few times. We wasn't making out or nothing.'

'You didn't tell me that.'

'I didn't think about it.'

They sat eating for a few moments.

'I don't get it,' Fay said.

'Don't get what?' Reena reached for some sugar packets and another one of those little cups of milk they give you in such a place.

'You said he don't let nobody mess with you. What about what that girl Cheryl was doing with that guy? He had to ask for it, didn't he?'

'That's different,' Reena said. 'She works there.'

'I don't understand,' Fay said.

'What don't you understand, honey?'

Fay put her fork down and picked up her milk and held it.

'Does people just come in there and ask for it? Why don't he beat em up like he did them guys who were talkin to me?'

'Look,' Reena said. She pulled out the flask again, this time from a purse. She had an empty cup on the seat and she poured into it, then put the flask back. 'A girl lets a man know if she's available. If he talks to her right. They work out the price before they go back to where I got dressed. Aaron just keeps the trouble out of there. I ain't never seen nobody whip him. Take it from me, he's a bad motherfucker. But you don't work there. And those guys were bothering you. He's got rules, like . . . he heard what that guy said to you.' She waved a hand and sipped.

'He don't know me. Why did he take up for me?'

Reena set her cup on the table and then picked it up and drank from it again. Fay watched her lips while she talked to the cup.

269

'He likes for people to behave when they come in there. If a girl and a guy want to go back and get it on and he pays her, there won't be no trouble. If she's willing, it's cool. But don't start no trouble cause he'll throw your ass out in the parking lot.' She looked up, 'I tell you what. He likes you.'

Fay kept eating when she saw him coming back around the corner. He brought his plate to the table and set it down.

'I'll be back in a minute,' he said, and walked away. Fay looked after him.

'Where's he going?' she said.

'Bathroom probably.' Reena drank some more of her coffee and bit off some more bacon.

'What makes you think he likes me?'

'I can just tell. I tell you what, you could do a lot worse down here than to latch on to Aaron Forrest.'

She didn't say anything for a minute. Some walking babies were moving around the steam table, jabbering, their young harried mother trying to herd them, fix their plates, balancing an infant on her hip at the same time. The infant was holding a bottle and once in a while it would turn it up and take a swig. It gave Fay a toothless grin and waved the bottle at her. Fay waved back, a small movement with her fingers while she smiled.

'Ain't that a cute baby?' she said to Reena.

'They're all cute when they're little.' She sighed and set her coffee down. 'I got to get home and see about mine. We still got to get that milk, too.'

'Where you gonna get it at?'

'I'll get Aaron to take me back to my car and we'll stop by the store. He just didn't want me to drive home drunk.'

'You all right now?'

'Yeah. I'm all right. I figure they're home by now. Chuck was supposed to take em over to his mother's this afternoon.'

Fay picked up her milk and drank some of it. She

could see Aaron coming through a pair of stainless steel doors at the back of the room.

'I heard y'all this afternoon sometime.'

'You hear us arguing?'

'Sort of. I was pretty sleepy and I went back to sleep.'

She wanted to ask her again about the man who had come to the trailer and taken the money from her, and hit her, and knocked her down in the floor. But Aaron was sliding into the seat opposite them now, picking up his fork and his napkin.

'They got some good food here,' he said, and started eating again.

'It is good,' Fay said.

Some more people were coming into the restaurant now and it was starting to fill up with noise and talk. Waitresses were moving among the tables in their black pants and white shirts and aprons. Fay wondered if she could get on here, waiting tables. It didn't look like there was anything to it. She'd been watching them to see what they did. It looked like all they did was bring coffee and water and write down the orders and then bring the orders when they were ready. She knew she could do that.

'I got to get home, Aaron,' Reena said. 'I got to see about the kids.'

He kept on eating, but he nodded.

'I'll get you back quick as I finish.' He looked up at Fay. 'You got a place to stay?'

She glanced over at Reena but Reena wouldn't look at her.

'Well,' she said. 'I sorta been stayin up at Reena's. I ain't really got a place of my own yet. I just got in town yesterday.'

'You need a place?' He didn't raise his head when he said that, just kept on eating and sipping at his coffee.

She didn't know what to say. Reena bumped her leg under the table but she still didn't look at her, so she didn't know what she was trying to tell her. Aaron seemed nice now. He hadn't seemed nice when he'd

271

gotten ahold of those guys in the bar. And then she remembered him coming over when she'd first walked in
and asking her if she'd like to sit down. And all men
weren't like Chris Dodd, were they? They couldn't be,
could they? Weren't there probably good ones and bad
ones anywhere you went? Look at her daddy. Look at
Sam. Look at the guy who hit Reena.

'You got a place in mind?' she said.

'Might have,' he said. 'It's a little ways out of town.
But I could give you a ride back in the morning.'

'You ought to go with him, Fay,' said Reena. 'Aaron's
got a nice place over at Pass Christian. It's out there
close to the harbor. I bet you'd like it.'

'My mama lives out there,' he said. 'She's got one of
those bed and breakfast places. It's an old house but
she's fixed it up pretty good. She don't have much
company through the week so I could get you in cheap.
Maybe even real cheap.'

He smiled and she saw then that he had a nice smile.

'It's so crowded in my little place,' Reena said. 'I bet
Aaron would take you back and let you get your other
clothes, wouldn't you, Aaron?'

'Up at your place?'

'Yeah.'

'Sure,' he said. 'I mean you don't have to go out there.
You can go back to Reena's if you want to. It's strictly
up to you.'

He picked up a biscuit and wiped the rest of the
gravy off his plate and put it in his mouth and dusted
his hands together to show that he was through. He
sipped a little more coffee and then dabbed at his lips
with his napkin and put it on the table. He reached for
his billfold and pulled it out and signaled to the waitress at the next table. 'Check,' he said.

She came over with it in a minute and he picked it
up and glanced at it and then pulled out a five and a
one and put them under a salt shaker.

'Y'all ready?'

'I am,' Reena said.

'How much is my part?' Fay said, and started to reach for the check. He closed his hand over it just as she reached for it and he picked up her hand and shook it.

'On me,' he said, and then he got up. Reena nudged her with her shoulder and Fay picked up her purse and slid out of the booth. From the side of her mouth, going down the aisle following his broad black back, Reena said, 'Don't look a gift horse in the mouth.'

Fay didn't know what that meant but she followed him on up to the register anyway.

Sitting under a tall pole with a bright light mounted on top of it she looked out over the parking lot and the white lines drawn across it. Aaron was rewinding a tape in the deck, his eyes intent upon the little green arrow mounted in the player. He pushed a button and a tune started up. She recognized the voice of George Jones.

He leaned back in the seat and said, 'You like old George?'

'Yeah. I do,' she said. 'He's real good.'

'Shit, he's the best. I saw him one time up in Tupelo, years ago. You ever been to Tupelo?'

'Naw,' she said. 'I ain't never been there.'

He nodded and kept quiet, listening to the music. There were some big rings on his fingers and Fay could see the edge of what looked like a gold bracelet peeking out from the edge of his cuff. She couldn't stop looking at his hands, couldn't stop thinking about the strength that was in them. She didn't know what to do but she knew she was going to have to decide something before they got back to Reena's car. And that wouldn't be long. She'd said she was only going inside the supermarket for some milk and bread and a few other things. But she'd been gone for ten minutes already and Fay couldn't see anything of her through the plate glass windows, just a few customers inside, cashiers standing at their idle registers and talking to one another.

The music kept playing and Fay tried to listen to the

words, but she kept thinking about Sam. He was probably working now or just getting off and going home to that empty house. She wished she had it to do over again. Maybe there might have been some other way she could have handled it. But it wasn't going to do any good to keep on worrying about it. Maybe when she got someplace where she could stay she could write Sam and let him know that she was OK. But she knew he'd probably come looking for her if he ever found out where she was. And what would happen then, she didn't know. He might take her back. Back to face what she'd done? It was just too hard to know, to even guess. She wanted somebody to tell all these things to. There hadn't been a chance with Reena just yet.

Aaron wasn't watching her. He was tapping his fingers gently on his knee, keeping time with the music. He'd stopped at a store on the way over here and bought some cigars and they were sticking out of his shirt pocket.

'I like your boots,' she said.

He turned his head.

'Oh yeah? Thanks. I kinda like em myself.'

She wished there was some way she could talk to Reena for a few minutes alone, but there probably wasn't going to be any chance for that. What if he got her out to this place and tried something like Chris Dodd had done? There wouldn't be any fighting this guy off. He was just too big and strong. A man like him could do just about whatever he wanted to with a woman. Probably be better to just go on home with Reena. That was the safe thing. Then maybe she could look for a job somewhere tomorrow.

'You want me to go up there to one of those machines and get you a Coke or something?' Aaron said.

She could see a bank of them standing beside the double glass doors of the supermarket, but she shook her head.

'No, thank you, I'm fine.'

He opened his door and the light came on. He slid his

legs out and looked back for a moment.

'I think I'm gonna go see if they've got any lemonade. You sure you don't want something?' He got up and closed the door and looked back in.

'Well. I guess I might take a Coke if they've got one. If it ain't no trouble.'

He didn't answer, just walked away across the parking lot with his long stride. She watched him. He walked with his head bent a little and his arms swinging lightly. If she had known the word grace she would have said that word to describe his walk. When he got halfway to the machines Reena came out the double doors holding a paper sack. She walked over to him and said something to him and he stood there and talked for a few seconds and he handed her something that she put in her purse. Then she came on back to the El Camino and set the sack in the bed, just behind the rear window. She pulled out a pack of cigarettes and unwrapped them, fished in her skirt pocket for a lighter, then opened the door on her side. Fay scooted over to the middle. She could see Aaron putting some change into a drink machine and she knew she didn't have much time. She put her hand on Reena's arm just as she closed the door.

'Quick,' she said. 'Tell me what I need to do. He'll be back in a minute.'

Reena lit her smoke and blew a thin stream of smoke out the window. She was mad about something.

'What do you want to do?' she said.

'I don't know. I'm kind of scared to go off with him after the other night.'

'You mean that rapist motherfucker?'

'Yeah. I don't know Aaron either. Shit, I don't know nobody. Do you trust him?'

She looked past Reena's shoulder and saw him move to another machine. He bent over and placed a can on the concrete at his feet and reached into his pocket for some more change. Reena took another drag from her smoke and thumped her ashes out the window. Aaron bent over and picked up the can and turned. He had one in each hand now and he was heading back. Reena watched him for a moment and turned back to Fay.

'You'll be a hell of a lot safer with him than anybody else I know down here, believe me. He won't let anything happen to you. Why do you think he kicked the shit out of those guys in the bar? I told you he likes you.'

He was too close now for Fay to say anything else. She watched him come around the hood and then turned her eyes back to the front when he stopped and set a can on the roof and opened the door. His hand and arm came in and the hand was holding a Coke out to Fay.

'Thanks,' she said, and took it.

All the shops and stores along the beach road had shut down now, nothing but empty parking lots and dark windows. The only lights came from the few gas stations that were open around the clock.

'Dead as a hammer this time of night,' he said, to nobody in particular, and they didn't answer. He drove on through the rest of the green lights and put on his blinker to turn across both lanes and back into the parking lot of the Love Cage. It was empty except for Reena's car.

'I guess Arthur's done gone,' she said. She flipped her butt out the window when he brought the El Camino to a halt. Fay could feel both of them looking at her and she knew that she was expected to say something now.

'Well?' Reena said. 'You want to go back to that crackerbox with me or you want to sleep in a real bed for a change?'

Aaron looked away and out the window. He turned the music down. Reena nudged her leg with her knee, made a motion with her eyes, one that meant *Go with him*. Fay cleared her throat and turned her face to him.

'You don't think your mama will mind?' she said.

'Naw,' he said to the night outside the window. But then he looked back at her. 'You don't have to go if you don't want to.'

She sipped at the Coke, then put it back in her lap.

'OK,' she said. 'I believe I will.'

Reena opened her door immediately and got out.

'I'll see y'all in a minute,' she said, and reached into the bed for her groceries and started over to her car, fishing in her pocket for her keys. Fay sat close to him on the middle of the seat, reluctant to stay that close to him, but more reluctant to slide over to the other side and maybe have him think she didn't want to be that close to him.

He turned his head a fraction.

'You can move over if you want to.'

She scooted over a few inches and felt him studying her. Reena was getting into her car. She heard the engine start and then the headlights came on, then the backup lights.

'Say you got to get your suitcase?' he said.

'Yeah. It's up at Reena's. Won't take me but a minute to go in and get it.'

He was already turning the wheel. Reena's car swung around backward and then it stopped and came forward by them. He pulled it into drive and followed her out.

He didn't say anything through the other traffic lights and through the turn up the street or gliding up the hill under the street lamps and his silence made her nervous. She figured maybe he was just one of those people who didn't say much. That was OK. She could be that way too sometimes. There had been lots of times when she and Sam hadn't talked much, were comfortable enough with each other in their quiet.

Reena's taillights went out of sight ahead of them around a curve. The Jap pickup was there and when they pulled in behind Reena's car she could see a light burning in the front room. Aaron pushed his lights down on park and rested one elbow on the top of the door. Reena was getting out and Fay slid on over and opened the door.

'I'll be right back,' she said, and he nodded, a slight movement of his chin. She got out and shut the door on him.

Reena was getting her groceries out of the car and Fay waited for her and then closed the door for her.

'Come on in,' Reena said. They went across the yard and Reena opened the screen door. They stepped in. The children were wrapped in sheets and asleep, one of them on a small bed, the other one in the floor. The TV was playing and Chuck was reclining against the wall watching it with a beer in his hand. Eight or nine empty cans sat on the little table.

'Where the fuck you been?' he said. He looked at Fay and raised the beer to his mouth. She looked away.

'Working,' Reena said to him. 'Come on, Fay, let's get your suitcase.'

They started down the short hall and he said, 'Who's that out front?'

'Aaron,' Reena said, and turned the light switch on for the bedroom. Fay's suitcase was still there where she had left it. She shut it and fastened the latch.

'What's he doing out here?' Chuck said.

'He's picking up Fay,' Reena said. In a lower voice she said, 'You might ought to get on, honey. He's drunk. I'm glad you've got a good place to stay tonight.'

'You gonna be all right?' Fay said. She glanced out at Chuck and she could see him glaring at them.

'I'll be fine,' Reena said. 'He'll go to sleep after while and sleep it off. That's what I'm gonna do, too. Sleep it off.'

'OK. I guess I'll see you later. Sometime.'

'Sure. Take it easy.'

Fay turned with her suitcase in her hand. She hated to walk by Chuck. When she glanced at him again, going by, he stared at her with open hostility and turned up his beer again. She put her hand on the screen door and pushed it open and looked back once.

Reena was standing with her hand against the wall, and Chuck had set his beer down and was getting up, going toward her.

'Bye,' Fay said, and she didn't look anymore. The door flapped shut behind her and even before she got over to Aaron's vehicle she could hear the rising voices inside, the screams and the curses already starting up. She tried to block the sound from her ears. She put the suitcase into the bed and opened the door and got back in with Aaron.

'Get everything you need?' he said.

'Yeah. All I got's my purse and my suitcase.'

He backed into the street and then pulled out. She looked back at the little trailer and the dim light that was burning inside. She wondered what would ever become of her.

The road followed the natural curve of the beach and the water. Out there was only blackness and vague distant lights far away from shore. He left Biloxi and they went by the big sign she had seen that welcomed visitors to Gulfport and she saw again buildings and hotels she had seen on the way in with the truck driver. She felt like there hadn't been much choice. They were already crowded in Reena's place. She would have had to leave sooner or later anyway.

Aaron didn't talk much and it was hard for her to keep from taking little sidelong glances at him. He drove with one hand on the wheel and listened to songs on the radio. He asked her one time if she needed to stop and go to the bathroom or anything before they got out of Gulfport but she said she was fine.

When they'd left all the red lights and intersections behind, he pressed harder on the gas and kept his arm out the window with his hand resting on the roof. She saw more big houses with the dark trees in the yards and she saw shopping malls and liquor stores and seafood shops. Places that sold shrimp, places that sold shells. The road was well lit by lamps on poles and she swayed slightly in the curves with the motion of the El Camino. The tailpipes rumbled their low and throaty song in the night. On spits of land on the coastal side of the road there were big restaurants whose signs were still lit up. She smoked another cigarette and wondered how much longer it would take to get there. She was tired and had to fight against going to sleep in the seat. Once in a great while they met another vehicle, but mostly the road was deserted. It was uncomfortable sitting there with him with both of them so silent, but she had no idea what to say to him. She'd already told him she liked his boots.

'You all right?' he said, after a time.

'Yeah. I'm fine.'

He took one of the cigars from his pocket and stuck the end of it in his mouth. He bit off the end and spat it out the window. She watched him lick it with his tongue, rolling it and turning it, then he clenched it between his teeth and reached out his hand to push on the lighter.

'I figured you were. You just been so quiet I didn't know.'

'Well,' she said. 'I didn't know if you wanted to talk or not. You seem like one of them people who don't talk a whole lot. Sometimes.'

'I guess you got that right.'

She saw his eyes in the dashboard lights, heard the lighter pop out, a small red cherry moving in his hand and making a faint glow on his chin while he puffed on the cigar and got it going. He tapped the lighter on the edge of the ashtray and then stuck it back into its hole. He leaned his elbow on the door top and held the cigar between his thick fingers as he drove on through the night.

'It won't take us too much longer to get there,' he said. 'Then you can rest.'

'OK,' she said. 'Thank you.'

'Pass Christian's pretty nice,' he said. 'You'll probably like it better than Biloxi. It's quieter over here.

Probably ain't as much to do but there's not as many people either. That's what I like about it.'

She nodded and smiled but she knew he couldn't see it. She wondered how old his mother was. And what she'd think about him bringing somebody in this late. But she might be already asleep and wouldn't know it.

'You like livin down here?' she said.

'I was born here,' he said. 'Lived around here all my life. My dad used to have a shrimp boat and I worked on it when I was a kid.'

He put the cigar back in his mouth and puffed on it, then held it in his fingers again.

'Did you like that?' she said.

He didn't answer for a space of time and she thought maybe he wasn't going to. But when he spoke she could tell that he'd been thinking about his answer.

'It was a good way to live,' he said, finally. 'It was hard work. You had to get up early in the morning and go out while it was still dark. But it was a great feeling to be out on the water like that with my old man. The best part was seeing the nets come up because you never knew what you had besides shrimp. It might be anything in there, octopus, shrimp, fish. Daddy always let me pick out all the trash and throw it back. We'd get back in to the harbor about eleven or twelve and grade it out, take it and sell it. Clean the boat up, patch the nets, get it ready for the run the next morning. I did that for years. I'd probably be still doing it if things hadn't happened the way they did.'

He put the cigar back in his mouth and puffed on it, then held it in his hand again. She wanted to know more but didn't want to ask. He began to slow a little and she could see that they were coming into a speed zone where the signs were marked at forty-five miles an hour.

'Getting pretty close,' he said.

'I hope your mama don't care for me spendin the night.'

'She won't know nothing about it till in the morning. She goes to bed with the chickens.'

281

Now they began to pass by more big homes, most of them two-story with galleries on the top floors and tall columns out front, railed porches with the pale forms of furniture sitting vacant and shrouded in shadows. Huge trees everywhere, dark and brooding. He slowed a little more and pointed out to the left, where some dim lights burned.

'There's the harbor,' he said.

A flock of masts stuck up into the sky and he slowed the El Camino to a crawl to let her take a look. There was a plank walkway that extended out among the boats tied to the weathered posts and she could hear the faint song of wind singing through their rigging.

'Boy,' she said. 'It's a lot of em, ain't it?'

He had slowed almost to a stop. He nodded.

'Yep. Not as many as it used to be, though.'

There was a gravel lot where trucks were parked and where metal buildings stood. Under a lamp on a pole she could see a cat walking, then standing on its hind legs to paw at a garbage can. Out beyond that there was only the black and invisible sea. He took his foot off the brake and turned off the road.

'We're here,' he said.

'You mean right across the road from it?'

'Yep. I'll see if I can get you into a front room. She usually don't have much company on Sunday night.'

The drive went up a slight rise. She saw the house then. There was a miniature yard but the house rose up tall and white in the dark. Some candles were burning on holders on the front porch and she could see the windows on the third floor, the glass black with night. Some of the paint was flaking away on the side they were driving past and he said, 'Needs a little work done on it.'

'It's nice,' she said. 'It's really somethin.'

He didn't answer. He pulled into an open space behind the house, stopped, and put it in park and killed the lights and motor. He opened his door and started out.

'Come on,' he said, and she opened her door and got her purse off the seat beside her. By the time she got the door closed he had already come around and picked up her suitcase and was carrying it toward the house.

'Watch your step,' he said. There was a rail to hold on to and she held on to it. Through the glass doors she could see a kitchen and a big table covered with a cloth and beyond that a hall and tables and lamps and some upholstered chairs. He set the suitcase down and found some keys in his pocket and flipped through them until he found the one he wanted. He put it into the door and turned it and the door swung open. He pocketed the key and picked up her suitcase.

'Here we go,' he said.

She followed him, hesitantly, looking around. He let her get in and then shut the door behind her and locked it. He still had the cigar in his hand and he put the suitcase on top of the table and walked into the kitchen and turned on the light. She stood there by the table watching him.

'You want some coffee or something?' he said, and looked back at her.

'I don't know. You goin to make some?'

'I thought I might. I thought I might have a cup and sit out on the porch before I go to bed.'

'OK,' she said. 'I'll drink a cup if you're gonna make some.'

She saw him reach for an ashtray on the counter and put the burning cigar in it.

'Look around if you want to,' he said. 'She's got some pretty nice stuff in here.'

She walked around the edge of the table, touching the faded green cloth that covered it. It was sunken in the middle with a rim that ran around the outside edges and she realized suddenly that it was a pool table. The legs were made of dark wood and vines and leaves were carved into it, small birds and animals that perched on limbs or flew down through branches on flawless feathers.

'My lord,' she whispered, touching it reverently.

'You want to shoot some pool?' he said. She looked up at him and he was smiling. She smiled back and he gave a little laugh and went on with what he was doing, pouring at the sink, getting things from the cabinets. The cues were racked on one wall and she ran her fingers across them. She'd seen her daddy shoot one time, drunk and unsteady in a Georgia tonk, betting money he didn't have, ordering beer he couldn't pay for. She remembered them all being driven out into the rain by a big loud man. She could hear Aaron whistling a small sweet tune in the kitchen, a sound comforting to her ears. He seemed different now, calmer, happier. Not at all like he had been in the bar earlier. But she still feared him. Up the hall there were some doors and she wandered that way. Old photographs of the house she stood in were hung on a wall, the trees out front much younger then, women in long dresses standing on the steps, a horse hooked to a buggy waiting beside a bush. A picket fence that was not there now. She raised her face to look at the beadboard ceiling, thinking of how old this house must be. She wished she'd gone to school more. Just one more thing she'd missed out on because of her daddy, the chance to learn things, the history of places, old wars that were fought. She missed those channels on Sam's satellite dish, the stories about animals and other countries and little brown men who fished nets in the sea, other old ones who rode open boats across black water with their harpoons hoisted for whales. She wanted to know how old this place was. But when she looked around at the fragile tables with their thin legs and the lamps that sat on them with their yellowed globes and the wide planks in the floor, she knew that it was old. Old. Maybe it had been sitting here as long as that harbor across the road.

She walked up the hall to the front door. There was a big room off to the left with a cold fireplace and rugs and more chairs. Magazines scattered on a low table.

On the mantle over the fireplace slanted back in their frames stood the pictures of two young men. One of them was Aaron and the other one was the man who had beaten Reena and taken her money from her. Aaron wore a uniform in his picture. His red hair was clipped short. She remembered Reena saying that Aaron worked for his brother. But to her they looked nothing alike.

She turned at hearing a step and Aaron was standing at the edge of the room, the cigar in his fingers.

'It's making,' he said. 'You want to sit out on the porch till it gets ready?'

'Sure,' she said. 'Can I smoke out there?'

'You can smoke in here if you want to,' he said. 'Mama doesn't care, she smokes herself. I been trying to get her to quit but I finally gave up.'

From the porch she could see the stars clustered above the masts of the boats. She sat down across a table from him and lit her cigarette. He pushed an ash-tray over to her and she said thank you. She set her purse on the floor beside the chair. It was very pleasant there. A light breeze was coming off the water and the moving leaves waved shadows up and down the white columns in front of her. The wind sang in the rigging steadily, like a song that could lull you to sleep.

'It's like music,' she said.

'Yeah, it's pretty cool.'

There were potted plants scattered across the porch and baskets of ferns hung overhead. They spun and twisted slightly in the breeze. She could see the coal at the end of his cigar glowing when he pulled on it. She liked him.

'This looks like a real old house,' she said.

'Built in 1852 I think. Before the Civil War I know. Mama bought it about eighteen years ago. After Daddy died.'

'And she lets people stay here?'

'Yeah. Just overnight usually. She gets up early and fixes their breakfast. Toast and jelly and stuff. Eggs and bacon if they want it. It's got eight rooms for rent. I stay upstairs when I stay here.'

And what would happen to her tomorrow? He'd said he would take her back in the morning, but she knew she wouldn't know where to go when she got there. She couldn't just keep staying with Reena. Maybe she just needed to go back home. As bad as that sounded, she might have to. None of this would have happened if she hadn't left. She wouldn't have gotten to have loved Sam either. But at least she wouldn't be pregnant and so far away from her mother. Hell, who knew if they were even still there or not?

'You look like you got a lot on your mind,' he said.

She looked over at him. He was looking out toward the harbor and he was holding his cigar in his hand on his knee.

'I guess I do. I need to find me a job. A place to stay.'

'How'd you get down here?'

'I hitchhiked. Caught rides with people.'

'I used to do some of that,' he said. 'I didn't think anything about packing a few clothes when I was eighteen and heading out. To San Francisco or wherever. Montana. I hitchhiked all the way to Mexico one time and stayed down there two months. But I wouldn't do it now. Too many crazy motherfuckers running around out there now.'

'That's what a friend of mine told me one time,' she said.

The silence closed in again between them and they sat there in it for a while. Her cigarette was almost gone.

'I guess that coffee's ready,' he said, and he put the cigar in the ashtray and got up. She started up.

'Just keep your seat and I'll bring it out to you. How you like it?'

'Sugar and milk,' she said.

'One spoon?'

'Two. Please.'

He went across the boards of the porch and through the screen door. And should she just walk away from this too? Get up in the middle of the night and take her suitcase and head out again? She had to be someplace and settled when this baby came. She had to get to a doctor and have it seen about, find out how long it was going to take, find out how much time she had left. And that was going to cost money. The baby would need food, milk, clothes. Maybe medicine. She remembered how sick Calvin had always been before they got rid of him, how Gary would rock him and try to shush him when the old man was drunk and disorderly. Maybe that was why they got rid of him, because he was always so sick. But he seemed to have grown out of that right before they traded him off. There had been a brief time when he was happy, and would crawl around on the grass wherever they were, and let her hold him, play with him. Reckon where he was now?

She watched the boats in the harbor. She could see the nets gently waving, just barely. It would be nice to walk out there in the daytime and look around. Sam would like a place like this, crazy as he was about boats. And water and fishing.

She might never get to see him again. He'd never get to see his baby if that was so. She didn't even know what his address was. As many times as she'd ridden by that mailbox of his, the one his daughter had painted. It had some numbers on it but there hadn't been any reason for her to try and remember them. She'd never thought she'd one day need to write him a letter. What she guessed she'd thought was that she'd just kind of stay there forever.

She heard Aaron's steps in the hall and she turned her head slightly over her shoulder to watch him push open the screen door with his elbow. He had two cups in his hands and she could see them steaming. He set one down.

'It's hot, now,' he said, and handed her the other one.

'Thanks.'

'You're welcome. How you like it so far?'

She held the cup gingerly, resting the bottom lightly

287

on her palm and blowing across the rim of the cup with her fingers curled in the handle.

'It's real pretty,' she said.

'What time you need to go back tomorrow?'

'It don't matter I don't guess.'

'What are you gonna do?'

'I don't know. I guess I better look for a job somewhere.'

'Did you finish high school?'

'No. No I didn't.'

'How old are you?'

She started to lie and say that she was eighteen but she didn't want to lie to him.

'I'm seventeen,' she said.

A small cloud of smoke drifted in front of him and she could smell the cigar, the odor of it sharp in her nostrils. He took it back out of his mouth and sipped at the coffee again. She was aware all over again of how big he was.

'You in some kind of trouble,' he said, not as a question, which she thought it was at first, and then she saw that he already knew somehow, could just tell from talking to her and looking at her that what he'd said was fact.

'I'm gonna have a baby,' she said.

The silence drifted in again. She could hear the sound his lips made on the rim of the coffee cup and she could hear him inhale on the cigar.

One word from him: 'When?'

'I don't know. I just found out a few days ago.'

'You know who the daddy is?'

'Yeah.'

'Does he know?'

'Yeah, he knows.'

'But you left him anyway.'

'I had to.'

He turned the rest of the coffee up and drank it and tossed the dregs out in front of him. He stretched one leg out and then pulled it back, working his calf back

288

and forth, squeezing his kneecap with his hands. Then he drew his knee back up and turned his boot over on its side and ground the nub of the cigar out against it. He tossed the cigar behind a bush near the porch.

'Well it ain't none of my business,' he said. 'All I know about babies is that their mamas need their rest. You ready to get some sleep? Or you want to finish your coffee?'

'I'm ready,' she said, and stood up. He picked up his cup and they turned together and he held the screen door for her. He locked the front door, picked up her suitcase and from a board on the wall in the hall lifted a gold key attached to a piece of red plastic. He unlocked the door to a front room and opened the door and set her suitcase inside. She stood there, looking in.

He gave her the key.

'Sleep late as you want to,' he said. 'If you get up early just help yourself in the kitchen. I'll see Mama before you will probably and I'll tell her you're here. You need anything?'

'No. I'm fine. Thanks a lot. I really needed a place to stay tonight. It's mighty nice of you.'

'It's got its own bathroom and everything. If you want to catch some of that breeze you can raise the windows or open that front door in your room. I'd keep that screen door latched, though.' He backed up a few steps and started to unbutton his shirt. 'Well,' he said. 'Good night.'

'Good night,' she said.

He didn't look back. She saw him head back into the kitchen and she stepped into the room and closed the door. Then opened it again, looking for the latch. There was a small knob and she turned it and a metal bolt slid out. She was satisfied. She shut the door again and turned the knob. It was locked. And he was OK. He wasn't going to try anything.

One lamp was on in the room. She picked up her suitcase and put it on the bed. It was a nice bed with a canopy over the top and four tall posts of polished wood and a rug on the floor beside the bed.

She unsnapped the latches on the suitcase and went through her clothes for the one gown she'd packed, an old cotton one of Karen's that she'd found in a drawer one day. She looked at the curtains, holding the gown to her chest for a moment. She didn't think anybody could see in. She undressed silently and pulled the gown over her head and buttoned the three buttons on it and searched through her purse for her toothbrush and went into the bathroom. She stood there in front of the mirror brushing her teeth, looking into her eyes, watching the pale foam form on her lips. Overhead she could hear the creaking of one board. Two boards. Then silence. She cut the light off in the bathroom when she went out. Then stepped back, turned it on, put the rubber stopper into the drain on the sink and filled it halfway with warm water. She picked up her bra and panties from the floor and put them into the water to soak overnight. Maybe that would clean them a little bit. Early in the morning if she got up in time she could hang them somewhere to dry. She turned the light off again and went back into the bedroom and closed the suitcase and set it on the floor.

Standing at the window with her hand holding the curtain open she looked out into the night to see the ghostly masts standing aloft, and when she raised the window she could hear the wind still singing out there in the harbor, and after she had pulled back the coverlet and slipped in between crisp clean sheets and had fluffed the pillow to her liking and reached for the chain on the lamp and turned it off and had put her head back down into darkness, she could still hear it. She believed she could hear the boats creaking at their moorings.

'I miss you, Sam,' she said quietly, just to herself, just to hear it said, even if there was nobody there to listen.

Sometime during the night she heard a car pull in but it was lost somewhere in sleep and she barely wakened at all.

Monday she woke to nausea in the early morning hours when the big house was still quiet. She turned over onto her side and lay like that for a while, trying to make it go away, hoping it would, but then it came on stronger and she had to push back the covers suddenly and find the light switch in the bathroom and go to her knees on the tile floor next to the commode and hold her hair away from her face while she threw up. It left her heaving and trembling and without rising she pulled some toilet paper off the roll and wiped her mouth and spat strings of mucus into the cloudy water.

She leaned back on her bottom and her right leg, resting, waiting to see if it was going to come again.

She sat there long enough to know that it was over, thinking of the darkness outside and the distance back to Sam. In a way she wanted to go buy a newspaper and see if there was anything about Alesandra in it. In a way she was scared to. What difference was it going to make if it was in the paper or not? She got up and turned off the light when she went out.

She wasn't sleepy now. The clock beside the bed with its little digital numbers said 4:57. She didn't know at what hour daylight would arrive. It had been so long since she'd been up that early. Back when those boys had taken her to their trailer, she guessed. Days at Sam's house had been lazy, sleeping late, watching television, eating, lying out on the beach, swimming, eating again. She sat on the side of the bed and lit a cigarette. She saw the front door he'd been talking about and went over to it, unlocked it and opened it.

Through the screen door a sea breeze filled the room and cooled it, bowed the ruffles over the four poster bed, lifted strands of her hair and pushed them back. She stood there, looking out at the harbor, listening to the chiming in the riggings again, so close out there in the dark. There was nothing to stop her from getting dressed, easing out the door, heading down the highway again. And she had thought for all that time with Sam that she had been saved from all that forever, that the picking up and the moving was over and done with, nothing more than bad memories of days and nights in places she didn't want to be. But nothing had changed. She was again just like she'd always been. And maybe would always be. But there was one thing she could do, one nice thing she could have right now.

She soaked in the tub for thirty minutes, one leg over the rim, amazed that her belly looked the same as it always had. Once she was done in the tub she washed her hair with the shower, afraid the running water might be waking people up. With some hand soap she washed out her underwear in the sink and from the suitcase she pulled a clean sleeveless blouse and a neatly folded skirt. The blouse was a little bit wrinkled but she put it on anyway with clean panties and the last clean bra. Out the window she could see a pale streak of light that meant morning was near. She saw a few clothespins hanging on a short line. She carried the wet things out there just as she'd done at Reena's and hung them to dry.

Back in the bedroom there was nothing to do but sit on the bed and that got old fast. She was hungry, too, wanted a cup of coffee at least. There didn't seem to be anybody up when she stepped barefooted into the hall. She had combed her hair and pinned it back with a clip and she felt clean now and somehow able to go on and face this day and whatever it would eventually bring.

At the back doors she looked out at the dawn. She tried to move quietly, not make much noise. Once the light was on in the kitchen she found the coffeemaker and the coffee and figured out how to operate it.

It was full daylight by the time she got back to the front porch and the little round table. Pink light in the bay rising up over the masts and people already beginning to stir down on the docks. She watched a few boats pull out, watched the care they took backing out of their berths. And then the water foaming behind them when they got turned and headed out, reading the names written back there in flowing script: *Bettye's Ride, Mama's Dinghy, Rosa Hartsell*. Far out in the bay a sail unfurled, tiny figures working at their tasks, and she watched how the boat took the wind under its sail and began to move out. Such a thing she'd never seen before, and for a few brief moments she was happy that she had come all this way. It wasn't like she had imagined it all but it was better somehow, this time in the early morning before the people in the house sleeping would begin to stir.

She went back for another cup and thought about fixing something to eat, but decided again to wait until somebody, Aaron or his mother, got up and came down. Mainly she didn't want to make any noise.

So she was still sitting there on the front porch with her coffee and her cigarettes when the slow steps came down the hall, stopped, paused, came on again. The lock moved in the door. She turned around in her chair as it swung open. Then the screen door pushed out and a woman was standing there, studying her from inside the wire mesh. The woman stood there for so long that Fay began to get uncomfortable. And then without saying anything, she backed up and the door closed again.

Fay thought maybe she should have said something, good morning or something, but she'd been waiting for the woman to come on out. And was that Aaron's mother or somebody who was just staying here?

She wished Aaron would come on down, but as late as they'd stayed up, no telling how long he might sleep. If he worked late like that every night, he might do all his sleeping in the daytime.

293

She looked down into her cup and swirled the dregs of the coffee around. Another cup would be good but she believed she'd wait and see what happened next. The woman hadn't looked friendly and it bothered Fay that she hadn't said anything. Maybe this was her regular chair. Maybe this was where she sat every morning to drink her coffee and watch the boats across the road. But there were three others around the table, looked like she could sit in one of them.

She wished he'd get on down here.

Shit, she couldn't sit here all day. She had to start thinking about looking for a job. She never had asked for a job, didn't know how to go about it, didn't know the first thing about it. And what if they asked her a bunch of questions? There might be those forms to fill out. You might have to tell them all kinds of things, like where you were from, how old you were, all that shit, who's your mother and daddy? *Well my daddy's a drunk and my mama's a frigging fruitcake and they live in a little rotten cabin up in the woods and the floor's so dirty you can't stand to walk on it barefooted. And you have to be careful inside because the wasps keep building nests. Anything else you want to know?*

Shit, it looked hopeless. How was she even going to get around to someplace to ask?

Inside somebody said a word. A woman's voice. Another woman's voice answered it. Fay sat there, trying to hear what they were saying, but it was low and indistinct, like a child mumbling in her sleep. Somebody had to be fixing some breakfast in there. She wondered now if they'd let her eat.

About that time the door opened again. She hadn't heard any footsteps because this woman was barefooted. She was coming out from behind the door with a smile on her face and a long white cigarette in one hand, a cup of coffee in the other. Her hair was blond and some of it was piled on top of her head while other strands hung down the sides of her face and throat. It was the woman she had seen on the poster outside the strip joint. Aaron's main squeeze maybe? She was wearing a short yellow teddy trimmed with lace under a long flowing dressing gown. Her chest was big and her thighs smooth muscled and deeply tanned. Her toenails were red and her teeth were bright in the lipstick smile she gave Fay.

'Hello,' she said. 'I'm Gigi. Mind if I sit down?'

'Sure.' Fay scooted her chair over several inches as the woman flowed to the table and set her coffee down. She bent, her hand extended.

'You are?'

'I'm Fay,' Fay said, feeling stupid. She took the hand that was offered and shook it briefly.

'Isn't it a beautiful morning?' Gigi said, standing with her hand on one hip and gazing off across the road. Posing, looked to Fay like.

'It's pretty nice,' Fay said, looking down into her cup again, knowing there was some more in the kitchen. Or had been.

'Is there any more coffee in there?' she said.

'Oh yes,' she said bending from the waist to pick up hers. 'Arlene just put on a fresh pot. Did you meet Arlene?'

'Somebody come to the door a while ago. I didn't exactly meet her. Is that Aaron's mama?'

The eyes swiveled back on her.

'Ohh,' she said, holding the cup just beneath her moist-looking red lips. 'So you know Aaron?'

'I just met him last night,' Fay said. The woman hadn't moved a hair, was waiting for her to go on. 'He brought me out here and let me spend the night. I think he's supposed to give me a ride back to Biloxi sometime.'

'Is that right?' Gigi said. 'Well. That's interesting. Where may I ask did he find you?'

She knew well enough that she was being put down, but she didn't quite know what to do about it.

'I was in the bar.'

'The bar?'

'The club or whatever.'

'The club? I don't think I know any club Aaron goes to.'

'The strip joint, then. The place where he works.'

'I see,' Gigi said. She sipped at her coffee and gracefully pulled back one of the chairs at the table and sat down. She crossed one elegant leg over the other. Fay had to admit she was beautiful. And then she wondered what she was doing here. Where Aaron stayed. With his mother.

Gigi puffed at her long cigarette and Fay watched the ash hanging off the end of it. She pushed the ashtray over closer to her and Gigi smiled and nodded and delicately tipped the ash into it.

'I was in Memphis last night,' she said. 'I'm afraid I got in late.'

'I think I heard you pull in.'

'It was pretty late. But you were up?'

'I was awake. I didn't sleep too good. Strange place and all, you know. I kept hearin that wind in those boats.'

'Boats?'

Fay pointed with her chin. 'Those out there across the road.'

Gigi turned her head and Fay watched her profile as the hand with the cigarette went slowly to her mouth, watched how her cheeks hollowed slightly, how the red lips sucked at the little white tip, and then how she slowly exhaled.

'Oh,' she said. 'You mean those boats.'

'Yeah.'

She turned her face back to her and gave her that smile again.

'I don't pay much attention to them. Usually when I come out here I have other things on my mind.'

Fay didn't answer. She hated sitting out here with her.

'So,' Gigi said. 'How was it that Aaron happened to bring you out here if you don't mind me asking?'

'I don't know,' Fay said. 'I was just hangin out with this friend of mine, Reena . . .'

'Reena? Reena Mize?'

'Well, I don't know what her last name is. She never did tell me that.'

'Does she work where Aaron works?'

'Yeah . . .'

'That's Reena Mize.'

'Oh, you know her, huh?'

Gigi picked up her cup with her lacquered perfect fingernails entwined in the handle and took a sip, set it back down.

'I've had the pleasure of meeting her, yes.'

'I like her,' Fay said. 'She's been good to me. She let me stay with her some.'

'How nice of her.'

'She's got a couple of cute kids.'

'I don't doubt that. I wonder if they're legitimate.'

'What?'

'Nothing. So. Tell me. Are you a . . . did you just start working at the Love Cage?'

'Naw,' Fay said. 'I don't work there. I just went over to see Reena.'

Gigi put her cigarette in the ashtray and stretched her arms and gave an enormous yawn with her mouth wide open. After she finished she grabbed her head with her hands and moved it around her neck, swiveling her eyes from the floor to the ceiling. She finished by lacing her fingers together and turning them outward and flexing her knuckles. She smiled and picked up her cigarette and coffee cup again.

'Honey,' she said, without looking at Fay, but gazing instead out across the water, 'I don't mean to be indelicate, but I'm having a small problem here and I'd appreciate it if you'd bear with me for a moment.'

'OK,' Fay said.

'I'm having a small problem coming in and finding a strange woman here saying Aaron brought her home with him.'

'You mean me?'

'Yes. You.'

'What's a problem about that?'

'It just is. You sure you're not a dancer?'

'I'm not a dancer. Are you?'

'I'm not a dancer. I'm an artist.'

'An artist?'

'Yes. I was in the House of Vixens on Winchester last night. And I've been in several films.'

'You mean movies?'

'Yes. I've had several starring roles.'

'*Gol*ly,' Fay said. 'What's some of the names of em? I might have seen one on TV or somethin.'

'I don't think so,' Gigi said.

Fay just looked at her. She should have known that somebody that beautiful was likely to be famous. You could just tell it by looking at her. Women like her didn't walk down the street every day.

'But back to our little conversation, though. You wouldn't be . . . I'm searching for how to put this . . . you wouldn't be *involved* in any way with Aaron, would you?'

'Involved?'

'Precisely.'

Fay saw what she was getting at now. She thought she was fucking him. She almost laughed. But she saw that it could look like that, her sitting out here, him upstairs asleep. But all of a sudden she didn't care for the way this woman was treating her, with her fancy nightgown and her fancy cigarette-smoking. She had to be Aaron's girlfriend.

'I'm not messin around with Aaron,' she said. 'What's it to you? What would happen to me if I was?'

Gigi blew a cloud of smoke straight toward her, then stubbed out the cigarette without looking down.

'You might get some of that hair snatched out of your pretty little head, that's what.'

'Oh yeah?' Fay said. She leaned closer. 'You let me tell you somethin. That shit goes two ways. You mess

298

with me and I'll kick your ass up between your shoulder blades.'

Gigi didn't say anything else. She got up in a huff and grabbed her coffee cup and went back in, letting the screen door slam behind her.

Well she guessed she'd done it now. She was probably going straight upstairs to see Aaron and tell on her. She wished now she'd just gone ahead and slapped the shit out of her, really given her something to complain about. She couldn't see him with her, not that piece of fluff. But she was the kind that men probably just melted over. She probably just shook those big titties at them and they . . . same thing she'd done to Sam, dropping that towel. *What the hell'd you expect him to do, turn it down?*

She got up and stepped back inside the bedroom for just a moment to see what time it was. It was 6:17. He probably wouldn't get up for hours. And she didn't want to go back into that kitchen where that woman was if that was his mother. And sitting on the bed she knew she just couldn't keep sitting in there. What a fucking mess. She got up and went back out on the porch, looked at the table, then walked over to the steps and down them and out across the neat brick path that led to the street. Where it ended she stopped and spread her feet a little apart and put her hands in her pockets. The sun was up now and the sails of the boats out in the bay were bright with it.

What a life that would be, to be rich like that, rich enough to own a sailboat and go out messing around on a Monday morning instead of going into work like that. Sam might be out on the lake this morning. Or sleeping late probably because of the night shift. Or maybe out looking for her. She wondered if there was any way she could get in touch with him without getting into trouble. But what if he came after her or somebody came after her and it was trouble? Where would she run to then? *And you killed her. Ain't no two ways about that.*

She sat down on the step there and picked up a pebble and tossed it toward the street. It bounced and rolled. She squinted up into the morning, then turned her head and looked back at the house. Couldn't see anybody. Miss Bitch was probably right up there with Aaron now. Probably had a room they slept in together when they got through fucking. She probably wasn't nothing but a high-class whore. She hadn't seemed to think much of Reena. And what was the deal with Aaron's brother and her anyhow? What was he doing coming over there and beating her up and taking her money away from her? She wondered what would have happened if that Chuck had been there. And how did Reena get him out of the way at the right time when she wanted to fuck somebody?

The whole thing was too puzzling for anybody to be able to figure it out. She picked up a couple more pebbles and closed her hand over them loosely and rattled them around in her palm.

She opened her hand and picked up the pebbles one by one and tossed them across the street. Then she rested her wrists on her knees and let her hands hang down and just sat there.

She pulled her knees up and rested her chin on them. That sun was creeping up and getting hotter already. She wondered how many hours she had spent between rows of dirt with plants growing on them, fields of green and black out there around her, a whole world of it and nothing to do but keep on working and working and on into the afternoon when it was hottest and wanting to stop so badly, go up under a shade tree, drink some cool water. As far back as she could remember, she could remember that, that work of some kind that was always around them, and the other people around them, like the naked people she saw bathing in a river one time, and the place where they had all the horses, and the walking between the fields with hoes and rakes, even down on her knees in Georgia picking up pecans in the fall and gathering them in the folds of her dress to run and dump them into the bucket her mother carried before Calvin came.

But always in the summer there was that awful sun. And she didn't understand how they could have done that to her. To all of them.

She could hardly imagine a life without Sam now that she'd had one with him for a while. If she could make any one thing real and true it would be that Sam had never gotten into a bed with that woman.

She blew out a sigh and got up. She went back to the house and got her coffee cup and grabbed her smokes and lighter, opened the screen door and went in. He'd said for her to help herself. She wasn't very hungry, so she'd just get herself a biscuit. If that woman was back there, the first one, the one who hadn't said anything, if she was back there and still wouldn't say anything, she'd just introduce herself to her and tell her that Aaron had brought her out here and had told her to help herself. And if she didn't like it, fuck her. She'd fix some toast and jelly or something and take it out on the front porch and eat it by herself.

But when she got back to the kitchen there was nobody there. The coffeepot was full, cups and saucers and spoons and sugar and milk in a little silver pot beside it all laid out on a clean towel. Doughnuts of all kinds, chocolate icing, plain, some dusted with white flaky sugar, resting in a large wooden platter. In a warming pan on the stove was a high mound of scrambled eggs, crisp bacon and round sausage patties piled next to them. Beside the toaster a loaf of bread sat, and a handwritten card was propped against it saying HELP YOURSELF. There was a stack of plates and butter knives and napkins, jars of jelly and preserves, a tray of butter.

Her plate was piled high when she sat down again at the table on the front porch, a hot cup of coffee beside the plate, her napkin neatly in her lap as Amy had shown her. So much Amy had shown her. She'd really paid Amy back good, hadn't she. Hadn't got cold good and she was fucking Sam. Just stayed after him all the time and didn't ever get tired of it. Aaron and Gigi might be doing it up there right now.

She bent her head and started eating. Traffic was almost steady now on the road out there. It wouldn't be any trouble to finish eating and get her stuff together, get her underwear off the line, pack the suitcase and step out there with her thumb out. Go somewhere else.

She hated to be so wishy-washy. She knew a few people here. She wouldn't know anybody if she went somewhere else. Why not just take the ride back to town with him and look around for a job? If she couldn't find anything, well . . . well what? Sleep on a park bench. Or on the beach? Then a cop would come along would be her luck and want to know what she was doing and where she was going and what her name was and then he might go back to his cruiser and have some kind of list with her name on it . . . *Fay Jones. You just the one I'm looking for. Git yo ass in this here car.* Naw, that wouldn't do, that wouldn't do at all. She needed to keep her ass off the street for sure.

She kept eating. After a while she began to hear some voices inside, clumps and bumps. She lifted her head and listened for a few moments but she couldn't tell who it was or what they were saying. She heard a door open and close, sounded like maybe it was the back door. She cut a piece of sausage and put it in her mouth and chewed. The door slammed again. Within thirty seconds an engine started. Somebody was leaving. She hoped it was Gigi. A crunching of gravel slowly got louder and she could hear the car coming alongside the house and she looked up as the little red car rolled by. Some man driving it, the woman who had come to the screen door without saying anything in the passenger seat. The car stopped at the end of the drive and the left rear blinker came on. It pulled out and was gone, the motor noise rising a bit each time the driver shifted a gear. She picked up her coffee and sipped at it. After a minute she saw the car go down the beach road to the right, gathering speed.

'Good morning,' she heard. She sat up and looked. An older, pretty woman was standing beside the porch in green pants and a flowered blouse. She had some shears and a hat in her hands and she had on some gloves.

'Hey,' Fay said.

'Did you find some breakfast?' the lady said.

'Yes ma'am. It sure was good, too. Thank you.'

'I'm Arlene,' she said, and kind of waved one hand at her. 'If you need anything just let me know.'

'Yes ma'am. Thank you. My name's Fay.'

'I know,' she said. 'You just make yourself at home.' And then she turned away while Fay was still nodding and walked over to a bush out near the road and started whacking at it. Small limbs dropped from under the shears. Then heavy steps came down the hall. Aaron, it sounded like. She turned her head when the screen door pushed open and he came out, barefooted, wearing the black pants from last night with one of those ribbed undershirts that old men used to wear.

'Hey girl,' he said, and came over with a plate and a glass of orange juice.

'Hey,' she said.

'You already eat, huh?' He set his stuff down and pulled out a chair, then sat down in it. 'There's some more coffee if you want some.'

'I done had three cups.'

She sat there and watched him eat. He looked around, rubbing at his nose once in a while. Out in the yard his mother clipped away at the bush, then stepped back and looked at it. Shook her head. Leaned over. Snip snip.

'I heard you met Gigi,' he said, and he couldn't stop a small grin at his mouth. He picked up his orange juice and drank some of it.

Fay stretched out in the chair, her hands crossed over her belly. Wonder when she'd feel the baby kick?

'Yeah, I had that pleasure. She your girlfriend?'

'We've kind of got an arrangement,' he said.

'Oh.' She thought about things for a little while. 'What kind of movies she make?'

He raised his eyes to her with a small look of surprise.

'She mentioned that to you?'

'Yeah. She said she was an artist too.'

He forked up some eggs and took a bite of buttered toast.

'In her own mind I guess maybe she is. She's a stripper, no more, no less.' His face considered something contemplative for a moment. 'But I guess she's got more than most of them.' He looked up at her again. 'Except maybe you.'

He went on eating for a while and she let him eat. She didn't really know what to make of what he'd just said but she guessed she had to take it as a compliment. She wondered if Sam could whip him.

'What was you gonna do?'

'Do what?' she said.

'What was you gonna do, whip her ass?'

She looked out toward the bay, moved her hands up and down. Arlene was walking around the bush, squinting at it. Snip.

'She thought I was messin around with you.'

'She did?'

'Yep. That's what she thought cause I was out here and all.'

'You were just minding your own business.'

'Yeah.'

He picked up his napkin and wiped his mouth and dropped it in his lap again.

'Well she's upstairs pouting right now because I wouldn't throw you out.'

Fay nodded toward the yard.

'What does your mama think about her?'

'She's got a really efficient way of dealing with it. She just acts like she don't see her.'

'Your mama don't approve of a stripper girlfriend, huh?'

'Actually it's not that. She used to be one herself.'

Fay almost dropped her jaw then. She looked at the nice lady so busily clipping with the shears, straw hat, cloth slip-on shoes.

She leaned forward, whispered, 'Your mama? Was a stripper?'

'Yep. A damn good one, too, they say. Or at least my old man said. I have seen some of her show pictures. She was pretty fine.' He raised his chin and shouted, 'Wasn't you fine, Arlene? You's fine as frog hair wasn't you?'

She looked up at him, waved her hand, *shoo*. He laughed and scooped up some more eggs.

'I believe I will get me some more coffee,' Fay said. She got up with her cup. 'You want me to bring you one?'

'Yeah, sure,' he said. 'Just put a little milk in it.'

'All right.' She turned and started across the porch.

'How about getting me another piece of toast, too? With some butter on it? Please?'

'OK.' She nodded and went on in. She fixed the coffee and made the toast and buttered it. He'd finished his orange juice by the time she got back out front.

She set the cup down by his elbow and he said Thanks.

'You're welcome.' She settled in the chair again and looked at Arlene. Things weren't as bad now. Aaron was here and he was talking to her and his mother was right out there.

'I had a talk with Mama a while ago,' he said. He pushed his plate away and picked up the coffee. 'She could use a little help around here sometimes.'

Fay didn't say anything. This was a real house like Sam's. And it had many rooms. It had plenty of room. She didn't want to hope but couldn't help hoping. It was dry inside and it had a good roof on it and it was probably warm in the wintertime. If wintertime came to this place. Gray days she'd bet, no people on the beach, the birds still crying out and flapping.

'Nothing heavy,' he said. 'Worst you might have to do's help her take the screens off to wash them. Just cleaning mostly. It wouldn't take but a few hours a day. Making beds, putting toilet paper on the rolls. Can you cook?'

She thought about what she should say.

'Well, yeah. I mean yes I can. I know I can cook breakfast.'

He drank some of his coffee and put the cup back on the table. He looked at her cigarettes lying there. She thought for a moment that he was going to ask for one and then he picked up his cup again.

'Well,' he said. 'It wouldn't be every morning. She gets up and does it most of the time. But she's getting older and to me she works too hard. She's damn near seventy. Don't look it, though, does she?'

Fay watched Arlene still snipping around on the bush, trying to imagine what she had looked like fifty years before, young and beautiful.

'She seems to be pretty spry for her age,' she said.

'Hell, she's got a boyfriend.'

'Boyfriend?'

'You can't blame her for getting lonely. He's a pretty good old fart anyway, name's Henry. Got a big cattle ranch up here at Winona.' He flicked his eyes toward the bay for a moment. 'Got a big yacht his crew brings over here from Miami once in a while. You talk about a party when that thing gets here . . . boiled shrimp, oysters on the half shell . . . hell he's got so much damn money he don't even know how much he's got.'

He looked at her cigarettes again and said, 'Damn it, let me bum one of your cigarettes if you don't care.'

She pushed them toward him. 'Sure.'

He kept shaking his head while he tapped one out of the pack. 'I can't hardly stand a menthol but I just can't stand it no more.' She leaned forward and flicked her lighter. 'Thanks. Damn.' He exhaled smoke and looked at the tip of it. 'There goes eight days shot to shit.'

'What?' she said. 'You try to quit?'

'Hell yeah. That's what I was doing with those cigars last night. I'll have to go to the store in a minute now. But look here. What do you think about maybe helping her out a little around here?'

'You mean? Like a job?'

He seemed impatient then, leaned forward and flicked some ashes into the tray.

'Yeah, like a job. I mean.' He lowered his voice and seemed a little embarrassed. 'What you told me last night, the baby and all. Probably be hard for you to find a decent job over at Biloxi. Hard enough for somebody who's got a high school education. Mama's got plenty of room here. She's willing to let you stay here and she'll pay you something. I don't know how much. That's between you and her. It's her place. I just stay here sometimes.'

'Well sure,' she said, without any hesitation. 'I mean, if you're sure it's all right. You don't even know me hardly.'

'You'll be working for her, not me,' he said, and he stood up. 'You want to ride over to the store with me?'

He had changed into jeans and a yellow tank top. He'd swapped his cowboy boots for leather sandals. He had a pack of Marlboro Lights on the seat beside him now and they were cruising on down the beach road toward Bay St. Louis. He'd bought her some lemonade when she'd told him she liked it. She was leaning against the door sipping on it, the breeze coming in the windows and making her hair fly in all directions.

He turned his face to her, a cold beer in his hand.

'We can roll these windows up and turn on the air if you want to.'

'I'm fine,' she said. 'How long's the coast?'

'It's twenty-six miles if you count all the bays and everything. Pascagoula and Gautier and all that. You ever been over to Gulf Shores?'

'No,' she said. Where Chris Dodd was from. 'I ain't ever been over there.'

'Someday when we've both got some time, we might ride over there if you want to. There's some good waves to swim in. I mean if you want to go swimming. You can swim, can't you?'

'Yeah, I can swim,' she said, looking out through the windshield.

While she'd waited in the kitchen for him to change clothes, she'd heard some shouting upstairs, but he hadn't mentioned Gigi when he'd come down, so maybe they weren't all that tight. Maybe she only worked for Aaron or his brother. That was something else he hadn't said anything about, his brother. She still remembered what it sounded like to hear Reena hit the floor while she was standing out in that yard. There had to be some stuff going on that she didn't know about. Maybe a lot of things. But the point was there was a place to stay and a job. She was damn lucky and she knew it. She could put up with Gigi, hell, she'd try to be friends with her if she'd let her.

'I used to swim a lot up where I lived,' she said.

'Oh yeah? Where was that?'

'Up around Batesville. About halfway between Batesville and Oxford.'

'Did you have a house there or something?'

She shifted around in the seat. Didn't know if she was ready to talk to anybody about all this.

'Well, yeah, sort of. I was livin with this . . .' *Man? Guy? Fellow?* 'I was livin with this guy.'

Aaron wasn't looking at her. He lit his cigarette and studied the road.

'Not trying to be nosy or anything,' he said. 'Tell me to shut up if you want to. He the one that got you pregnant?'

'Well.' Long pause. She was embarrassed. 'Yeah.'

Now he did look at her.

'What? He didn't want to marry you?'

'It wasn't that,' she said, and picked with her fingernail at the rim of the can she was drinking from. 'We just . . . we just had some trouble.'

He waited for her to go on. Then, dismissing it, he said, 'Ain't none of my business anyway. I have to say I think the son of a bitch is crazy, though.'

She started to tell him more, wanted to tell him more, wanted so bad to tell *somebody* what she'd been through, but she didn't know if he was the right one.

'It wasn't really his fault,' she said, feeling helpless in trying to explain it, how it was, how good it had been, how she had felt safe and protected, and the nights of fishing and the days in the sun and the nights of loving and feeling that you belonged to somebody and a place nobody could run you off from. 'He didn't even know I was leavin him till I left.'

'You ain't heard from him?'

'Ain't no way for me to hear from him. He don't know where I'm at.'

'Well. You gonna try and get in touch with him?'

'I can't,' she said. 'It was bad trouble.'

He gave a little short laugh and said, 'Goddamn, what'd you do, kill somebody?'

When she didn't say anything, he turned his head slowly and studied her in maybe a new light. She drank some more of the lemonade and then started asking him some questions about the coast, like what kind of fish did they have down here, what kind of bait you used, all that.

309

Sam was almost back to his driveway when the dispatcher called him and told him to come back to Batesville.

'Goddamn it,' he said, and turned the car around at the first place he could find and went back down the road, back down to 6, over to Batesville, up the other road, wondering what they wanted and this late at night.

It was lit up brightly inside but it was nearly deserted. Nobody was out front at the window but he could hear the radio going. He walked back toward the break room and passed by the dispatcher's room. The new young woman who worked his shift was sitting back there with one mike keyed, saying something into it. She looked up at him and smiled and kept talking. She held up one finger for him to wait. He waited. He'd probably have to see McCollum tomorrow. The wheels moved fast sometimes. He'd waited all day, dreading a phone call that never came, telling him to come in early to talk to somebody, one of his bosses, maybe. He'd thought David Hall himself might come see him. Well they were probably just waiting on the autopsy results. He guessed there wasn't any hurry for them. But he knew he'd have to talk to somebody. Sometime.

The color was faded from the tiles in the floor, the baseboards scuffed. He looked up at the dingy ceiling tiles.

The girl was talking to some trooper who was having trouble finding something, sounded like, and she was trying to tell him where it was. The phone rang twice

310

and she picked it up and spoke into it and then another one rang. He decided he'd walk back and see if there was any coffee. She kept on talking.

At least there was one damn place in the building where you could smoke. One day he wouldn't even be able to do that probably. The red light was on in the coffee urn and he got a cup and held it under the nozzle and drew some.

He was about worn out and he sat down and listened to her talking. She had a nice voice. She was single, too. Probably about thirty. He smoked a cigarette. Once she rolled out into the hall on her chair and looked at him, waved with one hand, the phone cord over her shoulder. It didn't sound like she was talking to anybody official. She was murmuring too many phrases and laughing too much for that. She was keeping it down, though. Everybody knew that Grayton was a company man who brooked no bullshit. Joe Price would be lucky to keep his job and for sure they'd transfer him somewhere else now, maybe down to Lucedale or somewhere. They could stick him down around Jackson in all that traffic every day.

And what do you suppose they're going to do with you there, buddy boy, if they get you by the short hairs? He figured some price would have to be paid now. He didn't know if it would have to be public or not. Alesandra was going to be public. She was going to be in the papers tomorrow and he wondered if they would run a picture. And how would they get the picture? Her family would have to supply one. And what was her mother like, reckon? She must have had some of that same great beauty herself. Alesandra would have been loved, he knew that. One time he'd thought maybe he loved her. Now he knew he didn't. But in a very solid way he still felt a great fondness for her. He remembered the curve of her lips in a smile. He looked down. The coffee cup was empty, a skim of brown liquid on the bottom.

'I'm sorry, Sam,' she said. He looked up and she was

311

standing there with her hand out. 'I'm Loretta Rains. Didn't mean to keep you waiting.'

'That's all right.'

He stood and took her hand and it was warm, soft, small. Little dimples across the backs of her knuckles. Her face was tanned, a few freckles. She looked healthy in a uniform like this. The pants were tight on her.

'Did you have something for me?'

'Uh, yeah, afraid so. The chief wants to see you.'

'See me? You mean now?'

'Yes. He's waiting. I couldn't get off the radio and then the phone. He's in his office waiting for you.'

He could tell she hated to tell him all that because she had a look on her face like she was hurting him and it crossed his mind that maybe people were already talking about it. He hoped Jimmy Joe hadn't heard about it. He'd always thought so much of Amy. Used to come over like he did. He couldn't believe Grayton was in his office this time of night. He was in deep shit now maybe.

What the hell could he do but go in there? He went up the hall and turned the corner and walked across the carpet and down the other short hall. The door at the end was closed and he knocked on it, trying to get ready, trying to keep in mind that he had to keep Fay's name out of it if he could. They didn't know anything yet. He had to remember that. And if Fay was the one who killed Alesandra, was he strong enough to protect her? How could he know what to do without talking to her and finding out what happened? He heard Grayton call for him to come in.

Only the light behind the chief's desk was burning. He still had on his uniform shirt but he'd taken off his tie. The dome of his skull gleamed faintly in the soft light as if he'd oiled it. The walls were paneled with dark wood and there were two good chairs in front of the desk. Among the things on his desk Sam saw a Bible. Grayton was working at some papers and he looked up long enough to say, 'You can sit down.'

Sam took the chair on the right and sat there. Grayton looked up at him again and studied him with his calm flat eyes behind his little spectacles and Sam saw a depth of coldness there that he had not known about before. He struck him as a man who'd want the truth.

Grayton looked back down at what he was doing. Sam was glad. Whatever was coming might be very bad. A great change might take place right here very rapidly, a few years short of retirement. But there was money in the bank. The house was almost paid for. He tried to stop himself from getting too far ahead. Grayton was going to ask him what he knew about Alesandra and he was going to have to tell him. And he knew without asking that Grayton wouldn't want to hear about one of his troopers having an affair. Not with that Bible sitting on his desk he wouldn't.

'All right,' Grayton said, and let a pencil fall from his hand. He raised those cold eyes. 'What do you know about this woman at Sardis?'

He couldn't lie now and not lie later. And Tony had seen him with her. By now Grayton might know everything Tony did. He'd probably talked to him about all this.

'I've been knowing her for a little over a year,' he said. 'I met her over on Highway Four.'

'You stopped her?'

'Yes sir.'

Grayton waited, not blinking at all. Sam could see little specks of dust drifting in the beam of soft light behind him. Books in a shelf back there. Dim pictures of a woman and children, and others with still younger children. His family back there behind him, the ones he protected in his own right. And would he understand how it had been and how it came to be if he told him?

'Go ahead, Harris.'

'Well,' he said. 'We just got to know each other. We got to spending some time together.'

Grayton wasn't budging. He wasn't shifting around, he wasn't squeaking his chair, he wasn't doing

313

anything but listening. He was perfectly still except for his breathing, his round gut stirring. And there wasn't anything for him to do but go on. Dig his own grave if that's what it was.

'My wife and I . . . ,' he said. 'We . . . she drank a lot.' *Yeah blame her you son of a bitch.* 'We drifted apart.'

You will not mention Karen.

'Your daughter,' Grayton said. 'I remember that.'

'It happened years ago,' Sam said, and he put his arms over his chest. 'We didn't spend a lot of time with each other. We lived in a house together. That was all.'

Hell, wasn't that enough? If he wanted to know anything else he could just ask it. He didn't have to sit here and spill his guts. He wasn't accused of anything besides knowing her.

Grayton was still looking at him. Sam put his hands on his knees and sat there looking back at him. The weak voices of the radio and the dispatcher spoke beyond the wall. He guessed it went on all night. He knew it did. Somebody had to sit there all night and answer it, even on Christmas Eve. And especially on New Year's Eve. With two million drunks running loose.

'You've been with us a long time,' Grayton said.

'Yes sir. I have.'

It was very quiet in the room whenever the radio stopped its chatter.

'You've never been in any trouble with us, either, have you?'

'No sir. I haven't.'

Grayton swiveled his chair around so that he was turned sideways. Sam thought he might put his feet up on his desk but he didn't. He just looked at the wall for a while. He had his fingers joined over his belly. Behind him Sam could see a color picture of Grayton holding a fishing rod and a kid in a diaper.

'What went on between you and your wife's none of my business and I don't need or want to know about it because it's not important to your job. I mean you know what your job is, don't you?'

314

'Yes sir,' Sam said. 'I believe I do.'

'I've been married thirty-nine years,' Grayton said. 'Every time I've laid my head down to go to sleep next to a woman it's been the same woman.'

He turned his chair around and faced Sam. He picked up a rubber band from his desk and toyed with it.

'I'm getting older now. Should have done quit. But it's just money in the bank when you've been here long as I have. And I don't work as hard as I used to.'

Sam nodded, just listening.

'You're probably going to get formally questioned by the Panola County Sheriff's Department. Are you willing to go through that?'

He made his voice steady. 'Yes sir. If I have to.'

'You'll probably have to since you knew her . . . the way you did. Wife never did find out?'

He had to lower his eyes.

'No sir. She never did.'

'Well.' Grayton snapped the rubber band between his fingers a few times and then hung it on his thumb and stretched it out. 'If you're hiding anything you'd better tell me now. You don't know a thing about her being killed, right?'

He looked back up at him and into his eyes. They didn't look cold anymore, just old and tired. And Sam saw that he was right, that they should have already turned him out to pasture. But he thought that in his case, it might have been a lucky thing, since old was sometimes soft, too.

'I don't know anything about it, sir. I'm just having a hard time dealing with the fact that she's dead.'

'What about her family? You know any of them?'

'No sir. I don't. She was from down around Clarksdale. She was Lebanese.'

'Yes. They said she was beautiful.'

'Yes sir, she was,' he said, and felt his eyes start to well, and then he pushed it back. There wasn't a bit of sense in her being dead. It wasn't necessary.

315

'You can go,' Grayton said, and then he turned his attention back to the things on his desk. He picked up a pen. That was all there was to it.

The day dawned gray and cool with a small wind rising. It reminded him of September mornings when he used to go dove hunting in the fields outside Verona when he was a kid. He dressed in jeans and leather boots and a button-down shirt with a pocket. He cut off everything in the house and made sure the eyes on the stove were off and the radio alarm and the coffeepot, that the answering machine was on in case anybody called while he was gone. The machine still had a recording on it that Amy had made but he hadn't been able to bring himself to erase it and put a new one on.

The sun was coming up when he pulled out on 6 and headed east, but it was shaded by clouds that moved slowly in gray shapes across the face of it. One of those mornings when you can't tell whether it's going to rain or not, when it might just start falling out of the sky without warning. But he hoped not because he figured he'd have to go down some dirt roads, and there were only street tires on the pickup.

He stopped at a station in Oxford for gas and bought some cigarettes and gum. It might wind up to be a wasted day but at least it was a place to start looking although he still thought there might not be much chance that she'd gone back to her family. After paying he turned the truck around in front of the pumps and went across the bridge and turned by the fire station and got onto the bypass.

Tula, Yocona, DeLay, out around there from the way she'd described it. But who knew if that was even where she'd lived? She talked like she'd only walked into it that one time and had walked out of it that one time. It might have been down near Paris or over toward Toccopola, Dogtown, Spring Hill. He didn't know those places well anyway, only cruised up and down the state highways that went near a few of them. He'd

316

have to get on the back roads, find the tiny stores where they might have traded, where somebody might know a Jones family who lived in the woods. Go to London Hill first, find the store. Those people might not even talk to him. You couldn't just go in and start asking questions in a little community like that, people were suspicious of strangers, some of them, anyway. Thing to do would be go in and get a Coke and stand around for a few minutes, comment on the weather. He guessed he could make up some kind of story, say he was looking for a place where some Jones man lived who had an old pickup or a good coondog for sale.

It was crazy to even head out like this. She didn't go back home. She'd have been trying to get as far away as possible, and to somewhere that the law wouldn't find her.

He turned onto an old patched asphalt road off the bypass and was immediately among growing suburbs with signposts at the ends of the lanes: Willow Cove, Oak Grove, Piney Drive. He didn't drive fast and he studied the things around him as he went. The county high school had added a wing and they were still bricking it, but the scaffolds were empty of men this morning and the piles of sand had been wetted by rain and the bricks sat deserted still in their ricks.

He remembered the place where the old sale barn had burned down. On the gravel lot there were new houses springing up, young trees planted and supported by wire guides and stakes. Oxford was growing outward all the time and he didn't feel like he was even in the country yet. Then he passed a small pasture and saw a couple of colts and mares standing under some trees and an old man moving slowly on a faded blue Ford tractor with his Bush Hog raised. The old man waved and Sam waved at him. The houses were farther apart here and there were four-wheelers parked in carports and dogs lying in the yards. In places weeds grew high along the sides of the road. He wished he'd gotten more coffee at that gas station. Here was a pen full of

317

young pigs and their bloated pink mother.

Through trees on the left and in a deep hollow he could see the glint of water, a big lake somebody had off in the woods down there. He guessed there were houses set way back off the road that he couldn't see, down some of these long driveways that seemed to lead off to nowhere. A place where you could let your dogs run loose and raise your kids away from the road. There was a nice new barn on the right and some red bulls were standing around it. Next to it in a scrubby pasture some goats stood grazing. Little goat babies scattered among them and two that faced off and butted at each other with their budding horns.

Now there were older houses with field equipment and big tractors in sheds out beside them. In one field hay sat rolled and ready to be picked up, but nobody much seemed to be moving this morning. He wasn't meeting much traffic, only a solitary vehicle once in a while whose driver would lift a languid hand, as did he.

The road curved often and it was shaded on both sides by tall trees where grapevines hung with clusters of green fruit. Muscadines and possum grapes. Dogwoods and thickets of pines. Oaks and hickories and sweet gum and sycamore. Now there were hollows of hardwood timber and in between them lay fields of cotton and soybeans. More pastures, most of them holding large numbers of cows, black, white, spotted. Old farmhouses that sat back from the road with their neat vegetable gardens out beside them, the pole beans staked, the tomato vines tied up with strips of cloth. He saw a big doe standing at the edge of a patch of underbrush, and a small flash of brown hair that might have been her fawn, but he didn't see any spots. He unwrapped a piece of the gum and started chewing it. It still looked rainy over in the south, right where he was headed.

He came into a bottom with three bridges where he'd worked a bad wreck one time, five or six years back, a murderous affair at noon one August day where people were trapped and screaming and others in smashed steel dead mute and bloody. You couldn't tell now by looking at that place that it had ever happened. Time washed things away but he knew it wasn't going to wash Amy or Alesandra or Fay or Karen.

After he drove a few more miles he began to see the big fields of corn and milo with their tasseled heads standing still under the weight of the morning dew, the broad green leaves at rest. Three deer grazed midway down a row, their bodies stark brown against the surrounding plants. He began to see more gardens and more farm equipment, more barns and pastures and cows. He saw one store coming up but he slowed down and as he watched it he saw that it was closed, looked like it had been for years. The glass in the pumps was broken out and two junked cars sat to one side. A small brown dog stood in front of the island and watched him pass, sniffed the air as if it would catch his scent.

It didn't seem any fun going to work now. There was nothing to come home to anymore and the house stayed so quiet that he usually kept the radio or the television on just to have what seemed like some company. He hadn't even been out in his boat lately and his fishing rods stood unused in the corner of the deck where he and Fay had always put them when they got through. What was she doing for money and was she getting anything to eat? No telling who might have picked her up or where she could be by now. The longer he drove the more he convinced himself that it was useless looking for her out here. But he wasn't far from Yocona by now and he decided that he would go on and look around some anyway, just to be able to say to himself that he had. In the back of his mind the small thought of driving to the coast today had been hiding and trying to come out. But he should have headed that way already if he was going to do that, it was a long drive. And he knew better than to think that even if he drove all the way down there and she was there, he'd be lucky

319

enough to see her standing on a street corner or walking on the beach.

He turned off to the right on a secondary road just past the Baptist church and went across an old bridge high above the river, looking down into the gutted banks as he drove by. On the other side somebody was plowing a field with a wide disk and a big green John Deere tractor with a cab. Then he was climbing hills again and going past thick stands of hardwood timber that stood on the steep sides of hills and the greenery was so thick that he couldn't see very far down in there. A box turtle was trying to cross the road and he straddled it with the tires and spared it.

On a high and windswept hill where a walking girl had been picked up one night by some boys with a load of catfish, he looked off to the left and saw the open and majestic expanse of the Yocona River bottom, the emerald trees growing, a pasture of jade hills dotted with the white forms of Charolais cows grazing. Far down below there lay big fields of cotton and beyond that more timber and beyond that the pale gray sky and the clouds that melded in it and one tiny speck of silver that was a water tank at Toccopola. And that was as close as he could get that day to where she once had been.

The weekend passed and he went back to work on Monday. He was still on nights and going in at four and getting off at twelve-thirty or one depending on what happened and how busy the nights were. He wasn't eating enough and was drinking too much when he came in and he knew it but didn't really give a shit either. He knew he'd have to go look again soon. She was somewhere. But he knew where. Probably the coast. And if he didn't find her there he didn't know where to start looking for her next. The world was so big and there were too many places to go. Or hide.

Monday evening they did a roadblock down near Marks looking for some prisoners that had gotten away from a satellite camp over by the Sunflower River and it was the kind of thing he didn't like, the kind of thing where you had to consciously stop yourself from going for your gun when you saw a carload of rough-looking old boys sitting back there in the line. But nothing happened, they didn't find them, only spent two hours and forty minutes getting licenses from old ladies and checking their tags and handing the licenses back and everybody asked the same questions, farmers and boys alike, sweet young things with carloads of screaming younguns or fishermen with their boats trailered behind them trying to keep from reeking their beer breath into his face:

'Y'all after them scaped convicks?'

'Yessir, sure are, that's what's going on, you ain't been drinking, have you?'

'No sir, not me, cept I had a couple beers a while ago.'

'How long ago?'

'Bout three hours. You know which way they headed?'

'Not right now, sure don't, now get home, you hear?'

'Yes sir, sure will, we headed that way right now.'

'Y'all catch anything?'

'We got a pretty nice mess.'

He rode back up into his district just when the sun was starting down and went to a barbecue shack on the other side of Sardis and got a sandwich and a big bag of fries. He ate in the cruiser with the radar going but he'd parked intentionally in a place where the drivers could see him in plenty of time to slow down, so he didn't catch anybody, but it gave him time to eat supper in peace. Once dark came he pulled on his lights and rode through Highway 4 over to 7 and went through the kingdom of kudzu again where he had first taken Fay that afternoon and marveled that it had only been a few months since that time. He met some speeders but only flashed his blue lights at them and could see the red brake lights in his rearview rocketing them down to a safer speed.

After he'd cruised for a while he decided to pull off the road just north of the Tallahatchie River bridge into a stand of pines that shielded him from southbound traffic very well. It was at the end of a long straight stretch where the trucks sometimes came roaring up with a full head of steam to tackle the hills that lay outside Oxford and sitting in that spot and hidden he could get them pretty easily sometimes. It was just more money for the state. And the state would be a ruthless motherfucker if they got after him.

He slowed and turned off the road and then backed up the short lane of dirt into the looming pines with dust rising from his taillights, doused his headlights and spoke to Loretta at Batesville, checking in with his position and what he was doing. She was more than casually interested, he thought, but he wasn't. Even now she put a teasing lilt into her voice answering him.

And she did have a fine ass. He finished saying what he had to say and hung up the mike. The engine hummed and the dash lights glowed with a pale blue luminescence. He wanted a beer and he wished he was home.

All the cars heading north slowed down when they saw him, even some of the ones going the speed limit. One time he almost started after a smoking junktrap with one headlight and a muffler throwing sparks up from the highway but let it go on for a reason he could not explain to himself, something to do with the old man and the girl in the Ford Pinto. Something like letting the ones with the hardest luck have one more break. If he could.

He turned the FM radio on and punched it to the country station in Tupelo and listened to it low enough to keep his ear on the radio chatter from Batesville and the patrol cars out on the roads. Squawks and sputters, voices sometimes speaking in static. Men alone out on the road like him. For some reason the truckers weren't speeding tonight. But he knew well enough too that when the first one had passed him he had picked up the mike of his CB radio and called back on a channel to others behind him. He could imagine the conversation:

'Hey Lone Ranger, we got a bear in the bushes up here bout a mile past the bridge, ten four?'

And then somebody would come back:

'That's a big ten four Rocky Raccoon, thanks for the info, catch you on the flip side, over and out.'

Those truckers got bored, nothing but endless miles of road with white lines down the center. No wonder they wanted to get to where they were going as soon as they could and get on home to their families. Sit out in the swing under the shade tree and drink a cold beer. Take the kids fishing. At one time it had almost been like that for him. But he and Amy had had such different ideas about how to raise Karen. All that time and what was it worth now?

He rolled the window down and lit a cigarette. He'd been trying to cut down and had been doing pretty good, but whenever he got to drinking beer it seemed like he smoked twice as much so he guessed it didn't matter.

Fay could be in a truck. Fay might have already been in a truck.

He was shocked to find that he'd gone to sleep when he realized the radio was speaking to him. He sat up and picked up the mike and turned his lights on. The news was bad from the sweet voice on the radio: a gasoline tanker had crashed five miles south of Holly Springs. He reached his hand out for the switch that operated the blue lights and pulled it down into gear even while she was still talking.

He got it headed that way and turned on the siren for good measure and pushed his foot down hard and he could see the cars pulling off the sides of the road already. By the time he had it up to eighty he was hoping some brokedick wouldn't decide to try and pass on the Tallahatchie River bridge. What was that boy's name that jumped off?

He went through the cars screaming where they sat pulled off or over and once he got around the curve at the Marshall County line where the first beer store stood, the one that sold the good ribs, he pushed it down even harder and hoped for no stray dogs blissfully trotting.

It never failed to amaze him how fast you could eat up some road going this speed. Trees and houses just shot by, blurred bullets of image that were gone. Cresting hills he let off but as soon as he saw clear road ahead he nailed it again. It was almost as if they all knew he was coming through. And when the traffic meeting him began to bunch up again he knew he was getting close. He eased off the gas pedal and shut the siren down and the main question on his mind was whether or not it was leaking.

Then all of a sudden he didn't meet any more cars and the road was eerily empty. Up ahead, just beyond the last rise, the pulse of blue lights faded and glowed in the night air. He went over the hill and there was the first car, a highway patrol unit in front of a stopped line of cars that looked two miles long.

'God almighty,' he said, and picked up the mike and told the dispatcher that he was 10-6.

He was down to fifty by now and he swung to the left and went around the cars, trying to see where the patrolman was standing. It was dark down ahead. He could just see the shiny bulk of the tanker in the middle of the road like a beached whale. He could feel the hair prickle on the back of his neck and he wondered where all the fire trucks were. The radio was filled with chatter, other channels, all excited voices trying to speak over screaming sirens, other emergency vehicles that were still en route. If the road was totally blocked then all the fire trucks from Holly Springs were on the other side of the truck. He wondered if anybody had put in a call for some units from Oxford but he guessed he'd find that out soon enough.

Some people were out of their cars, looking. Some of them even on the left-hand side of the road watching down toward there. Don't step out in front of me. A few were near the edge of the road and he slammed on his brakes and rolled down his window to yell at a young boy and two girls standing there smoking cigarettes: 'Get back over there in your car and sit down! And put those cigarettes out!'

They did it, quick.

The officer was standing near the open door of his cruiser, watching him. He pulled up and the officer trotted around. It was Joe Price, he of the hair trigger, Deadeye Dick they'd been calling him around the station lately. His hat was off and he leaned in toward the car.

'It's bad, Sam,' he said. 'The driver's pinned. You smell it?'

It was all around, a withering odor of petroleum fumes that sickened him.

'Yeah, I smell it.'

'You can go on down or you can stay up here with me. It's up to you.'

'What's our plan?'

'Hell if I know. I've got em stopped up here and they've got everything backed up about three miles on the other side. They can't bring a fire truck in too close, muffler might set it off or something.'

'What're they doing about the driver?'

Joe coughed and momentarily balled his fist at his mouth. Sam knew he didn't shake easily but he looked shook.

'They's some boys down there from Holly Springs Fire Department trying to get him out with hand tools but I don't know how much luck they're having.'

He stood up to look down that way and Sam looked with him. He could see lights flickering around the cab, small yellow spots of light that moved jerkily over the crushed steel.

'There's a car under it and somebody's in it but there ain't nothing left of him. Or her. Don't know who it is yet.'

'Was he loaded?'

'Not all the way. He just had dumped a load in Byhalia and was headed back to Oxford to get some more. We think there's about a thousand gallons left but it ain't all run out in the ditch yet. But they's gas all over everything down there. It ruptured when it rolled.'

'I guess I'll go down there,' Sam said.

Joe stood watching him. The people in the cars watched them both to see what these men would do.

'All right,' Joe said finally. 'They told me to stay up here or I'd go with you.'

'I know you would.'

The odor of gasoline got stronger and stronger. What it looked like was that the truck had rolled and come to rest on the tires but the trailer was on its side. He turned on his flashlight and shined it ahead of him and now he could hear voices talking in desperation, the boys from the fire department who were working feverishly to free the driver.

Joe hadn't been lying about the car. It was not even recognizable as a car unless you counted the tiny Plymouth emblem that was nestled up next to one of the blown tractor tires, that and some shattered plastic that was lying in the road, a few bits of glass that sparkled when he ran the beam of his light over the debris. The rest of it was simply a mass of crushed metal no higher than his knee. He thought the car might once have been burgundy. He didn't look to see if he could view the person inside it.

There were only three firefighters, wearing turnout pants and black T-shirts with HSFD printed on the back of them. One was inside the cab, on the other side of the driver, prying with something. The second one was standing on the fuel tank beside the open door. The other one was holding the light for them. Sam could hear them, panting, their voices strained, edged high with adrenaline:

Son of a bitch!
It won't move.
Try to . . .
I'm tryin damn it!
This piece of steel here . . .
I'm pushin hard as I can.
Shit, it ain't gonna work.

He could hear the driver moaning, too, and could see him, his face covered with blood and the white broken bone stuck out like a jagged stick from the swelling flesh of his ankle, his head back in the seat with his Adam's apple protruding and the one arm he could see hanging down from his side. His left arm. A wedding ring on his finger. The nails and the hand drenched in blood.

The driver turned his face and looked at Sam. He had a deep cut on his forehead that was leaking blood down into his pale blue eyes. The ear on the left side of his head was almost torn off, hung there by one little piece of meat where blood welled and seeped.

'Please, mister,' he said very clearly. 'Just tell these boys to cut my foot off. I know they got an ax. I can live with one foot.'

'We're going to get you out,' Sam said, but when he leaned over the driver's lap and looked down into the mass of torn steel where the other firefighter knelt, the foot was swallowed up in what looked to be the rear of the bell housing and some other pieces of metal that were twisted and bent.

'I been trying to get these boys to do it and they won't do it,' the driver said. All of this said and done in a reek of gasoline so heavy it made Sam dizzy and sick to his stomach at the same time. He saw that what the man was talking about made perfect sense: lose the foot as long as he could live the rest of his life before the gas flowed on down the ditch and found an ignition source. It made sense, but he couldn't do it. It wasn't worth thinking about. It was probably the thing to do but he couldn't do it. He said so.

Sam walked down the side of the tanker to the rear. The hole in the tank was up on the side and the gas had almost stopped flowing but it had dripped all over the road and Sam was standing in it. He stepped over to the ditch and went around the back side and back there it was much worse. The grass in the ditch was wet with gasoline and the smell of it almost put him on his knees. That was when he saw the smudge pots.

They were down the road, hard to see, set just below the level of the road where a blinking barricade stood, some kind of road construction he guessed. He turned to run and realized he couldn't run and that when it lit up it would light up there at the same moment it lit up here. He started running for them, as hard as he could go, not knowing how long it would take for the fumes to seep down there where the baby flames stood smoking in their pots, leftover things from older days, antiques, and he thought he might have a chance to smother them out if he could just reach them in time, but then the world went orange and black like Halloween and the road he was on lit up bright as daylight for one moment and the force of it blew him across the road into the opposite ditch where he could feel his hair scorching and the shirt melting on his back.

He pushed himself up on his hands and saw the whole road consumed and living in bright yellow fire and the truck back up the road in flames, saw one of the firefighters with his arms aflame stagger across the highway and fall flailing at himself into the grass. He was almost tempted to just lie back down and cover his head with his arms. Save himself. But then he was running back, the fire on his left cooking the side of his face, and he saw the door open on the cab and the other firefighter tumbled out, running crazily, his pants on fire, beating at himself as the other one had. He ran by Sam shouting something and Sam reached out and grabbed him and tripped him and threw him down and ripped off what was left of his uniform shirt and rolled him on the highway until he was out and smoking and then he was up again and going around the nose of the cab and he saw the second firefighter then on his back in the highway, already charred black and not moving. The third one was moving in the ditch, moaning. But the driver was still alive, that was the thing of it. He had been badly burned by the blast but somewhat protected by being inside the cab, but when Sam drew close he could see that the cab itself was on fire, and the driver was sitting in the midst of it, and for one awful moment he looked at Sam and then screamed with every bit of air he had left in his lungs: *'Shoot me for God's sake!'*

The road itself was burning where he stood at the edge of the pool of fire but already that fire was dying down, the fuel being consumed, and he put his hand up over his face and spread his fingers and tried to get closer, but the heat was just too great. He stood there,

wavering, and he could hear Joe Price yelling something at him that he couldn't understand or try to, but
all he could focus on was the yellow face of the driver
where the fire inside the cab was cooking him quickly
to death. He kept screaming for Sam to do it and he did
put his hand on his revolver and tried to get closer, but
already he could feel that most of his hair was gone and
that his skin was blistering.

The driver made one last plea: 'Shoot me oh God put
me out of it!'

That was the last thing he said. A pocket of flame
roared up and engulfed him even as the fire trucks
screamed in from both sides and the men jumped off
with the hoses swelling and started putting water on
the truck and the dead smoking boy in the road, and
Sam couldn't take his eyes off what he had already
seen.

He was in the hospital for five days. His hands were the worst, from where he had thrown the old firefighter down and smothered the flames, and the young doctor told him he'd been lucky, only second degree in spots that still hurt like shit, he knew, but, 'Hell, look, bud, that hair on your head'll grow back.' The doctor was amused that it had even blistered his dick through his pants: 'Hey Hopalong, lucky as a shithouse mouse, can't grow a new tallywhacker you know.' It had blistered the fronts of his legs, and places you wouldn't have thought, like the back of his head and under his left arm, a raw red angry place there. Fire does crazy shit, man, the doctor told him, sitting on the edge of his bed, letting Sam sneak a cigarette once in a while at the hospital just off 55 at Sardis. Some days they talked tractors and fishing. The doc had a place near Jerry Lee Lewis at Nesbitt and invited him up for bream.

His buddies brought milkshakes from the Sonic and fat chili dogs with cheese and helped him eat while his hands were still in the bandages. By the fourth day he was out in the coffee shop carefully playing cards and drinking coffee with an old codger who was dying of cancer, and who told him that he used to race pigeons in New York State when he was just a boy.

A sleek nurse with black hair that reminded him of Amy's came in one night at two and woke him gently with her soft hands and tried to get his pajamas open but he sent her away and turned back to his pillow and his troubled dreams, his burned hands cradling each other.

Joe Price came in one day after a round of golf and brought him a half pint of Wild Turkey that they smuggled out to a little patch of grass and a table with ashtrays. Joe said there was plenty of talk and Sam didn't ask about what.

He read in the *Panola County Times* about Alesandra. They didn't have her picture. Another piece told the fire story.

And late at night when the halls were dark and the TVs were shut down for the day and the nurses were squeaking their way up the tiled floors in their white rubber-soled shoes and he was lying in his bed with his hands hurting and knowing it was a small thing compared to the old man from New York, he imagined carrying the gas-truck driver to safety, the fire ax in his hand, blood trailing them in drops that dotted the yellow bars in the road.

Now she was heading across the water in a narrow skiff with an old outboard chugging. She trailed her hand in the afternoon waves and thought only of Sam. She watched Aaron's back in the sunlight and the muscles that moved in it and she watched his arms and the tendons and veins that lived there and then felt hot all over and ready to get there and have this new one inside her because she knew already what they were going to do. He skirted the edge of the beach and pulled in and landed the boat easily against the sand, killed the motor, stepped out and waited. Once she was out he pulled the skiff on in, tilted up the motor and left it.

It was still hot while they walked across the sand. He stopped one time and kissed her hard and deep. She pushed her woman's bone against him.

'I bet you don't even know how fine you are,' he said, and drew back from her and looked down into her eyes. He turned and caught her by the hand and pulled her on.

There was a path that went through pine trees and the mosquitoes were bad. She fanned them away from her face but still they bit. The pine needles felt good under her feet. She barely saw the birds that were singing in the trees, only felt his hand pulling her on. Soon she stepped beside him and slipped his arm around her waist and tried to lean her head against him as they walked.

She saw the cabin before they got to it. There was a low deck and a nice pond and two aluminum boats tethered to the dock, fishing poles upright in a stand like umbrellas in a store. She watched him pull keys from his pocket and then they were across the gravel path and up to the door and he was opening it and they went inside. A dark room where the blinds were drawn but she could see just fine. It was cool in there and the bed he led her to was freshly made and then she was pulling at her clothes and at his and kissing him and he lay down with her and she was ready and a little crazy and when he slid it in she smiled, open and free.

'God,' she whispered. 'Don't that feel wonderful?'

He agreed that it did. He turned her gently on her left side and pillowed her head with his hand and moved her top leg up and slid into her deeper. He began to move against her and she closed her eyes and held on to his arm. If there was anything better than this she didn't know what it could be. But she wouldn't let him hurt the baby.

Long after that when they were settled and satisfied and comfortable they smoked cigarettes lazily. She began to tell him about Chris Dodd. He listened without expression, one arm over his head holding the pillow, the big muscle relaxed, and he didn't seem like it bothered him that much. He only said, 'I'll take care of it for you.'

Later they dressed and went out. She stopped to wait for him to lock the door and saw bream schooling up out in the pond. He saw her watching them and stopped beside her.

'We'll come back one day and give em a try if you want to,' he said. She smiled up at him.

'I'd like that. I can dress em. Cook em too,' she said. 'I need to cook for you sometime. I'd like to.'

'Sounds good to me.'

He put his arm around her shoulders and they went back up the path toward the boat and the beach.

He went about the business of throwing Gigi out as soon as they got back. She sat on the porch and listened. There was some screaming that went on upstairs and some doors were slammed and then more screaming and then steps clumping down the steep stairs she'd seen and then the back door slammed. In less than a minute a motor started. The car came from around the side of the house and Gigi stopped and yelled some things from inside the safety of it. When Fay started up from her chair she hauled ass, flipping her off as she went. The little car got smaller down the road and then Aaron came out.

'Where's your mama?' Fay said.

'I don't know. Let's eat.'

She reached into the Arby's bag and lifted out his food and his tea and gave it to him. He unwrapped it immediately and started eating. She should have been hungry but she only nibbled at some of the fries and ate about half the sandwich. Finally she pushed it away.

'What's the matter?' he said. 'You ain't hungry?'

'I guess not.'

'Hell, you ain't had anything since breakfast.'

'I ate all I want,' she said.

'Well if you ain't going to eat the rest of that roast beef let me have it.'

She pushed it over.

'You want the french fries too?'

'Might as well.'

She slid them over and got up with the rest of her tea and wandered across the porch. Boats were moving out in the water just as they had that morning and people in shorts and swimsuits were walking on the dock.

She turned her head to look at his broad back. He was chewing and picking up french fries one at a time from the table. He seemed different now again, so much so that she was almost uneasy speaking to him. Yet he'd been so kind and gentle inside the cabin.

'Can we go over there sometime?'

He looked up, his jaws moving slowly.

'Where?'

'Over there. Across the road. Maybe look at some of them boats?'

335

Already he was nodding, still picking up the fries.

'Sure. Anytime you want to.'

'After while?'

'Well . . . I need to run over to Biloxi after while.'

'What you got to do?'

'Check on things.'

'Can I go?'

He turned his head slowly, pushed back from the table slightly and took a drink of his tea.

'What you want to go over there for?'

There was something his eyes did sometimes, a way they seemed to look all the way through her, as if they were searching for either honesty or lies in her words. She didn't look away, though. She'd been to bed with him now. It looked like maybe she was going to stay with him for now so she was going to have to get to know him, find out what he was all about.

'I don't know. Just to be with you.' She thought that ought to be enough.

He picked up one more french fry and chewed it.

'I don't know how much I want you hanging around there.'

'What you gonna tell your mother about us?'

'Nothing. Any more questions?'

'Yeah. Just one, though.'

'What's that?'

'Why are you such a fuckin asshole sometimes?'

He studied her for a long time. Then he got up and walked to the other end of the porch, put his hands on his hips, and stood looking down on the traffic on the road. She moved to the steps and sat down and put her arms around her knees. She didn't look around when she heard him coming back, but when he knelt beside her she felt his big hand light like a little bird on her shoulder. And then his hand was cupping her chin and turning her face to him. She could see the slightest bit of rough stubble on his chin and cheeks where he needed to shave again, a little lighter than his hair, but she could also see that all the anger had gone out of his eyes. He looked like he was sorry. He leaned forward and kissed her.

'I just got upset over what you told me about that guy. Hey. That ain't your fault, OK?'

'I know that. I know it wasn't my fault. I did kiss him, though.'

He shook his head without taking his eyes off hers.

'It don't make no difference. Come on and go with me. You can get you a shower and I'll go up and take mine and shave. Can you be ready in twenty minutes?'

'Sure.'

There were already some cars and trucks in the parking lot when they pulled in and stopped. The sky was cloudy and Aaron rolled up the windows before he shut off the El Camino. Fay got out with her purse and smoothed the front of the short black dress she had found upstairs, then he came around and got her by the hand and they walked to the front door. Gigi's picture was gone.

Aaron stood there, looking at where it had been.

'Looks like she picked it up on her way out,' he said.

Inside it was dim and full of smoke and people drinking. The stage was lit but nobody was dancing. Music was playing and the colored lights were revolving but she guessed maybe the dancing girls didn't start this early. Aaron led her to the bar and pulled out a stool for her. A different bartender was on duty now and as she looked around she saw two waitresses watching her and talking about her.

'I got some stuff to take care of back here,' Aaron said. 'It may take me a while but we'll go get something to eat when I get done, OK?'

'OK,' she said. He summoned the bartender.

'Harry, just give her whatever she wants, all right?'

He gave her one pat halfway down her back and walked away, behind the bar and through that rear door. She watched it close and then the bartender was standing in front of her.

'What can I get for you?' he said.

'You got a cold beer?'

'Sure do. Bud OK?'

'Bud's fine.'

He turned to get it and she reached into her purse for her cigarettes and lighter. She set her purse on the floor beside her stool and lit up. The waitress who had first served her that Sunday night walked by with a tray in her hands and murmured, 'You work fast, honey,' and went on across the room.

The bartender opened the beer and set it in front of her and brought her an ashtray. Then he turned away and started talking to a couple of men down at the end of the bar. She sat there and sipped her beer. It was very cold. She smoked her cigarette and listened to a couple of songs. Once she saw the bartender step to a small black box with blue lights mounted above a beer cooler and change out a tape. She wished they'd play some country but it was mostly all rock.

She looked at the beer can and knew again that she'd have to cut down on her drinking pretty soon. She didn't really want to, but she was going to have to ask Aaron if he could take her to a doctor one day and see if she could find out when the baby was supposed to come. If she could have gotten to spend a little more time with Reena she could have asked her some questions about what happened to you when you had a baby, since she'd already had two.

She stubbed out her smoke and drank some more of the beer. More people started coming in, the door admitting brief shafts of light each time somebody opened it. But when the door closed, the room would settle back into that premature darkness that she was beginning to get used to already. She was trying not to think about what she'd done to Sam. She guessed she wasn't good enough for him. Him worried about her up there and her down here fucking somebody already. She wondered what would happen if by some miracle Sam found out where she was and came in here to get her.

'How you doing? Need another beer?'

She looked up from her thoughts to see the bartender facing her from where he was mixing drinks for some other customers.

'I'm fine for now. Thanks.'

He nodded and went back to his work. A few of the men along the bar glanced at her or looked longingly at her but nobody came over to try and buy her a drink or talk to her. She wondered if that was because they had seen her walk in with Aaron. She wouldn't have minded having somebody to talk to. She thought she might try to talk to the waitress if she came back by, but she'd been over in a far corner talking to two men at a table for a while and was still over there. It didn't matter. She'd just sit here and drink her beer and wait for Aaron to get through with his business back there, whatever it was.

She thought about this afternoon. It had been so good she wanted to do it again as soon as they could and maybe that would be tonight. Maybe he'd move her to the room upstairs. There was a balcony up there. She'd be able to go down to the kitchen and get her coffee and then go back up and sit out there and look at the boats and the water.

She thought about Gigi some. She probably wasn't nothing but a high-class whore. And then she thought: *What about you, girl? You ain't no better. You fucked him just for a place to stay.* But she told herself that this was different. She didn't strip off her clothes for any man who walked through the door of this place.

She started drinking a little faster, just from having to think about all the stuff in her head. She finished her beer and called to the bartender for another and he brought it. More people were coming in and she saw a man in an orange suit and a black tie come from the back and set up a tall stool near the door. He had a roll of money in his hand thick enough to choke a goat, like Aaron that first night. And then she saw the waitresses start going among the tables, evidently asking for money, because some men started handing it over and others finished their drinks and got up and went out. It was getting close to showtime. She saw now that they didn't look for free.

She checked her watch and saw that she'd been in here forty minutes already. She would have thought he'd be back out by now but she didn't know anything to do other than just wait on him. She was starting to get hungry and she was hoping he'd take her somewhere they had some good food. Eat a good supper, go back to his house and make love again, that would be nice. She was happy to keep helping Arlene around the house. She liked making the beds, putting out towels, cooking in the kitchen. It might even turn out to be like having a real home again. But still she couldn't help thinking about Sam.

The door opened back there and she looked at it expectantly, but it wasn't Aaron, only some girl she hadn't seen before, a tall girl with brown hair and white undergarments who stepped to the end of the bar and called to the bartender for a shot of whiskey. The girl looked up at a clock on the wall and the bartender brought the shot. She leaned her head back and downed it and wiped her mouth, then looked over at Fay. Fay smiled and nodded at her but the girl had no expression on her face at all. After a moment the girl looked away.

People kept coming in and the noise level of the talk was starting to rise over the music. The man at the door was taking money from everybody who came in now. The bartender turned the music up a little louder. The girl with the brown hair had a beer in her hand now and she was drinking it fast. The bartender went over and said something to her. She said something back and started to lift the beer again, but with a quick move he took the beer away from her and pointed to the tables. Fay heard a few sharp words, then the girl tossed her hair back from her face and turned and walked toward some drunks at a table in the center of the room. The next time Fay looked over there, the girl had taken off her top and was dancing between the spread legs of a young man with a drink in his hand who was gazing up at her like somebody might have just warped him in the head with a two by four. Other customers at the table were leaning over and stuffing bills into the low waistband of her little panties. Now she wore a different look on her face, one that said Come fuck me because I like it.

Gradually, one by one, other girls began to emerge from the rear door. A few of them were the same ones Fay had seen that first night. She saw the girl who had been down on her knees. Each of them stopped by the bar and had a quick drink before they went out among the tables. The front door kept opening and closing and the roll of bills in the doorman's hand was getting thicker. She ordered another beer. She kept looking for Reena but she didn't see her.

He'd been gone too long. Way too long. It looked like he would come on out and at least see about her, see if she was doing OK. She thought about those rooms back there and what went on in them.

She smoked another cigarette and kept sitting there. The waitress she had talked to that night finally came back by with an empty tray and stopped.

'How you doing?' she said. 'Fay, right?'

'Yeah, Fay. I'm fine. You all right?'

'Oh yeah. You fixing to start working here?'

'I don't reckon so. Why?'

The waitress pulled a pencil from her pocket and scratched behind one of her ears with it, then slid the tray down and held it on her hip like some women hold their babies. She was chewing gum and she smiled now.

'Oh, I don't know. You seem to be pretty good friends with Reena. And now you come in with the big man. How long you been in town?'

Fay picked up her beer and took a drink from it. She turned on her stool and set the beer on her closed legs.

The air conditioning was cranked down so far she could feel goose pimples forming on her arms.

'A week or so. You seen Reena?'

'Not tonight. She may be in later. I don't know what her schedule is this week. You need anything?'

Fay lifted her beer slightly.

'I'm fine.'

'OK,' the girl said, and stuck her pencil back in her pocket. 'My name's Wanda. Maybe we can have a drink sometime and shoot the shit. Maybe me and you and Reena could get together sometime.'

'OK,' Fay said, and the girl moved off.

It was loud and smoky now. When she glanced back over her shoulder she saw that the bar had nearly filled up. People had pulled tables together and there was much laughing and talking. Alongside Fay people had crowded in but nobody seemed to be paying any attention to her. Then the lights dimmed on the stage and the first dancer stepped up. It was the girl with brown hair that she had seen come from the back and get the shot of whiskey. Some slow guitar music that Fay didn't know started up, and the girl was already moving to it. The level of talk in the room dropped as the eyes of the men turned toward her. She had bent her knees slightly and she was swaying with the music as if the guitar man was there and playing only for her. She turned on her long legs and moved her hips from side to side and even Fay had to admit that she was pretty fine. The guitar player started singing a sad lament to a lost lover and the red dress she had been wearing one night, and Fay listened to the words and heard the fingers move on the strings and watched the girl interpret the song through the movement of her body. She danced smoothly on her high heels and the money started hitting the stage all around her, though she seemed to give no notice of it or even of anybody else in that packed and smoky room. Bills that had been wadded and thrown rained on her, glanced off her arms, her legs, rolled between her shoes. The colored

342

lights whirled on her and spun around the dark walls and showered her hair with all their different hues, and she kept on dancing. The guitar wailed and screamed and the player offered up his voice and matched it until it all rose up together into a place that was somewhere beyond heartbreak, a place that was all loss and sadness and desperation, and then it stopped and the room went black. There was a great amount of clapping and whistling, calls for more, but when the lights came back on the money was gone and so was she.

Finally Fay had to get up and go to the bathroom. She asked a drunk next to her to save her seat and he said he would, and she took her purse with her. She noticed the bartender watching her when she went around the end of the bar and through the door to the bathrooms. Some sullen girl was in there putting on some eye shadow. Fay spoke to her but she didn't say anything, just kept frowning into the mirror and putting the stuff on. Fay stepped into the stall and did her business and when she came back out the girl had left. She went back to her bar stool and sat down and debated over getting another beer. She was pretty hungry now and wished she'd eaten more of the sandwich. She ordered another beer and got the bartender to give her a small bag of potato chips, but they were so hot she could hardly eat them and she left most of them on the bar still in the bag. She smoked another cigarette and saw that it had been an hour and a half now. She kept watching the rear door. Once in a while a girl would go back there. Sometimes a man would. The men would stay gone about ten minutes and then come back. Wanda came by a few times but Fay could see how busy she was. She walked fast and had a sheaf of bills stuffed in her apron pocket.

Aaron had been gone just way too long now and she was about ready to ask the bartender if he'd mind going to see about him, but he was working so hard back there mixing drinks and hauling out bottles and cans of beer for the waitresses that she was afraid to. She thought about going outside, just to get out of the smoke and noise for a while.

The rear door opened again and there stood the man who had taken Reena's money away from her. Aaron's brother. She saw his eyes move onto her and she froze, then quickly looked away. She didn't want him coming over at all and she wanted Aaron to come back right now. But then between heartbeats he was moving toward her. A man standing next to her stepped away from the bar and Aaron's brother slid in. He didn't look at her at first, only rapped his knuckles on the wood to get the bartender's attention. She didn't look around, but in the pause between the end of one song and the start of another she could hear the liquor going down his throat, could hear him swallowing. And then she had to look at him. He was smiling with uneven broken teeth and lips that looked too red for a man's. He was close enough that she could smell his breath and it was awful. He wore jeans, a green T-shirt under a sport coat. His hair was slicked straight back, just the way Aaron wore his, and there was a slight resemblance between them. She knew somehow that this man and Aaron had different fathers, same mother. Arlene was in the structure of the facial bones, the straight hair, the look in the eyes. But he was nowhere as big as Aaron.

'How you doing, Fay?' he said. 'Why don't you let me buy you a drink?'

'I've got one,' she said weakly, but he reached out and took it from her hand and hefted its weight.

'Feels about empty to me,' he said. 'Why don't you let me order you something?'

She just nodded. The bartender stood there waiting.

'Fix her something fruity, Harry,' he said. 'Something sweet she'll like. Can you do that for us?'

The bartender bent his head curtly and took the empty can from him and threw it into the trash. He turned to his bottles back there and selected a few and started mixing. Aaron's brother turned back to her and rested his elbow on the bar with his drink in his hand.

'You know who I am, don't you?'

'I know who you are. I don't know your name.'

He extended his hand. She looked down at it. The nails were not those of a working man. They were neater than her own. His fingers bore heavy rings of gold and jewels winked there in the small light from the bar.

'I'm Cully,' he said. 'I think you've met my mother. Arlene?'

She felt she had to take the hand. When it closed around hers it felt cool and clammy. She turned loose of it as soon as she could.

'I remember you,' she said.

'And I remember you.' He turned his face away for a moment. 'How's that drink coming back there, Harry?'

For answer the bartender set it in front of her. It was in a tall straight glass and it was colored like lemonade with the faintest pink cloud floating at the top of the glass. A long straw stuck out.

'Try it,' Cully said. 'See what you think.'

'Do you know where Aaron is?' she said.

He didn't answer at first. He just kept looking at her. She couldn't take his eyes, so she looked away, back toward the rear door.

'He'll be out after while,' he said. He urged her gently, a light push with his finger against her arm. 'Try your drink. I had Harry make it special just for you.'

She picked it up. It was very cold in her hand. She bent forward and put her mouth around the straw and sipped at it. It was sweet and delicious, slightly sour, a kind of flavor that made you automatically want more. She took another big sip and set it back down.

'It's good,' she said, looking at him again. 'Thank you.'

'That's the spirit. Drink up, kid.'

For want of something to say, something to do, she reached back into her purse and pulled out her cigarettes again. Before she even got one out of the pack he had struck his lighter and held it out. She dipped her head, nodded her thanks, lit it. Sat back and blew a long plume of white smoke toward the ceiling.

He was already close but he moved in a little closer. He held his glass just below his lips, looking over the rim of it at her. Something about her seemed to amuse him.

'I think I made a bad first impression on you,' he said. 'Hate to get started off on the wrong foot like that.'

'What'd you want to hit Reena for?'

He laughed to himself. He looked down at his glass and swirled the ice in it, then took another sip. The song ended and another one started up. Fay turned her head for just a moment and saw another dancer move onto the stage and begin to move. She reached for the drink again.

Cully extended one finger and stroked the back of her hand. She pulled it back. He didn't look up.

'Let me tell you some things about people in the world like Reena,' he said.

'You didn't have to hit her in the eye.'

'Oh I didn't?'

'It's a chickenshit thing for a man to do.'

His finger crept over to her hand again. This time she held it still on her glass. The finger moved. It rubbed in circles while he talked.

'You can't run a place like this and let people steal from you.'

'What'd she steal?'

'That bitch? Goddamn money, what do you think?'

'She said you took hers.'

He laughed again and twisted a ring. He looked around in the bar, a tiny smile fixed on his lips. He lifted a hand and waved at somebody, then turned back to her. The finger etched faint trails on her hand. She picked up the drink and took another sip.

'I didn't take any money from her,' he said. 'I just got what was mine. She didn't want to give it up, so . . .'

346

His words trailed off and then he said, 'Put it like this, we had a little conversation about it. I probably should have kicked her ass a lot worse than I did.'

'What about Chuck? What if he'd been there?'

He chortled in his throat and turned the drink up and finished it and slammed the glass down on the bar loud enough to get the attention of the bartender, who didn't do anything but reach and get it and pitch the ice toward the sink and start mixing another one.

'Where's Aaron at?' she said.

'I can get you a good job,' he said. 'Maybe some movie work later on. Get you in front of the camera, see how you do.'

She didn't believe any of that shit. He'd gotten her name from Aaron, or from Reena, and he was just a mean man who hit women. And did worse than that to them maybe too. A man like her daddy.

The bartender set the fresh drink up on the bar and Cully put his hand around it. Fay stubbed her cigarette out. She was ready to get the hell out of here. Right now.

'Can you go tell Aaron I'm ready to go?' she said.

'Why don't you go tell him yourself?' he said, and turned his back and walked away from her. She sat watching him. He stopped and looked back. The drink was in her hand and it was still cold and she took another sip from it. She could feel it hitting her already and maybe he saw something that caused him to come back to her. The music was still playing and she didn't see how it could get any louder. It had begun to beat inside her head with a sound that made her ears throb, small percussions that were going off inside her brain, a beat that she could feel even in the pulse of her blood. Getting drunk. And not caring. The place you slip from where you know what is right and the place you slide into where you just don't give a shit. Maybe that's what he saw.

She looked at the drink. It was almost empty. She finished it off. Somehow he was beside her again and handing the glass back to the bartender. Later she would remember him filling it again and setting it before her, and she would remember the noise and the lights, but would have only the vaguest memory of Aaron coming out from behind the bar to where she sat, and fragments of a drunken conversation:

'Goddamn, what's done happened to you?'

'Drunk,' she said. 'Drunk and don't give a rat's ass. We got to go fuck, baby, we got to go eat, baby.'

And vaguely him getting his arm around her and hauling her off the stool, half carrying her toward the front door, his back under her hand wet with sweat. A drunken altercation, more heads busted and shoved into the front door, folks leaping out of the way and Aaron and his brother back in the middle of it while she sat at a table with her head lolling and trying to light a cigarette and firing up the wrong end and dropping it on the floor and watching the two of them knocking people over chairs and finally a shot fired into a wall or a ceiling and then somebody being kicked into what looked like death in the parking lot while she hung on to the El Camino and tried to hold herself up. And some place miles down a road where he held her head and helped her puke and getting it on her like that night in the trailer with that fishboy. Conway and the Twitty Birds wailed on the tape deck. She lifted her eyes to the stars and saw them and the carpet of black in which they lay. Laying her head on his thigh and reading the green numbers on the dash and feeling him lift the beer to his mouth again and again, the pop of the lighter, the little red eye coming out as he turned it and the wind rushing in through the windows to cool her sweaty brow. Another time when she lay alone with the Chevy not moving and wondering where she was, a black place again, then waking up to hear clearly Merle Haggard singing her back into the sweet blackness. And she went to it gladly, whispering only one word just before: 'Sam.'

She woke on her bed at Arlene's house with the curtains and blinds drawn and her head pounding. She felt between her legs. Something sticky, something wet. She was naked but for her blouse and bra. She pushed back the covers and sat up and held her head with her hands. She swung her legs over and felt it coming and barely made it to the bathroom on time, a cold sweat breaking out on her face while her stomach contracted and gave up what little it had in it, over and over, until the bitter taste of her bile rose up in her throat. On her knees she grabbed a water glass and filled it from the sink and then threw that up, too.

'God,' she said. 'Fuck.'

She didn't leave the bathroom until it had passed. Holding on to the door frame she spied her panties lying on the floor and went to them, picked them up, sniffed at the crotch as if that would tell her what had transpired. She got clean ones out of a drawer where she had stashed them and slipped them on and sat back down on the bed. She saw her skirt on a chair. She made no move to fetch it. Her purse was on the floor beside the door and she got it and sat back down with it, fingered the clasp and then opened it. Her cigarettes were in there, one left in the pack. She found her lighter but was loath to light the last one. Not until she had a cup of coffee at least. She put the cigarette back in the pack and set it down on the bedside table with the lighter.

She went back into the bathroom and brushed her teeth. After she got through with that she washed her face with cold water and combed her hair. She wanted a shower or a bath but she wanted coffee worse, so she found a pair of her shorts and put them on and slipped her feet into her sandals and got the cigarette and the lighter and opened the door to the hall. Dead silence. Somebody had taken her watch off her wrist and she went back to the room and found it on a cedar chest where a small lace doily sat beside small tin cups and antique truck toys. She picked it up and slipped it on. It was two-fifteen in the afternoon.

There didn't seem to be a soul in the house. She made coffee and looked through some drawers for some more cigarettes but couldn't find any. She seemed to remember a store down the road a ways. She sat down and waited for the coffee. When it was ready she poured a cup and put sugar in it and milk from the icebox and looked at some cold pastries in there but decided against them. When she had the coffee in front of her and it had cooled down a little she lit her last cigarette and smoked it while she drank the coffee. It went too quick.

'Well shit,' she said. She stood up and drank the rest of the coffee and turned the pot off. Back in the room she was staying in she got her purse and let herself out the front door and went across the porch and down the steps and stopped at the road. She didn't remember which way the store lay, but she thought it was back to the east. Same old shit. Walking again. At least she was used to it.

It was two miles to the store, actually a Shell station but she knew they sold cigarettes. She still had some money left. She went in and got a bottle of orange juice and two packs of smokes and paid and went back outside and opened the orange juice and felt an instant something crank up inside her when it hit her stomach. Right away she opened a pack of the cigarettes and lit one. It seemed a hassle to walk back down the road drinking the orange juice so she stepped down to the curbing just outside the station and sat down.

She could see the water from there, could see the birds veering up and down in the air. Cars passed on the road and the wind moved through her hair. The juice was cold and good and men and boys kept going into the gas station and coming out of it and they all looked at her sitting there in her shorts. Most looked on the way in. All of them looked on the way out. Some of them looked at her through the glass.

By the time she finished the juice she was feeling a lot better and thought she'd go back to the house and find something to eat.

Cars passed her on the road. She didn't stick her thumb out. Two miles was nothing. Boys in pickups blew their horns at her. She just smiled and kept walking but was careful not to wave.

By late evening she'd found some tomato juice in the fridge and some vodka in a kitchen cabinet and ice in the bin and had fixed herself something to sip. She took it out in the backyard.

When she heard a vehicle pulling in she knew it was Aaron. She didn't even turn her head. Not until it stopped and she heard the door open and slam shut. When she turned he was already going up the steps into the house.

If there had been a chair back there anywhere she would have sat down in it. She walked in circles back there, sipping at her drink. It looked like he'd come out and see about her. It looked like he would have said something before he went into the house.

She went over to her purse and picked it up and carried it with her around the side of the house, up the gravel drive, and looked at the paint flaking and peeling away in white curving pieces. She turned the corner and went across the front yard close to the porch and climbed the steps and sat down on them. Her usual place she guessed. Most of the boats were in now but people were still moving around on the dock. The birds were still sailing.

Most of the drink was gone and it was watery. She finished it off and set it down beside her. She heard his steps in the house. She could hear him moving around in there and she wondered what he was doing. It was wrong to be here with him.

She could leave and try to get back to Sam. Get her things, walk out the door, never look back. Get somewhere and find a phone and get an operator to help her and get his number, call him, tell him where she was, see what he sounded like. Find out if it was safe to tell him where she was first.

In the movies they could trace numbers. But what if you were calling from a gas station or something? And you just walked away from it once you had hung up? They couldn't catch you then could they?

'Fuck it,' she muttered. She picked up the glass and went over to the front door and opened it and walked up the hall. It was quiet in there and she thought of how old this house was and of how long it had stood here. Through wars. Through the deaths of the untold number of people who had once slept in it or made love in it or maybe died. When she stopped beside the big room where all the old things were he was standing with his back turned to the hall, just standing there with his forearm resting on the mantle over the fireplace and looking down into the empty hearth. He must have heard her but he didn't turn. And she didn't know whether to speak to him or not. She waited for a while, less than a minute, probably, but he didn't turn or give any indication that he knew she was there. So she went on into the kitchen and fixed herself another drink. A bottle of whiskey was sitting on the counter beside an open can of Coke.

She looked back up that way. She could go quick. She could be out on the road in less than five minutes. But the road led only to places she didn't know. At least she knew this place a little bit. And in that tiny moment

352

she decided to stay. She opened the cabinet door and reached for the bottle again.

Just before dark she saw him walk across the street to find her sitting on the wharf with her feet hanging over the side. He was barefooted, had a drink in his hand. His cigarettes were jammed into his pocket. The shirt he wore was blue denim and the sleeves had been hacked from it so that the slabs of his arms with their freckles and pale red hair looked enormous, and were. He squatted down beside her and didn't say anything for a minute, just looked off into the expanse of the Gulf and studied it. Finally he leaned back and sat down on the boards next to her and crossed his legs.

'Well,' he said. 'How's your hangover?'

'It's better now. Did you fuck me last night while I was passed out or was it somebody else?'

He looked up at her and seemed surprised.

'Hell, you wasn't passed out. You were asking me for it. You don't remember it?'

'I don't remember much. I remember a little about when we left. Did y'all get in a fight?'

'Y'all who?'

'Your brother. Cully. And you.'

He scratched the back of his head, looked like he was trying to remember. He looked out across the ocean.

'I don't guess you remember that shit either.'

'What was in that drink he give me?'

'Hell if I know. You was already shitfaced when I come out. Somebody started a fight on the way out. When I was trying to get you into my car. Cully like to broke his toe kicking him.'

'I remember that.'

'And some bastard had a pistol and shot at us. Some sumbitch who claimed Julie robbed him.'

She let some time pass, let the birds cry some more.

'Seems like it's always a lot of trouble over there,' she said.

He nodded and looked down at the planks he was sitting on.

'I tried to get you not to go.'

'Don't you ever leave me alone again with your brother. You hear me?'

'Well what am I supposed to do?'

'I don't know. I don't care neither. I just don't want to be around the son of a bitch.'

He raised his hands in a backing-off gesture.

'All right, damn. Take it easy.'

She sat there in silence and looked at him. The wind had risen and his carefully combed hair was blowing loose and it was longer than she'd thought. She reached one hand out and rubbed her fingers against his cheek and then took them away. He scooted closer.

'Listen. Mama's gone up to Winona for a couple of days to stay with Henry. Her boyfriend. She left me a note but I didn't find it and then she called. His ticker's been acting up. She ain't got any guests and I want to get out of town for a few days. You up for it?'

'Where we going?'

He pulled back from her and looked out across the water. He pulled his cigarettes and lighter from his pocket. When he looked back at her there was nothing showing on his face.

'Gulf Shores,' he said. 'I done called for a reservation. We can get into the Best Western right on the beach if we get there tonight.'

'I need to go to the doctor sometime,' she said.

'I know you do. We'll do that when we get back. But let's go over for a couple of days and lay on the beach and eat some oysters. Few days ain't gonna make no difference about you seeing the doctor. Is it?'

'I reckon not,' she said. 'I just need to go sometime.'

'All right, then.' He stood up and reached out his hand to her. He took her back across the road, watching for traffic both ways and holding tightly to her hand, and she went back into the house and took a shower and washed her hair and packed her swimming suit and some clothes and underwear into her suitcase. Got her toothbrush.

While she was checking to see that she had everything in her suitcase she heard something pull in. She stepped back out into the hall and saw Aaron talking to a man in a pickup, a new Dodge, tan and brown, with a big camper hull bolted over the bed. It was Arthur, the bartender, that Aaron was talking to. She saw them raise the hatch on the camper hull and stand there looking and talking. Then they closed it and Aaron handed him a set of keys and Arthur got into the El Camino that was parked under the old oak tree and he left.

She went back to the room and got her suitcase. She set it down in the hall and walked over to the front door and turned the bolt in it, checked it. She went back to her suitcase and picked it up and carried it to the back door. Aaron was getting a few beers from the icebox and he asked her if she wanted one.

'Not right now,' she said. She stood there waiting. It was just dark and the yard light had come on so that she could see a sort of blue glow over the gravel out there.

'You ready?' he said.

'Yeah. I've got all my stuff. I locked the front door.'

'Good,' he said. 'Let's go, then. We'll be there in about two hours.'

She went out and stood on the back porch and watched him turn out a few lights and then come out with the keys and put one of them into the lock on the back door and turn it and check it. He helped her down the steps and opened the hatch and put her suitcase in and slammed it shut and then opened the door on the pickup for her and went around to the other side and slid in and cranked it up.

'How come we're going in this?' she said.

'More room,' he said, pulling on the headlights and rolling down his window so that he could see how to back around. 'Plus if it rains your stuff won't get wet like it would in the Camino.'

355

It was full dark now. The headlights showed the gravel on the drive and the peeling paint on the side of the house and he pulled out to the street and down the hill to the coastal road and pointed it east. He had to wait for two cars and then he mashed down on the gas and they headed out. He opened a beer and pushed a tape into the deck. She looked over at the gas gauge. It was full.

He reached out for her leg and she slid closer to him in the seat.

'Rest if you want to,' he said. She put her head back and leaned against him.

'Do you have any of the movies she made?' she said.

'Who?'

'Gigi.'

He waited so long to answer that she thought he wasn't going to. But finally he said, 'That ain't nothing you need to see.'

Book 3

Joe Price picked him up at the hospital in his cruiser and drove him home down the lake road with the trees standing under their masses of leaves, the shade beneath, the dark forms of spotted horses flicking their tails at flies, and horned bulls chewing their cuds while rocking their horns gently and lying in the cool black dirt. Farmhouses, fences, tall waving grass and people with mowers in their yards.

'We done took your car home,' Joe said, and glanced at himself in the mirror. Some of the troopers called him Pretty Boy and never behind his back. 'I guess you got some more time off now, huh?'

'I reckon so,' Sam said. 'How about pulling in up here and let me get some smokes before I get home?'

'I will if you'll pick me up somethin cool to drink while you're in there, sport.' He put on his blinker and slowed going into the curve. Boats were for sale out to the side of the store, party barges with colored fabric tops and aluminum rails and big pontoons. Joe stopped right in front of the door to let him out.

'What you want? A Coke?'

'Yeah. Can you get out that door?'

'I ain't that damn crippled,' he said, and got out.

A boy was tending the register and he got two short ones in green glass bottles and a pack of cigarettes and paid. The cruiser door was still open when he went back out.

After they'd been on the road for another mile or so Price answered something on the radio, but Sam wasn't paying any attention. Tomorrow was a week since they'd found Alesandra. Fay'd had a week to get some-where. And he'd had a week to get ready to talk to somebody from the sheriff's department. That day they'd sat out behind the hospital sipping the whiskey Joe had told him there was plenty of talk around the department. But he hadn't wanted to ask any questions. He'd wanted to keep Fay's name out of it. He was hoping that maybe Tony McCollum would just forget about her and be satisfied with the answer he'd given him at the boat landing.

Price was studying him now, sipping his Coke, want-ing to ask him something, he could tell. Joe'd been careful with his questions about Alesandra and Sam had given him short answers that let him know he needed to shut up about it. They had the windows cracked and some wind was whipping the short ruff of Price's hair.

He guessed Joe couldn't stand it.

'They called you?' he said, glancing at him while he drove.

'Who?'

'Hell, you know who. Don't try to bullshit a bull-shitter.'

'You mean the sheriff's department?'

Price took another sip of his Coke and rested the bottle on his creased trousers. He had on a really nice gun. He flashed his lights at an oncoming car and it slowed.

'Asshole,' he said, to the person in the car. 'I mean Tony. Our boy Tony who's so hot to get on the highway patrol. You knew that, didn't you?'

He thought about it for a few seconds.

'Naw.'

'Well he is. He aspires to be one of us.'

Some more road went by. Somebody was raking hay in a field. They entered the park boundary and drove by the lower lake. It was jammed with campers and tents. He slowed at the curve where the spillway went under the road and Sam looked down to see people in work clothes and shorts and T-shirts fishing over the rail.

'What do you think that means?' he said.

'Oh, I don't know.' Price tooled the car around the curve lazily. 'Might be he's ambitious. Grayton wouldn't let him come over to the hospital. He wanted to. Tried to.'

'Now how you know all this?' Sam said.

'Shoot,' Joe said. 'Little birdies fly around. Once in a while one comes around and shits right on your head.'

Sam waited. They turned left to go up on the levee.

'Loretta told me,' he said. 'She saw it.'

'I met her one time.'

'She's a fine piece of ass ain't she?'

Sam nodded. 'She looks pretty fine. I don't know how fine her piece of ass is.'

'You'd probly skeet off before you ever got it in, buddy boy. If I was you, I'd be looking for Tony pretty soon.'

'I already told you, Joe. I don't know what happened.'

Price just nodded. They went on down the road and stopped to get the papers at the end of his driveway. He got out in his yard and Joe waved going out the drive with his sunglasses and his shiny cruiser, the tires crunching in the gravel and one hand hanging out the window, his fingers spread to grab the wind.

It was the hottest sun she'd ever felt. Kneeling there in the sand wearing the white visor he'd bought her the night before at a local Wal-Mart she watched him talking to the browned boy with the tattoos who furnished umbrellas and foam pads for the wooden recliners that were rented by the day. Aaron pulled money from the pocket of his white shorts and gave it to the boy, who picked up a big blue umbrella and together they headed over to where she was.

She turned her head and gazed out at the water. The waves were rolling in high breakers and even though it was only nine o'clock in the morning the sand was covered with people – children, swimmers, and waders. Out in the dark green swells she saw the humped backs of dolphins coursing up and down. She'd thought they were sharks until Aaron laughed and hugged her with one arm and went to talk to the boy with the umbrellas.

Now he came over and tipped his hat to her and said Good morning ma'am and she smiled and got up and waited. There were two of the wooden recliners and another boy came jogging with the foam pads and put them down, one on each, and the other boy stepped between the recliners and started wedging the umbrella down deep into the sand. Aaron rubbed her back with his hand.

'I went ahead and got it for two days,' he said. 'Cheaper that way. You think you can take two days of this?'

She looked around. As far as she could see up the

beach both ways there were big hotels and decks and houses and restaurants that backed almost to the edge of the water. People walking and wading everywhere or just lying on their towels, sitting in their beach chairs, reclining under their umbrellas.

'This is great,' she said. 'I can tell I'm gonna hate to leave already.'

He just laughed. He was in a good mood, had been ever since last night when they'd first pulled into town. He'd left her in the truck right in front of the hotel lobby just long enough to check in and get the key, then he'd gotten back in with her and took her to a place called Coconut Wally's where they had to stand in line for ten minutes before they could get a table. But once they were seated there were tall frosted margaritas and fat fried oysters. She ate them this time and was surprised how good they were. She had boiled red shrimp on beds of ice and cocktail sauce with horseradish. And then back at the hotel they moved with each other in the darkened room with only the moonlight showing through the opened curtains on the third floor.

Naked in the room she'd sat just at the edge of the sliding glass doors that opened on to the balcony and looked out at the rolling water, at the people still walking, still collecting shells, while the television played silently behind her and Aaron slept and the waves spoke out there.

Now the boy had the umbrella up and there was shade to lie under. The boy bent with a piece of chalk and wrote FORREST on a green plate at the back of one of the recliners and then he was gone.

'Well come on,' Aaron said, and he bent to pick up the cooler and the radio he'd bought. She had a new mesh bag with suntan lotion and potato chips and sandwiches, her brush. Two big towels lay folded at her feet. She picked them up and got the bag and they slid in under the shade on the recliners, but then she told him to get back up and put a towel across each one and then they lay down. Aaron moved the umbrella a little where the sun was burning down on her feet.

'That better?' he said.

'Yeah. Thanks. This is nice.'

He reached into the cooler for a cold beer and brought it out, ice clinging to the sides of it. He popped the top and drank some of it, leaned his head back.

'Shit,' he said. 'We may stay three days.'

Fay was fiddling with the radio, trying to find a good station.

'You got my sunglasses?'

'Here.'

He slipped them on and lay still. Just for a moment he did. Then he got up and pulled off his shorts and laid them at the foot of his recliner and lay back down in his green trunks. She looked at him.

'How much you weigh, Aaron?'

'About two sixty most of the time. How about handing me my cigarettes, baby?' She handed them. 'I drop a little in the summertime cause it's so hot. I'm down to about two forty right now. But I'll pick it back up this winter.'

'How come you're so much bigger than Cully?'

Careful questions, as if the answers didn't matter much. Just making conversation. He seemed OK with it.

'Cully's daddy wasn't as big as my daddy. My daddy was about six foot three. He weighed damn near three hundred pounds. Genetics, you know? Like horses. Or dogs. Or, I don't know, gorillas.'

He pulled down his sunglasses from his eyes for a moment and smiled at her, then pushed them back up.

'So he ain't your whole brother?'

'My whole brother? That's a good one. He's really my half brother. Mama was married to Cully's daddy and he got killed in a car crash in North Carolina. I think Cully was about four or five when she married Daddy. They met in New Orleans, got married after a week. She said it was love at first sight. You believe in that?'

She was still messing with the radio. There was a lot of static on it and then a station came in clear as a bell and she pushed the antenna on out and set it down. Rock and roll. She liked it. Made her want to dance.

'I don't know,' she said. 'I kind of think you need to get to know somebody first.'

He nodded and pulled one leg up and looked out over the beach. He seemed happy. She knew by now that he would let you in for a while and then shut you out, that there were different sides to him.

'Well,' he said. 'I guess there's a lot to be said for that.'

About that time out of the corner of her vision she saw the plane coming. She shifted onto her side and watched it come. It was a pale tan, and out behind it hung a string of red letters that read FOOD FUN AJAX DINER NIGHTLY. The plane flew slowly and far up there she could see the pilot, just a dark blob against the cockpit window facing her. It was only about a hundred feet high. It droned. It flew the length of the beach and she watched it until it turned and went off into nothingness.

'We'll take a ride this afternoon,' he said. 'Show you some of the country.'

'I may just want to lay here.'

'I think we'll take a ride,' he said.

They had lunch at three o'clock after showers and some hard fucking on a soft bed. He hadn't mentioned Gigi and she hadn't said anything about her. The place was cool and dark and he called bartenders and waitresses by name but didn't introduce her to anybody. He ordered a steak medium rare and she had a salad and a hamburger. She drank iced tea and noticed that he drank only water. Not like him, from what she knew of him. He only ate about half of what he had and seemed nervous and preoccupied. He tapped his fingers on the table. She finished eating and pushed her plate away and he stood up and she got her purse and followed him to the register where he paid cash and left a tip for the waitress. Then they got back into the truck.

For a long time they had been following a sand road that seemed to lead nowhere. There had been houses earlier on the road but they had left them all behind and now there were some dumps with cast-off washing machines and crates of bottles and the road was rutted. The truck dipped and swayed. He drove carefully. By and by she began to see the ocean out there and far far off what she recognized as the beach where their hotel was. She had asked where they were going but he hadn't answered and she didn't ask again.

Finally the road ran out and there was just a turn-around where he pulled in and backed the truck up and shut it off. He looked over at her, his hand still on the ignition key, his eyes blank behind the sunglasses.

'Get on out,' he said. 'I wouldn't want you to miss this.'

She did as he said but she had to pee. She told him so and he pointed to some bushes behind her. Going over to them she looked back once and saw him raising the hatch on the back of the camper hull. The grass was high in the sand and she didn't figure anybody was around anywhere.

She made her way back through the tall grass to see him leaning against the fender with a beer sitting on the hood. Next to it was a gun with a long barrel, a thing fixed on the top like the deer rifle Sam had kept in his cabinet in the hall at his house. Aaron looked at her and then turned his eyes back to the sky and the bay. She couldn't imagine what. Then she heard the plane droning off in the distance.

'*Don't*,' she said, and took only one step forward, but he raised a finger to his lips for a moment. Far off she could see it coming, the red plastic letters fluttering out behind it, a tiny thing like a toy set aloft by a child's hand.

'How you know?' she said. 'How you know it's the right one? What if it's some other guy?'

'Not a chance,' he said. He picked up the rifle and slipped his shades off and fitted his eye to the scope. 'I called the airfield. I got this motherfucker's number.'

It came over the beach with the engine noise growing louder and she saw now that Aaron was waiting for it to turn. She watched him track it with the barrel and she saw him push a black button behind the trigger just as the plane banked and started to come past them seventy yards out, looking very big and sounding powerful. The rifle boomed, and boomed, and boomed, knocking his shoulder back, and the plane dipped crazily, righted itself to not quite level, and then a wing pointed downward and it began to fall.

And Christopher Justin Dodd in his high berth above the white beach saw glass splinter beside his face and then another round punched a hole through his shoulder. It passed through his collarbone on the other side and then blood was running out from the bottom of his sleeve. His hands wavered on the stick. He tried to make his feet do something. The last solidpoint caught him dead through the third rib and then the earth and sky swapped places. He felt the plane heeling over and was helpless to stop it. When the ocean came running to meet his starboard wing he did not know that he lay bleeding for a stolen piece of ass. For a brief moment he thought he saw the black shining back of a swimming dolphin. And then the world went totally dizzy and he knew in his final moments that he was going in for the last time.

It was hard on her, seeing it. Once they were back on the highway she moved over next to the door and wouldn't look at him. He didn't seem to care, only sipped his beer and looked casually out at the seafood restaurants and the big shops where they sold shells from Philippine waters. The sky was the color of a robin's egg and once they got back into the city limits the traffic was terrible.

367

'What you want to do?' he said, finally. 'You want to go to a bar? There's some good ones around here. Or we could drive on over to the Flora-Bama.'

She sat on the seat with her legs crossed and her arms crossed over her lap.

'I think I'd like to go back to the room and lay down for a while.'

He studied her for a moment, stopped at a red light, the blinker going. 'Suit yourself,' he said.

'How you know it was him?' she said. 'How you know you didn't shoot somebody who . . . how you know it was him?'

She wished she hadn't told him now. She could have kept it to herself.

'I made some phone calls,' he said. 'While you were sitting out front getting drunk.'

'I wouldn't have got drunk if you hadn't left me out there by myself. Your brother's the one that got me drunk.'

The light changed and he stepped on the gas hard and turned the corner. They were back on the main strip now. Cars all over the place, people trying to cross the road in shorts and swimsuits, old ladies in terry cloth robes that stopped halfway down their sad thighs and the old men with them with eyeglasses and white hair on their paunches.

'So what?' he said. 'Are we fighting already?'

'I guess goddamn we are.'

'Well I'll just drop you off at the room and you can sull up or whatever. I'm gonna find me a place to have a couple of drinks and I think I'll go swimming about dark. What, are you wanting to go back or something?'

'I ain't said that.'

'Well what the fuck is it then? Did you not want the son of a bitch dead? You said yourself you started to run over him. You think that bastard ought to get away with something like that?'

'I don't know.'

'Well what do you know?'

'Nothin, I don't guess.'

She could tell he was getting mad. He stopped in the road in front of the hotel and put the blinker on again. Traffic was speeding toward them, a long barely broken line of it. *Tic, tic, tic* went the blinker. She thought she was going to throw up. He stamped it hard and cut in front of an oncoming truck that blew its horn. Aaron stuck up his finger and muttered, 'Fuck you,' then swung into the parking lot. He pulled around to the door where the luggage carts sat and shoved it up into park. He dug into the pocket of his shorts and pulled out a key for their room. He put it in her hand. She sat there looking at it. He had one arm curled over the steering wheel and he was looking through the windshield at the hotel next to theirs.

'What kind of a man would I be if I didn't take care of somebody who messed over you?'

'I just didn't think you had to kill him.'

'Well. I did.'

'I guess you did,' she said, and opened the door, but he reached out for her arm and squeezed it tight.

'Look,' he said. 'We can end it right here. Is that what you want?'

It was hot out in the parking lot. She could feel the heat seeping in through the open door even while she was cooled by the vents in the air conditioner that were blowing onto her face.

'No.'

'Then straighten up, goddamn it.'

She sat there on the edge of the seat. He hadn't hurt her with his fingers and even now they were slacking off, lessening, easing their grip on her.

'I think I just want to go lay down for a while.'

He nodded and turned loose of her. He picked up a green polo shirt that was on the seat and slipped it over his head, worked his arms through the sleeves and pulled it down across his belly. He rubbed at his mouth with his fingers.

'All right. Go on up to the room and lay down and

rest for a while. I'm gonna go have a few drinks and I'll come back. Then we can decide where you want to go eat supper.'

'I thought you wanted to go swimming.'

'We can do that too. I'll be back in an hour or an hour and a half. OK?'

'OK.'

'Fay?'

'What?'

'Nothing. Just go on up and rest.'

She got out and shut the door gently. He pulled away. She stood there in the overhang of the parking garage and the shade it lent and watched the end of the pickup go around the corner where the indoor swimming pool was and where through the glass windows she could see children swimming and splashing. Then she turned and went deeper into the shade, across the concrete that had been wetted by the feet of the guests, toward the stairs that led up to their room.

Son of a bitch got just what he needed. The bastard ought not done that to her. And maybe he shouldn't have done it in front of her. It would have been easy enough to leave her in the room or on the beach, tell her he was going down the road for some cigarettes and another six-pack. But he'd wanted her to see it. He'd wanted her to know that he could take care of her. But now she was all fucked up with it and acted almost like she even felt sorry for the son of a bitch.

He got off the main drag and turned down one of the little roads that were lined with oyster shells and people were already standing outside restaurants, women in dresses and the men wearing shorts. He didn't like having the rifle back there but as long as he didn't fuck up, get drunk or hit somebody or weave, nobody was going to pull him over and hassle him. She'd get over it. They could go out for a nice meal tonight somewhere and have a lobster or something.

He cruised down one street and turned off on

another. A cop car was waiting at a stop sign. He pulled up, stopped, kept his eyes straight ahead. The cop went on. You just had to be cool. You could get away with almost anything as long as you were cool. People hauling dope halfway across the country and speeding because they were nervous. But don't mess up and they don't usually pull you over. Even if you do have two pounds of cocaine in the trunk. The trooper who had stopped him outside Clarksdale last year had only been unlucky. He still remembered the cop's nameplate: Banks.

He saw the place and wheeled in, parked it, shut off the motor and considered the pistol under the seat. He sat there for a moment, thinking about it. Finally he just reached over and locked the other door and got out and grabbed his smokes. He shut the driver's door and locked it and checked to be sure that it was locked. It was. He went on in.

A guy he knew vaguely named Pinky was still behind the bar and he swung one hand and shook with Aaron when he sat down.

'What up, bro?' Pinky said. 'Ain't seen you in a while.'

'I ain't been here in a while.'

'How's your brother?'

'He's fine. Y'all got any on the half shell?'

The bartender mopped at the bar with a wet rag. He was big shouldered and like Aaron his nose had been punched more than once. He seemed good-natured.

'Right back here, all you want. How many you need?'

He thought for a moment. Dinner later but maybe real later, depending on how she was, if she felt like going out. So go ahead and eat.

'Let me have a dozen and a Maker's Mark on the rocks. Make it a double.'

'You got it,' he said, and he turned away, said something through a wooden opening at the back of the bar, and started making the drink. Aaron kept his eyes on the bottles behind the bar and didn't look around.

When Pinky set the drink in front of him he reached for it. He picked it up and sipped it. He looked at his watch. It was almost six o'clock. He wanted to hurry up and get this over with and get on back. Find some decent place to eat supper. And maybe tonight they could walk on the beach if she wanted to.

Pinky mixed a drink for somebody at the end of the bar and took it and a Heineken and a Miller down there and got the money and made change and closed the register and when he was finished he came back over to Aaron. He leaned on his hands.

'What's happening in Biloxi?'

'Nothing,' Aaron said. 'Same old shit. Hot as a son of a bitch. Like always.'

'Where's that blonde you had over here that time? You still sporting her around?'

'Nah.' He pushed his glass around on its napkin. 'She's done went on to greener pastures.'

Pinky stuck his fingernail between his two front teeth and picked at something.

'Damn she was fine. You ain't got her phone number on you have you?'

'What's the special today?' Aaron said.

Pinky pointed. 'It's over there on the board.' Aaron looked. He'd come past it on the way in without glancing at it. A large chalkboard on legs sat just past the register and it listed the catch of the day or whatever was on sale. Aaron sipped his drink. The girl behind the register was one he'd seen before but he didn't know her. He watched her smile at the people she was waiting on. She was tall and had a red ribbon in her hair and she wore a short flowered dress over good legs and Aaron thought she was fine but not as fine as Fay. He had to hold on to her. Maybe he could watch his temper a little better. He didn't want to run her away. The only thing was that baby. He didn't know what to do about that.

There it was, on the board at the bottom: Bonita, stuffed or fried, blackened or broiled. He noticed that it was $11.95 and came with a house salad, choice of potato, bread and soup.

Hell. Maybe he needed to bring Fay over here and let her eat. He'd always heard they had good food.

He glanced at his watch again and saw how slowly the time was moving by. It was always like this. He'd told Fay he'd be back in an hour and a half at the latest. And shit, only thirty minutes had gone by. He was ready to rock and roll with it.

The oysters came sliding through the panel on a big brown platter and Pinky put them in front of him. Aaron ordered another drink and tore open a pack of crackers and stirred some extra horseradish into the small cup of cocktail sauce and scooped the first one from the shell. Pinky stood back and watched him eat like a man who was scared to speak.

It was not quite dark when he walked down to the wharf where Smilin' Jack's restaurant was perched on the hillside above him. He'd slipped on a pair of red jogging pants from the back of the truck and the .380 was tucked snugly into the waistband of them, the green polo shirt pulled down over the butt of it. He was ready.

He saw her, *Bonita*, riding at her mooring and a dark man perched on the wide white deck, making like he was polishing the chrome. The money was in a green USMC gym bag in Aaron's right hand. He stopped on the planks and looked back up at the restaurant. He could see people sitting in there and bartenders mixing drinks. Folks about to have supper. Well, they had their deal and he had his.

The dark man stood up and stopped his makeshift polishing when Aaron stopped in front of the boat.

'Where's Frank?' Aaron said.

The man motioned with his head. 'Inside.'

Aaron stepped closer. 'Can I come aboard?'

'Come aboard.'

He wasn't happy that he had his sandals on. Deck shoes would have been better. It was easy to fall off one of these slick son of a bitches and bust your ass. He made an awkward large step up to the bow. He'd take Fay out to dinner. Make some sweet love with her later on. Maybe go back to Pass Christian later on.

'I'll have to frisk you,' the dark man said.

'Fuck that shit,' Aaron said, and pulled out his piece and showed it. He didn't point it, but the man put his hands halfway up and took a step back.

'Frank,' he called.

'Put your hands down!' Aaron said. 'Tell him to get his ass out here.'

When the man saw that he wasn't about to get shot, he gave Aaron a murderous look and took two more steps back and put his hands down and went down the steps into the cabin. Aaron waited, holding the pistol alongside his thigh. He held it covered with his hand and he didn't think that any of the people who were wandering back up to the restaurant could see it. He looked at the boats. Some ran to sixty feet and they were fine and high, some with tall towers that lay sleek and gleaming in the last light that was rapidly fading from the sky.

He waited for about a minute. The dark man stepped back up to the top of the ladder and paused there.

'You got to come inside,' he said. 'Frank don't want to conduct business out here.'

He didn't much want to. But he could set Fay up, get her to the doctor, make her comfortable. Buy some clothes for her, whatever she wanted.

'But you got to put that pistol away. We're all friends here.'

Yeah, right. He raised the pistol.

'Let's do this shit instead. You go back down nice and easy and I'll follow you.'

The man stood there, didn't even raise his hands this time. He spat. Aaron thought he looked like a man who needed a little lesson.

'Any shit starts,' he said, 'you'll be the first one that gets it.'

'This the way you treat our hospitality?' the dark man said.

'Fuck your hospitality. Let's just do the deal and then we can all live happily ever after.'

The man turned. He went back down the steps. Aaron followed him down. He could see the lights of the cabin ahead and he could see two people standing by a table. When he stepped into the cabin he saw they were holding guns in their hands. And Frank was standing there, his arms crossed over his chest, a cold cigar in his mouth, the dope on the table before him. Moths batted around the single light bulb hanging from the teakwood ceiling.

'We don't want no trouble, Aaron,' he said.

'Neither do I. I got the money. Here it is.'

He pitched the gym bag, and it landed on the table next to some of the bricks of dope. He watched the other two.

'Ain't no need for you to come in like this, Aaron. I thought I'd fix you a drink.'

'I got somebody waiting on me.' He scanned the room, trying to see everything at once. The big boy on the left who looked like a skinhead held a Colt revolver. The Vietnamese next to him held a .45 auto and had a bad scar down the whole side of his face. 'Let's just get it over with and I'll be on my way.'

He waited, on a hair trigger now. It wasn't up to him. It was up to them. 'They better not point those guns at me,' he said.

'Yet you come in with yours,' Frank said.

'I don't trust none of you motherfuckers.'

Frank didn't take his eyes off him. But he tried to put a different look on his face. 'Sure you don't want a drink, Aaron?'

'I'm fine.'

'I got some Wild Turkey over here. I've been wanting to see you. Find out where those red snappers are biting.'

'Ask somebody who knows,' Aaron said.

Frank smiled and pulled out some of the money and riffled the bills slowly with his fingers. He stepped over to the bar and picked up the bottle of whiskey and held it up.

'You don't care if I have one, do you?'

'All I want's my dope,' Aaron said. 'Where's the rest of it?'

Frank had ice and a glass. He poured slowly.

'That's all we've got for you today.'

'Why?'

Frank stopped pouring and looked up. He capped the bottle and set it down.

'We had a little trouble down in Boca Raton last week. DEA boys. The big load slipped by them.' He smiled and picked up the glass and sipped from it. 'Unfortunately about half of yours was on the one they caught. Look at it this way. Even a blind hog finds an acorn once in a while.'

'Shit,' Aaron said. He relaxed, and then they did.

'How about taking half that money out of the bag for us, Bao?'

The Vietnamese put away his gun and moved to the table and started taking out money and counting it. What he kept he put in an ordinary grocery store sack. What he left he put back in the bag and then zipped it shut. The skinhead turned around and sat down.

'How come I get cut out?' Aaron said. 'My money's just as green as anybody else's.'

Frank swirled the whiskey around in the ice and smelled of it.

'Priorities, Aaron. Things bigger than you. Best not to ask too many questions. Now unless you want a drink you'd better be going. It's almost time for our other company to get here.'

The Vietnamese picked up the bag and held it out to him. He took it and looked down at the gun in his hand.

'One more thing, Aaron.'

'Yeah? What?'

Frank was holding the glass up to his lips and he sipped from it. Bao handed him his dope.

'Don't spend all that money in one place.'

'Fuck you,' he said, and he went on out.

She'd gone down to the beach to sit there on her towel and watch the waves come crashing in. They didn't seem to slow down any after dark. He was late but she'd known when he'd told her that he'd be back in an hour and a half that he wouldn't be. He was up to something, she didn't even want to know what. People were walking along the beach, couples holding hands, small girls and boys with buckets, their mothers trailing along after them, laughter and talking against the sound of the constantly crashing waves and all she could think about was that plane going down. But he was probably already dead by then. She thought about this: A person who had been inside her was now dead.

When he came up she didn't hear him at first. His feet made no noise in the sand. But she felt his hand on her shoulder like that little bird lighting again and turned her face to see him looking down on her.

'Hey,' he said.

'Hey.' She was glad to see him, still.

'You get some rest?'

'I slept some. I took a nap. I come down here right before dark. It's different then. It's nice.'

'I'm gonna slip in and swim just a little bit.'

She watched him take off the red jogging pants and walk down to the water. Just before he went in he took off the green shirt and tossed it back. She could see the form of him moving out there and she didn't have any idea what she was doing with him. She watched him play in the water for a while and then he came out.

'Let's go up to the room,' he said.

'OK.'

She picked up her towel and shook the sand from it and looked over her shoulder at him and saw him picking up his clothes. They went back across the beach, up

377

the steps to the hotel deck where they washed their feet from a sprayer and hung the nozzle back up. There was a big hot tub and a swimming pool with a waterfall where kids were splashing and yelling. They went across the boards to the stairs and up them. There were some people in the hall once they got to the landing, a knot of them, and when they got past them she took out the key and opened the door, then went to the glass door that opened on to the balcony and stepped out there to see the people still walking and wading. She felt like she could stay in this place forever, this place of sand and wind so close to the rolling water.

'How about going down to the truck for me?' he said. He pulled his keys from his pocket and held out a small shiny one to her. 'This one opens the hatch. There's two bags in there. Bring em back up here while I use the bathroom. Please.'

'Let me put some clothes on.'

'All right.'

She picked up a pair of shorts from the floor and slipped them on, and grabbed a T-shirt of Aaron's and pulled it on. She slipped her feet into her sandals and took the key from him. He let her out and she went back down the hall.

The lights were on in the parking lot. She found the truck close to the street, facing out, and she fingered the little key in her hand as she went up to it. For just a moment before she opened it she thought about what she was doing and wondered what was in the bags. Then she went ahead and put the key into the lock and turned it and turned the handle to open it. The bags were close to her hand. The blue bag was kind of heavy. She pulled it out and set it at her feet and grabbed the small bag and set it down, too. Then she closed the hatch and relocked it and checked it, pocketed the keys.

It was hard carrying the big bag on one side and the small one on the other. She was walking kind of lopsided. But she made it back through the parking lot and past the luggage carts where he had let her out earlier and went back up the stairs. Once she had to move aside and let some people pass. The big bag was bumping her knee with each riser. Once she got into the hall on their floor it was easier. The door to their room was open. She stepped inside and put the bags down and shut the door.

'Lock that door,' she heard him say from the bathroom. She turned and twisted the bolt. Put the chain on too.

She could hear the water running. She looked at the bathroom door. It was open but it sounded like he was in the shower. Quickly she bent over and unzipped the small bag. What she saw made her suck in her breath. It was more money than she had ever seen, bundles and bundles of it, too much to count. She zipped it shut and kept looking at it. But she was almost bursting to know what was in the other one. She looked at the door again. The water was still running. And what would he do even if he caught her? She bent over and unzipped the other bag. She didn't know what it was even after she looked at it. She reached in. Among blocks of some strange brown weed that were wrapped in clear plastic lay other ones, smaller, covered with shiny foil. She picked one up and sniffed at it. It had no odor. And about the size of the little blocks of chewing tobacco she could remember seeing her daddy buy in years past.

'It's hash,' he said, and she looked up to see him standing at the door of the bathroom with a towel around him. She sat on the bed.

'Hash? Is that what you said?'

He reached for his cigarettes and lighter lying on the dresser. He lit a smoke and dropped the pack and the lighter back on the dresser. He leaned against the wall.

'I don't mean the corn beef kind. I got a pipe in my suitcase if you want to get stoned.'

She sat there holding it on her lap. It seemed

hard-packed, dense. She creased it with her thumbnail. Then looked up.

'I'm afraid to mess with it. The baby.'

'Oh. Well I'll mess with it then.'

She put the foil package aside as he walked over to her. He knelt beside her legs. She put her hands on his arm and rubbed at the thick veins outlined against the freckled skin on his forearm. He kissed her.

'Listen,' he said, and he got up and sat on the bed next to her. 'Did you see that store next door?'

'That little gas station?'

'Yeah. Walk over there why don't you and get me some more cigarettes.'

'All right.'

'How about making me a drink first? Have we got any ice left?'

She got up and looked into the plastic bucket that sat next to the television set. Some melted cubes still floated in the water.

'There's a little. You want some whiskey?'

'Yeah, it's right there on the—'

'I see it.'

She got a clean glass from the bathroom and with her fingers scooped chunks of ice into it. She picked up the bottle of bourbon and poured the glass half full and took it to him. He took a drink and got an ashtray and sat back down. She went to the bathroom and brushed her hair, and when she came out he was still sitting there.

'There's some money in the pocket of my shorts over there,' he said. 'Or take one of them hundred-dollar bills out of that bag, I don't care. Get that pipe out of my suitcase first though. Please.'

She went over to it where it lay open on a wood rack with a navy cloth top. His underwear and razor were in there, aftershave lotion, a toothbrush and paste.

'It's in that little pocket.'

She unzipped it and reached in and her fingers found it. She brought out a small pipe carved from dark wood.

380

He was tearing at one of the packages with his teeth. He ripped off one corner of the foil and spat it on the floor.

'Might as well see if it's any good or not. How about handing me my lighter?'

She watched him load the pipe with chunks of something dense and near black. When he had it filled and lit, the bowl glowed and she saw him take in a big breath of smoke. After he held it in for a while he blew it out. He offered her the pipe.

'Tastes like some good stuff,' he said.

She shook her head. 'I don't want any.'

He nodded reflectively. 'All right.' He drew on the pipe again. She reached for his shorts on the floor and went into one of the pockets and found his money clip with some bills folded into it.

'I'll be back in a little bit.'

He didn't look up from the pipe. 'Pull that door shut behind you.'

'I will.'

She went out and he heard the door latch shut behind her. He sat there pulling on the pipe and it was starting to take hold. He took another hit and then laid it aside and reached into the money bag for the .380. He checked to see that it was loaded, easing back on the slide until he could see the cartridge case dully shining in the chamber. Then he let it snap shut and checked the safety to see that it was on and put the pistol down beside him on the bed.

His clean underwear was in a drawer right across from him and he leaned up and opened it and found a pair of boxer shorts and slipped them on. Then he reached for his drink and sat holding it and sipping it. It wouldn't take her ten minutes to walk over there and get the cigarettes and come back. But waiting made him nervous, always had. It might not be a good idea to spend the night here now. He knew getting high was making him paranoid but he reasoned that even if he'd been straight there would still be things to worry about.

Somebody could have seen his pickup near there at that time well enough to call in a description of it to the cops. He could imagine what it had looked like out there at the beach: cruisers all over the place, ambulances maybe, lights flashing, asshole people standing around gawking. It would be on the ten o' clock news from Mobile, reporters talking into microphones, some detective being interviewed, maybe even people from the beach still in their swimsuits who might have heard the shots. Or seen it go down. Fuck. Plenty of people saw it go down. It might be best to just go.

So he got up and pulled on some jeans and got his feet into a pair of tennis shoes and tied them and sat back down on the bed to wait for her knock on the door. He had made up his mind that they needed to go and soon. Get back to Pass Christian. Get back safe.

He picked up his drink and sipped it. Then he reached for the pipe beside him. He had enough dope to last him now for months and plenty to sell, too. He kind of wished now he'd just gone ahead and slapped the shit out of Frank. Fay would be back in a little bit, and she was kind of like a dog. He thought he had her figured out. All you had to do was just pet her a little bit once in a while and she'd be all right.

She came back in and then she kissed him all over his face and checked the locked doors and got them both naked on the bed and crawled on top of him. She rode him and could control him and his gasps that way and learned that and her heart softened for him again and she wondered with him going in and out of her was it just the pleasure that he brought to her, or would any other man do just as well? She knew by then that every man was not made the same, inside or out. Black dark came and lifted the moon and she rode him in the light it made in the room.

And then there was the long drive back home, up past and through the pine forests and the million tiny stores and the places that sold shells or fishing gear or fixed boats and motorcycles and the endless bars and package stores and grocery stores, places to get your palm read, your arm or your chest tattooed, places that sold four-wheelers and all the signs that lined the highway advertising something else for you to buy until she nodded and then slipped down in the seat next to him and put her head on his thigh. She felt his hand, a warm caress at her face, trailing through her hair, into the roots of it, touching her scalp, the tip of one of her nipples, then finally resting on her shoulder.

'Aaron?'

'Yeah baby.'

She didn't know whether to ask or not. He seemed nice now. And she wanted to. She needed to know.

'Would you take me somewhere one day if I asked you to?'

He had a beer between his legs and he picked it up and took a sip of it.

'I reckon I would. Where is it?'

'It's a long way from here,' she said to his leg.

'How long?'

'Long way.'

'I mean, like, three thousand miles?'

'No. It's not that far. Just back up where I come from.'

He was quiet for a few moments. Maybe she shouldn't have asked after all.

'Sure,' he said. 'When you want to go?'

'I don't know. Just sometime. It don't have to be no time soon.'

'Well,' he said. 'You let me know.'

'OK.'

The dash lights were glowing up above her and she could see the little dial on the radio in the cassette deck. She could see a red wire and a yellow wire hanging down. She could see the black tape wrapped around the wires. She could hear the steady rhythm of the joints in the road hammering at the tires. His leg was beneath her head. Like sleeping in the pickup with her head on her mother's lap one of those nights so long ago, going who knew where again to be hungry some more.

'Where is it?' he said.

'Just a place I used to stay.'

'You mean back up north?'

'Yeah. The place I come from.'

'Sure, baby,' he said, and he patted her again.

'Now you just sleep, OK? Get some rest and I'll have you back home in two hours. We'll get in our own bed.'

'Yeah.' She closed her eyes and felt the pickup move smoothly through the night and across the land, the tires a rocking whisper now, *slow down, everything's OK, maybe the trouble's over, ease off, sleep . . .*

He hadn't been home an hour when McCollum called him. He said he wanted to come over in a few days and talk to him. So Sam started looking for him to show up, but he didn't. Just dreading it was the worst part and he needed to get it over with. Do something. Do anything. Find out where the hell she was.

But days passed and nobody came down the driveway. He had to go back to the doctor and get his bandages changed and the doctor sat on a stool and talked to him.

'You ought to come up and go fishing with me. I was on a bream bed other day, caught seventeen before I lost the first cricket. Old Jerry Lee's fished in my pond before. You ever heard him play the piano?'

He'd already taken the old bandages off and now he was finishing with the new ones. He taped a last piece down.

'I don't guess I have,' Sam said.

'Shoot. That son of a gun's good. He used to play up at the Embers in Memphis when I was about fifteen years old. We used to slip in there and see him. I saw Elvis in there one night.'

'Is that right?'

'Well it might have been an Elvis impersonator. It was back when Elvis was still alive. But he looked just like Elvis. Sounded just like Elvis. Far as I'm concerned it was Elvis. That's what I tell myself anyway. You remember where you were when Elvis died?'

Sam remembered.

'Yeah. I was checking licenses down on Three-fifteen. Had a drunk pulled over. I got back in my car and had the drunk in the backseat and somebody called over the radio and told it. The chief got all over their ass.'

The doctor mused, sitting on his little stainless steel stool. He was a clandestine smoker and now he pulled one out and fired it up. He offered the pack to Sam but he waved it away. The doctor smoked Virginia Slim Lights or something like that.

'Course, you know,' the doctor went on. 'Everybody knows where they were at when Elvis died. It was like Jesus Christ, kind of, wasn't it?'

'I guess it was,' Sam said, and started putting his shirt back on.

The doctor said, 'Did you ever see him anywhere?'

'No. I never did.'

'I never did either except for that one time up in Memphis. But that was a long time ago.'

Sam finished dressing and then buckled his belt.

'Well,' he said. 'I guess I'll get on. I appreciate everything you've done for me, Howard.'

The doctor stood up and took a drag, thumped his ashes into the trash can where he'd thrown the bandages.

'Shit, Sam, anytime. Come on up and go fishing with me sometime. The Killer might be out there one day, you never can tell.'

'I'll do it,' Sam said, but he knew he never would. He liked the doctor but when this was over he wouldn't want anything to remind him of these last weeks and he wanted to try and forget as best he could about the burning man in the truck. And the charred boy in the road. McCollum was coming to see him. He kept thinking about that.

He shook hands carefully with the doctor and went down the clean white halls of the hospital and jingled the keys in his hand. His truck was sitting in bright sunlight in a pool of heat and he unlocked the door and slid onto a hot seat. As soon as he had it cranked up he turned on the air conditioner full blast and sat there until it cooled off a little. He'd sold Amy's shop the day before to the two girls who had worked for her, Suzy and Amber. He could have probably gotten more for it if he'd turned it over to a real estate agency, but he'd wanted to be rid of it and had let them have it for a hundred and thirty-five thousand. The check was in the bank and the billfold in his back pocket was packed full of hundred-dollar bills. Just in case he needed anything.

He backed out of the parking slot carefully, retrieving his Ray-Bans from the visor and slipping them on. The dash vents were roaring cold air directly into his face and he drove to the end of the parking lot and stopped. Looked both ways. He pulled out and turned right and went two hundred yards and put on his blinker just as he got to the gas station. He stopped under the metal roof and shut off the truck and got out.

He felt pretty good, considering. He took off the gas cap and put it on top of the bed wall and turned on the pump and put the nozzle in. He locked it down at a slow flow and watched the numbers rolling on the pump for a few seconds, then went on inside.

Ludell was behind the register with a few customers in front of her. She was short and wide and today she had on a blond wig. Some days she wore a red one.

'Hey sugar,' she said.

'Hey Ludell. You got any catfish?'

Her blunt fingers moved nimbly over the keys and she reached up for a pack of cigarettes.

'Yeah but you better git it now.'

He went around the people waiting and looked into the warmer. There were seven or eight fillets left. Plenty. He didn't need but two or three.

He turned away and went down to the beer coolers and stood there for a second, then opened a glass door and reached in slowly for a six-pack of Michelob. He moved to the chip rack and stood there studying the bags, then reached for some barbecued pig skins. Something to munch on sometime. He'd figured maybe she'd write him. Hell, did she know the address? By the time he got back up to the register there was only one person left and he was paying. Ludell took the money and gave him his change and the guy shuffled toward the door lugging his sack of dog food. Sam set his beer up on the counter and reached for his billfold.

'You get them bandages changed?' she said.

'Yeah, just now.'

'Let me see em over here a minute, baby doll.'

He smiled and put his billfold on the counter and held his hands out. He'd known her since she was sixteen and had a two-year-old baby that she kept behind the counter. Now she was twenty-five and had four more but none of them were in today. She turned his hands this way and that, examining them critically.

'That ain't too bad,' she said.

'No. Not too bad.'

'You got to be more careful. Can you cook and stuff?'

'I manage. Can I have some of that catfish?'

'You can when I'm done holdin hands with you. When you gonna take me out like I been askin?'

She turned loose of one of his hands but held the other one in a static handshake, massaging the length of his thumb with hers, studying the bandages. A few of the buttons on her knit pullover were undone and she was showing about ten inches of dark cleavage.

'I don't know,' he said, and began to mumble some stuff about trying to take it easy.

'Huh,' she said. 'You take me out I'll show you a good time. I can drive and everything. And you ain't never seen me git dressed up.'

'Maybe we can take a ride sometime, Ludell.'

'Well don't just think about it, do it. I take off every day at four. Sharp. And you know where I stay. I'll send them younguns over to Ruthie's.'

'Where they at now?'

'Over at Ruthie's. How much catfish you need?'

When he got back out to his truck he went around to the driver's side and opened the door and set the sack on the seat, then took the nozzle out, replaced it on the pump and put the cap back on the gas tank. He had a cold one open by the time he pulled out of the station. Thinking about everything so much made him want to drink more. There was some relief in it.

He took some long swallows once he was on the road back to his house and reached in and tore off a piece of the fish and took a bite. His new bandages were going to get grease on them. Unless he used rubber gloves. But Ludell had put some napkins in the sack and he got one to wipe his fingers on. He was thinking he might just find an empty picnic table under a shade tree on the lower lake and eat there.

The road was newly overlaid and a deep black with stark white lines along the shoulders but they hadn't put in the center line yet. He slowed down when he saw the road crew but they were stopped, he guessed to reload with paint, and they moved him through with a red flag. He waved.

He tried to remember when it had been that he'd taken Fay down this road and he knew it was the day they buried Amy but now the date wouldn't come to him. He couldn't see how he could have failed to mark it in his mind. He gave his head a slight shake and took another long drink from his beer. He still had enough time off to head south and get a hotel room somewhere down there. If he left on a morning he could be there easy before dark. He could just be a tourist for a few days. Nobody had to know that he was a cop. It wouldn't be any problem. It was a slim chance but at least it was a chance. There was no telling where she was but he knew he wouldn't be able to sit around the house by himself for long. Hell no. He had to look for her. Lost people got found sometimes.

The road was curvy and sometimes he met cars and trucks towing pop-up campers or boats or trailers hauling four-wheelers. It was this way now every day in the summer.

Where the road forked he kept going straight and rolled through the curve at the base of the levee and looked up at the tractors mowing the back bank at a steep slant. He didn't want that job. He didn't know how they kept from rolling over and he knew that sometimes they did.

He cut his speed and started looking for a good spot under some of the trees. He took the second road in and cut his speed to ten miles per hour. The road ran under the trees and it was shady and relatively cool there. He cut his air conditioner off and rolled down his window. People were everywhere wearing shorts and swimming suits, tending their fires or blowing up air mattresses for waiting children or just sitting in lawn chairs eating and drinking. A peaceful camp of humans. He liked them this way. He didn't like them the other ways he so often saw them.

There were a couple of empty tables but they were close to where people were camped. He didn't want to get too close to anybody if he could help it. He slowed enough that a person walking beside him could keep up and just kept watching around him. But soon the road curved back toward the dam and he drove back out to the highway and stopped. Two trucks were coming from the right and one put on its blinker and turned in beside him and the other one kept going. He pulled out behind it, taking a sip of his beer, checking things out in his rearview mirror. It was an almost constant habit when he was in the cruiser, a thing born of long years of driving. He felt sometimes like he'd spent two thirds of his life behind the wheel of a car, the same roads over and over.

At the next place he turned in again and drove into another grove of trees. This one didn't look so full. It looked pretty full over close to the beach, but he didn't go that far. He saw five or six tables off to the left and he turned slowly off the asphalt into the grass and drove the pickup carefully over to the closest one and stopped and shut it off.

There was a good breeze blowing there and he set his stuff down and stepped over the concrete seat and eased down. He put both feet under the table. The catfish was still hot and he pulled out the white bag that held it and reached in for some packets of ketchup like those you get from a burger dude. Napkins too. Ludell had always had the hots for him. A lot of women liked cops and he guessed there was something about the uniform or the authority or something he never had been able to figure out.

He wished he had some lemon juice. Just didn't seem right without it. But it was only a gas station. The Michelob was about to get warm so he finished it and tossed the bottle toward an open fifty-five-gallon drum with a plastic liner and it sailed in. He opened another one and threw the cap at it but missed. He got up and walked over there and picked it up and put it in the garbage.

After he finished eating, he opened another beer and he got back in his truck. He backed out and pointed it toward home, but then turned and went back across the base of the dam so that he could drive around the curve and take the upper fork and then ease across the levee before sundown and look at the water.

It was still bright with sun and the ski rigs were busy working across the waves. He could see the red bluff where his house sat once he got a third of the way across. The speed limit was thirty but there was nobody behind him so he slowed to a crawl. He had the window open and the breeze was blowing in and they had Johnny Rodriguez on the radio singing about a woman who had a hillbilly heart. He thought he knew one like that but Fay would have lost a part of her life if she'd stayed with him, that's what came to him. Never would have gotten to run around with boys in souped-up junkers, never would have kissed a boy with beer on his breath on some dim road in a pine forest, never

391

would have hung out with single people her own age or gone to movies or had dates or talked on the telephone to her friends and girlfriends or slept over with them. Never would have gotten to ski with young friends like those he could see down below streaking across the lake and gleaming wetly in the joy of their youth.

So lost in thought he was that the horn on the car blared before he even saw it and he jerked the wheel to the right as the car came by, the people in it studying him with strange looks. Somebody was behind him now, too. He sped up some and watched the road a little better. Far out in the distance the trees lined the borders of the lake like faint green velvet, but the water was too choppy to mirror those images. Never before late evening or morning.

She would have just gone straight to being married and a mother. And now if he couldn't find her she was going to go ahead and be a mother without the marriage. Unless she got rid of it. Would she do that? Did he even know her well enough to be able to decide if she'd do something like that or not? But she'd spoken fondly of children, that much he knew. He didn't think she'd get rid of it.

Why wouldn't she come back or at least call and let him know she was OK or where to come get her? Hell, if nothing else, just to let him know she was alive. Because there was always that to think about, too. Somebody could grab her. It happened.

The beer was almost warm by the time he got to the end of the levee. He finished it and dropped the bottle on the rubber mat on the passenger side and settled his hand on the wheel and sped up once he got out of the thirty mile an hour zone. Four curves and he was turning down the road that led to his driveway. He stopped by the mailbox and lowered the lid and it was crammed with magazines and bills and circulars. He had to reach twice to get it all and pile it up on the seat beside him. A little more of the bird was gone now. It was down to about half a bird. He guessed one day before it was all completely gone he ought to take it down and put it in the house and get a new one. Soon. He'd do that soon.

He wasn't expecting company but he had some when he pulled into the yard and parked. A red Olds '88 convertible was parked behind his patrol car and on the porch steps sipping a wine cooler was the little thing whose voice was so sweet when she answered him on his radio. She had on a pair of white jeans and a red-checked shirt whose tails were knotted about her midriff. It was the first time he'd ever seen her out of uniform and he could tell she filled the jeans pretty good.

He got out with the rest of the beer and left the mail on the seat. She was sitting there grinning at him when he put one foot on the first step.

'Hey Sam. I thought I'd come by. Hope you don't care.'

'I don't care, Loretta. How'd you find me?'

'I just asked around.'

Jimmy Joe had told her, maybe Joe Price. She was just a little bit drunk and grinning. Not too drunk. She was just about to slide over the edge. He didn't know if he wanted her to. It would be so easy to slide himself.

'You ain't drinking and driving are you, Loretta?'

'Look who's asking,' she said, pointing to his beer.

'I ain't drunk,' he said, and went up the steps and stopped beside her.

'Neither am I.'

'I may get that way, though. Why don't you get up and come on in? How long you been out here?'

Once in the house she excused herself quickly to go to the bathroom and he nodded toward it. He put the beer in the icebox and pulled out a canned Coke and got ice from the bin and put it in a glass. There was a cabinet beside the icebox high up where he kept his liquor and he reached up for a fifth of Evan Williams and pulled it down and tore the seal with his teeth and the bottle made a bubbling noise when he tipped plenty of whiskey in. It was a big glass. He popped the Coke open and poured it full. He set the can down and picked up the drink and sipped it. It was too strong but that was OK, standing there sipping it, looking down the hall to where she had gone.

He stepped over to the glass door and opened it. Out on the deck he leaned on the rail and looked at the water for a minute and then sat down at the table and put his feet up and lit a cigarette. He heard her call for him and he hollered at her and she came to the door holding on to her wine cooler.

'You like those things?' he said.

'They're good,' she said, and walked out onto the deck. She'd already kicked her sandals off somewhere. Her toenails were painted a bright crimson. She had pretty feet. And when she went to the rail and lifted her drink and leaned forward he knew she was letting him get a good look at her rear end, the tight white denim framing and sculpting her bottom. He looked at the seam that ran down between her legs. And who knew, once he had two or three drinks? Would it matter? Would it make anything better than it was now and would it comfort him any?

She turned. Maybe she was a spy sent by the department to try and get him to talk. He wondered what it would be like to get her in there on the couch and just fuck the living hell out of her. Fuck her brains out. Just get drunk and fuck all night long and not worry about a damn thing. Just get numb.

'How's your hands?' she said.

'They're better.'

'I've missed seeing you get your coffee. I hope nothing else happens to you.'

'I do too.'

She probably wanted to ask about Alesandra. She wandered across the deck, letting him watch her.

'You sure got a nice place here.'

'Thank you. I like it myself.'

She went to the railing on the other side of the steps and leaned up against it.

'You been fishing any?'

'Not lately. Not with these hands the way they've been.'

'Oh.' She nodded and drank some more while he sipped at his bourbon. He couldn't think of a single reason she'd be over here if it wasn't fucking.

'Why don't you sit down?' he said.

'OK,' she said quietly. She came over and pulled out a chair and sat down and then scooted it and turned it so that she was facing him.

'What's been happening at work?'

'Aw nothin. Same old shit.'

'Did they ever do anything to Joe Price?'

'You mean over that stuff with that woman?'

'Yeah.'

'Three days suspension. Was all that true?'

He thumped some ashes onto the deck. His drink was nestled comfortably in the folds of his pants.

'I don't know what you heard. You can't ever tell about all these rumors.'

'I heard he had some woman in his patrol car. That ain't all I heard, either.'

'I don't know,' he said, and grinned. 'I wasn't there.'

'I've heard a lot of stuff about him.'

'Is that right?'

'He's hit on me before.'

'I'm not surprised.'

She looked at him funny for a second or two and then a sly smile eased onto her face. She put one foot up on the arm of his chair and just barely touched the hair on his forearm with her big toe. She turned up the rest of the wine cooler and drained it.

'You want me to make you a drink?' he said.

'I don't know. What you got?'

'I've got some whiskey.'

She made a face. 'I don't much like whiskey.'

'Well,' he said, 'I've got some Cuervo in the house and I think there's a can of margarita mix in the freezer. I could make you a frozen margarita in the blender.'

'Yeah,' she said. 'I love those. We go over to the Best Western in Oxford sometimes and get those. They have two-for-one night for ladies on Wednesdays.'

'Who do you go with?'

'Some of my girlfriends.'

'You don't get in any trouble over there, do you?'

'Shit,' she said. 'We get in all kinds of trouble.'

He got up with his drink and went around the table.

'It may take me a few minutes,' he said. 'You can wait on me if you want to or come in with me either one.'

She was already getting up. 'I'll just go in with you.'

He turned the light on in the kitchen and bent to a low cabinet door and found the blender and plugged it in. She leaned on the counter watching. In the freezer he found the can of concentrate and in the cabinet he shoved some whiskey bottles aside and reached in for the tequila. In a few minutes he had a pale green ice slush whirring inside the blender. He cut it off and found a big wine glass and poured it full. He'd put three whole shots of Cuervo into the blender so she could have a couple more. She'd probably be drinking whiskey by that time. He wondered if he had food here.

She made it as far as getting his pants open and he was hard and couldn't help that because he'd been kissing her for a while and trying to stop, but now he pulled her head up before she could get her mouth on him, when it would be too late.

She'd dimmed the lights earlier and now she knelt on the floor and looked up at him as he fastened his pants back together. Her blouse was open, her bra in disarray because her thick nipples had been in his mouth. She was breathing hard.

'What's wrong?' she said.

'Nothing.' He got up from the couch and picked up his glass from the floor, almost dropped it, then got a good grip on it and carried it over to the sink where the bottle and cans stood. 'I just don't need to be doing this right now.' He opened the freezer top and reached in for an ice tray. He glanced at her. She hadn't moved.

'You don't like that?'

'You mean . . . ?'

'Yeah.'

What to tell this heaving woman? She was all revved up now. He was too and he was afraid to get too close to her again. Then he started to just forget the drink and go right back over there again. But he made his clumsy fingers shake out a few cubes into the glass.

'I like it fine,' he said.

'Then come back over here. I want you to fuck me.'

'I better not.'

'Please.'

He didn't answer her and she didn't say anything for a while. He knew it was embarrassing the shit out of her and he hadn't meant to do that. But nothing was going to make her feel better now.

'Because of that dead girl?' she said in a low voice.

And all lies were one. If you told one you might as well tell a million.

'Yeah,' he said, and he looked up at her long enough to see what looked like fear in her eyes.

'She was your lover.'

'Yes she was,' Sam said, and poured some whiskey into the glass. He'd be sure not to tell Joe Price about this. Or anybody. It was very quiet when she spoke again.

'I can make you feel better. I know I can.'

He topped off his drink with some Coke from a can that he'd already opened. It fizzed some then quit.

He could feel her watching him and he thought he could feel some pity coming his way.

'I guess I'm just not ready,' he said.

'Well fuck,' she said, and got up from the floor. 'God-damn it.' She was almost crying. 'How much of that whiskey you got left over there?'

When she passed out he lifted her from the couch and carried her back to his bed and dumped her on the right side, where she said something about shoes and rolled over and then was already beginning to snore while he arranged the covers for her. She seemed very innocent lying there. And then she started snoring louder and it caused him to groan at the thought of trying to lie down and sleep beside her.

Standing back in the kitchen in nothing but his blue jeans he pondered whether or not to have another drink. Instead he made coffee and locked the doors and pulled out sliced turkey and mayonnaise and bread and ate two sandwiches while he watched that old movie about the sea captain with one wooden leg and a top hat who at all costs was dead set on harpooning a big white whale.

Morning came through the glass doors, a glare rising across the railing of the deck and the actual ball itself sitting on top of it to shine right into his eyes when he blinked and came awake and groaned and turned over. *Please*, he thought. *Let her be gone.* And lying there knowing he wasn't going to be able to sleep anymore and the whole room around him lighting up he reasoned it would only take a peek over the top of the couch where he was lying to see how things were. He put it off, kept lying there trying to remember if he had heard anything during the night, noises of departure, doors closing. But nothing came to him. He remembered only stretching out, turning his face to the fabric of the couch's back. He sure hoped she was gone. He didn't want to have to mess with her as bad as he felt. But rotten ass luck would have it to where she'd slept solidly through the night, was still sprawled back there just like she had been when he'd gone back to check on her one last time. Or she'd want breakfast maybe. Jesus Christ. He wondered if he could go and get in Fay's bed now. He could lock the door. Loretta might bang on it. How his head would pound then. He turned over on his back and looked up at the ceiling. He was really glad he didn't fuck her.

All he had to do was raise up and look over the back of the couch. He knew it was still out there. The top was down on it, too. She didn't go back out there before she passed out. Dew would have already fallen on the seats. He knew the floorboard was probably full of McDonald's sacks and stuff. Gum wrappers. Plastic straws. He saw too often the things people left in their cars. Some of them even left their children in their cars.

She'll have a wet ass when she gets in it. Unless she stays long enough for the sun to dry them out.

He thought about waking her. It probably wasn't even seven o'clock, though. He guessed that beer in the fridge was cold by now. And he might as well go on and have a shower. Brush his teeth. But he was definitely kicking her ass out by ten o'clock.

At a little before eight he was showered and shaved and dressed in clean clothes, a T-shirt and shorts. He'd eased into his bedroom in his boxer shorts to go through the closet looking for his clothes, careful not to wake her. She'd been piled up under the covers, her head on one pillow, another clutched in her arms. Her snores were long and drawn out with a halting, choking sound vibrating through her nose and across her palate. He didn't know what he was going to do with her.

Now he picked up the towel from the bathroom floor and unlocked the front door and took it out into the yard with him and leaned over the sides of the convertible and wiped down the seats, turning the towel and mopping at the little beads of dew, the sun rising up over the house to send rays of light through the branches of the big pines. He hung the wet towel over the back of his pickup and went back in the house.

By peeking in on her again he could see through the crack of the door that she was balled up in the sheets now with her head under the pillow. She didn't move at all as he stood there looking at her the way he had done so many times with Fay. He eased the door shut and went back up to the kitchen.

He thought about making some breakfast but instead he picked up the rest of the drink he had fixed and finished it, sliding the limes out into the sink in a mush of red juice and melted ice cubes. He rinsed the glass and set it back in there and grabbed a beer from the icebox.

400

The sun was already hot out on the deck and he went down the stairs in his bare feet and stood for a minute on the low dock, drinking the beer and looking out across the water. He needed to get a cover for his big boat. Thinking about that dew on her car seats. He needed to go by Tri-County Marine one day and see if they had one that would fit it. Or could order one.

He went down the steps and walked along the fringe of the water. Dead branches and debris lay awash at the edge of the shore. A dead fish bleached a pale lemon and its eyeless sockets staring into the sun. He walked slowly and drank his beer. It was going to be another pretty day.

He stopped and stood facing the water with it almost touching his toes. He thought of Alesandra in that boat that night, of the rain that had fallen on her. He wished he could find out what time it had happened. In the autopsy report, probably, but probably no way for him to get his hands on it. Maybe if he ever talked to Tony McCollum he could find out. But knowing that wasn't going to tell him where Fay was now.

There was plenty of driftwood on down the little beach, ivory limbs twisted in a nest of roots. A breeze was blowing into his face off the lake and he sipped from the bottle. He glanced back toward the house. He guessed he'd have to go in there and get her up. If she'd get up. She might be one of those people who had to have thirteen hours of sleep or be in some shitty mood.

The empty place where she used to lie next to him and never beyond the reach of his hand, her hair pulled over her face. The thing that gnawed at him was worrying that he might never see that again.

He wandered, looking and drinking the beer. He'd already run all kinds of scenes through his head, trying to imagine what had gone on that night. Had it happened here? Or in the house? Had there been blood washed away that he hadn't seen?

It could have happened right here, behind the house.

Alesandra might have come over in her boat and waited for Fay to come out. What was McCollum waiting on?

He was going to drive himself crazy thinking about all of it. And what if people started asking questions about Fay? He didn't know if Grayton had seen her at Amy's funeral or not. But Tony had. And Tony could tell Grayton if he was that kind of guy, a guy who'd help hurt somebody if it would improve his own situation.

The beer was about empty, and the foam in the bottom didn't taste good. He tossed the bottle up into the bushes that stood in the ragged grass going up the hill, and the sun winked on something shiny lying in the sand. He walked over and looked down for a long time. Then he bent over and picked up one of them. He held it up, squinting at the tiny numbers of the end of the case, trying to tell what caliber it was.

She didn't know where she was when she first woke up, then saw Arlene's ceiling and Arlene's walls. Her hand as soon as she moved it touched his broad back. His arm was out from under the covers. He breathed through his mouth. She rolled over and tried to go back to sleep. The curtains were drawn and she didn't know what time it was. She could hear cars on the road outside. She remembered going upstairs.

She touched her belly and then scratched at the tangle of hair below it. She stretched in the bed and yawned, then shivered slightly and pressed her face up against his back. He had lots of freckles. She closed her eyes, breathing him in. His skin was warm. She slept again.

Later she woke and he was gone from the bed. She got up and washed her face and the morning sickness didn't come. She was glad for that but she had not been able to get the image of the falling plane out of her mind. Her face in the mirror looked pale and thin.

In the bedroom she pulled her gown over her head and looked down at her breasts. They were growing. She touched one with her finger, indented the flesh just above the nipple. She cupped them in her hands, lifted them, felt their weight. They were getting heavier. She had to get to a doctor.

Through the glass doors near the kitchen she could see him sitting on the back steps, drinking coffee. On the counter the pot was nearly full, the red warning light shining. She fixed herself a cup. There was no food laid out. Arlene still gone and no guests to feed

403

and she'd never seen Aaron cook anything. He seemed to live mostly on food from burger joints.

She went out balancing the hot cup in the palm of her hand, then switched to holding the handle when it almost burned her skin. He didn't turn. He was wearing only a pair of jeans.

'Hey,' she said.

He turned briefly. 'Hey.'

There was a white iron table out there on the back porch with two chairs next to it. She pulled one out and sat down, put her coffee on the table. The truck was gone and the El Camino was back, parked under the old oak.

'Where's the truck?' she said.

'Arthur's done come and got it.'

She sipped at her coffee, studying his long red hair, thinking about the little girl in Reena's trailer and how she looked. Already getting tall.

'You sleep all right?' she said.

'Yeah. Fine.'

'I was give out. I just barely remember us comin in. I woke up one time and you were still asleep. I guess you got on up.'

'Yep,' he said.

'I love to sleep late. Don't you?'

'I don't sleep too much,' he said. 'I have nightmares. Bad ones. Always have.'

'I've heard you talkin in your sleep before.'

'Only time I sleep good's when I'm drunk.'

She didn't know what to say. He was acting like he was in one of his moods again and already it seemed to her that she was being trained in how to act around him when he was like this. So she sat there quiet and drank her coffee, just watching him. For a while she did. She couldn't just sit there and not try to talk to him.

'When's your mama gonna come back?'

'It's gonna be a while longer, I guess. She left a message on the machine.'

'How's Henry?'

'She didn't say.'

She leaned back and crossed her legs. There was no need in trying to make him talk to her if he didn't want to. He drank some more of his coffee, then put his knees together and held the cup with both hands. He sat that way for a long time. There were so many questions in her mind. She wanted to ask him about her doctor's visit but now wasn't the time. Didn't seem to be.

'When you want to take that trip?'

She'd been thinking about looking in the icebox to see if she could find something for breakfast when he spoke.

'Trip?'

'Yeah.' He turned and leaned his back against the rail post. 'Back up north. When you want to go?'

'I don't care. Whenever you get time.'

'What are you looking for?'

'I don't rightly know,' she said. 'I guess I just want to see if my family's still there.'

He sipped the last of his coffee and poured out the dregs.

'Can you get ready pretty quick?'

'I reckon I can.'

By noon they were headed back toward Biloxi and the sun was high and bright on the water along the coastal highway. He had the air on low and he was drinking beer and smoking almost constantly. She had on a dress with nothing underneath it. His idea.

He turned at Gulfport and went through the old section of town and halted just short of the railroad tracks for a long train that was rocking heavily through the city with its rusted cars and flatbed trailers that held shiny green tractor motors winched down tight. She'd seen him put the gun under the seat, had seen the nylon bag with the zipper go under there, too, probably some more of the dope and the pipe, she figured. Their clothes were in two suitcases in the back end.

He made good time and seemed to know when to

slow down to avoid the troopers that were sometimes hidden in thickets of pine or on the other side of hills. She asked him how he knew and he said he watched the trucks, that if the trucks were passing him it was time to speed up. She saw again country she had seen on the way down and remembered roadside stands filled with watermelons and ripe tomatoes and purple hull peas and saw them again too.

By midafternoon they had left behind the boat lots and seafood shops and the reminders of the environment of those who lived near the sea. They went now through hills of pine trees where the highway was laid out straight for miles ahead and distant points were seen and finally reached and others seen and reached again. They slowed down for small towns along the way. He talked to her and she slid closer to him on the seat and put her hand on his leg.

He stopped in Hattiesburg to get them something to eat and to put more gas in the El Camino and they both went to the bathroom. He bought barbecue sandwiches and hot dogs and chips and another twelve-pack of Miller, a few cans of lemonade for her. They pulled out of the gas station with the food on a big napkin between them.

He kept his foot hard on the gas and they made Jackson after rush hour and swept on through the masses of cars and hotels and signs, him weaving in and out until it made her nervous. But he was a good driver and before long they were leaving the restaurants and tire shops behind. They went past Canton and Vaiden and Winona and she read the green sign that told the miles to Grenada. The sun was walking across the sky above them and she didn't know if he meant to make it before dark all the way out there. But he did. He turned off I-55 at the Coffeeville exit and pushed the El Camino hard even on this two-lane road. All the cops seemed to have left the country. He went past the turnoff to Coffeeville without slowing and skirted Water Valley and followed the hills and curves up into Lafayette

County and stopped at the stop sign at the junction of 7 and 9. From there on she had to direct him, north toward Oxford, then off onto a badly patched and bumpy secondary road, past a roadside sawmill and trailers perched on bladed hillsides. She had him take another right just before the sun started going down and she told him to hurry. He did. In a long bottom where cotton was planted on both sides of the road he pushed it up to ninety and then eased off as they went over the hills where old farmhouses stood, the yards now filled with rotting round bales of hay, past stunted cows in muddy pens, past acres of scrub oak and pine and on across to another highway and another stop sign. She told him to hang a right, that they were getting close now. They went five more miles and he slowed for a thirty-five miles an hour zone, a church, a community center and baseball field. A hundred yards past that she told him to turn right again and he drove a little slower now. He asked for another beer and she got him one. It was all hills now until they leveled out in a long bottom where cotton stretched almost as far as the eye could see. At a line of trees she told him to slow down and he turned right across from the church where she had eaten that first night.

'You didn't say it was a dirt road,' he said.

'It ain't far.'

'At least it ain't muddy.'

She nodded and chewed at her bottom lip, then reached back and got a beer for herself. He muttered when he had to slow to a crawl to cross one of the wooden bridges. She was watching anxiously ahead for the field road. They were in a creek bottom and she knew they had to get up on the next hill. He slowed to cross another bridge and he looked down into the shallow water as he passed over it.

'Who in the hell lives back in here?' he said.

'Nobody but them. Nobody but us that I knew of.'

'Is there a store around here anywhere?'

'On up the road.'

'What'd you do when you needed something from the store?'

'Walked.'

He was quiet then. He rolled his window down and hung his arm out. The gravel rattled against the underside of the Chevy and crunched under the tires. She told him to slow down.

'Shit, I'm already slowed down.'

'There it is!' she said, pointing. 'Pull in there.'

Standing where it had not stood before was a new steel gate, a chain hooked around a new creosoted post. He pulled up to the gate and stopped, then turned to her.

'Whose land's this?'

'I don't know.'

'Is it posted?'

'What's that?'

'It means no trespassing. I don't want somebody jumping my ass about going onto posted land.'

'I don't know if it's posted or not,' she said.

He looked down the road and reached for the gearshift.

'I'm gonna back down there to that wide spot in the road.'

Instead he cut the wheel sharply and backed almost into the ditch, then turned the wheel the other way and got it turned around and eased down the hill and pulled it in next to a clean little pea patch that somebody had tended well and parked it there. Without saying anything about it he got the pistol from under the seat. It was in a smooth black holster and he slipped it into the waistband of his pants in back and pulled the shirt over it, drained the beer in his hand and pitched it into the weeds. He got a fresh one and held her hand walking up the road back to the gate. It wasn't locked, only the chain looped around the post and one link hooked past the head of a twenty-penny nail. He got her to hold his beer while he removed the chain and opened the gate for her and then closed it back behind them and refastened the chain. He reached for his beer.

The dust along the fields of young beans was fine and pale gray, gentle explosions puffing beneath their feet as they walked. She stopped once and took her sandals off to feel the soft dirt on her toes. The sun was down now and the evening air had darkened. They flushed small flocks of doves from the bordering pines and they went singing and weaving low across the fields on their pointed wings to vanish into the deep green foliage on the other side. Frogs cheered from the trees and the crickets started up. As she had heard a million times.

'Almost dark,' he said.

'It ain't much further. We got some light left.'

And so they had. Now they were at the path, but a line of wreckage had swept around it, bulldozed stumps and raw torn earth, lumps of blue clay and red dirt balled up on the dozer tracks. On up a ways the dozer's path cut across their own. As if somebody had wanted to make a new road in here. They went across the rough ground and walked on the old path again, and now she could see up ahead a wide clearing where only a narrow one had been before.

Maybe he sensed some apprehension on her part because he walked slower and let her go on ahead.

She stopped to put her sandals back on and looked back at him once. He lifted his beer can, said, 'I'm coming.' She walked on ahead and stopped. It was only by looking at a big cedar tree that had stood at the rear of the house that she knew she was in the right place. But there was nothing left of the house, only a chewed patch of ground, a few shattered stumps.

'What is it?' he said, when he stopped beside her. He'd seen the look on her face: disbelief and maybe even fear.

'It's gone,' she said.

The sink was full of dirty dishes from where he'd cooked Loretta's breakfast but he didn't try to mess with them. Maybe he'd have to get some rubber gloves after all.

The damn house was getting kind of dirty too. Some of his clothes were lying around and the kitchen floor needed sweeping. Sitting in front of the television with a glass of ice water he was about bored out of his head. Nothing on but a bunch of baseball games and he didn't know one team from another. He liked the boxing. He was a big fan of Roberto Duran's.

Loretta had been gone for about an hour. But he looked for her to be back sometime without any doubt. And probably without any warning. He'd looked at her ass while it was walking her back to her car and had some definitely dirty thoughts. What if she caught him drunk?

He took a long nap in his own bed on mussed covers. He could smell Loretta's perfume on the pillow and it made him dream of Fay and being inside her as if it were real and then he was coming and could feel the hot spurts on his belly but could not wake from his dream either and slept on and had fragments of others, one where somebody shot him, and when he did wake it was with clammy underwear and a vague feeling almost like he'd been on a drunk.

He stripped and showered, holding his hands out from the spray. He looked at his body and saw again that he was growing old. There wasn't any way he could soap himself up so he just let the water wash over him for a while and did with that.

He dressed in clean clothes from the closet after his shave, bits of tissue paper on his nicked chin. It wasn't dark when he went out the door but the sun had gone down some minutes before.

And he almost didn't go back in to catch the phone. He'd turned the answering machine off, and it was ringing in there, and he knew it might be trouble, but then another part of him wanted to face it and if there was punishment take it, only get it to where he could go and find her and bring her back home. That was all.

It was them. They wanted him over in David Hall's office in Batesville. They wanted to know if he could be there in thirty minutes. He said he could.

She'd been mostly silent on the ride into town and now that full dark had come, her face was softly lit by the glow of the dash lights. He had put a Patsy Cline tape in and after a few songs had played, he'd asked her if she liked that, and she'd nodded and said a quiet Yes. He had his window down and he rested his elbow on top of the door, glancing up at the rearview mirror once in a while, sipping yet another beer.

'Is there someplace in Oxford we can get some decent food?'

'I don't know,' she said. 'I don't know much about Oxford.'

He dimmed his lights for an oncoming car and then put them back on bright when the car had passed.

'I thought you said you lived up around here.'

'I didn't live in Oxford.'

He drove in silence for a minute. He guessed she was bummed out. From what little he knew about her family it looked to him like she ought to been saying good riddance. Living out in the fucking woods like that. Ticks and bugs. On a damn dirt road. He glanced over at her but she didn't turn her face to him, just kept sitting like she had been, with her legs pulled up under her and her head leaned up against the window glass.

'Is that door locked?'

'Yeah. It's locked.'

'I wouldn't want you falling out or nothing. I knew a guy that happened to one time. Him and another guy was going down the road about forty and he was leaned up against the door and fell out.'

He waited for her to ask him what had happened, but she didn't.

'Don't you want to know what happened to him?'

'What happened to him?'

'Hell. It skinned about all the hide off his ass.'

'Looks like it woulda killed him.'

'Looks like it, don't it?'

The road was newly overlaid and curvy and the sides of it were lined with trees, sometimes gullies filled with kudzu.

He leaned over and touched her hand, then straightened up as he met another car that made a bad noise as it went past him.

'Why don't you lighten up?' he said.

'Lighten up.' She looked down and crossed her arms in her lap and held her elbows.

He guessed she'd just have to work it out on her own. He was willing to talk if she wanted to. But he wasn't going to force her. Sometimes she talked about them and sometimes she didn't.

'Well,' he said. 'I don't guess you know of where a hotel might be, do you?'

'Not right off. We could drive around and look I guess.'

'They ought to have a Ramada or something. We can find us someplace to eat. Ask the desk clerk if nothing else. They always know where everything's at.'

She nodded but didn't say anything.

'Is it just cause they're gone? Is that what you're so upset about?'

'It's that, too,' she said. 'But I don't know where they went to. They could be anywhere.'

'What about you, wild child? Hell, you left.'

'I had to.'

'It was that bad?'

'Yeah. It was that bad.'

He kept driving and sipping at his beer. He liked these country roads like this. Some people had ponds out behind their houses or green pastures holding

413

Holstein calves. He was glad to be away from the coast for a few days. It was a nice change. Gigi was gone but he wouldn't miss her. Even after all the time they had spent together he had barely known her. He'd never liked the way other men had looked at her or how she had welcomed it. There had been some good weekends with her in New Orleans over the last year. But she couldn't settle with one man. And for her there was no future in what she did, never had been. She would just go through a whole lot of men and then one day she'd be old.

He remembered her being shaken by a painting on the wall of the Saturn Bar in New Orleans, an oil of the devil rafting a whore down to hell through an ocean of flame, her hair on fire. She'd gotten drunk and cried and then had gotten even drunker and puked, moaning about how she didn't want to wind up down there. He'd told her she'd better change her line of work, then.

He finished the beer he was drinking and gave the can an overhead toss across the roof of the El Camino. It made a slight *clink* on a speed limit sign. Fay came out of her ball against the door. She rubbed at her face and then slid over in the seat closer to him.

'You want another beer?' she said.

'I don't know. How close are we to town?'

'Probly ten minutes or so.'

'Hell, I'll just wait,' he said. 'I need to piss like a race-horse right now. What you want for supper?'

'It don't matter to me. Anything's fine with me.'

'You tired?'

'Yeah. Pretty much. I think I'm sleepin more these days. I guess it's cause I'm pregnant. I never did need a whole lot of sleep before.'

'You're just tired,' he said, glancing at her. 'We've been going a whole lot here lately. You can get a good night's sleep and we'll head back tomorrow. OK?'

She didn't answer at first, just looked out through the windshield and twisted some strands of her hair through her fingers.

414

'What is it?' he said.

'Nothin.'

That was the way they were sometimes. You knew damn good and well they had something on their mind but they wouldn't just come right out and say what it was. You had to dig it out of them. You had to show concern. Maybe she wanted him to hang around and help her look for her family. What the hell did all that feel like to her?

'What is it?' he said again.

'You'd think it was silly.'

'I might not. Why don't you tell me what it is?'

She squeezed up close to him. He could feel one of those big titties pressed up against his arm like a puppydog's nose. That was another thing women did, mashed one of their titties up against you, some of them, anyway, even if they didn't know you that well. It was nice of them.

'I don't know,' she said. 'I just wondered if we maybe drove around some tomorrow if we might see some of em somewhere. Maybe goin down the road or somethin. Seems like that's all we used to do.'

He thought it over for a minute. It would be a waste of time for sure, but he reckoned there was really nothing pressing that he had to get back to in Biloxi or Pass Christian. He'd already left a message on the answering machine at Arlene's house that would tell people that they weren't booking any guests for a few days. Cully didn't know where he was but Cully didn't have to know where he was every damn minute either.

It might be good to show her that he wanted to help her if she needed him to. They all needed something. And once you found out what that thing was it was easier to keep them happy. Then if you kept them happy maybe they wouldn't bitch and raise hell about a bunch of old shit that wasn't even important. She hadn't been that way at all. She didn't ask for much and this was a small favor. And what was he going to do when he got back but just go right back to the club and drink some more and watch for fights to start and somebody to throw out? They could stay gone a while longer.

In a long stretch of straight road they went around a pickup with its flashers going for a tall Massey-Ferguson that was hauling a hay baler along at about twenty. He could see the dark image of somebody up in the glassed-in cab and he could see the cleated tires turning in a blur. The farmer driving it waved and Aaron put up a hand and waved back and then sped into the next curve and the tractor and the pickup trailing it were lost from sight. He glanced at her and saw the swell of her breasts against the thin cloth of the dress. This one was worth keeping happy. Another day was only one more day.

'Well,' he said. 'We get us a hotel, I can call down to Henry's and see if Mama's still there. I guess we could drive around some tomorrow. I don't guess you've got any idea where they might've headed to.'

'Naw,' she said. 'It ain't no tellin. I just thought it might make me feel better if I just knew I tried to see em somewhere.' She looked down at her lap and then turned her face to him. 'We wasn't much of a family I don't reckon but I wonder about my brother and my little sister. How they're doin. You know?'

'We'll look around some,' he said, and that was it.

He checked them into the Holiday Inn downtown while she waited in the covered drive. He came out with a room key and got back into the El Camino and handed it to her.

'They said it was in the back.'

He'd left it running and he pulled it into gear and drove through a gap in the building and then stopped and looked around at the doors for a matching number.

'Looka there,' she said.

'Oh yeah,' he said. 'They got a pool.' He nodded toward the parking lot in back where there was a

416

square of blue water, some kids splashing around in it under the lights. 'Well hell,' he said. 'Where's it . . . there it is.'

He pulled forward between slanted white lines and eased to a stop just short of a low brick wall and shut it off. She was already opening her door and getting out with her purse.

'You want to lock it?'

He considered it, a brief hesitation.

'Well . . . let me get this.'

He bent inside the vehicle and pulled out the zippered bag and then leaned over the bed and opened his suitcase and dropped the bag in there.

'OK. You can go ahead and lock it.'

She pushed the button and slammed the door. Her suitcase was lying on the bed and she picked it up when he shut his door. He got the rest of the beer in the cardboard carton and his own suitcase and she followed him over to the stairs and up them. They turned at the second floor and walked past rooms on the left, a railing on the right, down to 216 where she set her suitcase down and put the key into the lock and turned it. She pushed open the door and got the key from it and picked up her suitcase again. He came in behind her and set the beer down. The room was half in darkness for a moment and then he stopped at the table and turned on the lamp. There were two big beds and a low table with a color television sitting on it, a bathroom and open closet at the back.

'Home sweet home,' he said.

'I reckon so.' She let go of her suitcase and kicked off her sandals and crawled onto the bed with her purse. He tossed his suitcase on the other bed and went into the bathroom and shut the door. It was quiet in the room and she could hear the water running out of him into the toilet. It ran for a long time. Then the toilet flushed and he came back out and moved his suitcase to the table beside the TV set. He had a plastic bucket in his hand.

'I'm gonna go find the ice machine,' he said, and he went out, easing the door to so that it wouldn't lock behind him. She saw the remote lying on top of the television and got up and fetched it, then sat back down on the bed and pulled a pillow out from under the covers and propped it behind her back and looked at the remote and punched a button and the TV came on. Cartoons. She saw arrows on the remote and pushed one of them. News. She kept her thumb on it and ran through the channels, an old Western, a game show, a comedy, nothing she wanted to see. She pushed the button again and turned it off.

It didn't make any sense to go looking for them. They wouldn't find them. Even if they did, what difference would it make? What could she say to them that she hadn't already said?

She heard his steps coming back toward the room and he stepped in and shut the door. He slammed the empty bucket down on top of the television.

'Goddamn place ain't even got any ice.'

'What'd you want some for?'

'Fix me a drink after I found the Coke machine. I bet this place has a bar.' He walked over to the telephone and looked at it for a second and then picked up the handset and pushed a button. He waited awhile before anybody answered. He talked to somebody and said Thank you and hung it up. 'They got a lounge downstairs. Why don't you put on some more clothes and we'll go get us a drink or two.'

He started to turn away and was pulling his shirt off when she spoke.

'I thought we was gonna go eat.'

He dropped the shirt on the floor and put his suitcase back on the bed and sat down beside it.

'We are. I want a drink or two first, though. Long drive, you know.'

'It's past nine,' she said. 'How long does eatin places stay open around here?'

She saw him almost lose it and then get control of it.

In a gentle tone he said, 'Now how would I know, Fay? I'm gonna clean up and get high and then I'm going down to the lounge. A lounge is my favorite environment. If you ain't noticed. I'm gonna have a few drinks.' He stood up and started taking off his jeans. 'You don't have to go with me if you don't want to.'

She watched him without speaking. She saw him snatch a towel off a rack of them back there. The bathroom door shut and then the water came on. Well shit. She didn't want to stay up here by herself.

She got up and unbuttoned a button on her dress and then another one and then a man walking by the window looked in at her and almost stopped. She leaned for the cord and closed the curtain quickly, then took off her clothes and found some more in her suitcase and dressed in them and was sitting quietly at the table when he came out with his hair wet, wearing the towel around him. She didn't know why he bothered to cover himself up. He didn't say anything to her and she watched him while he got the little bag from the suitcase and packed the pipe with hash and lit it. He eased down to sit on the bed and she studied his upper body again, the width and thickness of his chest and those arms that caused second glances from people everywhere they went. There was no way Sam could whip him even if he found her. Even if he was looking for her. She was so close to him now. It was only about ten or twelve miles out there.

She watched him smoke the dope and she watched him slide a flat pint of bourbon from the suitcase and she watched him twist the top off and take a long drink of the brown liquor and she watched him load the pipe again and smoke it down until the smoke died away. Then he put everything back into the suitcase and pulled clean folded jeans from it and slipped them on and put his brown leather loafers on and there was a nice pale green shirt in there that he slipped on, a thin belt coiled somewhere that he put around his waist after he tucked the shirt into his jeans. He got all the stuff from the pockets of his other clothes and combed his hair at the mirror in the little alcove off the bathroom. He buckled on a watch from inside the suitcase and patted his pockets to make sure he had everything. He picked up the room key.

'Let's go,' he said. She got up and followed him, taking only her purse with her. He held the door open for her and she said a quiet Thank you and he pulled it shut behind them and stuck the key in his pocket. The kids had gone from the pool now and the water was smoothing out, only lightly lapping at the edge of the concrete rim that formed it.

They went back down the steps and stepped into the parking lot and turned the corner at the last room. The asphalt court in front was filled with cars and pickups and vans. She was hoping he wouldn't want to stay long. She was really hungry and she wanted more than anything to just go to bed. He seemed to be in another one of his moods and she didn't know if she'd be able to talk to him or not. She didn't know if she even wanted to talk to him or not. Sometimes when he smoked that stuff he talked a little crazy and didn't make sense about things. Just looking at him right now you could tell there was something wrong with him. But he wasn't even paying any attention to her. He stopped just short of the door of the lounge and pulled a tiny plastic bottle from his pocket, took off the cap, then leaned his head back and squirted a few drops into the corner of each eye.

'What's that?' she said.

'Visine. Keeps my eyes from getting red. So everybody can't tell I'm fucked up. Do I look fucked up to you?'

She didn't know how to answer that. She didn't want to make him mad. So she lied.

'You look OK to me.'

'All right, then.' He put the cap on the bottle and stuck it back in his pocket and held the door open for her. Inside it was cold and dark with neon lights glowing softly behind the bar and on beer signs hung on the walls. It looked comfortable. There were round tables and overstuffed chairs scattered throughout the room. A group of people were watching a baseball game on a big-screen TV. Some soft music was coming from speakers set behind the bar and three men and one woman were sitting on padded stools there.

'Let's just set at the bar,' Aaron said, and he didn't wait to see what she said but just moved over to the corner and pulled out a stool and sat down. She followed him, pulled a stool out, set her purse down after getting her cigarettes and lighter out.

There was a big black bartender behind the bar and he moved over to them, smiling.

'How you folks doing tonight?' he said.

'Pretty good,' Aaron said.

'What can I get for y'all?'

Aaron thought for a second. 'Let me have a double Maker's Mark and Coke.'

'And you, ma'am?'

Thinking about the baby again she said, 'Can I just have a Coke please?'

'Sure can,' the bartender said, and turned away to fix their drinks. Aaron looked at her.

'You don't want a beer or nothing?'

'A Coke's fine. I been drinking too much lately anyway. You know.'

'Know what?' Aaron said.

She lowered her voice. 'I mean with the baby and all. It's probly not good for it.' She started to say something else to him about needing to go to the doctor, but again it seemed like this wouldn't be the right time.

They watched the bartender making Aaron's drink. After he had it ready he pulled a straw from a box and stuck it into the drink and capped it with his finger. He put the straw in his mouth and tasted what was in it, nodded to himself, took the straw out and threw it away, then put a clean one in it and served it. He scooped a tall glass full of ice and filled it with Coke and set it in front of her.

'Can we start a tab?' Aaron said.

'Sure can,' the bartender said. 'Y'all staying here?'

'Yeah. We're up in two-sixteen.'

'I can put it on your room bill if you want me to.'

'That'll be fine,' Aaron said, and the bartender told them to let him know if they needed anything. He went over to a popcorn machine and filled a woven basket full and set it between them.

'Thanks,' Fay said, and reached for a handful. She'd had it so few times in her life that it was really a special treat, covered with butter and pretty salty. She ate some more of it and it seemed to make her hungrier. A Heineken clock behind the bar showed fifteen till ten. She figured they probably wouldn't be able to get anything but hamburgers if they waited much longer. But she could tell that Aaron was very content where he was. He lit a cigarette and swiveled on the stool and watched the ball game for a few minutes. She guessed he didn't have anything to say to her. It was embarrassing.

She kept thinking about how close she was to Sam's house. Would it be possible to slip away from Aaron and go back to the room and get somebody to help her find his number and call him? Ask him what was going on, if it was safe for her to come back? She kept seeing that plane go down. That bag full of money and the one full of dope. The way he'd slammed those two guys' heads together and the sound Reena's body had made when it hit the floor that morning.

She looked at Aaron from the corner of her eye and he seemed to be moving to some tune he heard only inside his head. His knee was jiggling a little and he was pulling hard on his cigarette. His eyes seemed fixed and glassy on the TV screen. He turned to her suddenly.

'You got a driver's license?'

'No,' she said. 'I never did get one. I was almost ready to try when I left there.'

'I guess your boyfriend was gonna help you get it.'

'That's right. He was.'

Half his drink was already gone and he turned it up again. She hoped he wouldn't turn mean to her now about Sam.

'I was thinking you could go get us something to eat if you had your driver's license.'

'I wish I did,' she said. 'I've done got pretty hungry.'

'Yeah,' he said, then turned away, finished his drink, and called to the bartender again. In just a few moments he had a fresh drink in front of him. He stubbed out his cigarette in an ashtray and looked at the bottles behind the bar. He leaned a little closer to her. 'I done caught a hell of a buzz,' he said. 'I don't want to be driving around this town where I don't know anybody. Can you drive at all?'

'Yeah. I can drive. I've drove a good bit. I just never did get my license.'

'Think you could drive somewhere and get us something to eat and bring it back over here? Cause it's too late to find a restaurant open anywhere probably.'

She was sure hungry. But she didn't know if she ought to do this or not.

'I mean, hell, you could find a hamburger joint or something somewhere. Drive around long enough you could.'

'Well,' she said. 'I don't know. What if they caught me drivin without a driver's license?'

'Fuck. Just don't do nothin wrong, they won't stop you.'

'What if they do and they find that gun under the seat?'

He must have forgotten about that because he leaned back away from her and said, 'Oh yeah. Yeah, that wouldn't be cool. We need to stay cool.'

She didn't say anything and he turned back around on his stool to the TV, muttering something about definitely needing to stay cool. She wished he hadn't gotten messed up like this. And if he kept sitting here drinking she didn't know what might happen.

Nothing happened for a while. They kept sitting

there and the clock's hands moved past ten o'clock. Some of the people got up when the ball game ended and made their way to the bar and paid their tabs and went out the door. Aaron took longer to finish his second drink and then ordered a third one. Her Coke had melted all the ice in the glass and sat untouched in front of her. The bartender asked her if she wanted another one but she just smiled and shook her head. She was so hungry now that it was starting to give her a headache. She remembered that happening to her a lot when she was younger and there was hardly ever anything to eat in the work camps.

'We need to eat,' she finally said.

He swiveled back around on his stool and put his elbows up on the bar.

'Yeah, I know it. You gonna have to go get it.'

And suddenly there it was. Sam had been meaning to let her drive in town some, but they never had gotten around to that. There were still lots of things she didn't know, like when to signal for a turn and who had the right of way where and she didn't know anything yet about parallel parking. She knew gas on the left, brake on the right. But she couldn't let on.

'You goin with me?' she said.

'What you need me for?'

She leaned close to him and whispered, 'I don't want to drive around with that gun in the car.'

He looked from side to side and then spoke to her without looking at her: 'Then just take it out of the fucking car, Fay, and put it in the room. Here.' He leaned back and went into his pocket for the room key and the car keys and a crumpled wad of bills. He dropped them into her hand.

She sat there looking down at all of it. She could see the corner of a ten-dollar bill and some fives and ones. It looked like plenty. But he hadn't said what he wanted. She asked him.

'I don't care. Anything. A hamburger. I don't give a shit what it is, I just need to get some food in my

424

stomach. Can't drink on a empty belly, it'll eat your guts out. That's what Daddy said.'

She closed her hand around the things he'd given her and slowly got off her stool.

'Well,' she said. 'OK. I don't know how long it'll take me to find someplace. You gonna stay here?'

'Yeah. Just stop back by and get me.'

She bent and picked up her purse from the floor and put her cigarettes and lighter into it. She looked around in the room for a moment. The bartender was moving among the tables, picking up empty drink glasses and emptying ashtrays into a small garbage can he carried with him. He looked up and saw her and said, 'You ain't leavin us this early, are you?'

Something about his smile made her smile back, and she walked closer to him.

'I was gonna go get us somethin to eat. You know where there's some hamburger places around here close?'

'Aw yeah,' he said, never stopping his work, moving along as he talked. 'You go out west of town here there's all kinds of eatin places.'

'Out west?' she said.

He straightened and pointed.

'Yes ma'am. Just go on up to the square and hang a right and keep on goin. Go through, let's see . . .' He paused to think. 'Bout three or four red lights and you'll be right in the middle of em. Burger King Burger Chef McDonald's, all them places.'

'Thank you,' she said.

'You welcome.' He went back to his cleaning and she turned to the door. When she looked back, Aaron was lighting another cigarette and talking to a woman who had come in and sat down next to him.

She pushed open the door and went back into the night. Going across the asphalt court she stuck the money into her purse and kept out the car keys and the room key. Just stick the gun in her purse, that'd be the thing to do.

425

The pool water had settled now and was reflecting back the lights that were mounted above it. One couple was sitting in chairs close to each other, talking quietly and drinking beer from cans. She could feel them watching her as she went past but when she walked by the brick wall in front of the El Camino they couldn't see her anymore. She stopped beside the driver's door and took a good look around. She didn't see anybody and she couldn't hear anything but a few cars moving on the streets that ran along the side and front of the hotel. She found the key and slid it into the door lock. The interior light came on when she opened it and she squatted inside the door's shelter, feeling under the seat for the gun. He had put it in a black nylon holster and she slipped it into her purse and stood up, relocked the door and closed it. She looked around again. There was nobody about.

In the room she put the pistol under one of the pillows and used the bathroom. There was a memo pad and a pen with the hotel's name on it and she put both of them into her purse. Then she went back down to the El Camino. When she got it cranked, the first thing she did was check to see how much gas it had in it.

She kept it on fifty and most cars passed her. By the time she was five miles out of town she had gotten the hang of dimming her lights for oncoming cars and watching for traffic in the rearview mirror. She thought she remembered where the turnoff was and she kept looking ahead for it, passing familiar houses and road signs, things they had driven by together so many times. What if he was home? What would she say to him now? Would she be able to look him in the face and would he be able to tell just by looking at her that she'd been with another man? And what would she say about Alesandra? All she wanted was a chance to explain.

The brown signs announcing the location of the state park showed up in her headlights soon enough and she slowed down some, looking ahead for the turnoff, lots of cars and trucks passing her now. There it was, just up ahead. She put her blinker on and touched her foot to the brake, steering with both hands, the wind coming in the window to make her hair flutter around her face. The pipes rumbled when she let off the gas and turned onto the lake road, and then they rumbled again with that low and throaty bellow when she stepped back on the gas. It hadn't been hard to get him to bring her back.

In three or four minutes she was turning onto the road Sam lived on, and she saw the mailbox with its faded and flaking paint and turned in beside it. She stopped off the road for a minute to think. She never had gone down the driveway by herself and she went slowly, the headlights picking out the shapes of the pine trees and lighting the dark curves ahead, nosing ever lower into the forest and then straightening and climbing the hill. And then the headlights swept the side of the house and turned on the cruiser sitting there, the stripes down the sides glowing. The truck was gone. The house was black inside except for a dim glow somewhere in the kitchen. She took a deep breath and went to open her door, then stopped and put the gearshift into reverse and backed the El Camino up where the headlights would shine on the steps. She put it up in park and got out.

The night wind was warm and she lifted her face to see it move through the big pines around the house. She climbed the steps and leaned her face close to the door to look inside. That dim glow she had seen was the light in the vent hood over the stove, and she couldn't see another light on anywhere. She knocked several times, knowing it was hopeless, knowing he wasn't there. She leaned her forehead into the door glass and put both hands up beside her face. How long could Aaron sit there and drink before he noticed that she'd been gone too long? She had counted on Sam being here. He could have taken care of everything.

They could have done something, figured something out. He could have told her what had happened since she'd been gone, if it was safe for her to come back. But now she couldn't do anything. Nothing except leave him a note maybe.

And this little piece of paper in her purse, where would she put it and what if the wind came along hard and blew it away? Or what if Sam had been made to tell the other cops her name and one of them came along here to see Sam while he was gone and found the note? And crazy she knew to think up all this stuff but wasn't there someplace she could put it where maybe nobody but him would see it? And she looked down the steps to the cruiser.

The damn pen wouldn't write.

'Son of a bitch!' she said, and threw it down. She looked in her purse, knowing she didn't have anything else. She was standing next to the cruiser and she wouldn't be able to hear anybody coming with the El Camino idling there, those pipes. What the hell could she do? She wondered if maybe there was something she could use to write with in his car. Same damn one he'd brought her home in. She opened the driver's door and the light came on.

There was a clipboard on the front seat and it had a bunch of pens clipped to it, one real fat pen. She leaned over and got it. The memo pad from the Holiday Inn was so small.

There was a beer carton in the back of the El Camino. She ripped off a big piece of it and wrote on the back:

Sam, I'm in Pass Christian. Across from the boats. Please come get me if it's safe.

She looked at what she had written. It didn't seem enough somehow. She needed to look into his eyes. The headlights shone on her and she added something else.

I love you. Be careful.

She signed her name to it and put it where he sat. She closed the door and the light went off. Then she hurried, hurried, trying to get back before it was too late.

There were only three of them waiting for him. He was glad he hadn't been drinking. David Hall was sitting behind his desk and Tony McCollum was leaning against the wall in a room full of stark bright light. The sheriff's office was not made for comfort, just his desk and a few cheap chairs and two file cabinets. Grayton was in the corner, and he wasn't saying anything. Their talk had ceased as he'd stepped into the room. But David came out from around the desk and shook hands with him and got him in a chair and then went back behind his desk and sat down. He cleared his throat.

'Autopsy reports, Sam,' he said, and nudged some papers on his desk as if he'd push them across, but he didn't. 'We need to know what you know about this woman they found.'

He looked at his chief, who looked pretty pissed. And he knew that he was walking on dangerous ground. If they were going to get him by the short hairs, this was where they would grab him.

'Why don't you ask him about that girl who was at his wife's funeral, David?'

McCollum had his arms folded and he was in civvies, boots and jeans and a pullover V-neck, but he hadn't forgotten his pistol. It was a little one in one of those little holsters. Looked like it would be good for shooting chipmunks up close or other small varmints.

'I reckon I can handle this, Tony.'

The sheriff had one finger at the corner of his mouth. Sam had heard about the day he had jumped into a frozen pond, breaking ice to get to a little girl who had

430

fallen in. But she died soon after he pulled her out. There was one gray streak in his black hair and he still looked like a boy. McCollum shut up.

He tried to relax. He had to remember that he hadn't done anything to get Alesandra killed except take up with Fay. After he'd taken up with Alesandra.

'I told Tony . . .' He started again. 'I told Tony that morning I didn't know anything about it. I told Chief Grayton too. And that's the truth.'

Then David acted like he didn't want to look at him and he thought he might be in trouble. He glanced at Grayton, who seemed to be turning to stone.

'We ain't got a single suspect, Sam.' David was nodding to himself, assuring himself that this was so. 'Do you know anybody or can you think of anybody who'da had cause to do her harm?'

'Nobody,' he said. 'I don't know of anybody who would have killed her.'

Well, he'd said that. Now later if they found out about Fay they might make something of it. He had to keep her name out of it.

David cut his eyes toward Tony.

'I was told there was a girl with you at your wife's funeral. Which I want to say I was sorry to miss. I was up in Michigan.'

'I know you were,' Sam said. He was afraid his heart was going to fail him because it felt weak in his chest and he could almost feel a hammer coming down.

'Who was that?'

'It was a friend of ours.'

It got deadly quiet. He kept his eyes on David.

'The dead woman was your friend?'

'Yes.'

'Lover,' Tony said.

'Why don't you keep your fucking mouth shut?' Sam said.

McCollum came off the wall.

'Why don't you fucking make me?'

Sam started out of his seat and David stood up.

431

'Quit it,' he said. 'Go get some coffee, Tony.'

McCollum relaxed and walked by Sam with a smirk. He went out and his boot steps faded up the hall.

'Where's this girl now?' David said, and he knew they had him. It was payment somehow. He never had cried for Alesandra. Had hardly mourned her. Now by God he'd pay.

'She's gone,' he said, had to say. 'She only lived with us for a while.'

'How old is this girl?' Grayton said.

He didn't want to look at him. He had to.

'I think she's seventeen.'

'Was she still living with you after your wife died?'

He just nodded. And Grayton's face began to blush a deep red. He got up.

'The state of Mississippi don't put up with this shit. I want you in my office. In the morning. Ten o'clock.'

'Yes sir,' he said, and Grayton went out. He heard him speak to McCollum out there. He looked back at David. They were going to find out now. They already knew. They were going to pull his life open and put it in the paper.

Again she woke alone in a strange place. She was almost getting used to it. The curtains were drawn and the room was dark, but she could see the mess on the table from where they had eaten the hamburgers she'd picked up on the west side of town. Napkins and foil-backed wrappers were scattered on the plastic surface, the empty paper cups of Coke.

She pushed the covers back and sat up. Her head was hurting even though she hadn't drunk anything. She wouldn't have thought he'd be up and gone somewhere but he was. The sex had been rough and he had hurt her. She felt raw and chafed between her legs. He hadn't even finished but had passed out lying on top of her. It had been all she could do to push him off and away from her, and she remembered that his head had hit the table beside the bed, although he hadn't seemed to feel it.

She got up and turned on a lamp and went to the bathroom and sat down on the commode and put her face into her hands while she peed. After she'd finished she went to the sink and ran some cold water over her face and looked at herself in the mirror. She had to get to a doctor. She had to. And he'd probably be hungover now, and in a bad mood.

She found some underwear and clothes and put them on without taking a shower. All she wanted right now was some coffee. She saw her sandals on the floor beside the bed and slipped her feet into them. The room key was lying in the middle of the hamburger mess and she put it in her pocket and got her sunglasses and went out the door. For a moment she stopped at the rail and looked down at the pool and there he was, swimming lazy laps, his coffee cup and cigarettes on a table behind him. She watched him. His long muscled arms stroked through the water and his feet kicked small splashes behind him. The pool was not very big and he had to keep turning. Why couldn't she just pack her stuff right now and walk on down the street and hide somewhere for a while? She could hitchhike back out to Sam's and wait for him. He'd have to come back to the cruiser sometime. He'd have to go back to work sometime. But she was scared of what she didn't know. The police. Alesandra had probably been in the papers.

He might be in trouble. It was too big a chance to take, to try and see him again. It might not even be safe to walk down the street here. She'd seen those movies where cops got people in a room and made them confess to their crimes. There was no way to know yet what might have happened. So what was she going to do? Stay with Aaron? Have this baby down there? And then do what? What if he got tired of her? Or decided he didn't want to be around a baby? Look where Reena had wound up. Living in that little tin box.

Maybe she shouldn't have left the note in his car like that. It wasn't even a note. It was like a sign telling anybody who wanted to look in that window where she was and now it was a whole new thing to worry about. They might have been able to work something out, the two of them, together. They might even could have called it self-defense. She'd seen that on the movies, too. If he guessed what happened, and tried to cover up for her, it might cost him his job. She'd heard him say he was getting pretty close to retirement because he'd started so young. All those years. All that time he'd put in working before she came along. Some of it even before she was born.

It didn't look like there was anything else to do right now but just go on back down to the coast with him, and try to make the best of it. But no matter if he was in a bad mood or not, she had to talk to him about going to a doctor. She couldn't put it off any longer. Wasn't going to.

He was still swimming. She went down the walk above the parking lot and turned the corner and walked down the stairs and over to the pool. When he saw her coming he stopped swimming and climbed up the aluminum ladder and pulled himself out of the water. He reached for a towel and wiped droplets from his face. He didn't seem to want to look her in the eye. Maybe he was vaguely remembering being so rough with her in the bed. By the time she got over to him he had sat down in a chair beneath a poolside umbrella that was opened over the table and was sipping at the rest of his coffee.

'Hey,' she said, standing in the sunshine.

'Hey. You sleep good?'

'I reckon so. Where'd you find that coffee?'

He nodded toward the front and reached for his smokes.

'Up front in there past the desk. They got some doughnuts and stuff if you want some. You wouldn't want to bring me another cup, would you?'

'I reckon I would,' she said. 'Up there where you went in to get the room?'

'Yeah. Those double glass doors up there.'

She left him there and went across the parking lot and under the shade of the building, walking past the bumpers of cars with out-of-state tags, pickups with camper beds, the back ends filled with luggage and junk. It was cool inside the lobby and she smiled at the desk clerk and saw the table set up against the far wall. She found the cups and poured two of them and stirred sugar and milk into them and carried them down to the end of the table where pastries and doughnuts were. She got a napkin and wrapped one doughnut in it and found some tops for the coffee and got it all up in her hands and pushed against the

435

double glass doors with her back and pushed her way outside.

He was leaned back in the chair with his eyes closed when she set the stuff on the table. She pulled the other chair under the shade of the umbrella and sat down. She looked at him. He was just reclining there. She pulled the top off her coffee and sipped at it. The glare was bright off the water and she was glad for the sunglasses.

'There's your coffee,' she said.

'Yeah, thanks.' He didn't open his eyes and she wondered if he was going to say anything about last night, how he'd been in the bed. For one frightening moment she had been reminded of her daddy and then she had made herself shut it out of her mind. She remembered his breath, the smell of the liquor that had been on it: both of them.

She drank some more of her coffee and lit a cigarette.

'I guess I got a little drunk last night, huh?'

She leaned back in the chair and crossed her legs. A fly lit on her knee and she brushed it away.

'More'n a little, I'd say. I'm surprised you're even up this early.'

'I had to get up,' he said. 'I felt so damn bad I had to get in this pool and sweat some of that poison out of me. Always makes me feel better.'

'I don't know how you could sweat in a pool,' she said.

'Tell me again what took you so long to get back with the food,' he said, and then he sat up and opened his eyes and reached for his coffee. He slipped his shades on and drank from the cup. His other big hand hung loose and unflexed from the arm of the chair.

'I told you,' she said. 'I didn't know where I was and I got turned around. I had a hard time findin a place that was open.'

'Mm hm,' he said. He wasn't looking at her and he was making her nervous. 'Bartender was hollering last

436

call when you finally got back. That's midnight in Oxford. I thought you left close to ten-thirty.'

'I don't know what time it was exactly,' she said quickly, because she didn't want him to say what she suddenly knew he was going to say.

'I thought maybe you drove out to see your old boyfriend since we's in the neighborhood.'

'Why would I do that?' she said automatically.

He turned his head to her. 'You tell me. Bartender told me it wouldn't take you twenty minutes to go get something to eat and come back.'

'Well he knows where everything is around here,' she said. 'I didn't now where nothin was. And I was nervous drivin. I told you I didn't have no driver's license.'

'But your boyfriend showed you how to drive. Right?'

It was quiet out there. She could feel the heat from the concrete rising onto her legs.

'A little,' she said. 'He showed me a little.'

He raised his sunglasses from his eyes and stared at her like that first night.

'Let me tell you something, Fay.'

His gaze disheartened her and she had to look down.

'What?' she said. She was scared to look at him at all now.

'Don't you ever lie to me. You hear me?'

'I hear you.'

'Don't you *never* lie to me.'

She didn't say anything, couldn't think of what to say.

'Are we straight on that?'

'Yes.'

'You sure?'

'Yes,' she said, almost in a whisper. 'Yes, I'm sure.'

'All right, then,' he said, and he picked up his cigarettes and lighter and put the towel over his shoulder. He started walking back toward the hotel across the hot concrete and she noted that he didn't even flinch. After

437

he'd taken ten steps he stopped and turned back to her.

'Well?' he said. 'You coming?'

'Where we going?'

'Ride around and look for your ragged-ass family awhile before we go back home I reckon. Come on.'

He turned away and started walking again and she got up slowly to follow him.

By noon they had been in the El Camino for over two hours, riding and looking, cruising up and down the hot and baking blacktop roads. He'd bought beer and iced it down in a cheap foam cooler and she had started drinking again herself just because she felt so bad. After the talk at the pool she'd been scared to bring it up about the baby and the trip to the doctor. She couldn't understand how he had known where she'd gone. She guessed she'd thought that with him sitting there drinking he wouldn't keep track of the time or would be so drunk by the time she got back that he wouldn't even care or even know how much time had passed.

They stopped in someplace in a country community north of town and had plate lunches of vegetables and pork chops and she noticed that he paid no attention to the wary stares of field workers and farmers eating their lunches on stools beside them. He'd been quiet most of the morning and he seemed to be able to drink beer all day without it ever having any effect on him.

Back in the car he took a brief detour into Marshall County and bought some more beer and pickled eggs and put the beer into the cooler and drove back into Lafayette County.

They cruised roads she'd never seen before, went past cattle farms and fish ponds and farmhouses set back from the road and crossed over rivers and climbed hills where yellow machines gouged the living trees from the earth. They rode past lush hollows of green timber, the road shaded and looking cool, drove past brackish pools of stagnant water where turtles and moccasins sunned themselves on logs and lily pads grew. Sun-browned boys with fishing poles casting into the black water. She couldn't think of anything to say to him. They saw nothing of her family.

When finally the sun had gone over in the sky he pulled off on a side road and got out.

'You need to go to the woods?' he said, just before he opened the door. She nodded that she did and scooted out, walked up the road and stepped away from it and squatted beneath a tree, feeling the heat in the weeds, watching a patch of blue sky through the needles of towering pine.

When she had finished and walked back, he was standing beside the El Camino, opening a fresh beer. He looked at her for a moment and then turned the can up to his mouth. He took it down and stood watching a field of cotton below them, the straight rows shimmering out there in the heat.

'Well,' he said. 'I reckon we better head back. If you're ready.'

'Yeah,' she said, fighting against letting him see the tears she knew could come. 'I reckon I'm ready.'

'You don't have to go,' he said.

She studied his face, the bunched arm and the hand that held the beer and stood there knowing how much she liked those hands on her, and how, at times, she believed herself safe in those arms.

'I can leave you here and drive off,' he said. 'I mean you was walking when you found me. You won't be no worse off, Fay. Hell,' he said, half to himself. 'You might even be better.'

He turned his head to wait for her answer. And she thought about it only for a second because that was the last thing she wanted, to be alone again and walking. That and the devil you know against the one you don't. She ducked her head, got into the car, closed the door.

He wouldn't tell David Hall anything about her and the next morning Grayton relieved him of duty, with pay, for thirty more days. He said the bottom of it would be gotten to.

He was out of there by ten minutes after ten, standing with his bum hands in the middle of the parking lot. They hadn't asked for the car back but Grayton had said they'd come get it if they needed it. People were looking at him through the windows of their offices. He tried to see Loretta but couldn't.

The car that was parked behind his cruiser in the yard was an older model Mercedes, a deeply polished gray. It looked as if someone who had loved the car had taken care of it. And Sam wondered if that was him sitting on the steps.

All he wanted was to go in the house and get a beer out of the icebox. He checked the plates when he pulled past it to park his pickup: Coahoma County. The Delta. Little towns like Friar's Point and Bobo. Clarksdale too.

Some older man, a well-dressed man, lounging there with his forearms on his thighs and his hands holding each other and his tanned and dark-haired shins showing above his good socks from where he'd hitched his slacks to sit down and wait. He hoped he wasn't a salesman. Son of a bitches came around sometimes when you were trying to go fishing or do some yard work and wanted you to stop everything you were doing and let them sell you something and he just flat never had made time for that and hadn't ever really worried about hurting their feelings over it. It would probably get to where they'd be eventually selling shit over the phone and would worry the hell out of you like that. But maybe by then they'd come up with something that showed who was calling before you ever picked it up. He hoped whoever it was wasn't anybody who was kin to Alesandra. His hair was as gray as the car, like steel that had been polished not too brightly.

He stopped the truck out past the cruiser and saw that towel still back there when he got out. From when he'd wiped down Loretta's seats. And hell she might show back up sometime. Damn. He could hardly see anything but Grayton's face. And he kept remembering the words over and over again. The bottom of it. Oh yeah.

He reached for the towel and got it. It was wet but it wasn't wet enough to have to wring the water from it. He saw the man starting to stand up and he nodded and shook some dirt from the towel, being careful with his hands. He didn't need this shit right now and wasn't going to put up with this shit right now whatever it was.

He folded the towel, kind of, and the man came down from the steps and waited for him, actually kind of blocking his way, not a big man, probably in his early sixties but still solid with muscle and his eyes a dark brown. And he knew then who he was. Alesandra was all in his face, and the way he moved. Gold rings on his fingers, on his veined heavy hands, what looked like a very expensive watch.

Sam stopped. There was still twenty feet between them. Had she gotten her temper from him? Old Daddy done found him now. His gun was in the house. Just in case anything happened.

'I'm Rubin Farris,' the man said. 'Are you the cop Alesandra was seeing?'

'Yes. I am. I'm very sorry about Alesandra.'

'We've done buried her,' he said. 'I don't think I saw you there.'

'I know how you feel,' Sam said.

Alesandra's daddy took two steps closer.

'Don't you tell me that. Don't you tell me how I feel. Cause you don't know a *goddamn* thing about how I feel.'

The shade they stood in was dotted with spots of sun through the leaves. It was cool, even.

'I had a girl that died,' Sam said. 'So I know what it feels like.'

'Oh yeah?' her daddy said, and Sam saw one tear leak

out. He was sniffling, too, he could hear it.

'Well tell me this. Was she fucking some married cop when she died?'

Sam dropped the towel and took two steps toward him.

'She was fifteen years old for your information, mister. Now I know you're upset.'

'Did you see her dead?'

'You mean my daughter?'

'Yes I mean your daughter.'

He looked at the ground for a bit. He spoke quietly.

'Yeah I saw her dead. She was dead when I got to her. She was in a wreck.'

Alesandra's daddy wiped at his nose and turned sideways a little. He looked at the house.

'Well,' he said. He started shaking his head. He seemed to be at a loss for words. He tried to say something several times. Finally he turned back around. 'It's a hell of a thing to have to look at. Ain't it?'

Sam looked down at his feet for a few moments. Then he looked her daddy in the eye, and it wasn't hard to do. He'd probably not lived a perfect life either. But the pain that was in there, that was what was hard to look at. All that anger was still in there behind it, but an unhealable hole that had been torn out of him was gaping and open for the world to see. And Sam had to stand there and listen to him cry. There wasn't anything he could do. Just hang his head and listen to it. It went on and on and on and finally began to dry up. He went ahead and lit a cigarette and leaned against the trunk of the cruiser. So they'd buried her. He'd known they would have by now. He'd already known that one time but his thoughts now were jumbled sometimes and things would pass in and out without a lot of order some days. He thought his gun was in the house. Hell he didn't know where it was. In the bedroom maybe. Maybe it was on the coffee table. There was too much to think about these days.

'I can't fight too good today,' Sam said, and he held

up his hands. 'If you want to wait till later it'll be OK with me. I was married. I did wrong.'

Alesandra's daddy closed his eyes for a second only.

'It's not that. That's part of it. She was fifteen?'

'Yeah. She'd be nineteen now.'

He'd die and go to hell right here before he said anything about Alesandra shooting at Fay that day because it would hurt her daddy. All done water washed under the bridge and the bridge washed out too. Too much old shit to worry about and the only thing to worry about was just getting through with everything whatever it amounted to and just get on the road and go look for her, *I'm headed to Biloxi*, that's what she'd said first time he ever laid eyes on her.

'They told me about your wife,' Mr Farris said. 'I've got a new wife now. She's young. I traded in my old wife for her. That's what Alesandra said. They never did get along. Alesandra was already grown. She was already wild. She was wild when she was sixteen.'

'You want to come in?' Sam said.

'You've lost three people close to you. I've only lost one. They had your picture in the paper. From the fire.'

'I didn't see it,' Sam said. 'I didn't want to.'

The birds were calling out there in the trees. He could hear something going down the road out by the highway.

'Are you in trouble over all this? Are you going to lose your job over it?'

Sam walked a little closer. He took a drag on his cigarette and blew the smoke out.

'I don't know, Mr Farris. I don't know what's going to happen now.'

'Would you tell me something if I asked you?'

'Yessir. I guess. If I could.'

'Would you be honest with me, though? Would you tell me the truth?'

'Yessir. Yes. I will.'

'She wasn't a bad girl, was she? I know she ran around and drank. But she wasn't mean, was she? She

444

never did hurt anybody or try to hurt anybody, did she?'

'No sir,' he said, and something got thick in his throat. 'She wasn't a bad girl. She didn't hurt anybody that I know of. And I'm awful sorry that she's dead. It's hard to talk about this with you.'

He waited a few moments.

'You could come in if you want to. I could fix you a cup of coffee or something. I was just about to have a beer. I had to go see my boss this morning.'

'I've got to get on,' he said, and he looked at his watch. 'I've got business in New York this afternoon.' He turned as if he were going to leave. 'You can't stop living unless you just do it all at once.'

Sam didn't have an answer for that. He watched him walk around the back of the shiny car and stop by the trunk. He flicked at something on the paint with one finger, then looked at his finger.

'I came over here to try to knock the hell out of you. Or make you tell me who could have killed her. It just don't make sense, you know?'

'Yeah. I know.'

'And the cops won't tell you anything. Just found in a boat dead. Shot in the face two times. But you couldn't tell it on her in the casket.'

Sam took a few more steps toward the house.

'You want to come in?'

Her daddy walked on around the rear fender and up to the door and stopped there. He put his fingers on the handle. Just about to pull on it and go on. Get on to whatever he had that was so damn important he had to take care of so far away.

'I heard there was some business about a girl. Another girl. A younger girl.'

'Sounds like you've been talking to some people.'

'I've talked to everybody I can. I'm going to talk to everybody I can. All the way up to the governor if that's what it takes to find out who killed my baby. Wouldn't you?'

445

'I guess so,' Sam said.

'You should, too,' he said, and opened the door. 'If she meant anything to you at all. She did mean something to you, didn't she?'

Sam didn't say anything.

'Well didn't she?'

'Yes. She did.'

There was more he wanted to say. It was easy to see that he was a man who was used to being listened to.

'I hope so. I hope you didn't get her killed over something you were doing. Because it's going to come out whatever it is. And if it does, and I hear about it . . .'

Sam flipped his cigarette butt away and walked on closer to the house, and stopped when he was right across the car from him.

'There's no need in threatening me, Mr Farris. There ain't a damn thing you can scare me with. You ain't got a damn thing. Nothing.'

And in a way that was a relief itself. There was nobody who was going to stop him from going on in the house and getting a cold beer out of the icebox. That was going to be such a small and uncomplicated thing, a thing that would feel a little good. The only thing that mattered was to find Fay.

Her daddy must have seen that what he said was true. He got in the car and shut the door and started the engine. He slipped on some Ray-Bans and glanced up.

'I just wish I knew what happened,' he said. 'Even knowing my daughter was going to bed with a married state trooper is not as bad as not knowing that.'

He turned the wheel and his head and backed up, then made a neat turnaround and pulled out of there, winding up through the pines on the other side of the growing grass on the sides of the drive. Sam watched the gray paint until it was up the hill and gone. He stood there until he heard nothing else.

He looked up. It was getting hotter now and inside the house it would be cool. He'd just go in there and get him a beer. That was all he had to do. He could have

446

another one after that if he needed it. He went up the steps, knowing that son of a bitch McCollum had told him where he lived. He was like a goddamn pit bull, he wasn't going to stop. And by God he might be made to. He could be. If he had to be.

And then all that fell away from him. He was sorry for his mistakes but he was tired of being sorry for them. He didn't want but one thing. Besides that cold beer.

He drove fast and didn't speak much to her. It seemed to her that whatever good thing they might have once had a chance at having was fading away in a hurry. She stayed on her side of the seat and after a while it was as if she wasn't even in there at all. She had decided that tonight she would leave, would lie awake until he slept or went somewhere or did something, and she would pack her suitcase and leave walking again, try to head back north. She could have been away from him already. All she would have had to do was just walk away from the Holiday Inn and keep walking. Even if she hadn't caught a ride, in a night's time she could have walked back to Sam's, curled up on his steps, waited for him to come in. But that wasn't what she'd done and now she was in the Chevy with him again and each minute that passed just put more and more miles between them.

At first the radio station had been clear and strong, but as they went deeper south it had started to fade and she had messed with the knob, trying to retune it to something else, but after a few minutes of whining and squealing from the radio he had reached over and snapped it off.

She knew she'd never see her family again now. They had gone on somewhere, to some other place on down the road, and there was no telling where that place was. Maybe it was just as well. There probably wasn't anything she could do for them and she knew there was nothing that they could do for her. But still she felt the loss of them. And now she would always wonder whatever had become of them.

Sam would have understood and she would have been able to talk to him about it, if he'd been the one who had driven her out there to see that empty place. This man just kept his eyes straight ahead and watched the road, sipped at his beer, lit one cigarette after another, drove in silence. She didn't know what she'd done that pissed him off so bad.

They had been driving for over an hour now, and she was going to have to go to the bathroom again before long. She started watching the roadside signs that told the distance to towns on ahead. There were always gas stations at those turnoffs. They always had bathrooms. She didn't want to make him any madder, but when the time came she'd have to say something.

She thought about trying to be nice to him, see if she could get him to soften up. But glancing at him sideways she didn't like the look on his face and was reluctant to say anything.

The traffic wasn't bad along this stretch of the highway and Aaron passed everything he came up behind. Once in a great while she saw state troopers across the median, going the other way, but if he gave any notice to them he didn't show it by letting off the gas any. She wondered what his hurry was. Right before they'd left the hotel she had come out of the bathroom and had seen him on the phone, but she couldn't tell who he was talking to and he had ended his conversation quickly.

A blue sign advertised a roadside rest stop up ahead but on the bottom of the sign were the words NO RESTROOMS.

After a few more miles they passed the rest stop and she could see a lot of trucks and cars pulled over. When they got to the other end of it, trucks were entering the highway, and Aaron had to move over for them. She glanced over at the speedometer. He was doing nearly eighty and she knew the pistol was back under the seat and wondered what he'd do if some cop pulled him

449

over for speeding. She knew they could search cars if they had a reason to. Sam had told her that much. He'd told her a lot of things, and one of them was that it was illegal to have a gun hidden in your vehicle. He'd said that was called carrying a concealed weapon. He'd said you could get sent to the pen for that.

And she was still wondering about Gigi. There must have been something going on between them, the way she'd acted that one morning. The jealousy she'd shown. What was it that Aaron had said? *We've kind of got an arrangement.* What the hell did that mean? She knew she'd been upstairs with him and she wondered how long that had been going on. She didn't know for a *fact* that they'd been sleeping together, but it sure had looked that way. Now she didn't know. And did it make any difference anyway?

She was going to have to pee before long. Her bladder was really full now. She was going to have to say something about stopping before long, whether it made him mad or not. If he didn't stop before long she was going to wet herself right here in the seat.

It was strange sometimes, the way he seemed to know what she was thinking: 'You need to go to the bathroom or anything?'

She looked over at him. 'Yeah. I'd like to stop somewhere if we could.'

'How soon?'

'Pretty soon.'

'You hungry?'

She thought about it and then nodded.

'I could eat somethin I guess.'

He glanced at his watch and then finished the beer he was drinking, dropped it on the floorboard on her side with a few other cans.

'I'll throw that shit out when we stop,' he said. 'There's a Stuckey's on up here where you can use the bathroom and get something to eat. About ten minutes. Can you make it that long?'

'Yeah. I can make it that long.'

'I'm getting a little hungry myself.'

She moved over a little closer to him in the seat. She didn't like driving down the road with him like this and not talking.

'Slide on over if you want to,' he said.

She did. There were all those questions, but there were questions back up north, too. It was hard to decide what she wanted to do. If it would be safe to go back to Sam, she wanted to go back to Sam. But if it wasn't how was she supposed to find out? There didn't seem to be any safe way to find out. Maybe she just needed to let some more time pass.

Aaron put his arm around her and she snuggled into him. He wasn't hard to be around when he wasn't in a bad mood. He was even kind sometimes. She liked being around him at those times. But she didn't understand why he'd just go off sometimes, for no reason. Maybe he got tired of dealing with women all the time in the bar. He usually seemed pretty good when he was out at Arlene's, but he seemed to have a pretty short fuse in the bar. He probably worried about the cops busting them all the time. And it looked like the cops would know what went on in there. It looked like people would talk, especially the ones he threw out of there after he busted their heads.

His hand reached around and touched one of her breasts, squeezed it tightly. She had to admit she liked it. His fingers moved around and stroked one of her nipples through the cloth. Her insides stirred. She leaned her head back on the seat while he rubbed her like a pet cat.

'You don't ever get enough, do you?' he said.

And what did it hurt to admit that?

'Not hardly.'

His fingers left her and he patted her on the shoulder.

'There's our turnoff,' he said.

She kept sitting close to him, liking the feel of him in spite of everything else.

They were going through Jackson now in rush hour traffic. Aaron cursed at it and drove slower because the cars were jammed almost bumper to bumper and some of the people drove in a manner that scared her, weaving in and out of traffic, hitting the brakes, stepping on the gas to rocket ahead and change lanes again. It made her so nervous that she couldn't see how he could stand to drive through it. There wouldn't be any way she'd be able to.

'Fucking place is crazy,' was all he said.

By the time the sun started to ease over in the sky to the west they were south of the capital and driving back through groves of pines and passing through small towns that slowed them down. She was hoping they'd make the coast before dark and look at the boats but now she didn't think they'd make it. She'd gotten used to doing that, to making some coffee late in the evening and sitting out on the front porch in one of the comfortable chairs, putting her cigarettes and lighter down there beside her cup and watching the birds across the road and the boats that were coming in and the people walking around out there and beyond it all the sea out there in the coming of night. Sometimes Aaron would be in the house, most times not. Most times he was over at Biloxi at the bar, taking care of who knew what.

She didn't ask many questions about it anymore. She had asked a few times if he had seen Reena but he'd always said no in a way that let Fay know he didn't want to talk about her. Because of the children probably. She'd seen what they ate. They didn't eat good. Maybe they were like her when she was little and there wasn't much to go around.

She wished she could see Reena. She missed her. It was always nice to have another woman to talk to, but after that last trip to the club, Aaron hadn't said anything to her about going back. And with Arlene gone now, and no people staying in the big house, there wasn't much to do when Aaron wasn't there.

'You going to work tonight?' she said.

He was watching the traffic ahead of him and he didn't take his eyes off it.

'I don't know. I probably need to go over for a while. I'll have to drop you off and clean up.'

'It was nice of you to drive me all the way up there,' she said. 'I know it's a long ways.'

'That's all right,' he said. 'I was ready to get away for a while anyway.'

The furniture stores and car dealerships and auto parts stores started thinning out again and the traffic started moving faster. Far ahead in the distance she could see some of the pine forests that lay between them and the coast.

'You like your job?'

He passed a couple of cars and she looked at the people inside them as they went past, wondered where they were going. There were so many people on the road. All the time. Sometimes it seemed to her that there were way too many people in the world.

'I don't like dealing with all them drunks,' he said. 'Somebody's always bitching about something. I get to listen to all that shit.'

The sun was shining almost painfully into her face and she lowered the visor in front of her. She made sure her door was locked and turned around and leaned against it.

'How'd you meet Gigi?' she said.

He was quiet for a long space of time and she wasn't sure if she'd said the wrong thing. But then he passed another car and looked into the rearview mirror and swung back into his lane.

'It wasn't hard,' he said. 'I saw her on the stage in Memphis one night and offered her more money to come down and work for me sometimes.'

'How long did she work for you?'

'It was close to a year, I guess. She'd go back and forth. We raised the cover charge two dollars a head the first night she danced. Cully was the one who got the bright idea of putting her picture out front. Gigi made us a lot of money. Made Cully a lot of money, rather.'

'Did she . . .' She didn't know how to put it. 'Did she do stuff with the customers?'

He glanced at her briefly, then turned back to watch where he was going.

'What do you mean?'

'You know what I mean.'

'What do you know about that?' he said.

She started to say that she didn't know anything about it, but then she remembered what he'd told her at the pool that morning about lying. And anyway, the whole question about Gigi meant she knew something about it.

'I just know stuff goes on over there.'

'What stuff?'

'Sex stuff.'

'And how do you know that?'

'I saw it. Back there in one of those rooms.'

He was quiet again for a bit. Then: 'When was this?'

'First night I went in there. I went back with Reena so she could get dressed.'

She watched him think that over for a while. He had sped back up by now and was again passing everything he could. Then for some reason he cut back on his speed and started letting other cars and trucks come around him.

'What goes on back there ain't no skin off my nose. I just keep the trouble out. That's all I do.' He looked at her now. 'I ain't no damn pimp.'

'I didn't say you was.'

He fired up a cigarette and cracked his window to let the smoke out.

'What my brother does is his business. I just work for him.'

He was getting a little riled up but he'd been mean to her too and she didn't have to just be quiet.

'That first mornin Gigi come down she acted like she owned you.'

454

'Don't nobody own me goddammit.' She saw him getting madder but she wasn't going to quit yet.

'Did you and her . . . ?'

'Hell yes I fucked her. So did half of Biloxi. So what?'

'Well why did she stay with you?'

'Because it was cheaper than putting her up in a hotel. Cause her ass loves that room service.'

'Oh.'

'You don't need to ask questions about Gigi. OK? There's no reason for you to ever bring her up again.'

Well. Since he put it that way.

'OK. I won't say nothin else about her.'

'Good. I'm glad to hear that.'

'I just can't see what you ever saw in her in the first place. That old bleached hair and all.'

'Fay?'

'Yeah?'

'You talk too much sometimes, baby.'

'I know it. My mama used to tell me to shut up all the time.'

It was dark when they pulled around to the back of the house. He got out and went up the steps to unlock the door and turn on some of the lights while she stepped out and stretched her legs and reached into the bed of the El Camino for her things. The porch light came on and she looked up to see him moving around in there. She heard the screen door flap and he came down the steps to get his suitcase.

'You got everything?'

'Yeah. I'm comin.'

She walked slowly and her legs were tired. He held the door for her and she nodded her thanks and carried her bag and her purse to a couch in the hall and set them down. She wasn't ready to climb those stairs just yet, but he went up them fast and said that he was going to go on and take a shower and get ready.

She got her cigarettes and lighter from the purse and went into the kitchen and turned on the lights, thought

455

she'd make some coffee and see what was in the refrigerator. The water came on upstairs and she heard it rattle in the pipes somewhere in the house, draining down through the old timbers and back into the ground.

Somebody needed to go get some groceries pretty soon. She wished Arlene would come on back. They'd done some shopping together a few times, going down the road to the Winn-Dixie in one of the shopping centers. Now the icebox held only a few dozen eggs and some canned biscuits and bacon and milk and juice on its racks. She pulled out the crisper bin and looked at the tomatoes and lettuce and onions down there, wondering what she could fix for her supper. She knew he wouldn't be in until late, probably. There was a pantry in the hall where Arlene kept her canned stuff and there were two freezers in a room behind the washing machine and the dryer where she kept steaks and chickens and pork chops and seafood. She guessed she could find something and thaw it out. But right now she wanted some coffee.

She measured the water and the coffee and poured it in the maker and turned it on. She sat down in a chair in the kitchen to wait. Faint noises came from upstairs and after a while the water stopped running. It would be quiet here after he left. But she could sit out on the front porch again and listen to the rigging songs.

She glanced up at the clock on the wall and saw that it was just a few minutes past nine. Would she hear him when he came in, when he slipped into the bed with her? Would she open her eyes coming awake and be surprised to see him there, his broad back turned, his red hair mussed on the pillow, and would she roll over in the sheets and snuggle into him and slip her hand between his arm and his ribs and hold him, listening to his deep and steady breathing like she used to do with Sam?

She wondered what she thought she was doing when

she already had a man who loved her. And the baby. She had to ask him now, before he got away again. She couldn't wait any longer. She had to get to the doctor. Some doctor. A doctor.

The coffee was ready now. She got up and poured a big cup and stirred some sugar into it. The milk in the icebox was still fresh and she put some in. She sat sipping it, smoking another cigarette, knowing it was bad for the baby. She'd have to quit.

She heard him coming down the stairs and she stubbed out her cigarette and took another drink of her coffee. He came across the hall, trailing his fingers across the covered pool table, and she smiled at him.

'You want some coffee?' she said. 'I got some fresh made here.'

He looked at his watch and went over to the cabinet.

'I got time for one cup I guess. What you gonna eat for supper?'

'I'll find somethin.'

'There ought to be some stuff in the freezer.'

'There is. But we need to get some groceries.'

He had a cup down and was pouring coffee into it. He had on a pair of jeans and his white boots again, a wine-colored shirt that she thought looked good on him.

'Maybe I can run you over to the store tomorrow. Why don't you remind me?'

'OK.'

'I wish Arlene would get on back. I hate for you to have to stay out here by yourself so much.'

'You know when she'll be back?'

'Pretty soon I hope.'

He brought his cup over to the table and pulled a chair back and sat down. She reached out a finger and wiped the side of his neck.

'What?'

'Shavin cream.' She smiled at him. 'You look nice.'

'Thanks.' He took a drink of his coffee and looked off to the side for a moment, then scooted the chair

457

sideways and crossed his legs. 'I'm hard to get along with sometimes.'

'Well,' she said. 'I don't know why you get like you do.'

He stuck his finger in his ear and moved it around in there for a few seconds, then looked at his nail.

'I just have a lot of stuff on my mind sometimes. You don't know what it's like to work over there.'

'Why do you stay there then?'

'Shit. I don't know what else I'd do if I didn't work there. It's a lot of headaches sometimes. But at least I'm not punching a clock. You ever had a real job?'

'I've had to work plenty,' she said. 'I've picked fruit and just about anything else you can pick. It's hard work. I've heard Mama talk about choppin cotton for four dollars a day. And pregnant. You wish you still caught shrimp?'

'Ah,' he said, and rubbed his chin. 'I don't know. It's a lot of work and it's not year-round. You've got to find something else to do in the off-season.' He smiled a small smile and took another sip of his coffee. 'Ain't no off-season in the naked lady business. Folks want to look at them every day that rolls around.'

There was something she'd been wondering about for a while. Just one of many things.

'How do y'all keep from gettin caught by the cops?'

He made a face. 'We been busted before for indecency. One time they got us for simulating sex acts they said. That wasn't nothing but Reena hunching on some guy in a chair. They've sent guys in plainclothes in a few times. Cully's got good lawyers and hell, this is Biloxi. It ain't as wild now as it used to be. Years ago. Arlene's told me some stories about the strippers in the old days.'

'I'm not talkin about the strippers. I'm talking about . . .'

'I know what you're talking about. I wish you'd get off of it. What goes on in the back rooms don't concern me. I just get sick of the damn noise sometimes.'

He got up and leaned over the table and kissed her and then took his cup to the sink. He walked out of the kitchen and up the hall and came back with a phone book in his hand. He put it on the table in front of her.

'Look through there and find you a doctor and call his office tomorrow. Tell em you need an appointment pretty soon. Have you told Arlene?'

She looked up.

'No. I didn't tell her. I'd been kinda wonderin about that, though. I didn't know what she'd say.'

'Well don't worry about it. Get that appointment set up and I'll take you over there and go in with you. OK?'

'OK.'

This sudden kindness made everything almost all right now. She got up and put her arms around him and she felt his hands take her shoulders. She stood for a moment, wrapped in the strength of him, and the wanting was quick and deep. She stepped back and pulled up her dress and pushed down her panties and shook them loose from her foot. She took him by the hand and pulled him down the two steps into the parlor, scooted her butt against the rim of the table and then lay back and pulled her dress up above her belly. She drew her knees up and opened her legs.

'You ever done it on a pool table?' she said.

He moved toward her, his eyes smiling, his fingers pulling at his belt.

'Damn, baby,' he said.

Now he was gone and the house was quiet. She'd found some frozen hamburger patties in the freezer and had set two of them out to thaw. There were some messages on the answering machine in the hall but she didn't know anything about messing with that so she left it alone.

She fixed her supper and ate in the kitchen and took a last cup of coffee out to the front porch and drank it there. The road was pretty quiet, and the harbor was silent except for the sound of the wind in the nets.

By eleven she was upstairs in the room she had

459

moved into with him. She took a long shower and washed her hair and then wrapped herself in a towel and sat on the bed to paint her toenails a dark red, her wet hair lying close against the back of her neck. She propped her feet in a chair to let her nails dry and when she was done she got up and dropped the towel on the floor and pulled some clean panties from a drawer. There was a short black nightie she had found hanging in the closet and figured was probably Gigi's. Before she put it on she looked at the tag in the back, holding it out where she could read it: *Frederick's of Hollywood*. Gigi had probably gotten it out there when she'd made some of those movies. She believed she liked wearing things like this.

She stood in front of an antique dresser with a mirror and spots of the backing had flaked off so that she resembled to herself an old picture standing there brushing her hair.

The walls in the room were beadboard and the big bed she shared now with Aaron was made of massive posts and so long he could stretch out to his full length. She already loved sleeping in it, having all that room. She'd locked all the doors and Aaron had his own key to let himself in. But she wasn't ready to go to bed. She wished she had some new magazines to read. She'd already read everything that was downstairs in the main sitting room where the pictures of Aaron and Cully stood on the mantle.

Aaron had a nice cabinet for his television in the room, up on a table so that they could watch it from the bed. A small VCR was hooked into it but she'd never seen him use it.

She propped some pillows up against the headboard and then thought of something and went downstairs and filled a glass with ice cubes, got a canned Coke, went back upstairs.

When she was nestled comfortably in the bed again she poured the drink over the ice cubes and waited for it to chill a bit and found the remote on the bedside table and turned it on. She wished there was a satellite system like the one Sam had at his house. Here there were only a few channels. Some old movie was playing and she watched it for a while but couldn't get into it, she'd already missed so much of it. A baseball game was on another channel, but the picture was fuzzy.

She drank some of her Coke and flipped it around, but she couldn't find anything she wanted to watch. She still wasn't sleepy. All that coffee.

She rolled over and pulled open the drawer on the bedside table, thinking she might find something to read, but there was nothing in there except for an old *High Times* and some insurance papers and some pens and pennies and a few yellowed handkerchiefs in a cellophane pack that looked ancient. She shut it and got up. She didn't want to just lie there. She thought if she could find something to read she could maybe just do that until she got sleepy. The phone book was downstairs and she guessed she could look up a doctor's number, but she'd have plenty of time to do that tomorrow. She wandered around the room. She never really had taken a good look around in it.

There were curtains on the windows and she fingered the clean lace trim. It would be nice to know how to sew stuff, maybe make some clothes. In Amy's magazines she'd seen where women did that.

She looked through a dresser's drawers but they held only Aaron's underwear and some T-shirts. Or she thought they did. One corner of something black and plastic caught her eye, almost buried beneath his white cotton briefs. Standing there knowing she shouldn't do it she went ahead and did. It was a black plastic box like the ones movies came in. She'd seen plenty of them at Sam's house. She'd even taken them out of the boxes and shoved them into the machine just before they sat down on the couch with some KFC or burgers from a fast food joint in Batesville or Oxford. Holding it in her hand and looking at it and wondering just what movie it held. A good love story? Or was it a tale of revenge? Something to watch anyway. He'd never told her not to go poking around. Wasn't anybody's business what she watched.

She took it out of the box and turned it over in her hand, studying it. It didn't have any kind of label on it telling what it was so what was it? You had to just stick it in and play it to see. Amy'd had some of those blank ones stacked up in a cabinet. Amy said some of them were videos of them out fishing and messing around on the lake. One was of a highway patrol picnic down at Grenada Lake. She'd told Fay she could watch that one if she wanted to see a bunch of cops getting drunk. She knew this was nothing like that. This was forbidden somehow simply by the unknowing of what it was. This might be like peeking in on somebody while they were sleeping, moving into their bedroom on quiet feet to stand watching them unaware of you in their dark safe room.

A little voice spoke, said *Don't do it*, even said *It don't belong to you*, but she didn't listen to that. She turned on the VCR and switched the channel on the TV around and put the tape into the machine and then pushed play. She went back to the bed and leaned up against the pillows again and reached for her drink. She took a big swallow and then turned back around to the television screen and then blew it out her nose, all over her nice new nightie.

The crowd seemed sullen and to Aaron it felt like one of those nights that came along for him once in a while, one of those times when he let himself get to thinking about things too much. That shit in Gulf Shores. He could have caught the pilot on the ground somewhere and let him off with nothing worse than a severe ass-whipping. But it had been such an easy thing to do. And he'd wanted her to see it, had in fact said it: *I wouldn't want you to miss this.*

He was sitting at the corner of the bar, sipping on a draft. Two empty shot glasses sat just past his elbow holding the squeezed pulps of limes. He wiped at his mouth with the edge of his thumbnail. Bobbi was on the stage and she turned her head and winked at him. He smiled a tiny smile. Some functioning drunks had some tables pulled together at the edge of the stage and he was keeping an eye on them while waiting to throw out the one nonfunctioning drunk who was sleeping with his head on a table in the corner, one arm hanging down. The music was throbbing through the smoky little dive, Clapton and friends working out on 'Bell Bottom Blues.' He liked Clapton.

He was breaking in a new guy behind the bar and he turned to him now. Somebody put a light hand on his shoulder but he didn't look yet to see who it was.

'Eddie. Two shots of Rumpleminz, bud.'

The bartender nodded and reached for a glass, then went to the old tin box that Aaron had salvaged from a shrimp man years ago. It was packed full of ground ice and they kept some of their liqueurs in there.

He looked over his shoulder then to see who was there and what she wanted, and Wanda was about to bust out the top of her waitress rig. He watched her eyes. They looked timid.

He felt her hand slide up his hip. He removed it.

'No touchy feely in the house,' he said. 'It ain't good for business. They get jealous.'

She pressed in tighter against him and set her drink on the bar beside his beer. She smelled real good.

'You want a quickie?' she said, like a married woman. 'I think the back room's empty.'

'Wanda Wanda,' he said, knowing people were watching. 'Wanda Hot Mama.'

She'd put on fresh lipstick and for thirty-three in that place she was not bad. She still had her figure and she knew about men. Then you'd get to talking to her in bed after it was over and she'd soften and you'd find out that she'd been raised in Alaska and that like some of them she pined to be in the movies and they meant the legitimate kind and they didn't understand that the world was full of beautiful girls, or that buying them to make them do whatever under the sun and in the world you wanted them to on film took no more than money or drugs or the right promises or even maybe just helping them out of a little spot of bad luck.

'Why ain't you been to see me?' she said. Her eyes were bright and wet and blue and there were jerky movements about her fingers. She fiddled with her cigarette and almost continually rubbed the tip of it in the ashtray or tapped at it. Had to have something to do.

'Busy,' he said. Not an unlikely story. The bartender set the shots down in a single glass and Aaron drained his beer. With a nod of his chin he said, ''Nother one.'

'I know what it is,' she said, and to him she looked like she was getting ready to pitch one of her little fits.

'Oh yeah,' he said. 'I'm sure you do.' He nodded toward the clock. 'Don't forget you got to start to work in thirty-five minutes. See the clock?'

She didn't bother to look and that pissed him off. She

was here to piss him off, he knew that. He picked up the glass that held the schnapps and sipped at it. Eddie finished refilling his beer and set it in front of him, then moved down the bar to wait on somebody.

'How come you don't come see me no more?' she said. She was beginning to get trembly all over now, not just her hands. He'd held her when she was cold one time, and her spine had shivered under his hands.

'You all right?' he said.

'You've been fucking that girl you brought in here, that Fay. You don't even care about me. Do you?'

He saw the reaction on her face when his eyes changed. He picked up his beer and took it and the schnapps as he moved toward the corner and spoke over his shoulder.

'Let's go out back,' he said. 'Go on and get this shit over with. We ain't gonna do it in here.'

He saw her taking that in and he could tell she wasn't ready for it.

'All right,' she said. 'Can I get me another drink?'

On the bar her drink sat half full.

'Sure,' he said. 'Get you another drink. Meet me out back behind the door.' He didn't wait for her or even look at her again but went around the edge of the bar and put his shoulder hard to the swinging door that was held shut by only a screen-door spring. He looked back over the room one more time before he went through it. One of the fluorescent bulbs was burned out in the hall and that was something else he'd have to do. Or maybe he could tell the new guy to do it. Some people were funny. They thought that if you hired them to do something they were only supposed to do that one thing and nothing else.

Cully's office door was closed and he stopped beside it and took a sip from the schnapps and set it on the floor. He rapped on the door with his knuckles and drank some of the beer. He licked foam off his lip.

From inside came a toneless 'What.' Aaron opened the door. A big girl with blond hair and tight white

465

stretch pants was fitting the cups of a dirty bra over the fat mounds of her surgically boosted tits and she looked appreciatively at Aaron and kept popping her gum. Cully had his feet propped on the desk, pale jaybird legs above his socks. The desk was cluttered worse than the room.

'You through?' Aaron said.

'Not yet. What's up?'

'I just need to talk to you sometime.'

The blonde reached for her top and slipped her arms through the sleeve holes and turned to face Aaron.

'Who's the Viking?' she said to Cully.

He smiled with his bad teeth and Aaron wondered again why he didn't go to the dentist and get the god-damn things fixed. His breath was like a septic tank. God knew how any of these girls stood to kiss him.

'That's my little brother,' Cully said.

'Little half brother. I'm Aaron.'

'Well my. You're just a big old thing ain't you?'

She was taking her time fastening the buttons on her blouse, but to Aaron she looked only fleshy and used and old. How many like her did he see in the space of a year?

'This is Kristy,' Cully said. 'She may go to work for us, what you think?'

Aaron sipped at his beer and watched her smile at him even as her hand went to Cully's ankle and touched it. He heard the door behind the bar swing shut.

'I don't know, give her a tryout, I guess. I got to go have a little talk with Wanda. I'll be back after I see what she says.'

He turned and reached for the doorknob as she started moving behind the desk. If he didn't get out the door pretty quick he'd probably have to watch her suck him off and he damn sure didn't want to see that shit.

He pulled it shut behind him. Wanda was pushing open the back door and she stood waiting for him, framed by the dark night behind her. The glare of the fluorescent bulb in the ceiling made harsh shadows under her eyes. He picked up the schnapps and she stood there until he came out. He kicked the brick over and she let the door to on it. Somebody had gotten one of the lawn chairs but there was a plastic milk crate ten feet away and he kicked it into position close to her and sat down on it.

'All right, Wanda. Sit down and let's get it over with. What you got a bug up your ass about?'

She didn't say. She wandered out from the building and looked toward the dark water and the wet sand that lay flat and slick out there. He took another sip of the schnapps and then nestled the glass carefully into the sand at his feet.

'If you ain't gonna use this lawn chair I'm gonna sit in it.'

'Go ahead,' she said, still facing away from him. He didn't like her turning her back on him like that. He didn't get up. He rested the beer glass on his knee. Why did they always have to fall in fucking love? Why wasn't just plain old fucking enough? Why did they have to get all these dreams going in their heads and mess everything up?

'I may just go somewhere else, Aaron.'

'Well,' he said, thinking it over. 'Don't let the door hit you in the ass.'

She whirled around.

'I never promised you a damn thing, Wanda.'

'What about that new one? You promise her anything?'

'That ain't none of your business. So don't go poking your nose into it.'

She took a few steps toward him. 'What you gonna do? Beat the shit out of me like you used to do Reena?'

He made one hand into a fist and she ducked her head and spun around and when she turned back she'd changed her tune.

'I'm sorry,' she said. 'Forget I said that.'

'You getting a big mouth, girl.'

467

'I didn't mean it. OK? I'm just upset. It's just that I miss you. I thought . . . I guess I thought we had something.'

He watched a tear leak out of the corner of her eye. It was probably a fake. People in movies learned how to do it so that meant other people could learn how to do it. It was always some shit like this. He knew he could take her back there right now and fuck her and she'd be happy but only for a while and it was only the short-term answer. Tomorrow or next week she'd be singing the same old tired shit again.

The silence gathered around them. The wind blew at his face while she sipped at her drink, her good brown legs muscled in the half dark. That had rocked him and held him tight. Sometimes the silence worked for him. Sometimes with a woman it was best to just be quiet.

He drank some more of the beer and lifted the glass of schnapps and drank from it again and finished it. He leaned over and set it against the foundation of the building, concrete blocks chipped and worn of their black paint. Trash and cigarette butts lay there alongside ripped foil packets that had held condoms. She sounded like she was talking to herself. In quiet. In wonder.

'I know a lot of shit on you. Child neglect. Selling dope. I let you talk me into making that tape. I even did that for you. And I don't know why. Cause you ain't nothing but a fucking loser.'

He set the beer glass down, got up with a sigh, and when she tried to run he caught her with no more trouble than a cat with a mouse in a closet. He was mindful that she had to work tonight.

His big hand cradled her jaw and throat and she dropped her drink. He looked into her eyes and gave her punches that went solidly into her ribs, high, middle, low. He hugged her to him and chopped her hard in a kidney, once.

'You fuck with me you'll do worse than piss blood,' he said. He had her up against the building by now, his

468

hand over her mouth, her pretty blue eyes wide with disbelief at the pain he was bringing her like a present or a place to live in. He shoved her face away and turned her loose and she stumbled along the wall and there by the light of a hotel up the beach and beyond the dark walkers and sitters on the beach she fell to her knees and then over onto her hands and propped herself there breathing deeply. Strands of her hair stood outlined in the backing light. He went over to his milk crate and picked up his beer and didn't watch her. She lowered herself into the sand and drew her legs up with her face turned away and stayed that way for a while. Serving drinks later she'd find grains still in her clothes, her hair.

After a while he finished the beer and he got up and went back inside to get another and find his stash and his pipe. He left the brick in the door so that she could get back inside, clean herself up, get ready to start waiting on the drunks.

That Wanda was on the tape, with two men at the same time. It looked like they were in a hotel room. It was a strange thing to her to watch. She could stop it and rewind it and watch them do everything again, over and over, endlessly. Breathlessly.

After a while she got hot and bothered and the more it went on the worse it got. She stopped it one time and went to the window and looked out but there were only the dark forms of the boats across the road. No lights from Aaron coming in. And maybe he'd be late. But she hoped not. Not now.

David Hall came to see him that afternoon. He was out on the deck drinking another beer and he wasn't careful where he was thumping his ashes. Or dropping his butts. There were eight or ten flat ones between his feet. But when he heard the car coming down the drive he got up and walked to the corner of the house and looked out there to see the shiny gold sedan pulling up behind his cruiser. He could see David behind the wheel. He set his beer down and went through the living room and opened the front door just as David was coming up to the steps. He stood there waiting for whatever else was going to visit him. He wondered if it might be possible to disappear into someplace like Nebraska.

But that wouldn't help him find her. David came on.

'Hey, Sam,' he said, when he got up next to the door. He didn't have a gun on. He was wearing blue jeans and black shoes and a red button-up shirt. 'I'm sorry to bother you at home.'

'That's all right,' Sam said, and stepped back from the door so that he could come on in. He'd always liked David and had been glad for him when he'd gotten elected the first time. 'I was just sitting out here having a beer or two. Come on out.'

He stopped halfway across the living room.

'Can I get you something to drink?'

'No thanks. Nothing for me,' he said, and kept on walking and went out through the sliding door.

'I'm gonna get me another beer,' Sam said, and he saw David nod and head toward a chair.

471

'Yeah, go ahead,' he said, and sat down. Sam watched him for a moment. He was looking out across the lake and he was wearing the same face he'd had on across his desk last night. The wheels were moving fast just as he'd been afraid they would.

He opened the icebox door and got the last beer from inside and carried it out. David had pulled one leg up and crossed it over the other. He had his fingers laced across his stomach. Part of the other beer was still left and he put the cold beer next to it. He'd have to go to the store if he wanted more now. This was his fourth or fifth, he couldn't remember. But it would only take a few minutes to go up the road to the store. He needed some cigarettes anyway.

He pulled another one from his pocket and lit it, then sat down and reached for the other beer. He turned it up but there was too much for one drink.

Out there past the deck the sky was clear and the sun floated high above. A good breeze was blowing, but he was looking forward to sundown, and cooler air. Maybe he could even go take a ride in his boat after while. After he got through talking to David about whatever it was he wanted to talk about. Maybe Fay had only gone to the other side of the lake and was hiding, and waiting, catching fish to live on. Were any of the rods and reels gone? The camp stove? He'd have to look. She might have gone to Tupelo. To Memphis. Maybe even Chicago by now.

'Sam, we got a problem. You know we do.'

He nodded in agreement and tipped the last of the beer down his throat. It was warm and made him want to gag. He quickly opened the other beer and took a good cold drink. He hadn't eaten breakfast this morning. Too nervous about going over to see Grayton. If he was going to keep drinking he needed to put something in his stomach.

'I mean something like this ain't going to go away if you just ignore it,' David said.

'Yeah. I know that.'

'It would make everything a lot easier on everybody if you'd just talk to me. Are you trying to protect her, Sam, is that what it is?'

He raised his eyes and stared at David.

'How do you know she did anything?' he said.

'I don't. But I'd like to talk to her.'

'Yeah,' he said, and took a drag off his smoke and let it out. The beer was cold in his other hand. 'So would I.'

David sat there for a minute without saying anything. He uncrossed his legs and put his hands on the arms of the chair.

'They'll fire you,' he said.

'Maybe they will.'

'Her daddy's got friends in high places. And he's making noise already.'

He remembered David from when he was a deputy sheriff, six or seven years back now. A good young cop.

'The Farris lady, Sam. The one they found in the boat. Did her and the one who lived here ever meet each other?'

'What does it matter?' Sam said.

David put his hands back across his belly. He looked like he was trying to relax.

'You're not that far from retirement, you know. What, a few years?'

'Something like that,' Sam said, and took another drink of his beer. It didn't seem right to be sitting out here this time of day. The sky didn't look right. Fay had killed her down there on the beach and the cartridges had ejected from the pistol and she'd never thought about that and had gotten her into the boat somehow and somehow had left it out there with Alesandra in it. She might have drifted for days until somebody found her. The boat could have floated into any little cove or patch of willows. The buzzards would have come. The flies would have buzzed over her. Had he gone fishing in the right place he might have found her himself.

'Are you willing to risk all that, Sam? Your job?

473

Your good name? If we find this girl and she did it, you might even have to do some time.'

'I've thought about all that,' Sam said, and he turned his head to look at David. 'Believe me. I've thought of just about everything you have. And I can't think of a reason strong enough to tell you her name.'

David stood up.

'Is that your last word, then?'

He tried to think if he had any other last words, but nothing would come to him.

'I guess it is,' he said.

Fay stopped the tape and went downstairs and opened the cabinet door that hid the liquor. She knew she shouldn't be drinking, but she was going to the doctor tomorrow. He even said he'd take her. She wished he was back here now. There wasn't any wine in there, only some whiskey and gin and vodka and tequila.

She looked at the whiskey. She didn't know if she'd like that or not. Sam drank it. Aaron drank it. She'd seen Reena drink it. What did Reena trying to kiss her mean? Did it mean anything? Would she have tried it again if she'd stayed with her some more? But she fucked men too.

All these girls knew about things she didn't know. They knew how to look sexy for a man. She never had tried to look sexy for Sam. She'd always just taken off all her clothes as soon as he got in the room with her. All that stuff down at the strip joint was teasing a man. She hadn't done that to Chris Dodd, had she? She hadn't teased him, had she? She didn't get him killed over something she'd done drunk, had she? No. Hell no. She hadn't teased him. She'd kissed him, yeah. But that son of a bitch had climbed up on top of her and taken some of her clothes off and spread her legs while she was passed out. Still . . . was that worth the whole rest of his life up there in that plane looking down?

The whiskey had a gob of what looked like red wax on the cap and some of it had dribbled and hardened down the side of the neck. It looked like only a sip or two had been taken out of a whole big bottle. Well. What did he do? He put Coke in it. Ice first.

She got some of both from their places and found a jelly glass up in the cabinet. She'd watched Sam. The ice was in there. She put some whiskey in the glass. It kind of just lay there on the bottom. It didn't look like much. She turned the bottle back up and poured it on up there a couple of inches. She wondered what it tasted like straight.

The fumes hit her nose when she held it close and sniffed. She sipped it. It tasted like some good wood if wood could taste good. Her old daddy, how he'd craved it. It burned a little but then the fire was gradually gone and there was just a warm glow left in her belly down there so close to that little one.

She almost poured it out, thinking about the baby suddenly, and then she thought about how much fun it was going to be, drinking and watching the tape, and getting hotter, just waiting for him to get home. She'd unzip him and get down on her knees first thing. He liked that.

Back up in the room she started the tape again and found her cigarettes and sat down. There were some dead spaces on the tape, places where fuzzy lines came across and made colored noise. Snippets of somebody sucking on something, too close to tell what it was, just a mouth and some skin.

She sipped at the drink and watched the screen. Some woman ran naked across a room. Somebody chased her but in clothes. The picture tilted, went over sideways. It panned the room at that crazy angle, bounced back, stopped, wobbled back and forth between a corner in a floor and a window.

Why hell this part wasn't interesting at all. She guessed they just made these things for people to watch and jack off to. But everybody was horny. If it hadn't been for getting sick she might have done it with that Jerry, but his breath smelled so bad and the way that woman treated that baby.

She wondered how many men one woman could have. In a whole lifetime, reckon how many there could be?

She sipped easily at the drink now. It was going down pretty smooth and it was the kind of thing where it got better and better. Like making love. It tasted good and it was really good with a cigarette. She might just have to have herself another one. Or she could just drink until Aaron came home and then quit, since there was the baby to think about. She could drink tonight and then tomorrow she would go see the doctor and then she wouldn't drink any more until after the baby came.

She was feeling pretty sexy now. She wanted him to do it to her in this nightie of Gigi's and then ask him who was the best.

Then the tape was back and it was different and Reena was lying on a bed. Fay recognized the bed since it was the same one she was lying on and both rooms were the same. Reena seemed to be waiting for something. Fay slowly sat up, and then somebody came into the frame with Reena, just his legs in front of the bed.

She held her breath, waiting to see who it was. But she already knew.

To Aaron it seemed that the crowd had begun to roll and surge and die back like waves against the beach, or out at sea. The smoke level had increased and the dark inside seemed to have gotten deeper and the music louder and he knew that he was steadily being driven deaf. He guessed that was what they meant by an environmental hazard.

He'd found his pipe stashed in the nylon bag in the back room and had locked the door and sat down on the bed, huffing at it until a knock had come at the door.

'Who is it?'

'It's Eddie,' said Eddie, muffled by the door.

Aaron reamed out the bowl of the hash pipe with the fingernail file on his clippers and pinched off another chunk and pressed it into the bowl. He held it up in front of his mouth, lighter poised.

'What is it, Eddie?' He fired up the lighter and moved the wavering blue-and-yellow flame close to the bowl. He touched fire to the stuff and pulled on it, and the chunk of hash slowly smoldered and glowed deep within itself.

'Bunch of these drunks out here,' Eddie said.

He sucked the smoke in and held it.

'Yeah?' he said.

'They won't keep their hands off Billie.'

Billie. He had to think. Was she the one with the knocker job or the short one with red hair and the big ass? He liked feeling this way, half drunk and starting to get high. A man needed it for a long night.

He blew the smoke out and up toward the ceiling and

rocked back on the bed. Damn. It was some good shit.

'Tell Cully.' He probably needed another hit. He considered it.

'I can't find Cully.'

'Well hell,' he said.

'What?'

'Nothing,' he said, raising his voice. 'Tell . . . who's out there?'

'Just me.'

He didn't want to have to fuck with this shit now. He wasn't even high yet. And here they were already trying to fuck it up. It didn't matter how many heads you busted, you always had to bust some more. Some damn people couldn't keep their dicks in their pockets.

'Well hold on,' he said finally. 'Or go on back out front. I'll be out in a minute.'

He heard Eddie say something in reply and then he must have gone away. People would be stealing beer if he didn't get back out there. He wondered where in the hell Cully was. He was probably hunching that Kristy in his office with the door locked. Looked like a nasty bitch to him. Cully liked them that way though.

He loaded the pipe again and set it down momentarily to rewrap the rest of the hash. He pulled up the leg of his jeans past the top of his right boot and wedged the dope down inside his sock.

The music was coming steady through the wall. He fired up his lighter and took two tremendous hits off the pipe, settled back on the bed, let it sink in. Then he shook his head and got up and stashed the pipe in the cabinet inside the tiny bathroom and went out front.

There was nothing going on that he could see. A chunky brunette had walked onto the stage and was dancing. Charlene, he thought her name was. Sometimes they came and went so fast he couldn't keep up with them.

Eddie was serving drinks when he went back to his stool at the bar and sat down. He looked over the crowd and a few faces turned toward him briefly, then looked away. Damned if he wasn't getting tore up. Or maybe down. He'd need to take it easy now and not drink much.

Eddie came over. 'You want another beer?'

'Yeah. What was going on?'

Eddie reached for a clean mug and started filling it at the tap.

'They left. I told em to get the hell out and they all took off.' He finished drawing the beer and set it in front of Aaron. 'Shot of that Rumpleminz?'

Aaron looked at the beer. Some more schnapps would be good with it. He wasn't drunk. Nowhere near it.

'Yeah, sure, let me have one.'

Eddie poured the shot and leaned over close to him. 'I wish I had about a pound of whatever the hell you're smoking, boss.'

Aaron reared back, looked up, smiled dimly.

'Oh yeah?'

'Yes sir.'

He considered it. Hell he'd thrown the assholes out. Saved him from doing it. Cully had hired him. He was clean-cut but that didn't mean he was a cop. And it wasn't like he didn't have plenty of the shit.

'You a straight-up man, Eddie?'

'Yes sir. I sure am.'

'Can you work high?'

'A monkey could do this blindfolded.'

'Well let me just come around there and relieve you of your post for a few minutes.'

Eddie nodded. 'All right,' he said.

Aaron bent over when he got behind the bar and retrieved the hash and palmed it over to Eddie.

'You seen the little room down the hall on the right?'

'Yeah, sure.'

'There's a pipe in the bathroom back there. It's stuck in there in the cabinet behind some makeup and shit. You got a lighter?'

Eddie was already pushing on the door behind the bar.

480

'I got one,' he said, and was gone. Aaron reached now for his beer and the glass and pulled them back over in front of him. He watched the crowd. They felt like trouble tonight. Some nights he could feel it and this was one of those times. Maybe it was the trouble that came in waves. Sometimes things seemed to float along smooth for a while, but never forever.

He picked up the schnapps and drank some of it, set it back. That shit was dynamite, he had to watch it.

Eddie stayed gone for a while. Aaron mixed some drinks and served a few beers to some customers. He didn't talk to them and they didn't talk to him other than to order.

He saw Wanda come through the door. She stopped at the stool in the corner and got up on it and sat there. Waiting for Eddie to get out of the back room where she could clean up probably. Fay wasn't any of her goddamn business. She knew what was good for her she'd keep her fucking nose out of it. Fuck you a few times they thought they owned you.

Here came Cully and the big blonde who was all smiles now. Aaron hoped he hadn't hired her fat ass to dance but he figured he probably had.

He turned around and found Eddie's stool and pulled it over to where he was and sat down on it.

Here they came over here now. Cully going to buy her a drink on the house probably. Impress her good.

'Shit let's give everbody one,' he mumbled.

They stopped in front of him. Cully had his hand on her shoulder.

'Well hell,' Aaron said. 'I guess y'all want a drink don't you? How bout a drink on the fucking house?'

'Two of em, little brother.' Cully was wearing the shit-eating grin he used whenever he latched on to a new one. The blonde teased the tip of her tongue around on her upper lip. He guessed she thought that was sexy. He guessed she thought that was supposed to let him know that she'd like to do something to him with her mouth now that she'd already let his brother have everything she had. Nasty bitch. If she'd fuck his brother for free she was a nasty bitch. Well it wasn't exactly free. It was for a job.

'All right,' he said. 'Got your thirst all worked up, have you? All ready for a little drink, are you?'

She didn't seem to know what to say. She tried to smile and glanced sidelong at Cully and put her hands on the bar. The polish on her fingernails was chipped, looked to Aaron like she might have just changed a tire. Cully just looked at him.

'Hell, I'll get it,' he said, and started around the end of the bar. Aaron pushed him back.

'Get outta here,' he said. 'I'm the goddamn bartender, what you want?'

'I want a goddamn drink,' Cully said, and started forward again. 'What the hell's wrong with you?' Aaron pushed him back.

'Stay out of back here,' he said. 'I'm the goddamn bartender.' He turned. 'Let's see. Glasses. Got to have some glasses before you can have a drink. That's the first fucking thing they teach you in bartender school.' He grabbed glasses and scooped them full of ice and looked up from where he was bent over. 'That's the first fucking thing *I* learned in bartender school.'

Cully was going back around to the front beside her. 'Bartender school my ass. I want a Beefeater on the rocks.'

Aaron grabbed the bottle from the rack of them back there.

'Just say when.' He upended it over the glass and poured one shot, then another, and had it almost up to the rim when Cully said, 'Whoa, goddamn.'

He served it to Cully and leaned to the woman.

'Now little lady, what can I do for you?'

'I don't know, how long's your tongue?'

'Uh uh,' Cully said, and put his arm around her. 'I saw you first.' They giggled.

The girl on the stage was finishing her number and some more people came in and Aaron was shaking his head to himself. He didn't know why his life had to be such a slime. Look at his ignorant-ass brother. If there was any worse scuzzball on the entire Gulf Coast he hadn't met him yet. Standing there hugging and kissing on this common whore who had probably fucked her way across the whole United States to him finally and was way past her best years if she'd ever had any and was still trying to look twenty-one. She probably *needed* a damn drink.

'Can you fix me a Tom Collins?' she said, ignoring Cully, going for her smokes, pulling one out, waiting for Aaron to light it. While Cully fumbled at his pocket he reached out with his lighter and gave her some fire. She looked into his eyes and blew smoke straight out. He stepped back.

'I don't know Tom Collins but I'll fix you a Bob Collins, how bout that?'

'Whatever you say, Aaron. Just long as it *tastes* good.'

Her eyes were trying to play with him. He managed to keep from rolling his and turned to the booze.

He thought he'd just build it as he went along. He poured two shots of some Absolut Citron into a tall glass and then scooped up some ice with his hand and dropped it in there and poured some sour mix into it and added some sugar and some lemon juice and stirred it good. Then he decided he'd shake it so he put it into a shaker and shook it good and then strained it back into the glass and dropped a little more ice in there. He gave it to her and didn't wait to see her taste it because the other thing was coming back in now, the other thing he'd been thinking about. Oh yeah. That thing. Cully started talking to her.

He looked around to see if there was anybody who needed throwing out. He was kind of hoping there was. Kicking somebody's ass right about now might just make him feel a little better because there was no doubt about it, Fay went to see the son of a bitch and there was no need in her trying to lie her way out of it. He knew how they'd lie. Lie in your face and fuck somebody else, *Oh honey no this stuff is all yours*.

Eddie came through the door and Wanda went out it. There was a break in the stage dancing and people started coming over to the bar.

'What's the matter with Wanda?' Cully said. 'Acts like somebody poked a sharp stick up her ass.'

'I guess parting ain't such sweet sorrow,' Aaron said.

Eddie came over and whispered: 'What you want me to do with this stuff?'

He looked across the bar. Customers were lining up.

'Give it here,' he said. He watched Cully watch him take the dope from Eddie and slide it down in his jeans pocket.

'Thanks,' Eddie said, and went to wait on the patrons.

'Anytime,' Aaron said. Lord have mercy he was toting a buzz. He was going to have to get over there in his corner and sit down. He picked up his beer mug and then took a hit of his schnapps. That shit was golden fire.

'I think I'll take up my post,' he said to nobody in particular, and moved over to it. He could feel Cully still watching him, but he didn't really give a shit.

He found a shelf for the glass and held on to the mug. The constant noise was something he rarely paid any attention to anymore, and it was only when the place was empty sometimes in the middle of the day that he remarked on the silence. Now there was a steady chatter of talk and the music kept on playing. He knew they'd all be drunk eventually. Somebody would get rowdy. Somebody would get a hard-on and wouldn't be able to make it with a certain girl or wouldn't have enough money to pay her or couldn't pass a short-arms inspection and would bump into somebody else who was drunk and had one reason or another to shove back and it was the same old shit over and over. He didn't care which one it was. All he was waiting for was the happening of it.

He withdrew into his dark corner and watched how

things would play themselves out. He was toting one motherhumper of a buzz. And Fay was the best of them all.

It was an hour later and he'd been to the bathroom and was coming out when he saw Cully's door open. He heard talking in there and Arthur came out. They spoke and Arthur went on by, out to the front.

He moved back that way. He'd left his whiskey up front. His clean boots moved over the dirty tiles in the floor. Cully was doing something with some papers when he leaned against the doorjamb. Cully didn't raise his head.

'Real cute, passing the shit out front. Why don't you just go up to the police department and walk in the lobby and do it there?'

'Like people don't know what goes on here.'

'Thanks to you sometimes. What about Wanda?'

'I had a little talk with her.'

'She ain't got shit to say now.'

'I don't blame her.'

Cully put down the papers and sipped from a drink that was sitting on his desk. The dripping glass had wetted the papers under it into big damp rings. He leaned back in his chair and studied Aaron.

'When you going to bring sweet thing over here and let her dance?' he said.

Aaron crossed his arms against his chest. 'Try a cold day in hell. She's been in here too much to suit me already.'

'What's the matter? You afraid you'll get her dirty? If she wasn't already she wouldn't be here.'

'You don't know that. I don't want her around you, that's for goddamn sure.'

Cully smiled. 'I bet she's got some good stuff.'

'You bastard. She's gonna have a baby.'

'Make her get rid of it so she can dance.'

'Fuck you. No.'

Cully's eyes weren't believing him now.

485

'Why?'

'Cause,' Aaron said. 'I don't want her around this . . .' He glanced around at the walls. 'This shit.'

He turned sideways. He needed to go back in there and smoke some more. It was starting to ease off some and he didn't want it to until it was time to go home. He wouldn't wake her. He'd let her sleep, let her baby sleep inside her. Get her to the doctor tomorrow. This one could turn out different from all the others. She was young and she was strong and nobody had ruined her yet. He thought there had only been that one guy. Hell, one guy. That was nothing. She was still learning.

'Maybe she'd like to try a little acting job.'

'Aw why don't you shut up about that shit?' Aaron said. 'You scared the hell outta her first time she seen you. She ain't gonna have nothing to do with you. I'll see to that.'

'If I sell it and make some money she might.'

He couldn't believe the stupid son of a bitch was still talking about it. He moved up a little closer.

'Listen. I ought to have my damn head examined for ever listening to you. I done told you all this shit. You ain't got nobody to sell it to. You ain't got no way to edit it or nothing or put a title on it. It ain't no movie. It's just a bunch of people fucking.'

Cully didn't speak for a while. He moved his chair some.

'You're saying you won't get tired of this one. Cause she's different, I suppose.'

'Yeah. She is.'

'I wish you'd tell me how.'

She *was* different. She was better somehow. She had that nice smile and her tits were the most wonderful things he'd seen in his whole life. And he knew already that he'd give plenty to be able to hang on to her. He *had* to hang on to her. That's all there was to it.

'That's all right,' he said. 'She just is.'

Cully lost interest. 'We'll see what kind of tune you

486

sing in a few months,' he said. 'Did Charlie ever come in to get on the door?'

'He's supposed to be here.'

'Will you go see? And come back and tell me if he's not. So I can call Willie or somebody to take up money?'

'Yeah, sure.'

'Close the door, please.'

He did. He walked across the hall and locked that one behind him and smoked some more dope and went back out front to see Charlie coming in. The crowd had grown a lot and he wasn't surprised at all to see Kristy up on the stage dancing and laughing with the cheering customers. The smoke hung above the shoulders of the customers in pooling layers that curled and eddied. A waitress walking through it would send it spinning, and then it would settle again. Kristy winked at him from the stage and he had to admit that she had some style and only needed to be about twenty years younger. She could do that thing with some tassels from the old school his mama had probably learned in, twirl one clockwise and the other one counter. Great shouts and whistles went up as the tassels spun.

Aaron laughed and looked up at her and smiled. He gave her the thumbs-up. Her weatherbeaten haunches gleamed in the stage lights for another night at least. And he guessed he couldn't blame her for trying. He glanced over at Arthur, who nodded and found the whiskey.

A honky-tonk on Grenada Lake and country music blaring. Sam sipped his drink at the end of the bar and watched the couples whirl and move on the dance floor. The lights were low out there and he didn't see anybody in there as old as him except for the bartender.

He didn't know what to do now. He guessed they'd call him again sometime.

She was just gone. *But Lord please.* He said that to himself on a bar stool with a glass of whiskey in his hand. He wasn't anywhere close to crying. People were out there dancing. Some of them, he knew, were in love. Some of them had to be and he could tell it from the way they looked at each other. Maybe she'd even fucked somebody else by now. It was possible. She might have found herself in a place where she might have had to. Or wanted to. She was so young. She wasn't no more than a child, really. He knew he shouldn't have done what he'd started doing with her. He knew he shouldn't have flirted back with Alesandra on that road that day. And he wished that he could bring back the time from before when Karen was still alive so that he could have another chance not to be so hard on her.

He bent his head. *Lord please. If You can. Let her come back. Or let me just see her one more time.*

He guessed a prayer was a prayer, no matter where you said it, even if you said it in a bar. He hoped that was so. He felt like people were looking at his hair. But he could pray in here if he wanted to.

When Cully got on top of Reena she couldn't watch it anymore. It was the way she turned her head and looked at whoever was running the camera. And with it taking place in here she figured she knew who that was. It was just like watching the boys from the camp on top of Barbara Lewis. She got up and turned it off.

She wasn't walking too good by now and her glass was almost empty. And she wasn't looking out the window for him to come home anymore either. If he could let them do that to her, right here in this bed, and putting it on a videotape, then there probably wasn't much else he wouldn't do. She thought back to when his eyes had scared her the first time she'd seen him. And she thought again about the booming of the rifle and how his shoulder had kicked back with each shot.

She weaved her way across to the door and she knew she had to be careful on the steps. They were steep and they were old and she knew she was pretty drunk. But all she had to do was hold on to the rail and take one step at a time and get down to the kitchen and mix another drink and then maybe she could go to sleep. When she got up tomorrow she could decide what she was going to do.

She took careful steps. The stairs were steep. The boards under the carpet, some of them weren't too steady, so she kept a good grip on the rail and went on down and into the kitchen and fixed another drink. She spilled a little. It didn't matter. Sam might be here any day now. He might just drive up in the front yard and park right out there and walk up on the porch and knock on the door. He was a highway patrolman and he could just tell Aaron that he had business with her. And he couldn't say nothing. She'd seen him kill somebody. The police all over Alabama were probably looking for him right now.

She could see it in her head. She'd just get her clothes and go right out the front door. She'd tell Sam everything. She'd tell him what happened with Alesandra. If she had to she'd even tell him that she'd gone to bed with Aaron, but she'd been lonely. And scared. And had needed somebody to hold her. She'd ask him to forgive her.

She sat in the kitchen with her legs spread apart in a chair and drank some more of the whiskey. She'd tell him she was sorry. And that she wouldn't ever do anything like that to him again.

She didn't know what to do. As much as she'd thought and thought she still didn't know what to do.

She finished the drink and then fixed another one. It was helping her think. But her smokes were upstairs.

She went back up slowly, one step at a time, holding on to the rail. She wasn't going to sleep with him tonight. Not after watching all that stuff on the tape. She'd get all her stuff, that's what she'd do. She'd move back into the other room and wait for Sam to come get her. And then they'd go back home. And then almost at the landing she made a misstep, lost her balance, tried to catch herself and couldn't.

It was past dawn when Aaron found her on the floor, sprawled in gray light coming through the tall windows to show her there on the polished pine boards sawn with crosscuts from logs snaked out with mules, dead and lain here all these years deaf and dead to the rhythm of the neighboring sea. It looked like she had rolled almost to the pool table and there was blood streaked on her thighs and a dark smeary puddle of it was what she lay sleeping in.

The lake seemed lonely this early in the morning and Sam stood with his hands in his pockets looking out over it. A thin low cloud hung out there.

He didn't know if he could go down there now. It might make it worse if they called for him and he was gone.

He was afraid now that whatever trouble in the world lay before her was beyond his reach to prevent. He just didn't know how she'd make it by herself. And then realized once more and sadly that wherever she was, she would not be alone for long unless she wanted it that way.

He wasn't going to give up hope. She might get in touch with him. There was always that to hope for. A phone call might come at any time when he least expected it. There was so much luck involved in living, the good along with the bad. So he hoped to have some good luck. It seemed not too much to ask.

She woke in a white room, short white curtains on the window. Her bed was at an angle where she couldn't see out the glass. Voices spoke beyond the walls and she knew something had happened but not what. She remembered knowing that she was ready to leave him. She was drinking in the kitchen. She thought she might have fallen down the stairs. Her legs were sore, her belly, her head. Something was plugged into her arm, a clear tube that led to a bag on a steel pole. It was a hospital, then.

A tray of food sat nearby. Pudding, milk, a banana. She waited for someone to come and tell her something.

She slept again and a nurse woke her, overweight, breathing hard, gray hair and glasses. She was the one who let her understand that the baby was gone now and that the doctor had cleaned out her womb.

Then he himself came in with his wavy hair and steel-rimmed spectacles and told her what he'd done to her. She had trouble looking him in the eye. He said there might be some bleeding for a few days but not to worry about it unless it became severe. He spoke quietly. He looked like he was sorry. And she was free to go.

The door closed behind him and the nurse finished unhooking the IV from her arm and she pulled the needle out and put a small bandage on the puncture. Then she left, too.

Fay's insides hurt but she got off the bed and found her clothes and got dressed slowly. She wondered how much milk she would have had and if it would have been enough and if she would have chosen that way to feed the baby. All those articles in Amy's magazines. Only knowing she had to see Aaron kept her from crying.

And in the hall he had absolutely nothing to say. It was just as well. She didn't want to talk to him anyway. She stood in a corner of the lobby while he paid the charges with one-hundred-dollar bills and got a receipt.

He helped her out to the El Camino after somebody on the staff offered her the use of a wheelchair and she refused it. It wasn't too hot yet in the parking lot and she was grateful for the clouds.

Driving through the streets she saw the copper glint of whiskers that lay along his jaw and she saw his big knuckles riding the steering wheel. She found her cigarettes in her purse and smoked one, the window cracked and her eyes steely and blind to the things that passed outside the glass. He wiped his right hand a few times on his jeans, his hand flat and the fingers spread. He drove with a nervousness she had never seen in him as the traffic picked up.

He stopped without asking at a roadside barbecue joint and went in quickly and got her a cup of coffee and brought it back out to her with a lid on it and extra packs of sugar clamped in his fingers. He didn't speak and neither did she.

It was too hot to drink. She held it and blew on it and blew on it and sipped lightly and still it scalded her tongue. When it got too hot to hold she switched it to her other hand.

And what were people made of and how did they come together to be what they were? What made you be bad or good? Why did good men die and bad men live? She kept seeing Cully on top of Reena. She kept thinking about those kids in that trailer and that dried bologna she'd found in the tiny refrigerator. She knew he had money. She knew he had guns. And probably more than one. Reena and Gigi, probably that Wanda, too. He'd gone through every one of them. And he'd go through her, too, if she let him.

'I can't believe I ever went to bed with you,' she said. 'You're about a sorry son of a bitch.'

And he must have agreed with her because he didn't say anything.

Sam started taking drives in the afternoons. He'd go up to the store and get some gas and maybe a six-pack and a bag of pig skins. A fresh pack of smokes. He'd ride down to Enid and look at the water and then pull around on the south side of the spillway and watch to see if the people were catching anything.

He was careful about drinking on the road. He knew you had to give a police officer a reason to stop you. Or be just in the wrong place at the wrong time and have to drive through a roadblock.

He listened to music on his truck radio without really hearing it, his ears ignoring the songs for the thing that lay like a stone in his mind.

She was so young. She was so much younger than him. People would have mistaken her for his daughter, their child for his grandchild. By the time Fay was thirty he'd be an old man almost.

And so he worked his way around to start thinking that she might be better off without him, maybe, just in case he never did see her again. But then he knew the forgetting her would go on forever and never die. Even when he lay dying he'd think of her and wonder what had ever happened to that family of hers, the ones she'd told him about who had lived in those woods.

And men. Why did they act the way they did? Here you were nice enough to offer them a really good piece of ass and what did they do? Turned it down over some whore who had wound up dead. He was going to get his ass in some bad hot water if he didn't talk to somebody pretty soon. People were already saying they were going to fire him. Joe Price said he believed Sam didn't know anything about it and she was sure that was so. It was just that talk about that girl, whoever she was. They were telling so many things. And Mr Grayton was in such a foul mood all the time now.

The top was down and Loretta's hair was blowing in the wind. Boys in sporty trucks honked at her when they passed and she just smiled. He wouldn't be expecting her back this quick. She shouldn't have drank so much that night and passed out like that. Almost every time she was off she was drinking something now, and there had already been that one scrape with Mister Jimmy Joe when he'd stopped her for weaving but all he'd done was fuss at her like he was her daddy and make her go in front of him all the way home, about fifteen miles, making sure she went in with his headlights shining out there on the road. She felt sorry for his old busted foot that always hurt him so much.

She pulled over when the first beer joint came up outside the city limits. She stopped the car close to the building and got out and went inside. The door closed behind her and the car sat there running. A little black smoke was jetting out of the dripping tailpipe. Traffic passed on the highway behind it.

She came back out a few minutes later with a sack in her hand and got back into the car with it. She backed up and pulled down across the sloped lot and looked back to see what was coming and then spun out, some rocks kicking across the asphalt, the tailpipe spouting some more black smoke.

She thought Sam would be good in bed. He had good hands, a nice mouth and he knew how to kiss. All some of them wanted was to just stick it in and hump a couple of times and then shoot off in you. What the hell good was that? Hell, she wanted to be kissed, she wanted to be touched, if they didn't know what she liked all they had to do was ask her. And it had been going so good with him, he hadn't had to ask her anything, and then, *poof*, he was gone. Not gone but over there making another drink. She should have just stripped naked right in front of him. Got on the couch and spread her legs. He might not have been able to stand it then.

There was a half-pint bottle of peppermint schnapps in an Igloo Playmate on the seat beside her and she pushed the lid back and took it out. Cold drops of water fell on her white pants. She got the top off and held it in the fingers she was holding on the steering wheel. There was nothing in her rearview mirror except for one truck topping a hill way behind her so she took a hit.

So. He wouldn't be looking for her back this soon. She'd just go over after while. Try it again and see how things went this time. He might have thought it over by now and wished he'd done something different.

The truck was closer now. But he was just a trucker. He'd probably look over at her when he passed. He might even blow at a woman in a convertible with the top down and her hair flying all over the place. She took another sip from the bottle and then screwed the cap back on tight. She decided she wouldn't put it back in the cooler just yet. It would stay cold for awhile, long enough to get a few more sips on down the road. She could slip it back into the cooler when it started getting too warm to drink.

The truck started closing the distance on a downhill grade and she saw it creep into the frame of her side mirror and then from the corner of her eye she saw the long red and shiny nose with its chrome bumper start to pull alongside. She picked up the beer from between her legs and took a drink.

She'd just have to try a little harder with Sam. She had to remember that he was a widower and that he'd probably been messing around with that woman before his wife ever got killed. She must have been really drunk to have driven right up under a log truck. And then this girl got killed so he had a lot on his mind. All this trouble he was in with the department. She knew she could get him calmed down if he'd just let her. Then maybe they could talk. He probably needed somebody to talk to. He was probably dying to have somebody to talk to.

The truck came to a rolling pace beside her and she looked up for a glance into the high window. She had on her green halter top and she could see that it was a grinning young man up there behind the wheel. She grinned back but she kept her eyes on the road. He rolled along beside her for a half mile or so, and then he blew the air horn and she waved at him without looking and he came on around her and then crossed over into her lane, and she saw the black smoke from the twin stacks when he shifted up into a higher gear and gained speed and started to pull away from her, the truck growing smaller in the growing distance between them, smaller, smaller, tiny, finally just a moving dot trailing a thin pipe of smoke.

Aaron put her back into the downstairs room she had first stayed in and she took a shower. He brought some of her clothes down and took a mop and bucket to the floor beside the pool table while she stood naked beneath the streaming water and blinked against the spray that was coming down into her face. She felt better after it was over. She kept looking down for what blood was still coming out of her.

She'd have to catch him asleep and get the car keys if it was locked or find the gun if it was not hidden under the seat but somewhere else. There might be all kinds of hiding places in a house this big and old. She might have to look every chance she got.

She dried herself in the bathroom and stood on a rug that somebody had made. There were yarn birds worked into it, colored figures somebody had formed with their hands. She wished she knew how to do stuff like that. She wished she knew more about being a woman.

Even if she knew how to sew birds into a little thing you stood on naked after your shower, would she ever have anybody of her own to show now? Did something like this mess up your insides? For good? The doctor hadn't said.

She cried then, finally, her eyes closed where nobody could see, leaning against the cabinet mirror with her sore belly up against the cool porcelain of the sink, droplets of water lying on her arms and shoulders and legs. She didn't make any noise much.

Pretty soon, when she was putting on some clothes, she heard the El Camino's pipes and they swept a wave of stereophonic rumbling along the side of the house that filled the air and vibrated in it and moved on out to the street and down the road.

Loretta thought it was time to go on over now. She hoped he was home. She was real interested in how things would go once she got over there. It might be totally different this time. You couldn't tell about men sometimes because they'd say one thing and then do another.

She had all her stuff. She had a teddy in a Wal-Mart overnight bag with toothbrush, makeup, extra cotton panties and cigarettes and Trojans. She had some Kama Sutra oil in there and some incense and two tightly rolled joints of sinsemilla she'd bought on Beale Street in Memphis. The lingerie was a black number with skimpy panties trimmed in red and she had a garter belt and stockings that matched. She had a pair of high heels in there too so that she could get dressed up all the way if she needed to.

She turned off onto the lake road and went up the hill with her hair blowing back. She took a glance at that bottle of schnapps riding there with her and picked it up and looked at it. It was over half gone but hell, so what? She got the cap off and turned it up again and then looked into her rearview mirror and saw two guys wearing ball caps trailing close behind her in a pickup with a boat behind it. She sped up. Assholes were watching her drink. Why didn't they find some other place to go riding around?

She put on her blinker and turned off and they whined past. She was looking for that mailbox. She unscrewed the schnapps and took another hit, then put the cap back on it and laid it on the seat. That mailbox was kind of hard to see, right in a curve. She kept driving, looking for it, went into a curve, saw it, hit the brakes too late and overcorrected it skidding with her eyes fixed and wide right into the mailbox and knocked the whole thing down amid some weird noise.

The dust was still settling when she got out and looked. Damn. Knocked it clean off at the ground. That was just fucking great. Now if he was home, she'd get to go down there and tell him she'd knocked his mail-box down. Or . . . tell him that his mailbox was down. She wondered if she had a dent in her car. If he was down there, he wouldn't know who hit it.

She stepped around to the front, holding her beer. Looking around. Right here on the side of the road where just anybody could come by and she *did* work for the highway patrol. She was actually an officer her-self even if she didn't carry a gun.

She turned the beer up and killed it, then tossed the can into the bushes behind his driveway. She looked at the bumper. It didn't have a scratch on it. Both fenders were OK. It was just that his mailbox was bent all to hell and the post was broken.

Weird mailbox too. She bent over and studied it. It looked like somebody had tried to paint something on it one time but most of it had flaked off. She studied some of the patches of paint, trying to figure out what they were. But there was just too much of it gone.

Well. She'd have to drag it out of the driveway if she wanted to get down it. She did that, laid it in the grass beside her car. She got in and shut the door and then wondered if that beer was still cold. And shit, she was still sticking out in the road. She moved it up, held her foot on the brake, reached down on the floorboard on the other side, where nestled against the hump seat sat the sack that held the beer, the top judiciously folded. Oh yeah. It was still cold. She opened it and eased rolling forward, thinking something like *Fuck his damn mailbox*.

It took her a few minutes to get down the drive

because it was so narrow. But she liked the way it twisted through the pines. Little bridge, then the house. Cool.

Well the truck was gone. Truck was gone and the cruiser was still there so no telling where he was. Unless somebody had his pickup and he was sitting in there in the house or something.

She cut her car off and got out with the beer. It was about the middle of the afternoon. It sure didn't look like anybody was around.

He had a nice place. Go skiing every weekend if you wanted to. She'd seen that big boat. Lord that'd be fun, ice down a bunch of beer and get out on the lake and cook hamburgers and get drunk and fuck. Swim if you wanted to, all the time, right here. Private beach down there, wouldn't be anybody coming up in there throwing out beer cans or anything. Run their ass off if they did.

House was new, wouldn't be too hard to keep clean probably. He was a man, he probably wasn't too picky about how clean the place was. It would be real nice to live here.

Maybe the timing was just bad. Maybe later on everything would settle down about this dead woman and he'd talk to them like they were wanting him to and everything would go back to normal for him and she could get to know him. She could take it slow if he needed her to. Not too slow. Slow for the first hour maybe. She could slip her teddy into her purse and have it in the house, be ready to slip into the bathroom and change when he wasn't looking.

She walked out by the edge of the yard, out by the trees, toward the cruiser. Big old trees. Good and shady. No yard much to mow. And he'd sold that beauty parlor of his wife's, and people said they'd heard he'd made out like a bandit, had gotten a whole lot more for it than they'd paid years ago they said, so he had plenty of money even if he did lose his job. Hell, if she could get in with him, she might not even have to work. She could probably just go ahead and retire since he'd probably find something else to do if they fired him anyway.

She stood there looking at his cruiser. It needed a wash job. Looked like a bunch of tree sap had dripped down on it. Every time she'd seen him in it, it had been clean.

Well there was no worry about the mailbox anyway. She could just come back later. Some other time when he was here. She could always call him and leave a message if he had an answering machine and he probably did. She thought they required him to have one. They didn't require her to have one but she had one. She could leave a message or write him a . . .

Sign. There was one on the seat of the cruiser. Looked like a piece of . . . beer carton.

She turned her face to the driveway behind her. It was absolutely quiet. She took a sip of her beer, cocked up the toe of one sandal, wiggled her foot on its heel and stood there reading it through the side glass. She read it twice. She looked up again. If he came in now she was just standing around here waiting for him.

She leaned on the car. It was that girl they'd been talking about. The one Tony told her had stayed with him. The one he'd seen at the funeral. The one Sam wouldn't tell them anything about.

She sipped her beer. She walked over to her car for the schnapps and her cigarettes and walked back up to where she'd been and leaned against the fender. She wondered how long it had been inside the car and why he hadn't found it before now. Maybe he had and had already left to go down there and get her. And maybe he just hadn't looked in the car in a few days. Or a week. She knew somebody from the department had brought it over here. Maybe he hadn't driven it since the fire.

She stood looking into Sam's woods and twisted the top off the bottle again. She turned a drink down her throat, felt the cast threads on the glass neck against her lips. It wasn't as cold now. It was almost gone.

So he'd kept not one woman on the side but two

women on the side. Sure fooled her. He'd never once offered to flirt with her. Well he was quiet. He wasn't like Joe Price, who would almost just come right out and ask for it.

What now? Go home? Sit in front of that TV by herself and drink some more beer? She was sick of that. She was sick of fucking these total strangers she met in all these bars. They didn't have any money and sometimes not even a job and why did she have to be so easy when she was drinking? She was tired of waking up with people she didn't know and seeing their dirty socks on the floor. She was tired of fucking these cowboys with big boots and big hats and little dicks and pleated shirts who sold insurance and drove jacked-up trucks with tires big enough for a tractor and set up so high you had to use a stepladder they carried around in the bed to climb up into the cab. She opened the door of the cruiser and reached in and got the sign and started tearing it into some smaller pieces. She was tired of a lot of things and just one more on the list was somebody she was trying to give her good loving to not wanting it.

When she had it into enough bits she carried it out toward the gravel beyond the car and squatted down and piled it up. It was hard to light at first but she just kept the lighter pushed up against the edge of the pile and soon enough it caught. She stood up and watched it burn. She looked up the hill. Nothing was coming. He wouldn't know anything about this. She'd still have a chance at him.

The little pieces of beer carton flared up for a while and then the flames subsided. She stood there until there was only a pile of thin black crispies. And she scattered them with her foot before she walked back up to the cruiser and closed the door.

Sam was driving, down on 32. He passed in and out of rain and back into it again, had to turn his wipers on and the cars and trucks that came by pulled running beads of water around their spinning wheels and the tires hissed as they passed and faded into the gray blur of rain in front of him.

He couldn't get making love with her out of his mind. That first time and all the times since then and how she had learned from him and had a joyful pride in her naked body and loved so much to show it to him. He drove thinking about all that, and the rain beat down, and the wipers slapped at it, and the red taillights in front of him were bleary and distorted. He thought he'd better go on home. Check to see if she'd called.

She eased herself down on the bed and propped both pillows up against the headboard and stretched out gratefully, raising her legs up slowly. The sun was bright out front but the heavy curtains didn't let too much of it in. She just wanted to stay here and rest. That would be the best thing for her. He was going to be real nice all the time for a while probably. She wondered if Arlene would come back right in the middle of all this.

She was thirsty but she didn't want to go out to the kitchen and get anything right now. Right now she just wanted to rest. She closed her eyes.

Cars were out on the road. She could hear them. She felt so sleepy now.

Why did that doctor have to go up in there? She hadn't understood a thing they'd told her. She'd never heard of such, didn't know all that was up inside her, embryos and stuff. Said they had to get it all cleaned out. She thought it all *had* come out. It looked like it had. She'd looked at it on her knees there by the pool table, before she'd passed out again. It was too small to tell anything about. About like a little tadpole the way it was shaped. It hadn't known nothing yet.

Had it?

It wasn't like it was a real person.

Was it?

It would have been, though. It already was. It was alive and it had been living in her. That was the main thing. It was alive.

Late in the evening Aaron knocked gently on the door to her room. There was no noise inside there. Nothing making even a peep. He put his ear up to the wood and listened. Goddamn rock and roll in Cully's joint had about run him deaf.

He didn't hear anything in there. He hated to knock again and wake her up if she was asleep. He turned quietly and went up the hall and sat down on the couch. He pushed some magazines off onto the floor and looked at them. Gardening stuff. Arlene was crazy about all that stuff. Can your own vegetables. Make pretty shit out of paper. Decorate the whole goddamn house with it. He pulled his pipe back out of his pocket. He had some more of the hash stuck down in his pocket and he stretched one leg out enough to get it out. He unwrapped it, still listening for her, then loaded the pipe and fired it up. He wished Arlene would come on home and maybe she could take care of her. He didn't know what to do with her. Leave her alone he guessed. Let her get well.

He sucked the smoke down and looked at the door. She was probably asleep. But how did he know she wasn't just lying in there with her eyes open, wide awake, listening to him out here, just didn't want him to know she was awake because she didn't want to talk to him? That was probably it.

She'd feel bad for a while over losing the baby probably. But it might be just as well. What kind of a chance would it have had and whose was it anyway? It wasn't his. Just like Reena's probably weren't his. It didn't matter that they had light-colored hair. Lots of little bastards running around had light-colored hair. Just because you fucked some woman for a while didn't mean you had to spend the rest of your life taking care of her rugrats.

She went to see him. Oh that burned his ass. That odometer had read 89106 that night when he'd parked it at the Holiday Inn and he knew because he'd looked and the next morning before he got in the pool it read 89145. Didn't nobody put no forty miles on a car driving it around Oxford looking for a hamburger. Well. He'd wanted to see what she'd do if she got close to him, and she'd done it. Went straight out there wherever it was and scoped out the hamburger joints on the way out or even picked it up then and took it with her. Had she seen him? Had she *fucked* him? Probably so. That was why he'd done it to her so hard. To make her be sorry for what she'd done to him behind his back. But if he could just keep his eye on her down here, everything would probably be all right. She could go back to helping Arlene sometime, whenever she came back. He didn't know how long it took a woman to get over something like this but he could find out.

He looked at the door again. Was she a good actor like Wanda? Was her whole story a lie? He didn't think it was. He thought she was just a country girl who didn't know anything about the world. He hoped she wasn't feeling too bad. He'd told himself all along he'd never get this close to one. And goddamn, now here he was. He guessed he was in fucking love with her. And the dope was kicking in. It was kicking in right nice right now. Oh yeah. She'd be all right. She'd get healed up. She'd be ready to do it again then. Shit. Hang on to her. Do it with her forever. Every night. Keep her away from that shithole where he worked. Keep her away from his stupid-ass brother.

He thought a drink would be pretty good now, so he

got up and went back to the kitchen and took down a glass and put some ice in it. The Maker's Mark was sitting out and he saw that a good bit was gone from it. He looked up at the stairs. Wonder it hadn't broke her fucking neck. Then where would he be?

And now on top of everything else it looked like you couldn't even go off and drive around for a while without some drunk son of a bitch running over your mailbox. He wished he'd been home. He wished he'd been in his uniform and had been around when this happened.

He got out and left the door open and walked around there. Somebody had moved it. Shit. He stood there looking around. There was one skid mark on the road, curving into here. Somebody coming from that way didn't knock the mailbox over here. So why'd they move it? Unless they wanted down his driveway. And there shouldn't have been anybody here. Unless Tony McCollum or somebody had come over.

It was misting rain on him. What if Loretta had come back over? God he hoped she wasn't down there waiting for him right now. If she was, she was probably the one who'd knocked his mailbox down. But he hoped she wasn't down there.

He stepped over in the wet grass and kind of leaned over looking at it. He straightened up and put his hands on his hips. The mailbox itself had a big dent in it. Hell. There on the gravel in the driveway were some chips of paint that had been knocked loose. He went over and tried to pick some of them up, but they flaked away in his hand. What did he want them for anyway? Keep them? Naw. He had enough bad memories already. He didn't need anything to remind him of them. And most of the time he tried to focus on the good ones anyway.

But he'd get the mailbox. He'd come back up here

before dark with the hammer and get those nails out of the board it was fastened to and take the box down to the house like he already should have done. The damn road was full of mailboxes, he didn't know why some asshole had to hit his.

He got back into his truck and put it into gear. She'd better not be down here waiting on him. She could go right back out a lot quicker than she'd come in. All he wanted was to get out of his truck and take off his boots and fix a drink and then start thinking about what to fix for supper. If he even had anything. The eating had gone to hell around here. He'd even kept that last piece of fried chicken Fay had cooked until it was just a withered brown nub and then he'd thrown it in the trash.

There was nothing but his cruiser sitting at his house. That was real good. He wheeled in and parked and got out. He'd have to get some music going as soon as he got back in or the television. When something was making some noise or you could hear people talking, it wasn't like company exactly but it was something to listen to while you were going over all the other stuff in your head. He had to keep remembering that she could always call. And he'd been leaving the answering machine on but there hadn't been any messages.

When he walked by the cruiser he just happened to look down and see an ink pen lying there beside the door. Hmmm. He stopped and picked it up. It was white with green letters and a green cap. He brought it up close to his face. Holiday Inn. Oxford, Miss. Right there on North Lamar. Bartender's name was Clyde. He'd been in the lounge and had a beer before. Folks came in there all the time and watched the ball games. And there was nothing strange about the pen except that he didn't remember ever having it. He looked through the window. His clipboard was in there and it always had a bunch of pens stuck on it, still did. But he didn't know where this one had come from.

And then he did. Somebody had probably dropped it

when they'd dropped off his car. He thought he'd see if it was any good because he could always use another pen. People borrowed them all the time and never gave them back.

He opened the door and reached in for the clipboard. There were some forms clipped to it and he took the pen and tried to draw some circles with it. Cheap son of a bitch wouldn't write. He tossed the clipboard back on the seat and shut the door and gave the pen a pitch toward the woods. But it was very light and it didn't travel very far. And he had more shit on his mind to worry about than damn ink pens.

And there was still Reena, oh yeah. Aaron had almost forgotten about her with all the stuff that was going on. She came up to him as he was locking his car in the parking lot and he stopped with his key in the door and looked down at her. She didn't say anything at first but he could see the wet tracks down her cheeks.

'Don't waste your breath,' he said, and turned the key and pulled it out.

'Baby,' she said. 'Please. Just listen to me for a minute. You'll do that, won't you?'

He didn't want to stop. Fay was asleep again now after he'd finally gone in and tried to talk to her and taken her in some food. But he wanted to get on in.

'Make it fast,' he said.

'I ain't been able to see you,' she said.

He didn't even want to look at her. He knew her so well.

'Sugar pie, there ain't nothing for you to see me about. I tried to get you the hell away from here a long time ago.'

'You mean when you were still taking care of me, Aaron? Is that what you mean?'

He faced her and backed up a step while traffic passed on the road. She didn't need to push him any now. He didn't want to hear anything about those kids now. And as bad as he'd seen her already, she looked like hell now. Hair hadn't even been combed and her tennis shoes were untied and the dirty dress looked like it had been pulled out of a pile. She rubbed her forearm with her hand, taking short steps closer. He looked around. Lots of cars were already in the parking lot. He needed to get on inside.

515

'Let me go in with you, Aaron. Maybe just get a beer or something? I need something bad, baby. Shot of whiskey. Couple of beers. Please. Just anything.'

He studied her not without sorrow for what she was now. Even fondness for what she had been. The last traces of it were almost gone, but there might still be time for somebody to see some of it if she stopped now, if she got it together by some miracle and hauled ass out of here and took the kids someplace else and got away from these fish bums she kept bringing home.

Then there was that thing about something being for old times' sake. He guessed this could be one of those times. But it needed to be the last one. She'd want money again. This little tramp would always want money again.

'Look what a favor I did you, Aaron. I got her for you, didn't I? And it only cost you five hundred bucks. I bet she's settled in out at Arlene's, ain't she? I bet it's still nice like it was.'

She was crying again, a weepy mess with strange hair.

'All right, damn it,' he said. 'Come around back.'

He didn't wait for her but went right in and among the people with the door letting a diminishing wedge of light come across the stage where the lights were dim and a girl was hard to see dancing and looking like she didn't know what was going on either. People were yelling about the lights, yelling for them to turn the lights up. Eddie was busy at the bar. Aaron waved at him even when he heard Eddie calling to him and went right on through the door behind the bar and down the hall, the door banging back behind him, its ratchet-down swivel of noise dying in a last rusty croak for a sup of oil.

He tried Cully's door and it was locked. He twisted the knob. Locked. His piece was behind his back, a fluffy sweatshirt with the sleeves gone over it. She was just getting to be too big a pain in the ass. He wished he knew some way he could just get rid of her. But messing with her was going to have to wait for him to get to his stash over here and he didn't even want to think about what might be going on out front with the lights.

He stepped to the back door and opened it. She was waiting in the sand, small waif now, luster gone from her eyes. She reminded him of a sparrow hanging around a doorstep in winter, hoping for crumbs.

'Get in,' he said, and she slipped past his wrist and outstretched arm, scooted in. He pulled the door shut, got her by the arm, and took her into the dressing room.

He locked that door behind them. There was an open bottle of whiskey on a table and she went straight for it. It was plain that she'd already gone through all the money he'd given her on that first night, when Fay was waiting for her to come out of the supermarket. And she evidently didn't even care about how she looked anymore. He remembered the good clothes she used to have and how she looked in them, how men turned their heads and watched her. Nobody would give her a second glance now. It wasn't all his fault.

Reena had the whiskey bottle turned up. And Fay wouldn't even talk to him. He'd opened the soup himself and put it in the pan and got it good and hot and took it in to her in a nice bowl on a plate with crackers and had propped up her pillows and offered to help her eat but she'd just shaken her head for him to leave her alone. So he'd left the soup. He'd tried to touch her, but she'd just drawn back and looked away. He hoped she'd eaten some of it.

He moved past Reena to the cabinet in the bathroom and got the stash out and pulled his pipe from his pocket. People were still yelling out front and they'd raised the volume on the music probably to drown out some of the yelling but that just made them yell louder. Fucking place.

He sat down on the edge of the bed. It hadn't been made up in who knew how long. He loaded the pipe and saw her watching him. She never had gotten too heavy into the dope. It had mostly been just the booze. He saw her slipping toward him and then she got down on her knees awkwardly and crawled over to him. He felt her touch at his ankle. She turned up the whiskey and took another drink from it.

The yelling out front stopped, chopped off short by something. The stage lights must have come back on. Good. Maybe they wouldn't knock on the door now.

Her hand went up into his shirt pocket from the floor, pulled out his cigarettes and lighter. He never had liked her doing that. A son of a bitch had done that to him on a boat dock one day when he was nineteen and he'd broken his fucking arm for him and told him to ask next time. He waited for her to light it and then got the lighter back and struck it over the bowl and pulled hard on it and the little nest of brown stickiness glowed and smoldered and he drew on it and pulled it deep into his lungs. There was just too much shit to deal with. She was mad at him because of the damn videotape. It had still been in the VCR and he'd backed it up far enough to make sure of what she'd seen. Had watched those images of this one or that one again for only a few seconds, because it seemed now to be the kind of thing you couldn't take back and once it was done it was. It was taking a picture of it. And it might be possible for almost anybody to see that picture. It might even go to other places in the world, maybe to be watched by foreign eyes, spoken over by foreign tongues.

He held his hand out for the bottle and she passed it reluctantly and watched him drink from it. He welcomed its fire. She had her hand out for it back and when he passed it over she turned it up, leaned toward him on the floor, the other arm holding her up, her thinner thighs showing in glimpses and even the dark thatch, the still perfectly usable mystery monkey.

She lowered the bottle and picked her other hand up and put the cigarette between her lips to draw on it. He could remember her feeding the first baby with one hanging from her lips. He hadn't even gone to the hospital with the second one because by then there had been others. There had always been others. A place like this stayed full of them because girls like this always moved on. All except this one.

Fay might not want to be around any of the women he'd been with. But Gigi was gone and Wanda might leave now, too. But this one. What would it take for her to leave? Not bad treatment, he knew that. He'd wiped his feet on her for so long she didn't even feel it anymore.

'You smoke that shit,' Reena said. 'You talk crazy. But you love that shit.'

He looked down on her.

'Fay saw your movie. Ain't that just great?'

'I'd like to see the part with me and you again,' she said.

'I don't think she got to that part.'

'You know I still got some good lovin for you, baby.'

He turned his head away from her.

'I don't need it.'

'You don't need it cause you got Fay now.' She nodded her head to agree with herself and her head started to sway, she already humming the words to a song the whiskey was writing in her brain. 'She's still pretty and young. She's still got her body. She ain't had any babies yet. Not yet. Aaron, can I have some money to buy me something to drink?'

And he looked down at her as if seeing her for the first time. He leaned toward her. Great howls rose beyond the satin teddies hanging by sixteen-penny nails driven into the wall, and the music was beating welcome on the air like a great velvet drum.

Fay slept and dreamed love near a field that bordered a creek where the water ran clear and moving schools of fish darted under the trees, a boy tall and lanky with black hair who drank their water with them from a tin dipper hung in a barrel, a rounded iceberg floating and bobbing in it, knocking deadly against the wet wood of the sides. He took her away at noon and she walked barefooted in a skirt and blouse into the cool shade with him and on a bed of soft grass he slid one leg at a time out of her panties and lay kissing her to make even nicer the opening of her blouse. And her legs were around him and she was filled up with him and the birds were fluttering up in the trees and bushes around them and the creek bubbled and made a kind of music with the wind that came through the limbs. They married and lived in a little brick house near a branch and the first baby wandered off into it and drowned because it didn't know how to swim. And she remembered her daddy telling her everybody needed to know how to swim and then Sam came out from behind him on a horse and she swung up with him and left her husband. The next time she looked over her shoulder they were riding through a high meadow where all manner of flowers reared their pretty faces to the sun and sometimes one brushed against her shoulder as if asking her to take it and she did and wove each into her hair. There was a cabin on a mountain where supper was ready. He had a red-and-white checked tablecloth and they ate with candles and wine and laughed in the candlelight, sat on the porch where the horses waited at the hitching rail and on the porch a bed with good quilts and clean sheets like those you get in a hotel and he loved her through the night because they were making another baby. She pulled him as far up inside herself as she could get him, leaned up and grabbed a handful of him on each side and pulled him in as deep as she could. And panted, twisting in her bed, small moans escaping her lips as they finished and more children appeared until sometime soon there was a whole snowy-headed flock of them, boys and girls with Zebcos and dolls. Or she'd have them all in the pool, a bobbing gang of them around like puddle ducks. They all seemed to be about the same size and their names are Frank, Freddy, Francisco, Florentine, Fonda, Felicia, Francis, Floyd, Faison, Ferlin.

In a few days she was stronger and could hobble around. She tried to fix her meals and eat when she knew he wasn't there. But it didn't always work.

Once he surprised her coming out of the upstairs bedroom where she had gone to look for the gun and he put his arm out and against the wall. But she only stared into his eyes for a few hard seconds and ducked under his arm and went past him, down the stairs, no wonder she'd fallen, the steps were loose and they creaked, and paint was falling from the ceiling in the hall, and sometimes she swept flakes of it up. He came down and she saw him going out the back door. She stood watching and listening and went back to looking for it. She looked in every cabinet and pulled the contents of them out and remembered how they'd been and put them exactly back in their order. She'd find money he'd left her in the kitchen under a plate and walk down the road to the gas station as the soreness slowly left her and she'd buy cigarettes or a cold can of lemonade and lean against a post with her sunglasses on watching the boats and the gulls.

Back at the house, she searched closets and ran her hand along the shelves in them and dislodged blankets and pillowcases but it was never there. Each drawer in the house was opened, looked through, the stuff taken out, put back in. It probably wasn't safe to go back to Sam and she wasn't going to prison over Alesandra.

He kept odd hours and she heard the slamming of doors in the middle of the night those last days.

She knew the gun was there. It was there somewhere.

She knew because when he was sober he was a very careful man, and in sober times he would have put it somewhere he could find it again if he needed it. But she could not find it.

She kept her own odd hours and crawled under the beds and pulled out the couches looking for secret spots or hidden doors. She thought there might be more than one gun. She found pens, coins, paper clips, phone numbers scratched on scraps of paper. She found petrified french fries and loose buttons.

She'd stop what she was doing suddenly and listen for him, and then she would go back to peeking behind dressers, pulling rugs back and looking under them, replacing the beds over them as they had been. It was simple. All she had to do was look in every possible place in the house until she ran into a lock. There was a crowbar in the utility room.

She found the money in an ordinary pasteboard box sitting under an old leather suitcase in a tall wardrobe in the upstairs room. There were dresses long musty and hanging in plastic bags with bodices of fake pearls and dipping necklines, the material thick and soft in her fingers. It was inside a couple of manila envelopes and when she looked in and saw it she knew that the gun had to be close by. If she'd learned one thing about him it was that these two things went together.

Dumped on the bed and even spread out there was a lot of it. She counted it, a little over eleven thousand. Then she put it back into the envelopes. She closed the wardrobe door. Then opened it again to look at something she'd glimpsed. A glossy poster stood hidden behind the dresses and she parted them with her hands and looked at it. A beautiful girl with dark shining hair and bright white teeth smiling out at the camera, one eye closed in a wink, all curves and skimpily clad in a torn T-shirt and her nipples pressed hard against the thin cloth, her hands tugging the hem of the shirt down to barely cover her, a Reena

523

from years past, a Reena that Aaron had known when she looked like this.

In the center of the room with the sound of the cars on the highway coming through the second-story windows she looked at the bed and imagined the two of them lying on it. She backed to the bed and sat down on it. He was on this side. She propped his pillow up and lay back against it. She could see what he saw from there. And where would he put it so that he could grab it quickly if he needed to?

So many times she had held on to the short posts in the headboard but not on his side. She put her hands back as she had done in the throes of their lovemaking and her fingers touched the smoothness of the leather holster that had been nailed back there and then the cool curves of a frame and a wooden grip and a deeply crosschecked spur for the hammer.

She made good time hitchhiking back to Biloxi. An older man with a smelly cigar and a rusty Jeep took her seven miles before he had to turn off, but she only had to walk about a hundred yards before a divorced lady in a fairly new Ford pickup stopped and gave her another ride. The woman started talking and kept on talking about an operation she was going to have done on her face to make her look younger. She seemed excited and scared. She told Fay that she could ride all the way to Jackson with her but she asked to be let out just this side of a red light in Biloxi and with the truck sitting in the midst of halted traffic she got out and thanked the lady and stepped away from the truck. She crossed the road before the light changed and when the truck moved away the woman lifted one hand and waved. Fay waved back, but she didn't think there was anything wrong with the face the lady already had.

The toys that belonged to Aaron's children still sat out front, but now they were broken, looked like some of them had been run over. They'd even left the steps. Fay wondered if that Chuck had gone with her. She hoped not.

'Hellfire,' she said, out loud and softly to herself, blinking the tears back. Traffic flowed on the road below.

She looked down the hill. There was a pay phone down there. She'd walked by it on the way up here. She'd seen people use them. You stuck a quarter in them.

What the hell. What the hell else was there to do now?

In that drowsy dreamy state that comes between dreams or in your afternoon nap Sam heard her talking to him and he stirred and moved his socked feet on the bed. He wasn't under the covers but he had Fay's pillow tucked close to his face because her scent had lingered on it, even through one night with Loretta's head on it. She talked to him in short sentences, and he could see her pointing and moving her fingers the way she did when she was telling something she was excited about, a movie she'd seen while he was away, a piece she'd read in a magazine, a show about a lone tigress in a deep green forest in India. She talked on and on and she had her swimming suit on and her belly was showing a little but she was still looking great. He had to get some baby food. Needed to stock up. The baby would need one of those baby life jackets. Here was a baby in the dream in a diaper and a sailor hat holding up a sign: GIRLS CAN FISH TOO. She kept talking and he kept lying there listening to her and her voice soothed him with the round vent in the white ceiling blowing cool air down on his splayed fingers, his lips open slightly, his chest falling and rising ever so slightly and then the message machine chirped a bright beep and he woke up. Then he sat up. Then he got up and ran up the hall to look. The little green light was winking at him, on and off.

She figured maybe a six or seven hour drive depending on if he was home and when he got the message. She tried not to let herself think beyond that.

Walking back by the beach she thought she would just sit on the porch. If Aaron came in she didn't have to tell him nothing. Tell him she was just sitting there. She sat out there all the time anyway. Or she had.

Trucks and cars passed her and she didn't put her thumb out, but it was going to be a long walk back if she didn't get a ride. She thought it was about twenty-something miles. Wasn't any way she could walk that far today. She didn't want to overdo it and start herself to bleeding again. But she couldn't stay with him anymore. She could get back some way and wait all night if she had to and see if Sam showed up. If he didn't, she could call him again from Arlene's.

It might take time. She had to remember that. He might be on duty and not be in until midnight or sometime. Or if they'd found Alesandra and found out he'd been messing around with her he might be in some trouble. If he didn't come tonight she'd just call back tomorrow. Maybe get him instead of the machine.

She kept walking and she didn't like being so close to the traffic, but sometimes there wasn't much room to get over.

Once a man in a car pulled over onto the shoulder a ways up and almost caused a wreck, vehicles swerving around him and horns blowing. He looked back and waved for her to come on up and get in with him, but she just stopped where she was and waited for him to go on. He didn't for a long time, just kept sitting there and waving, like he was hoping she'd change her mind and come on and get in with him, but she shook her head, looking at his face, dark, a curly head of black hair. Hair like Chris Dodd's. Finally he went on.

The beach was covered with people and it was getting on toward evening. The gun made her purse so much heavier and she was tired of carrying it. She had to have it. He wouldn't understand anything but the gun.

The breeze was blowing as always and it lifted her hair from the side of her face as she walked. Some boy waved out the window of a car to her, but she only looked at him for a moment and saw him waving, and then stopped looking at him. The horn blared on the car, the sound of it dimming as it went on down the highway. She kept walking. Same old shit.

The road went by under him like it was greased. He had his gun because she'd said there might be trouble. That she was sorry for the things she'd done. He didn't know what she'd done and he didn't care because getting down there as fast as he could in one piece was the only thing.

He was stopped twice in north Mississippi. One trooper pulled him over just past the Grenada exit on I-55 South but it was only Dago Petersen, wanting to know how everything was going for him. He'd followed him long enough to get his tag and since he knew he'd probably clocked him at something like ninety, he didn't mind sitting there and talking to Dago for a few minutes. After he told him he was going down to the coast for a few days to try and relax and forget about everything for a while, Dago told him he was sure sorry about what had happened to him, his wife, that gas truck crash. All that trouble. They'd all heard.

'They tellin all kind of shit on you, man,' he said, his arm up above him leaning on the cab, the wide brim of his hat shading his face. 'But I'm hopin everything'll turn out OK for you.' And he told him he'd see him later and walked back to his cruiser.

The deputy sheriff who'd hidden himself in the bushes south of Duck Hill only kept him for a second after he showed his badge, didn't even need all the explanation about how he was late for a meeting in Jackson and his cruiser was down, was already shaking his head that it was OK and for him to have a nice day, that he wouldn't have even stopped him if he'd known who he was, and he went on back to his cruiser, too.

Then he shot through Montgomery County and left it behind.

Aaron thought just take her somewhere now, maybe call an airline in Jackson and get two tickets somewhere, maybe down to Key West. Or he could take her to San Francisco and they could walk up and down the hilly streets with the little stores that had almost anything a person could want to buy, walk in the crowds of people with their different clothes and faces and their handbags and shoes. They could grab a cab out to the stadium and catch a ball game one afternoon, have hot dogs in the stands with tall waxed cups of beer, and she could get to see some of the country. There was plenty of money. He could spend some of it on her.

The crowd was low. The crowd was quiet. He sold two half-ounces of the grass and he kind of wanted to go back and check on her, see how she was doing. But he hated to leave. Cully was off somewhere and Arthur had called in that he wouldn't be able to come in until later on, so he'd had to call Eddie in to cover for him, and Eddie was pissed at having to work again tonight.

One good thing was No Wanda. No phone call, no nothing. So maybe her ass was gone too. Now. Maybe they were all gone now and he could tell her that, too, that he'd gotten rid of all of them if that's what was bothering her. Maybe she was having some weird time with it being in his room. But he didn't see why. He didn't know what difference it made where you did something like that. It was losing the baby. That's all it was. She'd get over it. She was stronger already. He'd seen her come in from her walking. Everything would be all right in a few more weeks. Once she got healed up.

He turned around to tell Eddie to fix him a drink and the front door opened and Cully walked in with Kristy. She had some classy new clothes on now, a short dress, her legs not too bad in the pantyhose.

They started to head toward the back and then Cully said something to her and then came on over to the bar. He stopped next to Aaron.

'Where the hell's everybody at?' he said.

Aaron looked out over the few tables that people were sitting around. There wasn't anybody on the stage now but Bobbi was supposed to be back there getting ready. He guessed they were going to have to kick her out before long. Her ass was just too fat. A few people had jeered at her and made her cry one time. It looked like the quality of the talent was going downhill fast.

'I don't know. They damn sure ain't here. I wish to hell I wasn't either.'

Eddie moved over in front of them and put his wet hands up on the bar.

'Y'all want something?'

'Give me two draft beers,' Cully said, and Eddie turned to get them. 'Well shit. Why don't you go home, then? Go fuck your pretty girlfriend?'

'Fix me a Turkey and Coke when you get a chance, Eddie,' Aaron said to him. 'When you get a chance. Please.'

Eddie nodded and watched the flow from the keg tap into one of the glasses. Aaron turned to face his half brother and scratched at the underside of his jaw with his finger. He didn't think his pretty girlfriend was ready for that. 'Aw hell,' he said. 'Ain't nobody to bounce but Eddie if I take off. Arthur ain't never come in yet.'

'Arthur'll be here in ten minutes,' Cully said, and he reached out for the two beers the bartender was setting down. 'Thanks, Eddie.'

'How you know?' Aaron said. He watched Eddie start mixing his drink back there.

Cully picked up one of the beers and sipped at it. Kristy had crossed her arms, a peevish look already on her face. Aaron glanced at her. Either hot to fuck or already had her meat hooks in him. Already had him whipped. They did it to him every time. And the nastiest one that walked through the front door next, that was the one he would want.

'He called me at the house a while ago. Said he'd be in at eight. Go on if you want to. We can handle it on a Tuesday night surely to God. But suit yourself.'

Aaron watched him. He picked up the other beer and walked away as Eddie slid the Turkey to his elbow. He watched Cully go over to her and motion with his head for her to go on ahead of him, and they walked behind the bar and she pushed against the swinging door and they went through it.

'Slow night, boss,' Eddie said. The music had been off for a few minutes and Aaron didn't mind it. Listening to the same ones over and over again every night, it burned you out. And they played it so loud. Cully claimed it made people drink more. And Aaron had said Yeah, but they can't hardly have a goddamn conversation.

'Yep.' He leaned on the bar and took a sip from the drink. 'You still want a little dab of that hash?'

Eddie looked anxious. 'I don't know,' he said. 'How much is it?'

What he ought to do was just go on home, then. She was probably watching television or something. He knew she still went up there and watched it because whenever he came in, whatever time it was, he felt it to see if it was still warm, and it almost always was.

'I can let you have a nice piece for eighty,' he said. 'Same stuff you smoked the other night. It got you high, didn't it?'

'Hell yeah,' Eddie was quick to say. 'I don't know if I can afford that much.'

Aaron took another drink.

'Well shit or get off the pot. That's a pun,' he said. 'A play on words.'

'You got it on you?'

'Hell yeah I got it on me. I can get it on me.'

The music cranked up again and the stage lights dimmed. But maybe it was still too soon to try talking to her. Maybe she just wanted to be left alone a while longer. He didn't know how long it took a woman to get over something like this. Not on the inside where the baby had been. On the inside where she felt things. There had been some women he'd liked a lot. But there had never been anything like this. No other woman had ever made him feel this way. He didn't want to be away from her any longer than he had to. Maybe he should just get her clean out of town. They didn't have to stay here. The world was full of places to go.

He thought he'd stick around a little longer. He thought he'd see what went down with Eddie here, and he took him to the back room and pulled an old olive U.S. Army footlocker from under the bed and got him out the hash and they smoked some of it quickly so that Eddie could get back to the bar, and Eddie did, and then he just sat back there by himself with the music climbing through the wall, and something thumping the wall in Cully's office, something thumping, and thumping, and thumping.

Man, he thought. *She's wearing his ass out.*

There was a mall along the beach and she'd seen it before. It had a movie theater and there was a marquee out front and they had three different ones showing. She stopped in the road and looked at it. There was a place to cross right down there.

She'd never really been to the movies. Sam had kept telling her he was going to take her to the show sometime. He talked about the popcorn, and about how good a movie was on a big screen like that. He said watching one on a videotape was nothing compared to seeing the same one in a theater. And even if he'd gotten the message right after she'd left it, it was still going to take him six or seven hours to get down here. She had to get back to Pass Christian. It would be dark by then. But she looked at a cab stopped at a stop sign down the street for just a moment.

She had money in her purse. She could find a movie down there that looked like a good one, go in and get her some popcorn. Even if he was driving right now he still wouldn't be here for a long time. And there wasn't any need in going all the way back over to Pass Christian this early and sitting over there on the front porch all by herself.

There was a pizza sign down there in the mall. They probably had a place where you could sit down and eat it, too. Kill some time. Watch a movie. Have some popcorn. See if it really looked that good up on the big screen. She bet it would.

He went through Carroll County and Holmes and Yazoo, past the towns like Vaiden and West and Durant, and Goodman and Pickens and Vaughan, always passing whatever it was, just having a sixth sense sometimes and knowing where to slow down because he was one of them and knew their times and a lot of their hiding places. He gassed up at a Texaco station in Canton and he didn't get any beer, just two chicken legs and a pack of cigarettes and a tall fountain Pepsi that he sipped from a straw. The traffic was light in Jackson and he hit 49 at Pearl and split off to the east to angle toward the middle of the coast where Gulfport sat almost dead center. Her voice was still alive. There was still breath in her and now somehow he'd get her to someplace where she'd be safe until whatever was going to happen happened, didn't matter if it was a Holiday Inn every night, by God he had enough money to pay for it. He might find somebody she could stay with until it was time for her to have the baby. He'd work it out, whatever it took. He could make up a name for her and tell it to David Hall, just a few short lies and nothing else. Keep her hid. Then what he didn't know. Worry about all that shit later. Just get his hands on her.

He went past Piney Woods, past D'lo and Mendenhall and Weathersby and Magee. He'd gone fishing one time in Magee with Earl Boatright, in a pond for crappie Earl had caught in Ross Barnett Reservoir and put in there. Three or four years ago and he hadn't seen Earl since. He might have retired by now.

It started getting dark and he had to pull his

headlights on. Already the gas gauge was starting its slow ride back to E. And he might not make it in on this tank. At this speed probably not. He wouldn't be able to see the troopers as easily now. But that didn't make him let off the gas any.

The first movie she went into was a bunch of fake Hollywood bullshit where tires squealed on a gravel road or somebody could shoot a car and it would blow up and it looked like any dumbass would know better than that. She didn't know how much it cost to make a movie but she figured it probably cost a good bit and it looked like if they were going to spend all that then they ought to try and make it not look and sound so fake. There was one place where some guy had a revolver and shot it about eleven times, she counted. Bunch of sirens, bunch of cars running up and down the road.

She got up twenty minutes into it and pushed open the padded door in the darkened back of the theater and went back up a dim hall and finally back into the bright lobby where somebody was vacuuming the carpeted floor and the kids who worked at the snack stand were talking to one another. One of them was sneaking a cigarette. The pizza had been pretty good but now she was kind of hungry again, so she wandered back out into the mall. Just killing time.

There were all kinds of shops. Shoe shops and clothing shops and toy stores. People in booths had all kinds of leather belts and they could put your name on one if you wanted one. She stopped and told the guy to put *Sam* on one and stood there and watched him make it. It took him about ten minutes and it cost her fifteen dollars but Aaron was still leaving money for her every day and she'd only been keeping it because she thought she might need it sometime. She had about three hundred dollars.

The man coiled the belt and put it in a bag for her and thanked her and then bent back to his bench.

She walked along, looking in the windows. People were sitting on benches here and there, and there were large plants in boxes or big vases. Somebody was sweeping the floor. Some old ladies in tennis shoes came by her walking fast and talking fast, flopping their hands back and forth to keep time with their strides and she wondered where they were going in such a hurry. She stopped to look at some jewelry and then she stopped to look at some stereos and they came by her again.

She sat on a bench and smoked a cigarette.

She bought a cone of strawberry ice cream and a cookie.

She talked to a little boy with white hair like in her dream.

Then she went back to the theater and paid again and started watching another movie, thinking, when that was done, when a few more hours had passed, she could get back over to Pass Christian and pack and wait for him to show up. She hoped he wouldn't show up while Aaron was there. But that was why she'd told him there might be trouble. She didn't figure Aaron was going to let her leave, not if he could help it. She thought he was probably in love with her.

He didn't stop in Hattiesburg except for the lights that caught him and he went on, through Perry County and down into Stone. Beyond that lay Harrison County, Gulfport, Biloxi, the ocean and the boats that drifted on it. Every mile that went by was one closer. Every house he passed was one more house behind him.

She asked the cabdriver to let her out on the side of the road so that she could walk up to the house. It looked dark up there. He pulled over into a driveway at an angle and turned on an overhead light. He was a black guy with an accent, long braided locks that hung down over his shoulders. And he was smoking something that smelled funny.

'Twenty dollas, please miss. All dark, you gettin out here?'

'I live here,' she said, and got the money out for him. Then remembered what Reena had said that time about tips and pulled out a five and gave it to him. His bright teeth gleamed when he smiled.

'Thank you ma'am, you a very kind lady. And a most scrumptious one if I may say so. You take good care of yourself now, you hear?'

'Yes. I will. Thank you,' she said, and she opened the door and got out. He sat there until she'd walked out of the path of his beams, going up the little drive, and then he pulled away.

The house looked spooky now, so dark upstairs. She watched the cab go down the road and turn around, the lights sweeping a circle in the road, then he pulled out fast and gunned it back toward Biloxi. The traffic was sparse.

Out there in the harbor the masts jutted, and the wind was still chiming in the nets. She hated to leave that. This would be a nice place if it wasn't for him.

She had to get her suitcase packed and she went into

the yard and down along the side of the house. The yard light wasn't on.

The house wasn't locked. The small light was on over the stove and it cast a dim glow over the stuff in the kitchen. She flipped some lights on and went up the hall and turned some on. The door to her room was open and somebody could have just walked in and taken whatever they wanted, and she was glad now that Arlene wasn't back yet. She turned on the lamp and put her purse on the bed, then locked herself in the bathroom and used it. When she got through she went back up the hall and up the stairs. She flipped the light on for the bedroom and stood on the landing looking down at the floor. There was still a sore place on her head, and one on her arm.

She made a few trips up and down, getting the rest of her things. In fifteen minutes she had everything she owned packed back into the suitcase. She zipped it shut and put it on the floor.

At the door she stopped and looked around. There was nothing else she needed.

She checked in the bathroom. An almost empty shampoo bottle sat on the sink. A comb that wasn't hers. Hairclips she'd found in the medicine cabinet. She told that room good-bye too.

She stopped in the hall and looked at the front door. She could make coffee and light the candles. Sit out front and watch for headlights to slow and turn in.

But just then she heard the low bellow of Aaron's exhaust pipes and reached for the door to the room and pulled it shut to hide the suitcase.

She was in the kitchen rinsing out the pot when his steps sounded on the back porch. Fuck him. She hadn't been talking to him. She didn't have to now. But she didn't know what she was going to do when Sam pulled up. If he pulled up. If he wasn't gone from home for a couple of days or something and hadn't gotten her message yet.

She was running clean water into it when he came in

543

through the back door. She could feel him looking at her but she didn't turn her head. She opened the coffee and started measuring some out.

'Hey,' he said.

'Hello.'

She didn't have to mess with him. She'd sit out on the front porch and drink some coffee until Sam drove up or she got too sleepy to sit there any longer and then she could just go to bed in the front room where she'd be able to hear him when he pulled in. The headlights might shine in. And when he got here, she'd just get in the truck and go with him. She didn't have to explain a damn thing to Aaron.

He closed the door and she heard it latch. He was making her nervous. Wondering what he was going to say. Hoping he'd just let her alone.

'You heard anything from Arlene?'

She put the coffee in the filter and put the little plastic thing that held it into the machine and then lifted the lid and poured in the water, put the pot under it and pushed the switch.

'No,' she said. Then she turned around. He was standing there with a bunch of flowers in his hand. She looked at them. They were nice flowers, blue ones and yellow ones with brown stripes across their petals. He stepped forward and held them out.

'Here,' he said. 'I went over to the mall and picked these up. I thought they might cheer you up a little.'

But she turned away from him and headed past him.

'Find somebody else to give em to,' she said, and went back to the bedroom for her cigarettes from her purse. She was careful with the door and got her purse and just took it with her. She didn't look back at him, just went out on the porch and set the purse in a chair.

She found her lighter and went to the candles and started lighting them. She glanced back in and saw him standing back there by the pool table. She didn't owe him anything. Not a damn thing. He'd let her have a place to stay for a while and she'd fucked him for a while so they were square minus one baby. If she hadn't been here she wouldn't have fallen down the stairs. She might be somewhere else, but she might still have the baby too.

She almost burned her finger on one that was slow to light. She moved to the others, lighting them one by one, until they were all flickering little yellow tongues of flame. If he came tonight, this is what he would see. All these candles lit for him.

She sat down in the chair and got out a cigarette and lit it. It would take the coffee a few minutes. There wasn't any need in him bringing her flowers. Not after all the shit he'd done.

He was walking around in there. She could hear his steps in the hall. She hoped maybe he'd just stay in there and not follow her out here.

The steps in the hall stopped. They sounded like they were close to her room. If he opened that door he was going to see her suitcase sitting there. She got up and went to the door and he was standing in the middle of the hall with his hands in his pockets. She went on in. When he looked up she knew what he knew.

'You're leaving,' he said. 'Ain't you?'

She stopped next to him. Just for a moment she did.

'Yeah. That's right. I am.'

He looked kind of bewildered and he turned in a little half circle, kind of swaying, his hands still jammed into his pockets. She could smell whiskey on him. His eyes were so red she knew he'd been smoking that dope again.

'I love you,' he said.

'I don't want to hear that.'

She started on by him and his hand lashed out like a snake and clamped on her arm, hard, right on the bruise that was still sore, and when she almost cried out and did close her eyes against the pain, he turned loose quick.

'I'm sorry, I didn't . . . I forgot your . . . Fuck.'

'Why don't you just let me alone?' she said, and she

545

went on by him, back down the hall, and he was following her.

'I didn't mean to hurt your arm,' he said.

She was rubbing on it as she went. She'd just be quiet. She didn't have to talk to his ass.

She went back into the kitchen but the coffee still wasn't ready. She turned around and he was right behind her. He reached out as if he were going to put his arms around her, and she watched what his face did when she pulled back from his touch. She remembered how she'd locked her legs around his freckled back and called out for him to give it to her harder. And shook and bounced on the bed and shoved it against him as hard and as fast as she could, and her hair wet with sweat at her temples, and her fingers clawing at him.

'I guess you've been in love before,' she said.

He wagged his chin and leaned against the wall.

'Not me.' He raised his eyes and looked at her. 'I guess I never did meet the right one.'

'But some of them loved you. Didn't they?'

'Yeah. So they said.'

'I know Reena did. She never did say it but I know she did.'

He turned his head. 'Your coffee's ready.' The flowers were lying on the pool table and he nodded to them. 'Don't you want your flowers?'

'You're crazy,' she said. 'You think you can just do whatever you want to. You won't even take care of your own kids. You think I'd stay with you, after what you did to Reena? What'd you do, run her off?'

She reached for the coffee and poured a cup and set it back on the warmer. He got down a cup.

'What do you mean run her off? Is she gone?'

'You know damn good and well she's gone,' she said, and she fixed her cup and dropped the spoon on the counter and walked out of the kitchen, and then she could hear him following her out to the porch.

She stopped and turned.

546

'Why don't you just stay in here?' she said. 'I don't want to talk to you no more.'

That was funny to him.

'My house,' he said.

'Your mama's house.'

'My mama.' And he smiled.

She turned her back on him and went out on the porch. She got her purse from the chair and sat down in it and set her cup on the arm.

He came out the door and walked past her to the edge of the steps and stood there holding the cup to his lips. The water was shining and rippling far out, a light burning at dockside.

'You got nowhere to go,' he said.

She leaned toward him for a moment.

'You don't know nothin. I do have somewhere to go.'

He turned around and gave her a hard look.

'Oh yeah. I hope you don't think you're gonna go back to where you came from. Because whatever shit you were in when you came down here, you're still in it up there. What'd you do, anyway? You might as well go on and tell me.'

There had only been that one time he'd asked about it. And she'd been glad of it. As many times as she'd *wanted* to tell somebody about it, she never had. Sam would be the only one who'd know that. And it was going to be hard to tell him.

'It just ain't none of your business,' she said. She picked up her coffee and tried to take a drink of it and it was still too hot.

A car came from the east, slowly, and it slowed even more as it got closer to the house. She followed it with her eyes, thought it was maybe going to turn in, and her heart almost started up to beat faster, and then the car sped up and went on.

When she looked at him he was watching her.

'What the hell?' he said. 'You expecting company?'

'No,' she said, but she didn't look at him when she said it, and he walked a little closer.

'How you planning on getting out of here?' he said. 'You gonna catch a ride out like you did in?'

'I don't know. I might.'

He leaned over and put his face right into hers, his eyes streaked with red blood vessels and his breath smelling sweet now like a peppermint boozehound's.

'Well I just wondered. You look just like somebody who's sitting here waiting on a ride. Is that what you're doing? You waiting on a ride?'

She had to lean away from him and her arm hit her coffee and knocked it to the porch, broke the cup, spattered her feet and his. He had his hand on her again, on her shoulder this time, and she tried to pull free, but he clamped down with the same force she'd seen him use to break that man's hand, and she had to freeze. She had to freeze or he would have made her hurt. It hit her: *This is how he does it.*

'Now don't you tell me something,' he said, and he leaned in and talked low into her ear. She was afraid he was going to hit her but he was still holding on to his coffee. Some of it sloshed on her leg and burned it. 'Don't you tell me you're sitting here on my front porch. Waiting for the son of a bitch that knocked you up in the first place to come down here and get you. At my house. You not gonna tell me that. Are you?'

She didn't answer. She couldn't believe that some person across the road wasn't seeing this or some neighbor down the street who was out on her porch. She knew better than to scream. He might kill her if she screamed. Break her neck with his hands.

'You *will* tell me the fucking truth,' he said, and he dropped his cup which also shattered and pulled her up out of the chair. It was punishment to fight. Two tries she found that out. As long as she walked straight toward the door where he was sending her, the pain stayed away. The second he felt her balk or try to get away from him, he clamped down. And the pain shot down into her legs and almost to her feet. He had ahold of something back there that hurt so bad when he mashed on it that she wouldn't have been able to stand it, she would have had to pass out. So it was a lot better to just go on in the door. Where none of the neighbors would see in case they'd been looking. She thought of the gun.

'Let me get my purse.'

He was behind her, guiding her.

'Fuck your purse.'

She went for it, but she didn't go far enough, only snatched at the strap enough to yank it off the chair when he jerked her back, and when it hit the porch floor it went *clunk*. He stopped.

His eyes lost the last little bit of that soft light they'd held. And she'd seen that look on his face before, the one he turned now on her.

'Well shit, sweet baby. What you got in your purse there, dumpling? Chunk of lead? Huh? You got to do me like this. Want to go back now and fuck the other guy that fucked you first, is that it? What's my sweet thing got in her purse that's so heavy, now?'

'Nothin.'

'Ooo we sound scared.'

He bent over and got it by the strap, and hefted it, throwing it up so that the strap slapped back down hard into his hand.

He chuckled, seemed pretty amused by it all.

'You know what this . . . know what this feels like? It feels like a fucking gun. That's exactly what it feels like. So let's just dump it out and . . .'

He lowered the purse and turned it over gently. His bedroom piece slid out, and it clattered and lay there among lipstick tubes and pieces of gum and a few nickels. He picked up the gun and stood there with it. Then he leaned in and whispered, amazed, infuriated:

'All you fucking whores are a*like*.'

The air was cooler now close to the coast and he could begin to even smell it. Boats were everywhere in yards and shops and there were places that sold motors and trailers and there were signs painted on sheets of plywood that advertised shrimp or charters for a day of fishing. The pine trees were a different kind here, and they grew low and close together in dark forests of themselves.

There was gas enough left to make it to Pass Christian, he thought. It was only a little below half a tank and the traffic wasn't bad. He hadn't been down here in a while. But he had been here plenty of times before. There wasn't much in Pass Christian, he thought, just a nice little town with some pretty old homes set up on some higher land across from the water. She'd said she was right across from the boats. A big white house her voice had said. He'd played the message three times and then written down everything on a piece of paper that was in his pocket. But he had it all in his head anyway. For the tenth time he glanced down at his Smith & Wesson, lying there quietly in its brown leather holster.

Too much road. Too many miles. When he got back with her there would be time to fix everything. Even if he had to take an early retirement he'd draw something, he didn't know how much. But there were other jobs. He wasn't too old to work somewhere else. Keep paying in his Social Security. Hell, he could commercial fish right behind the house. There was plenty he could do. He could get a piece of land at Pat's Bluff or somewhere and build a nice bait shop and have a grill where he could cook for people, sell beer and sandwiches, have plenty of fishing poles and stuff on hand. Once everything got straightened out they could. Or maybe it might be better for him to just go ahead and retire. Look at all the driving he had to do. He had to direct traffic for all the Ole Miss football games. He was out in bad weather a lot and there were all kinds of shit details they sent you on. And there were always the wrecks. Always some drunk son of a bitch who couldn't find his ass with both hands driving a car down the road and drinking some more. Some had bars in their cars.

There was plenty he could do. Just about anything was possible. He was getting pretty close now. Probably less than an hour.

After a while the green sign for Gulfport came up. He changed lanes and drove beneath a big metal arch across the highway. It wouldn't be much longer now.

The traffic moved around him. The radio played some tunes and he wasn't a bit sleepy, just wished he hadn't slept quite so long. Then he could have talked to her on the phone. But it wouldn't be long now. All he had to do was get to Gulfport and turn right.

The road kept moving under him, and the cars and trucks seemed to move aside for him, and he flew low and fast, going through the night with his taillights moving in a red blur.

She started fighting him when he pushed her through the door hard enough to send her against the wall and when he caught her with his hands he ripped her blouse and she got her hands up toward his face and raked a red groove down one of his cheeks but he slapped her and spun her into a corner next to a door in the hall. An umbrella stood at her knee. She grabbed it. Poking at him as he advanced, her breath coming fast, her arms shaking. He snatched it from her hand and flung it, waiting for her to come out of the corner. She started out like she was going to run, and when he moved to intercept her she launched her foot out and caught him square in the crotch. The breath oofed out of him and almost immediately he was on his knees. But when she went by him he reached out a hand anyway and caught her and pulled her down. The floor was hard on her back and she kicked at him as he dragged her to him, he himself curled almost into a ball and trying to throw up. She kicked him in the face. He was trying to get up onto his knees. He was trying to slide her up under him. And there the gun lay, where it had fallen from the back of his pants, and he was still hurting, and she turned on her side and sent her hand out for it and once she had it she swung herself back under his belly and holding it in both her little hands and thinking about her gone baby she went *boom boom boom* in the big hollow house.

After she rolled him off her and got up, Aaron lay there for a long time, listening to the sounds of her leaving. He was too weak to move much, and after she left there was only the sound of an occasional vehicle out on the road, and the wind singing in the nets. Up above him he could see that flakes of paint had fallen from the ceiling. And his mama still wasn't home yet.

The blood cooled on his shirt and there was so much of it. It kept coming. He tried pulling himself along on his belly toward the phone in the kitchen, but his strength was going. It came and went in waves. Sometimes he could pull himself a few inches. Sometimes he could not. He was able to get his hands on the gun where she'd dropped it.

He thought he dreamed, but then came to know that he had been only thinking about the daylight creeping up over the water to light the transom of his father's shrimp boat as it crawled rocking along off the coast and the houses he could see like this one sitting so far away.

After a while he gave up on getting to the telephone and pulled himself up against the wall to lean back with the gun between his bloody legs. The cigarettes in his pocket were soaked with blood and his weak fingers shook three or four of them out until he found one that still had some white on it. Then his lighter wouldn't work. His eyes were focused on it, his thumb striking on the wheel, the little spark it kept throwing up. It fired finally and he sucked the smoke in and leaned his head back against the wall.

Damn. All that fucking trouble for nothing.

He knew he was in shock. He was glad to be in shock. Shock was cool if shock was what it took not to feel what was wrong with him. He wished he had some of the hash. Or even a drink of the whiskey.

He saw the son of a bitch when he came in. He saw him outside at the screen door first. He eased the gun under his leg, hiding it beneath his knee. Old boyfriend come to retrieve his lost squeeze, eh? They'd see about that.

The door opened, and he came on in. He had a revolver in his hand and he stood there looking down on him for a long time. All of his hair had been cut off and his hands were pink with new skin like he'd been burned. Behind him a car went up the road, and the wind blew through the open door.

'Where's Fay?' he said, and Aaron pulled the gun from under his knee and raised it and squeezed the trigger. It kicked in his hand, and the shot was loud in the hall, and the guy with the revolver toppled backward into a table and knocked one of the antique lamps to the floor, where it broke into curved shards of painted glass. He must have fallen, because Aaron couldn't see him anymore. There were some noises, but he couldn't tell what they were.

He lay there bleeding and now his guts were on fire. Far off he could hear sirens screaming toward them. They rose slowly, threatening to overpower the wind singing in the riggings.

A gun roared once, twice, almost in his face, almost deafening, that close.

And wailing along the coastal road in the back of the ambulance he heard the siren going and the sound of it comforted him because it sounded just like the one in his cruiser. Probably made by the same company.

It was very bright in there and he was on his back on the gurney and the two of them were working over him with their pale rubber gloves so bloody. They were shaking their heads, but there was no need for them to get so upset. She was probably OK now. And he was just too tired.

EPILOGUE

One evening at the end of the summer, just before the gas lamps came on, a girl walked on the streets of the Old Square in New Orleans and drew the looks of men as she passed. They would stop and look at her and walk some more and stop and look back again. She moved among the drinkers and bars and the rich fragrances of Cuban food cooking, a zydeco beat on the air, the soothing notes of an accordion. She mingled with the talking people on Royal and looked at old coins and Civil War muskets or mummies in shop windows and she smiled as she walked. She stopped at a wide plate of glass to see people standing at a zinc bar eating oysters off their shells and drinking beer from tall brown bottles.

She came out of one bar with a plastic cup in her hand and went on up the street, smiling and ducking her head or brushing her hair to the side and stepping past the men who tried to stop her and talk to her. She did talk to some of them, but she kept moving, too. The dark came down a little bit but it didn't lessen the crowds in the streets. Somebody was selling postcards on a corner and she bought one.

On a cobbled avenue she saw the marquee in lights and when she got closer she looked at the women on the posters with brighter bulbs around their frames and they were wrapped in feather boas and sparkling sequins. People waiting outside called to her. In front of the door there was a man in a striped coat and a flat-brimmed straw hat. He had a silver-tipped cane and he was hailing walkers to stop in and see the girls. To this one he tipped his hat, called her by name. She handed him her empty cup, and then she went on in.

THE NEW CITY

Stephen Amidon

'A NOVEL TO DEVOUR AND BE DEVOURED BY'
Sunday Times

'RARE ASSURANCE, GRIPPING . . . THE STUFF OF TRAGEDY'
Sunday Telegraph

The time is the Watergate era, the place is a spanking new
American suburb with a rapidly widening racial fault line. Two
families, one black, one white, who have been close friends for
years, are about to be set by circumstance against each other in
the most primal way imaginable.

'A BRILLIANT STORYTELLER . . . SUPREME
CRAFTSMANSHIP'
Literary Review

'A HUGELY GRIPPING AND SATISFYING READ, FULL OF
ASTONISHING SET PIECES'
Time Out

'A POWERFULLY PLOTTED AMERICAN TRAGEDY . . . BRINGS
TO MIND THE INEXORABLE FALL-FROM-GRACE PLOT OF
TOM WOLFE'S *BONFIRE OF THE VANITIES*'
Amazon. co. uk

'A POWERFUL PAGE-TURNER'
New Statesman

'A UTOPIAN THRILLER . . . COMPOSED, ELEGANT AND
CONFIDENT'
Times Literary Supplement

'A POWERFUL EXPLORATION OF RACE, WEALTH AND
AMBITION'
Express

'AN IMPRESSIVE, HIGHLY INTELLIGENT NOVEL'
Scotsman

'EXTRAORDINARY . . . A COMPLEX NARRATIVE WITH
A SHARP AND URGENT PACE'
Independent

0 552 99915 6

BLACK SWAN

EDDIE'S BASTARD

William Kowalski

'A REMARKABLE DEBUT'
Time Out

Billy was deposited as an infant on the doorstep of
Thomas Mann's home in a simple wicker basket with a
plain two-word message pinned to his shawl reading
'Eddie's Bastard'. Eddie, Thomas's son, had been killed in
Vietnam three months earlier, and his father had given up
on life, having lost his only son. But now, suddenly,
Thomas has a grandson and an heir – if not to the once-
vast Mann fortune (for Thomas recklessly squandered
that in a foolhardy enterprise involving ostriches just
after his heroic return from the Second World War), then
at least to the long legacy of the Mann family stories,
stretching back to the Civil War.

In this rich, deeply resonant literary début, William
Kowalski explores the power of family, the meaning of
history, and the bonds of individuals united and divided
by love. By turns hilarious, thrilling and heart-breaking,
Eddie's Bastard is a novel that stays in the mind long
after the reading is over.

'CLEVER, EMOTIONAL STORYTELLING WITH
LAUGHS, TEARS, AND LOVE'
The Times

'A BOOK WRITTEN WITH SUCH ELEGANCE,
MATURITY AND HUMOUR IT IS DIFFICULT TO
BELIEVE THAT THE AUTHOR IS ONLY 28 YEARS OLD'
The Good Book Guide

'WICKEDLY FUNNY AND GENUINELY MOVING'
Attitude

0 552 99859 1

BLACK SWAN

A SELECTED LIST OF FINE WRITING AVAILABLE FROM BLACK SWAN

99915 6	THE NEW CITY	*Stephen Amidon*	£6.99
99820 6	FLANDERS	*Patricia Anthony*	£6.99
99532 0	SOPHIE	*Guy Burt*	£5.99
99824 9	THE DANDELION CLOCK	*Guy Burt*	£6.99
14698 6	INCONCEIVABLE	*Ben Elton*	£6.99
99609 2	FORREST GUMP	*Winston Groom*	£6.99
99681 5	A MAP OF THE WORLD	*Jane Hamilton*	£6.99
99847 8	WHAT WE DID ON OUR HOLIDAY	*John Harding*	£6.99
99204 6	THE CIDER HOUSE RULES	*John Irving*	£7.99
99205 4	THE WORLD ACCORDING TO GARP	*John Irving*	£7.99
99037 X	BEING THERE	*Jerzy Kosinski*	£5.99
99859 1	EDDIE'S BASTARD	*William Kowalski*	£6.99
99807 9	MONTENEGRO	*Starling Lawrence*	£6.99
99875 3	MAYBE THE MOON	*Armistead Maupin*	£6.99
99874 5	PAPER	*John McCabe*	£6.99
99762 5	THE LACK BROTHERS	*Malcolm McKay*	£6.99
99785 4	GOODNIGHT, NEBRASKA	*Tom McNeal*	£6.99
99536 3	IN THE PLACE OF FALLEN LEAVES	*Tim Pears*	£5.99
99718 8	IN A LAND OF PLENTY	*Tim Pears*	£6.99
99817 6	INK	*John Preston*	£6.99
99810 9	THE JUKEBOX QUEEN OF MALTA	*Nicholas Rinaldi*	£6.99
99777 3	THE SPARROW	*Mary Doria Russell*	£6.99
99811 7	CHILDREN OF GOD	*Mary Doria Russell*	£6.99
99122 8	THE HOUSE OF GOD	*Samuel Shem*	£7.99
99846 X	THE WAR ZONE	*Alexander Stuart*	£6.99
99366 2	THE ELECTRIC KOOL AID ACID TEST	*Tom Wolfe*	£7.99